P9-CCX-359

Place your initials here to remind you that you have read this book!			
BS			

DISCARD

ONSLAUGHT

Center Point
Large Print

Also by David Poyer and available from
Center Point Large Print:

The Whiteness of the Whale
Tipping Point

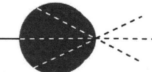

ONSLAUGHT

THE WAR WITH CHINA— THE OPENING BATTLE

David Poyer

CENTER POINT LARGE PRINT
THORNDIKE, MAINE

This Center Point Large Print edition
is published in the year 2018 by arrangement with
St. Martin's Press.

The text of this Large Print edition is unabridged.
In other aspects, this book may vary
from the original edition.
Printed in the United States of America
on permanent paper.
Set in 16-point Times New Roman type.

ISBN: 978-1-68324-812-5

Library of Congress Cataloging-in-Publication Data

Names: Poyer, David, author.
Title: Onslaught : the war with China- the opening battle / David Poyer.
Description: Center Point Large Print edition. | Thorndike, Maine :
    Center Point Large Print, 2018.
Identifiers: LCCN 2018009628 | ISBN 9781683248125
    (hardcover : alk. paper)
Subjects: LCSH: Large type books. | BISAC: FICTION / Sea Stories. |
    FICTION / Thrillers. | FICTION / Action & Adventure. |
    GSAFD: War stories. | Sea stories.
Classification: LCC PS3566.O978 O57 2018 | DDC 813/.54—dc23
LC record available at https://lccn.loc.gov/2018009628

It is time, Odysseus said, that I told you of the disastrous voyage that Zeus had willed.
—Homer

1
The East China Sea

The tiny, pale, crab-like animal had hatched only hours before. It scurried about a world it barely sensed. Tendrils of weed. Cool water, seething with microscopic prey. And arching above, a scatter of stars. The crab clambered here and there, fearful and greedy, grasping and eating. With only the faintest stirrings of thought.

Until it dimly felt some distant change. A high-pitched vibration, trilling through the translucent sea. It peered nearsightedly around, then returned to its instinctive seeking.

A shadow neared. The crab-thing paused again, eyestalks waving frantically.

A gentle wave lifted the sprig it perched on. It tensed. Sensing danger, yet not knowing what it feared.

An immense column of gray steel tore the universe apart, tumbling the creature over and over in a seething froth. It beat at the unsupporting sea with segmented legs, helpless in a hissing green.

Until something silver flashed in the darkness . . .

Silver, and *toothed* . . .

Leaning against the splinter shield of USS *Savo Island*, a tall, sandy-haired officer looked down at where a patch of seaweed, barely visible in the predawn darkness, had disappeared in the seethe of the bow wave. A cool wind blustered against his cheeks. The singsong keen of sonar drilled through steel.

On the horizon another shape raced eastward with the speeding cruiser. Neither showed running lights.

Eastward, toward impending battle . . .

"Good morning, Captain."

Captain Daniel V. Lenson, USN, turned, sighing inwardly, and returned his executive officer's salute.

Petite, humorless, and apparently immune to any need for sleep, Cheryl Staurulakis was the best second-in-command he'd ever had. Her pale hair was pulled back tightly, just visible under one of the black-and-olive shemaghs they'd bought in Dubai. Like him, she was in dark blue ship's coveralls. "Come on out, Exec. Geeks still down?"

"Geeks" was the Global Command and Control System. Staurulakis frowned down at a clipboard. "Uh, yessir. They either shot down our satellites or jammed them somehow."

"Which is also why we've lost GPS. All right, go ahead."

"We're in company with *Mitscher. Pittsburgh* is lane clearing fifty miles ahead. We'll rendevous with *Curtis Wilbur*, *Stuttgart*, and two Japanese destroyers. *Stuttgart* has fuel, an ammo reload, and a passenger for us—an NCIS agent."

Dan massaged his jaw. Someone aboard had abducted and raped one of the female petty officers, capping a series of sexual assaults. "Good. We can use his help; we need to nail this guy, fast. Names on the Japanese units yet? Capabilities?"

"No sir. Comms are still spotty. Heard anything from the States? Your wife? Your daughter?"

Dan shook his head as *Savo Island* rolled, as her bow wave creamed out below them, sparkling and gleaming with cold constellations. The Navy depended on satellites for communications, data transfer, remote targeting, and navigation. But since the outbreak of theater nuclear war, then China's attack on India across the Himalayas, most had been either shot down or hacked into uselessness.

On the other hand, Intel said all enemy reconnaissance assets, at least that the U.S. knew about, had been taken down as well.

Joint Operation Plan Sachel Advantage/Iron Noose was the contingency plan for a conflict with China. It had placed a carrier battle group in a blocking position north of Taiwan. But USS *George Washington* had struck two submarine-laid mines. Pacific Command had plugged Dan into the gap with an adaptive force package. The impending join-up would wcld six U.S.

and Japanese units into the Ryukyus Maritime Defense Coalition Task Group, with him in charge as Commander, Task Group 779.1.

A temporary commodore. He leaned back, squeezing his eyelids shut. Tuning his hearing to the steady roar of blowers and machinery, the murmuration of voices inside the pilothouse. Smelling, along with the dark sea, the ship scents of exhaust and fuel and fresh paint and the night baker making cookies. When he opened them, the top-heavy-looking superstructure towered against the dark sky. Her ID flags snapped in the wind, and the battle ensign streamed out straight.

The powerful radars of Aegis cruisers could detect and track over two hundred contacts simultaneously. But *Savo* fielded an even more impressive capability. Her upgraded combat system could lock on ballistic warheads screaming down from space. The hatches on foredeck and fantail covered Block 4 Standard missiles, along with antiaircraft, antiship, and Tomahawk land-attack rounds. He'd expended several of them trying to stop the nuclear exchange between India and Pakistan, but had been only partially successful.

With the U.S. sucked back into a reflare in the Mideast, China had come to Pakistan's aid with an attack on India. Now the dominos were toppling around the world. . . . He coughed into his fist. "We're crossdecking Dr. Schell, right,

Cheryl? We have to keep sterilizing those hot-water heaters."

"Chief engineer's on it." The ship's lead engineer, Bart Danenhower.

"How about the other antiballistic cruisers?"

"USS *Monocacy*'s en route from Guam, for a position south of Taiwan. *Hampton Roads* is finishing a hasty fitting-out in Pearl. She'll defend Manila, along with the rest of our old battle group. Once we're all in position, we can cover the inner island chain against missile attack."

Dan said, "If everything works perfectly, and we don't get overwhelmed."

Staurulakis murmured, "Yes sir. Also, our sub forces are moving closer inshore."

"Great. But Intel said most of the Chinese sub fleet's already vanished."

"Yeah . . . they're out here somewhere." Staurulakis squinted past him into the dark. "The U.S. and Indian navies have been directed to impose a blockade on China and the 'Opposed Powers.' No grain, no strategic materials, no oil."

Dan fiddled with his wedding ring, contemplating the paling sky. Not yet dawn; merely a lighter shade of black, as if a fluorescent light had been snapped on below the horizon.

A thousand miles to the west, a combined U.S./Vietnamese force was gathering. China's far-flung atolls, bases, and logistics in the South

China Sea would be vulnerable, as Japan's outposts had been in an earlier war. If the Chinese premier, Zhang Zurong, pushed southward, the allies—Vietnam, Indonesia, Malaysia—would fight to defend their claims there.

But if China could break through the *eastern* island chain, Zhang could pincer Taiwan, isolate South Korea, and neutralize Japan.

Dan's task group would be the last line of defense. If it failed, if *he* failed, the conflict might be enormously long and bloody . . . a fourth world war, if you counted the long twilit struggle with the Soviets as number three.

The aluminum gridwork underfoot rattled. "Captain. We join you out here?" The chief quartermaster, Van Gogh, cradled a sextant. Behind him was apple-cheeked Ensign Mytsalo.

"Morning stars, Chief? Sure, step into my office."

Van Gogh held it out. "Do the honors, Skipper?"

"I'm pretty rusty on a sextant, Chief—"

"Hey, we're all *rusty,* sir. We'll just do it over until we get it right."

Dan had to grin at that. "All right. Sure. XO, you might want to listen in. You'll be doing this too. If we don't get GPS back."

Staurulakis positioned herself beside the canvas-shrouded bulk of a machine gun as Van Gogh read off his calculations. Dan set the sextant to the elevation, sighted along the pelorus for the bearing, and found Sirius. The Dog Star. The brightest in the sky.

Muscle memory kicked in. He found the brace, tucked his elbows, and rocked the distant glitter in an arc, verniering it down with the micrometer drum until it just kissed the barely visible sea horizon. He twisted the lock nut. "Mark."

"Time: zero four fifty-one," Van Gogh intoned, clicking the stopwatch. "Elevation? We need to get these fast, Cap'n, sunup's a-comin'."

Dan hit the light button, and read it off the arm and the drum. From the pilothouse the junior officers gaped with holy awe, as if at some arcane ceremony. Van Gogh gave him the next bearing and elevation, in the hushed tones of an acolyte.

He lifted the apparatus that had guided mariners for centuries, and steadied it once more.

Dan's pimply mess attendant, Longley, brought up a tray at 0530. Sliced ham, eggs, and coffee. Dan ate perched in the command chair, groggily watching the sun blowtorch the curved horizon from ironglowing red to lily orange, then blazing gold. He'd only gotten uneasy naps in the padded leather chair.

His operations officer, Matthew Mills, came up as the radioman arrived with the morning traffic. Tall and fair, Mills could have graced a Harlequin cover. Dan flipped through the clipboard. *George*

Washington was still immobilized. . . . *Franklin Roosevelt* battle group was behind schedule . . .

And there they were, the first overt moves. The Chinese had occupied Quemoy and Matsu, Taiwan's last toeholds near the mainland. No casualties; Taipei had withdrawn its garrisons when the crisis had begun. More inflammatory were reports of landing craft, escorted by destroyers, approaching Uotsuri Jima, a Japanese island northeast of Taiwan. China had claimed the Senkaku group for decades, and gotten more assertive since General Zhang had bullied and murdered his way into the premiership.

He scribbled his initials and handed the clipboard back. Massaged his face, fighting for a casual tone. "Okay, Ops, we're gonna be joining in twelve hours. What've you come up with?"

Five straits gave China deepwater access to the western Pacific. The Soya, Tsugaru, Osumi, and Miyako straits, plus the Bashi Channel, south of Taiwan. The war plans assigned the northern-most three to Japanese forces. Dan would be responsible for holding the Miyako Strait, north of Taiwan and south of Okinawa.

"We have three missions," Mills said. "Air and ballistic missile defense of Taipei. Closing the channel to surface and subsurface passage. And providing strike support, as directed."

Dan shook his head. "If they wanted to sortie, they've had plenty of time."

14

"Right, but follow-on forces, refueling, rearming . . . they'll still need to transit. And if they attack Taiwan—"

"Okay, what's it look like ASW-wise?"

Mills pulled a chart from under his arm. "I talked to Chief Zotcher. We should have had bottom-sensor data, but that's satellite-uplinked—"

"So we don't have SOSUS?" Dan said, referring to the worldwide underwater listening system.

"You mean Seaweb? I'm trying to engineer a work-around. So the Japanese can pass information. But I haven't found the right button yet."

Examining the chart, Dan reflected sourly that this must be how it had felt after Pearl Harbor. Confusion, lack of communication, and frantic, too-late moves against an enemy with a solid plan and a clear goal. The Chinese were calling their operation "Breath of the Dragon." It was designed to send America reeling back, bleeding and dazed, leaving Beijing holding an impregnable rampart from Japan to the Philippines.

He didn't plan to mention the Three Hundred Spartans out loud, but Daniel V. Lenson might go down in history beside King Leonidas and George Armstrong Custer.

Mills ran a fingernail from Miyako Jima to

Okinawa. "We've got an eighty-nautical-mile gap. Strait's wider, but that's what's navigable submerged. Most of it's a thousand-plus feet, but a crooked channel to the north goes down to five hundred and fifty fathoms. The current's from left to right across our front, at about three knots."

"Did you talk to Rit Carpenter?"

"The sonarman?"

"He's also an ex-submariner. In diesel boats." And, unfortunately, one of the prime suspects in the rape. Dan leaned in his chair to hit the 21MC. "Sonar, CO."

"Sonar, aye."

"Ask Rit Carpenter to join me on the bridge?"

"Aye aye, sir."

He clicked off, then back on again. "This Chief Zotcher?"

"Yes sir."

"Can you shoot up here too? We need to get our ducks in a row. For when we get to the Miyako Gap."

They gathered in the navigation space just behind the pilothouse. A mussed, overweight Carpenter was saying, "Absolutely, Dan. That's where I'd position for a slow, quiet passage. Deep and silent as I could run."

"I concur." Zotcher nodded.

Dan adjusted the half-moon glasses he needed

16

now for fine print, and bent to the chart. "What's the red book say about operating depth? The new boats, the Songs, Hans, Shangs?"

Lieutenant Mills: "Max rated is around eleven hundred feet. Crush depth, the usual twenty-five percent below that. They have a shitload of diesel boats, too, Romeos and Mings, and the Kilos they bought from Russia. Depth limited, but still dangerous."

"Because they're so quiet. So why should they stick to this three-thousand-foot channel?"

"If they're proceeding without active sonar, they have to worry about terrain. They can't risk a collision. Not at max depth."

Dan sucked a breath, remembering skating across the bottom of the Persian Gulf in a stolen Iranian Kilo. "All right, makes sense. But I still want ears on the rest of the channel. How do we maximize coverage?"

The operations officer positioned a grease-penciled overlay atop the chart. "With *Mitscher* and *Curtis Wilbur*, along with the Japanese, we'll have enough helo assets and platforms for a sonobuoy barrier."

Dan studied the patterns, chewing his lip. A collocated grid, staggered, ranked in depth . . . there'd be blind zones near the coasts, but you had to balance sensor expenditure versus probability of detection. "Yeah, but for how long? We don't have unlimited assets."

17

"Right, gonna be iffy. Also, how're the helos going to lay without GPS? And where do we want *Pittsburgh*? Behind the barrier, or out front?"

"Let's let Captain Youngblood make that call." Dan sighed, stretching a kink out of his back. Along with the antisubmarine mission, he'd have to cover the antiair picture. Make certain *Savo* was positioned to intercept missiles aimed at the capital, Taipei. And hold the strait, until the FDR carrier battle group got there.

Conflicting demands, with a lot of moving parts. He'd have to juggle assets, be ready to skitter back and forth in front of the goal. Like playing lacrosse back at the Academy . . . "Okay, make it happen. Matt, also, I need a force balance between Taiwan and the mainland. Leave the Southern Fleet out; my guess is they'll be deploying defensively."

When the group broke up, Carpenter lingered. "Dan? A word?"

"Uh, yeah." He turned back. "What you got, Rit?"

The old sonarman lowered his voice. "About Petty Officer Terranova. You gotta know, it wasn't me."

Dan studied the sagging jowls, the silvery hair. Carpenter had served with him before. But that didn't mean Dan had crossed him off the suspect list. The submariner added, "Yeah, right, I brought that gang-bang game aboard. But you

18

know I don't go for round-eye pussy anyway."

"You like 'em young, Rit. That fifteen-year-old in Korea?"

Carpenter grimaced. "I pay as I go, Dan. Never needed to knock anybody around." He looked at the deck again, then squinted up. "I hope you get him. I like the Terror. It wasn't me."

Dan was mulling an answer when the officer of the deck stuck his head in. "Captain? You back here? Sir, Lieutenant Singhe, calling from Combat." The ensign's eyes were blown wide, cheeks sallow under scattered freckles. "Incoming aircraft, Skipper. She says, better get down there right away."

2
Somewhere in the Pacific

Master Chief Petty Officer Theodore Harlett Oberg was six foot two and no longer quite as lean as he'd once been. But he could still run twenty miles, swim five in the open ocean, bench his weight a dozen times, and do twenty pull-ups carrying a weapon and a basic load on his harness gear. His dirty blond hair was banded back in a ponytail. His light blue eyes never seemed to blink. But the first thing most people noticed were the scars radiating out from his nose. The doctors had said they could fix them, but he'd told them not to bother.

Just now Teddy was face to buttcrack with "Knobby" Swager, eighty feet underwater, in a steel escape chamber six feet across. Four other SEALs were crammed in too, faces and gear illuminated by a ruby glow. He checked his watch, then touched his gear lightly, to inventory. Rebreather. Bailout. Rifle. SIG. The thin-blade he'd carried for so long it was like a third thumbnail. The only weapon he'd had left above the Parachinar Valley, after his blood had frozen his handgun solid. The dry re-enriched gas he breathed now parched his throat. His left leg burned like it was thrust knee-deep into molten lead.

"One minute," said the in-hull circuit, deep in his ear.

Teddy eased his leg, panting a little into the mouthpiece.

A minute. More than enough time to remember another time he'd waited, encapsulated, with the carapace bolted down over fear. That had been in the Gulf. He'd had his doubts about those guys, a mixed bag of electron pushers, computer wonks, and retirees, headed up by a skinny bastard name of Lenson. Not what you'd call tier-one operators. But to Teddy's astonishment, K-79 had made it out.

He'd checked out of the Teams after that one. Tried to make The Movie. And almost had it. German financing. Liki Dittrich and Hanneline Muruzawa producing. Ewan McGregor, Colin Farrell, and Russell Crowe reading the script.

9/11 had derailed it, and he'd gotten back in. To Afghanistan. The Tora Bora assault, followed by the fucked-up Echo Platoon mission into the White Mountains. In the Safed Koh, the Ghilzai route across the Pak border. A shot-down helo. An old man, frozen rigid where he sat. A captured Dragunov, after Teddy'd lost his SR-25 falling down a fucking cliff. And one shot at the shadow in the fog that had to have been OBL himself.

He'd thought that was fade-out and credits. Dropping away into the oatmeal dark, the bitter snow. But a skinny, limp-dicked newbie had hiked back for him. Swager had manhandled him fifteen hundred feet back down to the extract LZ. Petty Officer First Class Swager now, in the chamber with him. Still kind of a limp dick, but one Teddy owed his life to.

That was where he'd gotten fucked up. His Achilles tendon, shredded in the fall down the mountainside. They'd had to graft in tendons from his shinbone, then fight some stubborn cipro-resistant Afghani infection. Three months in a cast, six months of physio. And limited duty since.

Until this. Probably his Last Fucking Hurrah. Then it'd be back to Salena. She'd stuck while his leg healed. He was almost forty. Too old for a top-tier operator. Time, maybe, to tackle LA again . . .

He was checking his watch again when the intercom came on.

"Opening," it said.

Days before, he'd leaned against an equipment cabinet as a gray-haired buzzcut in slacks and a polo shirt introduced himself. Retired Colonel Somebody, from the Marine Corps history office, had unrolled a topo to give the team a once-over of a curved small island, its beaches and lagoon, interior and relief. Then dimmed the lights, and brought up a PowerPoint slide.

"Early 1942. The Japanese controlled the

western Pacific. Their next goal was Australia. We planned to stop them by seizing the airfield they'd built on Guadalcanal. But a distraction was needed before the First Marine Division landed.

"The target was Makin Island. Well placed as a seaplane and reconnaissance base, on the eastern edge of the newly expanded empire. An attack here would divert the enemy and confuse him as to Allied intentions. Additional objectives were to collect intelligence, capture prisoners, and do all the damage possible to the installation.

"Evans Carlson's Second Marine Raider Battalion trained on mock-ups on Oahu. Intel predicted two hundred fifty defenders and a shore battery covering the lagoon. So the marines decided to land on the ocean side of the island."

A photo of a very old diesel submarine. Teddy had fidgeted, glancing at Knobby beside him. Whispered, "What is this, ancient history? We got rebreathers to rebuild."

The prof said, "The raiders embarked on two subs for the trip from Hawaii. The plan envisioned disembarking into rubber rafts at 0300, hitting the beach before dawn, and withdrawing no later than 2100 that same day.

"The weather was bad when they reached Makin, but they went ahead anyway. Unfortunately, heavy swells drowned the motors on the boats. The tide set the subs toward the reef. Carlson decided to abandon a simultaneous assault and began paddling toward the beach, ordering his men to follow.

"They made it ashore, but the boats landed scattered across a mile. Also, one man fired his rifle accidentally, losing the element of surprise."

Teddy caught Swager's eye. His buddy inclined his head slightly. They both frowned back at the screen, which now showed movement arrows and tactical symbols.

"The marines moved inland to the coastal road. The defenders, now alerted, engaged them in a fierce firefight near the hospital. They had machine guns, flamethrowers, and snipers.

"When dawn broke things got even worse. A troop transport and a patrol boat were coming in to the wharf. Carlson managed to pass this to the submarines. Fortunately, the subs managed to sink both ships with their deck guns.

"For the rest of the morning Carlson's men were pinned down by machine guns and snipers. That afternoon the Japanese bombed and strafed them, and landed reinforcements by seaplane. Though fighting hard, and holding against a banzai attack, Carlson had to pull back. He buried his dead and, as dark fell, withdrew to the beach to extract.

"This was when luck really turned against them. The heavy surf dumped the boats as they tried to paddle out. They lost nearly all their weapons and equipment, and finally gave up trying and established a perimeter just off the beach.

"Carlson called a meeting at midnight. His determination to fight on, even without adequate weapons or ammunition, meant most of his men might die in battle. But they accepted it.

"At dawn, some of the unwounded raiders fought through the surf and made it back to the subs, which had stayed despite Japanese air superiority. With the ocean-side surf still too high to get his wounded out, Carlson decided to try to escape via the lagoon side. After a terrific struggle, he managed to get his wounded and most of his men to the subs, using the remaining boats and a native outrigger canoe. Nine men were left behind, however. They were captured and beheaded."

The colonel looked at the overhead. "The Raiders destroyed a radio transmitter, gasoline, and other stores. The Japanese landed a thousand reinforcements on Makin, so the diversion worked. There was a PR bonus, too. Makin was the first offensive action by American forces. But there wasn't much gained for such heavy losses."

The colonel turned the projector off. "To summarize the lessons of the operation: The intel's probably going to be wrong. Surprise won't always work. Luck can cut both ways. And leadership is all-important."

He paused, then seemed to shrink, to lose his

classroom confidence. "I'm not sure why I was asked to give you this briefing. And probably it's best I don't know. But I can guess. So can you, probably. Thanks for your attention."

The light in the trunk turned green, then went out. A clunk, Teddy's ears popped, and the hatch unsealed. "All right, let's go," he said into his throat mike, and unplugged. One after the other, the team uncoiled. A black circle appeared above as the hatch powered open.

The open sea pulsed and flashed with light. They were surrounded, enmeshed in a coldly glowing net. Green and blue, it shaded off into a shimmering glow, as if they hovered high in the ionosphere, among the northern lights. The gossamer illumination snaked and swirled, like snow in the White Mountains.

Levering his fins, wincing at a flash of pain from the leg, Teddy rotated slowly, hanging in ultraviolet space.

A hundred yards away, a black whale-shape was emerging from the second sub. The swimmer delivery vehicle. Battery-driven, with its own sonar. Only one sub in the Pacific could transport it. But they needed more than the six SEALs it could carry to accomplish whatever their objective was.

Whatever that was. He still didn't know. Echo had been given a warning order, which let them gather equipment, conduct training, then do a rehearsal—this one, in fact. A Patrol Leader's Order would follow, to detail individual responsibilities. But nothing had specified their objective, beyond the generic "hostile beach" and that it involved sabotage, demolition, and intelligence collection. Maybe Commander Laughland knew. But he wasn't saying.

All Teddy had to go on was the briefing about Makin. That, and the fact that his investments had been wiped out.

His broker had called before they left Hawaii. An immense tide of short-selling. The markets had closed, but not before he'd lost everything his grandmother had left him. Since then, the snippets of news they got aboard the sub had made clear that things had gotten even worse. Shit, he'd never expected to have to live on his Navy retirement. In LA, that would be a grim prospect.

Snap out of it, Obie! Shaking his head, he sucked gas from the Dräger, mainlining oxygen until his bloodstream sang.

The beach gradient was shallow, and they figured the sand would be laced with listening devices and mines. The subs would have to stand off. The delivery vehicle would make two runs, dropping the first team, along with a homing sounder, at sixty feet, then going back for the second team. Once assembled, the force would

27

power the last miles in to shore with prop-driven scooters, towing weapons and equipment. After that . . .

He hovered, waiting, until the hatch cycled again with a thud that echoed through the sea. When it powered up he reached in.

The Package was five feet long, black, vaguely torpedo shaped, but with an annular bump or ring around its midpoint. Definitely not the usual satchels he'd gotten all too familiar with in Afghanistan, blowing down walls and doors.

He beckoned, and Swager got the other side— there were handles on it, to make it easier to maneuver, but even in water it was heavy as a bomb—and working together, they got it up and onto the curving steel hull. He secured the lift saddle on it and inflated it with gas from a bottle that dangled on a hose. It rose from the hull and he valved a little off, until it floated weightless, massive but balanced in the sea.

Another hand signal, and he and Swager swam it out into the void. The lights swirled around them. He saw now what they were. A massive tide of coelenterates, flashing like pulsars in the dark. A spiral of argon light rotated slowly, a blue galaxy in interstellar blackness. He put out a hand; the glow passed through his fingers without resistance, intangible, like smoke. Another cloud succeeded it, passing like snowflakes in utter silence.

A touch on his arm. Swager looked puzzled behind the flat plate of the mask. *What the fuck?* he gestured. Clanks and thuds echoed through the water as the SEALs clambered into the vehicle, stowed gear, and switched to the onboard breathing supply.

As the motors whirred into life, Teddy glanced toward the surface. Only sixty feet up, but totally black. No moon. No stars. Only the weird shimmer of that cold luminescence surrounded them, appearing, created, sweeping past, then vanishing forever, back into the void.

An hour later, crouched behind his carbine, he rose slowly from the sea. Facemask first, the fold-down backup sight of the SOP-modd'd M4 flipped up in front of his eye. For whatever reason, they'd been told to use only iron sights, to leave anything electronic (aside from night-vision devices, and the controllers in the rebreathers) on the sub.

Sand crunched as he waded forward. The shore ahead was black dark. Until he flipped down the goggles and powered them on. Then he made out the curved boles of palms. The slowly wavering fringe of leaves, caressed by a night wind. To their left, the solid ebony of impenetrable mangrove.

Exactly where they'd planned to land. Fallen trees lay scattered across the beach. The sand sloped upward and he leaned into it, ignoring the pain in his calf. Suddenly one of the logs stirred. He swung without thought and centered it in the sights as a shape heaved up and shook itself, then lumbered into a heavy, belly-swaying run.

He blew out and lowered the weapon, thumbing the safety back on. A hog, roused from slumber, making tracks away from the intruders who'd waded up out of the surf like Lovecraftian aliens.

Fading snorts and the muffled thunder of hooves on sand signaled the departure of other livestock. He swept the green-and-black field of view left to right. Aside from the pigs, and smaller shadows that were probably sand crabs, the beach was deserted. He raised an arm and pointed forward. Around him other silhouettes grew from the surf, took on human shapes, and became armed men, wading forward, bent under burdens of gear.

A dark figure emerged from the palms and strolled down to meet them. "All accounted for?" Commander Laughland snapped.

"First team, all present."

"Second, all here."

"Package one?"

"Over here," the first team leader called from down the beach.

"Package two here." Teddy and Swager leaned into the braided nylon yoked over their shoulders. The dark seal-bulk emerged behind them, the sea parting as it shouldered up.

30

The officer knelt, and a shielded flash glowed for a moment. He glanced up. "Any problems on the way in? Did Sandia get the buoyancy right?"

Sandia, Teddy thought. So it *was* nuclear. But, Jesus, couldn't they figure a better way to deliver a nuclear warhead than having fucking SEALs swim it ashore? And how long would the team have to get clear before it went off? He cleared his throat. "Maybe a tad light, but we can stick some of those wheel weights on it. Uh, not that I personally care, but are we gonna get any radiation exposure from this thing, Commander?"

Laughland frowned. "Radiation?"

Teddy coughed. Some officers never seemed to think enlisted, even master chiefs, were capable of thinking. But what was this black turd squeezed from the asshole of DoD? His only clue was a shipping tag, with a cryptology of bar codes and what might be a serial number: *TA-III No. 12.* "Uh, sir? Could be helpful down the road, if you'd share a little about what we're escorting, here."

"Once we're sealed, Teddy, I assure you, there'll be a full brief. Just can't do it now." Laughland stood, dusting sand off his knees. "All right, move inland. We've got an exercise area set up for a sandbox drill."

"Bury the gear, sir? The rebreathers? In case we need it again?"

"Right now we're thinking not. Destroy them.

Render inoperable. The extraction will be by boat."

"Yessir, just trying to think ahead. And . . . mines?"

Laughland halted in the dark. "Sea mines, Master Chief?"

"No sir. Land mines. Will the beach be swept before we land? Or do we need to build in the capability?"

Laughland looked away. "No need to worry, Master Chief. Just lock tight. Adapt and over-come. Hoo-ah?"

"Uh, yessir. Hoo-ah. But it's my job to worry. About what can go wrong. Like at Makin. Or Tora Bora."

"This isn't going to be like Makin."

"Hope not, sir. About the gear, again. If things happen to go to shit, we need to—"

"Just follow the plan, Master Chief." The commander's tone meant *end of discussion*. Teddy stared after him as he strode away up the beach.

Swager coalesced out of the dark. "What was that all about, Obie? He getting in your pants, or what?"

Teddy was spitting on the sand, trying to formulate some kind of smart-ass comeback, but none surfaced. He didn't like it. Didn't like the feel of the mission, didn't like whatever this black weight he towed was, didn't like being kept in the dark. It wasn't the SEAL way.

"Obie?" Swager muttered again.

"Ah, fuck it. Never mind." Teddy tightened up his harness gear. "Pile the gear on the beach. Simulate a demo charge on it. Then round 'em up, move 'em out, get 'em headed inland."

He turned the NVGs off. For a moment his dazzled gaze registered nothing.

Then, rising behind the palms . . . the stars. The banded radiance of the Milky Way, vibrating up there in the night like a billion glowing jellies tiding past.

His leg ached like a dying tooth. Makin had been a disaster, with heavy casualties. And was he going to be able to hack it, with a bad leg, his other injuries? He wasn't forty. Yet. But in the world of the Teams, that was getting to be past it.

But there wasn't much choice, it seemed like. The other Teams were in the spreading wildfire of the Mideast, back in Iraq, Lebanon, Syria, Yemen, or fighting the spreading Islamist nightmare in Africa.

But his worries seemed to recede as he blinked up at the distant lights wheeling in the sky. Not moving. Not even, really, thinking. Just being there.

Until at last he slung his carbine, and followed his men up the beach.

3
Washington, DC

Traffic was light on 66. Probably not a good sign, despite the rain. It was still early enough to be darkish, a little after six on a Tuesday. The wipers whipped back and forth. The gauge was down to a quarter tank; the gas stations had been closed for days. She touched the pedal, and the engine purred as she nudged another few yards ahead. Two roadblocks and vehicle checks so far, and the red strobes of yet another glared off wet asphalt ahead, at the entrance to the Theodore Roosevelt Bridge.

Blair Titus tapped manicured nails on the wheel and sighed. It usually took half an hour to the Pentagon this time of the morning. An hour to the Capitol and, for much of the past two years, forty-five minutes to SAIC headquarters in McLean, Virginia. That was from the house in Arlington, a redbrick colonial with three bedrooms and a family room in the basement. Her husband, Dan, had lined it with shelves, to turn it into a library and home office.

Its back window looked out over a garden planted in terraces down a steep slope, ending in pine forest. She'd planned to get things in order out there, once she'd left the Pentagon, but somehow never found the time. Now overgrown beds of rhododendrons and azaleas shadowed the Christmas ferns and trilliums and dogtooth violets. They blocked the broad stone steps littered with fallen twigs and rotting leaves.

On NPR, the commentator was retailing the financial news in funereal tones. The Dow had begun faltering weeks before, as the Indo-Pak war began. Then a system crash had taken down Wall Street, closing trading. The panic had spread. The president had closed the banks, a step not taken since 1933, and called an emergency meeting of the Federal Reserve. Parallel cyberattacks had shut down much of the power grid, Internet, credit card accounts, cell phones, and the central servers that processed transactions for gas stations, sending prices over fourteen dollars a gallon—payable only in cash. A fire had shut down a smokeless propellant plant in St. Marks, Florida, one that supplied over 90 percent of the Army's needs.

Yesterday the markets had reopened. But to the worst one-day loss in history. A Treasury bailout had summoned a brief rally, but when the House blocked further action, the bloodbath resumed. Even money market funds had lost over two hundred billion dollars as investors converted everything they could to cash.

On the radio, a Cambridge economist was discussing the average of the lowest quarter-end price-to-earnings ratio during panics and recessions from 1873 on. *"The Dow closed yesterday at 6299, the S&P below 500 for the first time since the previous century. The question is, what knock-on effects insurance losses and the disruption of normal trade with Asia will have in the event of a prolonged conflict in the Pacific. That explains the massive drops in valuation of the major insurers, along with electronics, computer manufacturers, and large retailers. The sole sector with positive movement is defense manufacturing."*

She could imagine how her foster dad must feel. He'd always believed in being 100 percent invested, betting on growth. Her own portfolio was more conservative, but still, she'd lost over half her net value. The market ran on confidence, and the American people seemed to have lost that altogether: in Congress, in their president, in their economy, even in themselves.

So far, the primary instinct seemed to be self-preservation.

Diane Rehm was reporting that combined Vietnamese and U.S. forces were threatening the Spratly Islands, in the South China Sea. Did that bring peace closer? Or push it out of reach? No one seemed to know. Just as she didn't know where Dan was. The last she'd heard, before the Internet collapsed, his ship was in the South China Sea. Beyond that, nothing for days. Zip on the news, silence from the Navy . . . but of course, rumors swirled.

On impulse, she pulled her cell from the center console. But the screen still read *no service.* Just like everyone else's.

The rain torrented down even harder as she reached the checkpoint at last. Sandbags. Orange plastic cones gleamed wet. An African-American guardsman waved her to a stop in front of a collapsible barrier, then did a double take and saluted. The Pentagon decal, still on her windshield. From the last administration, but it still showed three stars, her equivalent rank as undersecretary of defense. Rain brushed her cheek with cold fingers as she presented her identification. He handed it back, peered into the car. Her wipers slashed rain at him; he flinched; water dripped off the barrel of his rifle.

"Oh, I'm sorry. I'll turn those off—"

"Pop the trunk, please, ma'am. Where we headed this fine morning?"

"The Capitol. Armed Services Committee. I've been asked in to advise."

He nodded again, gaze lingering on the side of her head as, in the rearview, another trooper inspected her trunk. She brushed a blond lock back to cover her ear. The graft had taken, but imperfectly. The surgeons had warned her, ears were difficult.

The soldier behind her yelled something. The

guardsman stepped away and waved her through. "There'll be another pass point, on Constitution."

She'd been in the South Tower, interviewing with Cohn, Kennedy, when the first jet hit the North Tower. Had fled desperately down the crowded, smoky, jet-fuel-smelling stairwell. Pursued by claps of thunder, nearer and nearer, as the World Trade Center collapsed above her, one story imploding into the next, like a vengeful giant's approaching footsteps. Sometimes the joints between the concrete paving slabs in a highway would sound like it, car-*umph*, car-*umph*, and she had to pull off the road and talk herself down, or bolt a Xanax.

She'd spent seven hours in surgery, with broken ribs, a broken thigh, fractured pelvis, breaks in the arm, and internal injuries. The left eye saved, but the left ear burnt off. They'd "reconstructed" it, but it was still ugly, a reddened, twisted nub.

But as Dan would say, she was still in the game.

She came back to the present headed down Constitution, with traffic sparse, speed better than on a normal day. Taillights blurred and ran pink on the rainy windshield, and she turned the wipers back up. Less than a quarter tank now . . . Ahead in the dim dawn rose the white cupcaked dome of the Capitol. Her destination was beyond it, the Russell Senate Office Building. She'd worked there for years, first as a junior staffer, then as defense adviser to Bankey Talmadge.

She'd risen with Talmadge as he climbed the seniority ladder to chairman, and been staff director for four years before going to Defense as the Undersecretary.

Bankey had called last night, asking her to come in. The familiar, gruff, vaguely drunken voice. Half in the bag, as usual in the evenings. But Talmadge in the bag was still four times as smart as the average senator stone sober. "Mindy's good, but she's not you. I sorely need somebody who knows what's what. Any chance of temptin' you back from that egghead company?"

"You know that's not in the cards, Bankey. I've got to win this election."

"Oh, right, I forgot. Maryland, right? Is cash a problem? I got a little bit'a spare change I can swing from the party. If you need it."

A "little bit" for Talmadge meant several million. She'd salivated at the thought, then felt ashamed. Being from one of the oldest families in Maryland, she hadn't expected trouble raising funding. And at first it had gone well, thanks to her dad's contacts; Checkie had spent his life in banking. But she hadn't been able to give his friends the assurances they wanted, and then with the war, and the market crash, even the pledges she'd managed to garner had evaporated.

"Uh, sure, we can talk about that," she'd said. Grasping that, like a manumitted slave, she'd been bought back, at least for the duration.

The final cordon was at the foot of Capitol Hill, across from the seventies concrete waffle of the Labor Department. About the only building in Washington named after a woman. After another search and ID check, she headed for Senate parking. Which was full, but cars were parked on the grass. She left the Audi there.

"Hey, there's my favorite girl." Talmadge's cheeks were rosy, and even this early she could smell bourbon from across the room. "Grab a seat, Missy."

The senator's office was high-ceilinged, ornate, a stark contrast to the labyrinthine warren of cubicles and converted closets the staffers sweated in. "Missy" was his nickname for her. Blair smiled at Mindy, hoping she didn't take offense. Her old employer was one of the few remnants of the age of the dinosaurs, coeval with Barry Goldwater, Bob Dole, Robert Byrd, Strom Thurmond, the other Talmadge a distant cousin. . . . With the passage of decades his offices had grown larger, his perks greater, his clout colossal. Especially with defense contractors, whose purse strings the Armed Services Committee controlled.

The staffer was petite, brisk, with long glossy dark hair and a sharp little nose. Her squeaky voice was instantly irritating. "Hi there, Blair, how nice to meet you at last. Bankey always

40

talks about you. You're like, you know, the ex-mistress."

Talmadge reddened, rumbled in pleasure. How he loved the little double entendres. And his dalliances had indeed been legendary. Fortunately, Blair reflected, his follow-through had cooled before she'd come on the scene. "Heh heh . . . What say we get down to business. Missy—I mean, Mindy? Want to bring Missy up to speed? And then we'll maybe have a little refresher." He glanced at a chifforobe; Blair knew what that meant.

Mindy opened a folder. "The press is voicing doubts about Defense and the president's direction of the crisis. *WSJ* quotes you from day before yesterday. The polls are sobering. Between 75 and 80 percent of the public thinks we should stay neutral in the Pacific. Things haven't quite shaken down to party positions yet, but Fox is asking if we should consider war at all. After all, isn't Taiwan part of China?"

"The old isolationist wing," Talmadge grumbled.

"Yes, Senator. Some are asking, why not just hand it over? 'Taiwan's a lot closer to China than Hawaii is to California'—that kind of thing."

"That's gonna be interesting. The China Lobby versus the America Firsters."

"Senator?" It was Mary, Talmadge's blue-haired, stooped secretary. The office buzz

41

was that long ago, perhaps in the Ordovician age, there'd been a flame, but Blair had never heard them converse in other than the frostiest formality. Which indeed might confirm the rumor. "It's Mr. Herzog. Hello, Blair. Good to see you again."

" 'S'cuse me, gotta take this." He swung his chair toward the tall window that, thanks to four decades in the Senate, looked out on the Capitol grounds almost on a level with that building itself. In the cold light the trees stood motionless. "Hey there, Augie. What's shakin'?"

Mary asked her, "Is your husband still in the Navy, Blair?"

"Yes, he is. Commanding a cruiser. Out in the Pacific."

"Oh my. Really? I certainly hope . . . certainly hope things will settle down out there." She glanced at Talmadge, shook her head, and tiptoed out.

Talmadge hung up, muttering, "He's sellin' America short. Lookin' for a crisis, and hoping I'll help trigger it. Then we gotta print twenty or thirty billion more in fake money to pay him. . . ." The old man looked bewildered. "And the fella calls himself a patriot. This ain't how it used to be."

Mary, at the door again. "Mr. Callahan. Line two."

"London Callahan, or Seattle Callahan?"

"Seattle, sir."

Talmadge swiveled away again, and once more

only detached words bounced off the expanse of plate glass. "Billy? Hey, what's shakin'? Yeah . . . yeah. Real Buck Rogers, hey? But, you know, we wouldn't have them thangs until five, six years from now. . . . You could speed it up? How much? Yeah. Oh yeah? . . . Sure, build us some, if you can. I'll make sure you get paid."

When he hung up this time Blair caught his eye. "Exactly what did you need, Bankey? You wanted me here first thing."

"Well, you've kept your hand in. I could use your advice."

She glanced at Mindy. "You have a defense aide. Hu? Ku?"

"Hu. Caught short in LA, couldn't get back with all the airlines shut down. Like I say, you were at the Pentagon. How do we look, for this thing in the Pacific?"

She took a breath, organizing her thoughts, then launched into a recap. "The Pakistan-Indian nuclear exchange broke the escalation ceiling. I'm sure Premier Zhang knows eighty percent of our ground forces are bogged down in the Mideast. He's obviously judged this a good time to rebalance the power structure in Asia. Also, I suspect Ed Szerenci's partially to blame."

Mindy said, "The national security adviser?"

"I met with him just before this began. He seemed to think, better war now than later. Quoted me history, about Germany and Britain.

43

He began shooting down their reconnaissance satellites. They retaliated."

"An' now we're invading South China," Talmadge rumbled.

"Um, I didn't hear that." Blair frowned. "We're threatening the Spratlys. That's on the news. But that's a long way from the coast."

"The Paracels aren't," Mindy put in. "I hear that's the Joint Chiefs' plan. But, maybe more like a raid than an invasion. And that *is* classified."

Blair was about to ask how she knew, if it was so damn secret, but was forestalled by a tap at the door. A smooth-faced, very tall African-American in a gray suit stuck his head in. Talmadge called, "Hey, Hu. Glad ya could make it. They flyin' again?"

"Had to rent a car from Philly. Senator. Mindy. And this is—?" He lifted an eyebrow at Blair.

Mindy made the introductions. "Hu" Kuwalay, the defense assistant, picked up the conversation as if he'd been listening outside the door. "We face a difficulty, Senator. You've seen the polls. There's a considerable element with grave doubts about the president's direction of this crisis. After all, isn't Taiwan part of China?"

Blair said, "A lot of history, but we made a commitment to defend Taiwan."

Talmadge nodded heavily. "The Taiwan Relations Act of '79."

Blair said, "Correct. We would regard any attempt to reunify by force as a grave breach of the peace."

44

Kuwalay said, "But actually, the act you cite recognizes the People's Republic as the legitimate government of Taiwan. Yes, we 'regard' aggression as a 'breach of the peace,' but we're actually not pledged to intervene. Some members are asking, why not arrange a compromise? The way Britain handed over Hong Kong, and Beijing promised to maintain the rule of law. And by occupying the South China atolls, aren't we the real aggressor?"

Talmadge started to say something, probably his story about his face-off with Carter back in '79, but Blair jumped in first. "The question's bigger than that, um . . . Hu. You could have argued for a peaceful turnover when China was evolving toward democracy. But after Zhang's crackdown on dissidents, his attack on India . . . we have to defend our national interests. If they take Taiwan, South Korea's encircled, Japan's threatened. We lose everything we won in 1945: a stable Pacific, trading relationships, dependable allies."

"And if we lose?"

"I can't believe we can be defeated. We can give up, but that's not the same thing."

Kuwalay glanced at Talmadge, eyebrows lifted. "We keep getting calls. Longtime supporters. They've sustained huge losses in the downturn. And they're pointing out, we actually don't have a defense treaty with Taiwan. Like we have with Japan, South Korca, and thc Philippines."

Blair suppressed a sigh. "We already covered that. Once we throw the Taiwanese to the wolves, why should our other allies trust us? China will dominate the Pacific."

"That's the Pentagon talking, Ms. Titus." Kuwalay smiled loftily. "Not the Hill. We answer to our constituents. And they don't see why they should go without cheap goods from Walmart, and do without the Internet, and pay fourteen dollars for a gallon of gas, just so we can keep some distant island—"

"No!" She leaned forward, rapping the table. Mindy flinched. "Don't you get it? We've been through this before. The Civil War. Pearl Harbor. This isn't the time to buckle, Bankey! This is when you channel Abe Lincoln. Winston Churchill. Rally the country!"

Talmadge glanced at the liquor cabinet again. He tried to make a fist, but his hand shook. "I hear ya, honey, but . . . I may be getting a little too tired for a big old fight. Missy, I'll level with ya. Used to be, it took two, three years for the members to get restless with a war. Way it was over Vietnam. Or Iraq. Now it's two weeks in and they're talking compromise. Like Hu here says.

"We're gonna see a peace move. One way or another, I'm gonna have to take a position. Can I take a hard line, without the back bench bailing on me? And, hell, have we still got what it takes to fight for four, five years the way we used to?

46

Spend trillions, and take casualty figures in the thousands, the way we did in Korea? Do we have the production advantage we used to? This isn't the same country it was when I was a kid." He fiddled with a small donkey figurine. "Question is, which side do we come down on?"

"He also means, which side do *you* come down on," Kuwalay told her. "The senator has to take a position, *eventually,* but you're the one who's up for election *now.* Pro-war, antiwar—that's what they're going to ask on the campaign trail."

"Nobody's *pro*-war," Blair said. She started to finger her ear, but forced her hand down, casually, into her lap. "I certainly am not. But I don't think we're starting from a disadvantageous position. We have strong allies. Zhang faces internal resistance. And the blockade's got to hurt, sooner or later. No economy can run without oil, and the Navy has its foot on the hose."

"Oh, right." Talmadge looked confused. "Wasn't that your husband who testified? I read about that—"

Kuwalay cut in, "Of course, Blair, everything you say is true. From a strategic point of view. What I mean is, if the party chooses to oppose the administration on this war, it could cost you *our* support for your run."

The senator cleared his throat. Gazing dreamily at the ornate molding over his head, he tapped his fingers together. "Here's what we can do,

Blair. I'm committing five million dollars to your campaign. Run on that platform you just gave us. Kick the Chinks in the balls. Teach 'em not to mess with Uncle Sam. If you can carry Maryland with a hard line, I'll have a feel for how far I can drag the rest of the party. But you gotta hammer the administration, too. They're goin' nuts on the executive side. Attacking. Invading. Land war in Asia. That's crazy."

She thought it over. "It'll be a tough sell."

"If anyone can do it, you can. Still got contacts across the river?"

"Actually, I still consult."

"During your campaign?" Mindy looked disapproving. "Is that wise?"

"It's within the guidelines."

"That doesn't mean you can't be criticized."

"Oh, you're always gonna take flak." Talmadge flipped a hand. "Blair can take it. Put her in a cage with whoever, I'm bettin' she's the one walks out. Who is it now, Missy? Who ya up against? The incumbent?"

"No, he died. My opponent is one Gregory Beiderbaum. Ford dealer, state senator. Openly gay."

Talmadge looked startled by the last adjective, but recovered. "Uh-*huh*. That'll make it interestin'. Get you some coverage, right? Well, good. I guess we're—"

"Just a minute, there, Bankey." Blair laid a

48

finger on his sleeve. Leaned in close. Be his canary in the coal mine? Fine, but this was the time to name her price, and a dose of her perfume had always seemed to jog his memory. "And if I don't win? What then?"

"Why, then . . . then I give Claire a call. She listens to old Bankey. You know Claire, right? You'll be back in the Pentagon in no time."

"I'll hold you to that, Senator. I know your word is good."

"Allus has been. Well then . . . Give Mary your finance manager's name, she'll make the calls. Okay . . . we good?" He hoisted to his feet heavily, orienting toward the cabinet. "Anybody want anything . . . ?"

"Bankey, it's only nine o'clock," Mindy said primly.

"Honey, at my age, Jim Beam's the only way I keep that old blood pumping around." He squeezed Blair's arm. "That sailor-boy husband of yours don't know what he's missin'. Lettin' you run around loose."

The senator came in for a whiskey-smelling bear hug. She smiled and pecked his cheek, glad she didn't have to put up with his sexist crap anymore. It was all a game to him. Push her out on the board, and see if she survived. Yeah. It was a game.

Like the one they were playing with China.

49

4

Savo's Combat Information Center was an ice cave lit by screens of data. It smelled like a freshly unpacked television. Four aisles of consoles funneled data to four large-screen, full-color flat-panel displays. With a three-section wartime steaming watch, about half the consoles were manned.

Panting from the scramble down the ladder, Dan slid into the worn leather chair at the command desk. An icy breeze popped gooseflesh on his nape. He shrugged into the foul-weather jacket draped on the chair, squinting up. One screen was a blue blank, except for a blinking tab reading *GCCS feed failure*. The joint picture, air, sea, and land. Its absence left him blind outside the range of his own task group's sensors. The middle display was the air picture, from *Savo*'s own radars, plus shared data from *Mitscher* via a link.

Two contacts caught his attention. A pulsing yellow trefoil, MIL-STD-2525 Common Military symbology for Unknown Air, glowed to the northwest. Closer, a blue semicircle blinked on and off. The callouts tagged it as a Japanese Air Self-Defense Force antisubmarine patrol plane. Good; they'd have help closing the strait.

The eastern coast of Taiwan walled off the left of the screen. Nearly a straight line, without major ports, bays, or inlets. Behind it glowed an emeraldine sparkle, radar returns from rugged mountains.

The next screen was blank again, and that farthest to the right displayed video from a camera looking aft. The same lens that had nearly caught their rapist, the first time he'd pulled a female crew member into a secluded corner, threatened her with a knife, and masturbated on her. Now it showed only the white, smoothed wake across bright, heaving blue, and a curtain of low clouds.

The yellow trefoil blinked and changed to a red symbol: *hostile*. Dan checked the text readouts above the large-screen displays. Flickering green or orange, they presented the statuses of the various computers, combat systems, a weapons inventory, and radio call signs. He knew most of the numbers by heart.

This was his battle station, not the bridge. Ticos had a little armor, mainly around CIC and the computer room, but antiship warheads were designed to penetrate. By the time any enemy got in sight, he'd most likely already be dead, along with his crew. Blasted apart, burned alive, or sliced into ribbons by flying metal.

The sweet musk of sandalwood as the dark-haired woman at his side leaned in. Lieutenant

51

Amarpeet Singhe, *Savo*'s strike officer. A classic Indian beauty, with huge, dark eyes. But also a Wharton grad, and probably the smartest person aboard. Unfortunately, that had led her into more than one clash with the Chief's Mess. "See it, Skipper? Up to the northwest. Inbound a couple of minutes ago. Then it doglegged right."

He averted his eyes from the V in her partially unzipped coveralls. "I see it, Amy. And, look, next time, don't make it 'CO, report to CIC.' Just the situation, and let me decide whether I need to come down or not."

"Sorry, Captain. I just thought—"

"I know. Never mind. Range?"

"Two hundred miles. No IFF squawk."

"South of the Senkakus."

"Yes sir. Where the landing force was reported this morning."

"Anything from EW?" The electronic-warfare console, where a technician stared at a screen like a rabbit on ketamine. Eavesdropping on every radio and radar emission within hundreds of miles.

Singhe said, "One Type 245 Kobalt I-band surveillance radar. Correlates with H-6 Badger. Maritime recon, but may have a cruise-missile-launch capability."

The Chinese had picked up a lot of Soviet tactics and equipment for long-range maritime strikes. Including antiship missiles. Dan said, "It's covering the landings. Watching out for someone like us. But he's in the Japanese air-defense zone. Let's see how Tokyo reacts before we go to GQ on him. Watch for their fighters, out of Naha."

A raised voice from the Aegis console. "If we can see him, he already knows we're here."

Dan craned around to meet Donnie Wenck's slightly insane-looking bright blue stare. His blond cowlick was sticking up, and as usual his hair pushed the boundaries of the regs. Dan had worked with him on classified missions to Korea, the Philippines, and the Gulf. His spacy demeanor disguised a mastery of arcane software fixes. Dan had just promoted him to chief petty officer, to the displeasure of some. Wenck added, "All the power we're cranking out, five megawatts, we're like a fucking searchlight in a closet."

"Knowing it and doing something about it are two different things. If you detect a missile seeker, though, Amy, assign a Standard and take the archer down. Copy, TAO?"

The corners of Singhe's lips curled upward. "Roger that, Captain."

"Is that encoder gear on the Mark 86 getting fixed?" The fire-control system that controlled the forward and aft five-inchers. Guns were no longer a cruiser's primary armament, but they'd be useful if he had to take on patrol craft or missile boats. Or the landing craft that were, apparently, beaching troops to the northwest.

53

One of the ETs took that one. "Yessir, we have it in the micro-min repair shop. We're short on parts, though."

The downside of just-in-time inventories. The radars, in particular, were burning through spares. Power supply cards, analog-to-digital coverters, switch tubes, crossfield amplifiers. They'd been radiating at a high-duty cycle and peak power more or less 24/7 since the Indian Ocean . . . "Did you read Premier Zhang's ultimatum, Amy?"

Singhe pursed her lips. "I did, sir. One: no American ally will be attacked unless it attacks China, or refuses to provide rights of passage. Two: forces capable of delivering nuclear weapons will be dealt with 'by any means necessary.' Three: any act of aggression against Chinese soil will be answered by a similar level of destruction visited on the American homeland."

"He 'won't attack,' but they're landing on the Senkakus right now."

She shrugged, so gracefully he could imagine those smooth brown shoulders naked. "It doesn't matter what he says. We're at war."

"I agree. Do we have *Stuttgart* and *Curtis Wilbur* yet?"

"They're in radar silence. We won't pick them up until they push over our horizon."

Dan twisted back toward Wenck. "Donnie, how's the Terror doing?"

Wenck dropped his gaze. But murmured, "She's holding up, Skipper. But I'm gonna take her next watch."

Dan kept the command seat warm for the next hour, watching the screen gradually populate with additional aircraft and small surface units as *Savo*'s radars could peer farther over the curve of the planet, toward the mainland. Most clustered around the largest island in the Senkaku group, but there was a lot of air activity over the mainland. Anything the SPY-1 could paint at that range had to be at least medium-bomber size, and at a high altitude. So the coastal defenses were at a high state of alert. The EWs were reporting radar and comm activity from those bearings, too.

In contrast, little showed above Taiwan. They were husbanding their effort, no doubt. Like the lull before the Battle of Britain. No point burning fuel and maintenance hours, when their interceptors and fighters—mainly F-5s, F-16s, and Mirages—might soon be the only shield between them and invasion.

And so far, there was no sign of a Japanese response to the violation of their territory. He'd expected fighters, at least, but nothing showed on the screen.

Singhe had her head down in a reference on the ship's LAN. He watched her for a while, telling himself he was timing her glances at the screen, but in reality just admiring the curve of her neck, the way she brushed shining black hair back from her cheek.

Finally four surface contacts popped up to the north. Singhe spoke into her throat mike. The symbols contracted, then winked blue. Friendly surface. Callouts identified USS *Curtis Wilbur*, escorting *Stuttgart*. JDS *Kurama*. JDS *Chokai*.

"What's *Kurama*?" Dan asked her.

The keyboard rattled. "Wait one . . . Shirane class. Seventy-five hundred tons. They call it a 'helicopter destroyer.' ASROC up forward. Sea Sparrow for point defense. Hangar for two, maybe three helos. Optimized as an anti-submarine platform."

"Just what we need. How about *Chokai*?"

"Kongo-class guided-missile destroyer. Ninety-five hundred tons. Aegis-equipped. Basically, us, except for our antiballistic capability."

Dan nodded, impressed. Excellent fits for the mission. With three Aegis combatants, he could maintain an air picture from central Taiwan all the way to the Japanese mainland, and hold the line against anything short of an overwhelming air assault. With *Kurama*'s helos, plus his own, he could close the strait to submerged passage. A couple of frigates would have been nice, with low-frequency sonar "tails," but maybe he could do this with the forces he had. Hold the pass until the cavalry arrived.

But why weren't the Japanese responding in the Senkakus? The lines must be crackling between Washington and Tokyo. Or were the Japanese just going to roll over? They must know appeasement only encouraged aggressors. And if Zhang got an air base and missile batteries on the Senkakus, he'd have his jaws halfway around Taiwan. The islands were less than a hundred miles from the capital, and perfectly placed to interdict trade. Instead of a blockade strangling the mainland, the PRC could strangle Taiwan.

He got up and paced around, then was reminded by his stomach it was almost noon. He was desperately tired, but maybe food would help. "I'll be in the wardroom, then my at-sea cabin. Call me if anything changes."

Singhe murmured, "Aye aye," as if only half listening. He left her staring up at the screen, dark brows knitted.

Dr. Leo Schell plunked down next to him at lunch. The major from the Infectious Diseases branch at Fort Detrick had joined them in the Maldives, to find out why so many crew members were falling ill. He was out of his white lab coat and back in Army BDUs now. For the crossdeck to *Stuttgart*, Dan guessed. "Guess I should say so long now. Skipper."

They shook hands. "Thanks for helping out, Doc. I really appreciate it." Dan said. To the messman, "Toasted cheese? And a cup of the tomato soup. Thanks."

"I think you'll be in good shape now. None of the samples I took shows any *Legionella*."

"Okay, but how do we keep it from coming back?"

"Hyperchlorinate at least once a week to fifty ppm. I showed your medic, I mean, your corpsman, how to stain and test. If you get a recurrence, steam-clean again. And don't stress the crew. They need rest. Post-legionellosis syndrome; they're still under the weather from the outbreak."

Dan reflected sourly that battle steaming in a wartime environment was pretty much the definition of stressing the reduced-manning crew *Savo* had put to sea with. "Well, again, thanks. We'll be transferring you"—he tilted his wrist to check his watch—"in about two hours. *Stuttgart*'s on the radar. We'll crossdeck you by helo at the same time we rearm."

"Hey, I was hoping for one of those things you see in the movies, where they haul you across in a chair—"

"Helicopter," Dan said firmly. "Things could light up around here very quickly. Sure you don't want to stick around?"

"USAMRIID wants everybody back out of the field."

"In case something nasty breaks out at

home?" Before Schell could answer, the J-phone squealed. Dan reached for the handset under the table. "Captain."

Mytsalo's eager voice. *"Sir, officer of the deck. Request permission to strike eight bells on time."*

For just a moment, Dan felt disoriented. The eternal traditions, combined with the technology of the space age.

The scrape of a chair, and a rangy, spare civilian in slacks and a golf shirt dropped into a seat opposite him. Dan blinked. "Bill. We don't often see you in the wardroom."

Dr. William Noblos was a physicist, not a medical doctor. From Johns Hopkins, the main contractor for ALIS, *Savo*'s still-developmental ballistic-missile-defense subsystem. Noblos had been with them since the Med, though when he wasn't in CIC or in the Aegis spaces, he kept to his stateroom. Dan tried for a friendly tone. "We were discussing Leo's crossdecking this afternoon. Did you want to leave with him? *Stuttgart*'ll be headed back to Guam. You're a civilian, after all. And this is a war zone now."

Noblos pursed his lips modestly. "I owe it to the ship to stay. Your team isn't up to this, you know, Captain."

"Thought you said they were improving."

"I don't want to say they're dunces and you have no chance without my help. So I won't." Noblos sniffed, flicked a napkin open, laid it

59

across his lap, and looked expectantly at the mess attendant. "Dressing on the side. Don't let the bread touch the filling. . . . They're still in the dark on the Delta AM on the array face. I explained how to calculate and apply a bias-correction factor. Several times. I guess elementary calculus is beyond them."

"Chief Wenck's no dummy, Bill. I can't believe he's not picking up on the tuning issue."

Noblos shrugged. Dan contemplated saying something more, but finally didn't. The guy knew his stuff, but it was like dealing with an oncologist with a lousy bedside manner. Still, the scientist was probably the key to making *Savo*'s unpatched, un-updated system work at all. To achieve that, right now, he could put up with an egotistical asshole. Oh, yeah.

But as soon as this crisis was over, the guy was off his ship. And he'd be writing a scorching letter to Ballistic Missile Defense. Noblos belonged in the lab, not out where he had to interact with human beings.

Everyone not on watch mustered at 1300, on the just-cleared mess decks. Dan sat in front, as usual, as Staurulakis and then Mills presented an operational overview. Geo, weather conditions, current intelligence. Emissions-control posture. Unit sectors, *Savo*'s mission, and their rules of engagement.

He hitched forward when Mills reached the part he'd asked him to research: the overall balance, allied forces—including Taiwanese—versus those of the mainland.

"The first requirement for a cross-strait invasion is air superiority. That picture's adverse. Attack aircraft, fighters, and bombers number roughly six hundred versus three hundred, with follow-on reserves limited by airfield capacity, not airframes. If we add U.S. fighters out of Kadena and Iwakuni, the picture looks more even, six hundred to about four fifty. But the PRC still holds a numerical advantage, though their pilots may not be up to ours."

One of the chiefs lifted a hand. "How about the Japs? Are they going to get involved?"

Mills said, "If the *Japanese* stepped in, that would even the odds. But based on what we're seeing, they'll stand aside from a battle for Taiwan. Or, at least, hesitate before they commit. Like a couple of our other allies.

"Any other questions? . . . Okay. The other side also holds a sizable advantage over the Republic of China in submarines, about ten to one, and in surface ships and amphibious units. But they won't risk a crossing before the air war's decided.

"The most striking imbalance is in missiles. DIA estimates over a thousand ballistic missiles, most likely with conventional warheads, are targeted on Taiwan, to suppress defenses, take out

61

radars and command, and crater runways. Plus, between three and five hundred cruise missiles, although many of these may actually be for area denial rather than land attack."

He looked at Dan. Who nodded, considered for a moment, then asked, "What's the bottom line? The outcome? If they really commit to an invasion."

"I've read the studies. Force balance isn't the only issue. A lot of other factors are involved—sortie rates, munitions effectiveness, exchange ratios. The metrics are too variable to pick a winner. It'll be vicious. But if there's a bottom line it's probably . . . yes."

Cheryl Staurulakis said, "Yes, what? Ops?"

"The Chinese can seize the strait. Gain at least local air control. Enough to get a force across, and land."

They fell silent. Not too long after, the exec called attention on deck. Dan rose and left, and the gabble of discussion rose behind him.

He spent that afternoon on a damage-control self-assessment, getting into his oldest set of coveralls for a couple hours of low-crawling, flashlight in hand, along with each compartment's damage-control petty officer. They found closures that weren't watertight, misadjusted ventilation airflow alarms, and some other minor deficiencies and electrical hazards, which they fixed on the spot.

The automatic doors worked. The fire-suppression systems in the engine spaces tested out.

One message came through loud and clear, though he didn't comment on it: the dust 'n' rust were building up. Trash in the compartments. Dirty decks. Three-section watches, along with everyone being fagged from the aftereffects of the *Savo* Crud, probably made that inevitable. But all the inspection tags and maintenance were up to date.

A quick shower, a change to khakis, and at 1500 he held a ceremony on the bridge, pinning enlisted surface-warfare specialty pins—silver "water wings"—on eight petty officers, and getting pictures to send the families, when they got connectivity back. The rest of the day he put in with the Aegis, ASW, and strike teams, fine-tuning and double-checking the calculations they'd generated, and deconflicting them into an overall barrier plan for the task group.

His Hydra crackled as he lay melted into the chair in the little barbershop, all the way aft on the 1 level. The first time he'd felt relaxed all day. "Captain," he grunted into the radio. Hoping he hadn't been snoring while "Turbomouth," the ship's barber, cut his hair.

"Sir, Dave Branscombe, TAO. We have all units in VHF range. You wanted to be called."

"I'll be right up. Ask Matt to join us there if he's awake. But don't roust him if he's off-line."

The bridge was dark. A huge moon hung low, glittering coldly off three-foot seas kicked up by a steady wind from the west. From China . . . Lieutenant Garfinkle-Henriques, the supply officer, currently officer of the deck, oriented him, and reminded him the sonar tail was deployed, in case he wanted to maneuver.

Mills arrived lugging a three-ring binder stuffed with messages, ROEs, and references. They went over everything on the chart table. Then Dan picked up the handset. Cleared his throat, positioning the binder beneath the dim ruby pilot light and eyeing the call-sign board above the scuttlebutt. He pressed the Transmit button, and gave the encryption a chance to sync. "Steel Hammer, Cannoneer, this is Ringmaster, over. Request speak to your actuals. Over."

"Steel Hammer" was the call sign for *Curtis Wilbur*, "Cannoneer" for *Mitscher*. Dan would have to remember that he himself would be "Matador" as CO of *Savo Island*, but "Ringmaster" when he spoke as Commander, Ryukyus Task Group—in Navyspeak, CTG 779.1. The task group would be further subdivided into the Japanese units, Task Unit 779.1.1, and the U.S. ships as 779.1.2. Collectively, their call sign would be "Steeplechase."

"This is Steel Hammer. Stand by for actual. Over."

"Cannoneer, actual on-line. Over."

When both U.S. "actuals," the skippers themselves, were on the line he said slowly and clearly, "This is Ringmaster actual. Stand by. Break. Request Japanese Steeplechase units come up at this time. Over."

A few beats, then the crackle and beep of a new signal. *"This is Mount Yari, over."* The words were faintly accented, but understandable. Dan had decided he wouldn't insist on speaking to the COs, in case their best English speakers were already on the line.

"Mount Shiomi, over."

It took a couple of exchanges before he got them straight. "Mount Yari" was JDS *Kurama*, the helo carrier; "Mount Shiomi" was *Chokai*, the Aegis destroyer. When he had everything clarified, he began passing sector coordinates, taskings, and frequencies. Speaking slowly, line by line, and making them repeat back. Making sure there could be no mistake, no chance for collision or gaps in the coverage. Doing it the old way, before everything had gone to satellite-mediated chat. Mills followed along, nodding as Dan completed each ship's assignment.

When they were done, he took a deep breath. "This is Ringmaster. We're here to hold the line against any attack. The more fiercely we resist, the more effectively we deter further aggression."

He clicked off, thinking, *Jeez, that sounded pompous enough*. Then back on. "This will be the coordination frequency. Stay alert. Keep me informed. Also, be aware of blue submarine activity in Orange Zone, sectors Alfa to Charlie." *Pittsburgh*'s CO had chosen to patrol out front of the barrier, where quiet water and depths down to six thousand feet in the Okinawa Trough would give him better hunting. He hesitated, then concluded, "Ringmaster, out."

When he resocketed the handset, he found Cheryl Staurulakis at his elbow. "Hey, Exec. How'd that sound going out?"

"Uh, pretty stuffy."

"Yeah, got to come up with something catchier. Like '*Molon labe*' or 'England expects every man to do his duty.' "

"As long as it isn't Custer's last line," Mills said.

Dan squinted. "What was that, Ops?"

" 'Gatling guns? We don't need no stinking Gatling guns.' "

Staurulakis murmured, "He didn't really say that. Did he?"

Mills shrugged. "Not in so many words. But he had the chance to take them along, and he turned it down."

Dan grimaced. He found the HF handset in the dark, and reported to "Dreadnought"— Commander, Seventh Fleet, his tactical boss—

that the strait was closed. A bored-sounding watchstander gave him a roger.

He stood near the open wing door for quite a while after they went below, watching a baleful moon above a restless sea.

5
GNS *Stuttgart,* China Sea

The stocky woman in the flower-embroidered tunic and black head scarf dropped her bags on the deck of the hangar. She bent next to a stack of pallets and boxed parts, panting, hands on her knees, and blinked out at the gray ship a mile away. A helicopter hovered above its forecastle, lowering a gray container. The blue sea coursed between them like a massive conveyor belt, as if the ships floated fixed to each other by the black hose that dangled between. As if the ocean, not they, was moving.

She glanced back to find the crew eyeing her again. Germans. They'd kept their distance the whole time she'd been aboard. Not one offered to help, though she was burdened. And not exactly in the best of shape to be climbing around anymore.

Special Agent Aisha Ar-Rahim was in one of her traveling outfits. Under the long embroidered tunic, not quite an abaya, she wore cargo pants and a long-sleeved knit shirt, with Merrell hiking boots. And, yes, she was heavier than she should be, according to the NCIS. Her blood pressure was pushing the limit too. Not uncommon for black women her age, but her diet made her so hungry for salt that she dreamed about potato chips and Virginia peanuts. At her feet squatted a bulging carpetbag purse, a suitcase, and a black multipocketed 5.11 backpack. A second backpack held a high-resolution digital camera, a sixteen-inch expandable baton, and her "case cracker"—a laptop with an external video camera, for recording interviews. Also her SIG 9mm, with a spare magazine of 115-grain +p hollow-point rounds.

A clatter floated across the sea, and she straightened. A wasp-shape lifted, canted, and swiftly grew, trailing a sinking haze of exhaust. A rape case, following incidents of groping and sexual harassment. A ship in trouble, in the middle of a world in even bigger trouble. But being at war didn't mean you stopped investigating crimes.

She edged back out of the way as the helo lined up into its approach.

Aisha had grown up in Harlem and graduated from CCNY. She'd been a Naval Criminal Investigative Service agent for seventeen years. The NCIS looked into any crime involving naval personnel, grand theft to murder. It conducted criminal and counterintelligence investigations, ferreted out contract fraud, and did counter-narcotics work. At first, as one of the few agents who spoke Arabic, she'd worked counterterror, and helped bring to justice the leader of an insurgency in a country on the Red Sea. Then, based out of Bahrain as the Yemeni Referent, she had been part of a joint FBI/NCIS team assisting in the interrogation of a suspected Islamic Jihad member. She held two Civilian Service Awards and the Julie Cross Award for Women in Federal Law Enforcement.

But the director's commitment to promoting Muslims had seemed to fade. As had Aisha's wedding plans. She was shuttled to force protection, then back to Washington, in the Communications directorate. Where she pushed paper and wrote releases.

She'd hit the glass ceiling, which had never been high for agents who wore hijab. For a time, she'd contemplated resigning. But having a daughter starting school made you think twice about leaving a federal job.

Usually, GS-13s with her years in didn't go to sea. But if she volunteered for a float, they'd let her pick her next assignment. She could be the assistant resident, in Manhattan. Retire from there, and collect her pension while she and Tashaara lived in her mother's rent-controlled apartment on Adam Clayton Powell Boulevard. And then, maybe, start an online fashion business. "Plus Size Muslima"; she'd already submitted a trademark application.

She'd been comfortably ensconced on the

carrier, doing clearance interviews, investigating the occasional locker theft, and teaching an introductory Arabic class, when the message had come in from *Savo Island*. Agents routinely flew off the carrier to do investigations. But instead of five or six thousand men and women, the population of a carrier, a cruiser had a crew of fewer than three hundred.

She doubted it would take long to close this case.

There was one debarking passenger. His name tag read SCHELL. He nodded to her in the waiting area. "You've just come from *Savo Island*?" Aisha asked him.

"That's right."

She examined the caduceus on his lapel. "Medical?"

"Dr. Leo Schell. USAMRIID." They shook hands. "You must be the special agent they're expecting."

"I must be. Aisha Ar-Rahim. And what did they need a germ-warfare specialist for?"

Schell bared his teeth. "That's not all we do."

"So what *were* you doing over there?"

"No secret. They had an outbreak of legion-ellosis. We finally traced it to the hot-water systems."

"Ah. Should I not take showers, then?"

"They steam-cleaned everything. Pretty thoroughly. I think you'll be safe."

One of the flight-deck crewmen came over. He held out a cranial, a flight-deck helmet with ear protection, while looking doubtfully at her head scarf. "Fraulein Ar-Rahim? It is time to board. Please put this on."

"Thank you. Can I . . . possibly get some help carrying my gear?"

The crewman looked pained, but reluctantly took two of the lighter items. "I'll give you a hand," Schell said, and picked up one of the backpacks.

Outside, wind and sun. The familiar scorching stench of turbine exhaust. She and Schell heaved her luggage up the fold-down steps, where a flight-suited crewman took them. The doctor shouted something, head bent close to hers. She shook her head, shrugged, and patted his shoulder. Then grabbed the crewman's hand, and let him pull her up into the aircraft.

The helo was settling toward the cruiser when it canted abruptly, making her grab for the edge of her seat. The pilot corrected, a bit wildly, Aisha thought. He set the bird down so hard her chin slammed into her chest. The fuselage swayed and creaked. The crewman seemed to be absorbed in whatever was coming over his headphones. Only when their gazes met did he come to life. He sprang to the exit and dropped the ramp. "Out, we need to get you out!" he shouted, unbuckling her belt and shoving her toward where the sun flooded in. "We got to get back in the air."

When she looked back toward the ship she'd just left, she understood why.

On *Savo*'s bridge, Dan felt it as an attenuated jolt, a distant thump that arrived through steel first, then air.

"Torpedo detonation, bearing one seven five," Rit Carpenter said on the 21MC, at the same moment the lookouts reported an explosion. Dan wheeled, raising his glasses, to witness a black column mushrooming above the replenishment ship's afterdeck. It seemed to be on the far side from *Savo*, which would make the attacker—

Dan said rapidly, "OOD: Breakaway, breakaway! Right hard rudder. All ahead flank as soon as the stern clears. Stream the Nixie. Helo control: get Red Hawk back in the air. Vector to *Stuttgart*, then out along one five zero. Sonobuoys, MAD run. Boatswain: Sound general quarters! Set Zebra, Aegis to active, Goblin alert. Sea Whiz in automatic mode." He wanted his radars aimed low, alert for sub-launched missiles.

The boatswain, Nuckols, put it out over the 1MC, adding *"This is no drill"* as *Savo* heeled hard, building up speed.

Dan hit the 21MC lever. "Rit, why didn't we get a 'torpedo in the water' report?"

"Negat detection, Skipper. Some of these

73

new fish have a quiet setting. They run slow, practically no screw noise. First thing you know, their nose is up your ass."

"Just fucking great . . . Can you hear additional incomers now that you're alerted?"

"No guarantee. We'd have to go active."

"Start pinging. He's in torpedo range; we should be able to pick him up. Find this guy and let's kill him. Before he tries again."

One after the other, departments reported manned and ready. The bridge team finished donning flash gear. As Dan dropped his own hood over his head, his Hydra beeped. He snatched it up as he jogged to the far side of the pilothouse. *Savo* was kicking up a roostertail now, turbines and blowers whining, leaning as the rudder dug in. He picked up the VHF and got *Mitscher.* The destroyer was peeling off in the other direction.

Dan blinked down at the nav console. The torpedo had come from the south. *Inside* the barrier they were setting up. Did their attacker lie in that direction? The odds favored it, but they held no datum—no confirmed location of the sub—so he had to play the probabilities. The gear and weapons had changed since World War II, but antisubmarine tactics hadn't, not that much, with the exception of adding helicopters to the mix. Which evened the odds.

On the other hand . . . *one* torpedo? Most attacks were carried out in salvos. And there'd been three targets. Had the sub simply selected the biggest, pickled off one fish, and pulled the plug? If so, they might have a hard time digging him out. Like taking out a nest of ground wasps: well concealed, yet packing a painful sting. They'd have to proceed step by step. Take their time. He'd let *Mitscher* prosecute. Meanwhile, he'd stay between *Stuttgart* and the threat, in case of a reattack.

Or *was* the replenishment ship the higher-value unit? Maybe *Savo* herself was more valuable, now that her fuel tanks were nearly full, and the replacement missiles secured on her decks.

He grimaced, not wanting to admit that abandoning the stricken ship might be one of his options. That, if push came to shove, he might have to leave her to her fate.

"Bridge, Combat. Starting the plot here. Come to one three zero. Slow to sonar speed."

"Roger, Cheryl. You're parking us to block the threat bearing?"

"Correct, Skipper. Stand by."

Savo steadied on the new course, slowing to reduce self-noise. Cheryl Staurulakis had fleeted up from Ops to become the cruiser's second-in-command. If she had a flaw, it was that she kept reverting to operations officer. But right now, she was where she belonged. He hit Transmit. "XO, 202's on its way out the threat bearing. Put *Mitscher* where you want him and pass control

75

of 202. We stand off, he prosecutes." He debated going down to CIC himself, then dismissed it. He'd built a team. Now he had to trust them. "Take ASW command and nail this fucker down. I'm going to keep my head on the big picture."

The OOD, at his side. "Captain, distress call from *Stuttgart.*"

When he looked back, the replenishment ship was heeled to starboard. The smoke plume was bleeding off, its cap sheared by upper-atmosphere winds. He accepted the handset, but kept his attention on the radar screen; the enemy might poke a scope up, just to gloat. "This is *Savo* actual. Over."

"This is Captain Geisinger. We have taken a torpedo. Flooding. Fire. Request assistance."

"This is *Savo*. We are prosecuting the sub that torpedoed you. Over."

"That is good but . . . I need help here. Fire is out of control. If you cannot help, am abandoning in lifeboats. Over."

Dan held the handset suspended, racking his brain. The German sounded close to tears. But doctrine was crystal clear. Laying alongside to render assistance, without neutralizing the attacker, would just mean another ship got torpedoed. "This is *Savo*. Nailing this guy takes priority. You're on your own, Captain. If you have to abandon, do so in a timely and orderly manner. Over."

"This is Stuttgart. *I protest this decision. You are running away. You can save us. All I need is help. Firefighters."*

Dan almost snapped back at him, but just released the Transmit button. He felt cold, then hot. There didn't seem to be anything to "you're on your own" he could think to add.

He didn't always like being in command.

Aisha stared horrified at the burning, sinking ship, which she'd left only minutes before. But the cruiser was turning away . . . leaving it behind . . . *running.*

Someone seized her arm. "We need to clear the flight deck," a crew woman muttered. Grabbing her gear, she hustled Aisha down a ladder. Men and women in hoods and coveralls pelted by, laden with axes, coils of line, breathing gear. The woman led her into a side passageway, dumping her luggage helter-skelter in a corner. "Sick bay. Ma'am. Please stay here for the time being."

Aisha looked around. "I need to see the exec. Or the command master chief."

"Stay here," the woman said again. "Gotta go." She broke into a run, disappearing around a corner.

"Sir, CO of *Stuttgart,* calling you again."

Dan almost waved him off, then reluctantly accepted the greasy, warm handset. "This is *Savo,*" he said. "Over."

The return transmission was weaker than before, crackly. Probably a handheld. *"This is Geisinger. I am abandoning. Making too much water, too fast. Plus, the fire. But there are men still aboard. The after lifeboats . . . destroyed. They're trapped, on the afterdeck. We can't reach them. A helicopter could get them off."*

Dan studied the overhead as cold sweat prickled his back. "This is *Savo Island.* With regret, Captain. We are continuing to prosecute the contact."

"Your helicopter. There are five men up there. One of them I think is yours. Schell?"

Doctor Schell. Leo. The one who'd found what was killing his men, and helped them wipe it out. Dan scrubbed a hand over his face, and hardened his voice. "Once again, Captain, prosecuting the submarine has to take precedence. Once we're done, I'll send *Mitscher* to pick up survivors.

"God be with you, Captain. This is *Savo Island.* Out."

6

The turbines whined, the air intakes behind the bridge roared. *Savo* was racing northwest, departing the scene. *Stuttgart* had disappeared from the radar, leaving only scattered returns.

No one spoke on the bridge. Dan stood on the wing, gripping the binoculars so tight his fingers hurt. Staring back at the dark stain that still discolored the horizon.

The talker leaned out. "Captain? Red Hawk reports bingo fuel. No contact. Also, patrol air from Kadena's on its way to help prosecute."

"Very well." He drew a breath and let it out, forcing his gaze away from that dark blot. He wanted to stay, and nail whoever had fired that torpedo. The war was hot now.

But a commander had to stay above vengeance. Think coldly. Act rationally. The allies' sole ABM-capable unit in the Western Pacific didn't belong dawdling behind the barrier, trying to track down a single sub. He leaned in the doorway. "Air?"

"Captain." Aside from the one he was speaking to, everyone in the pilothouse was carefully not looking his way.

"Hot-refuel Red Hawk, then vector him back to the sinking site. SAR as many as they can. OOD, come to final course for our sector, as soon as you have it plotted."

They'd laid out the screen sectors in three ranks, or zones. The Yellow Zone stretched from the Chinese coast out two hundred nautical miles to the Okinawa Trench. Orange, for initial detection and tracking, stretched back from there fifty more miles.

Red, sixty miles deep, was the kill zone. Any submerged contact caught there would be prosecuted until destroyed.

Fortunately, he knew these waters. Had operated here during exercises. And, of course, the Navy maintained hydrographic and meteo-rological records on every navigable body of water on the globe. The main thermocline in the Orange and Red zones hovered at a hundred meters, if there was no mixing due to storms. Running the numbers, Rit Carpenter had come up with an average active detection range of twenty miles for a Song-class boat running quiet, as compared to a passive detection range of less than five.

That made Dan's choice easy, especially since *Savo* would have her radars blasting out full power for the ABM mission. All the units in the barrier would be pinging active, except for *Pittsburgh*, of course.

If anyone wanted to take him on, they'd have his address.

Carpenter had also predicted that the abyss to the north would provide enough depth excess that the deep isothermal layer would bend sound upward into a convergence zone. Playing off that, Dan had begun by placing his most capable antisub unit, *Kurama*, at the focus of the CZ, thirty miles back from the intersection of Orange and Red. To the left of that, facing the strait, *Chokai*. To her left in turn, *Mitscher*. *Curtis Wilbur* he placed deep in the Red Zone, a goalie, primed to pivot and sprint at short notice toward anyone penetrating the first line of defense. And finally, anchoring the chain off Miyako Jima, *Savo Island*.

Looking at the geometry for missile defense of Taipei, Dr. Noblos had advised them to displace *Savo* back thirty miles, to get a better intercept angle. Dan had agreed. He'd adjust the other stations, too, once they got the sonar conditions sussed out, but Seventh Fleet had signed off on their initial disposition.

He just hoped no more Red units had slipped through. And that soon, very soon, they could start getting JTIDS data from the AWACS.

A rattle on the ladder, and the blond shield of the exec's head bobbed into view. Dark stains underlined her eyes, and her coveralls were stained at the elbows with what looked like fuel oil . . . or, more disturbingly, dried blood. She was speaking into her Hydra, but clicked it off as she reached the wing. Calm blue eyes locked onto his. "Captain."

"XO. What've we got?"

"CIC called me about recovering the survivors."

"202 will hot refuel and go back. Most of them made it to the boats. We'll lily-pad them to Okinawa, to get them home."

"That's good. The crew's kind of . . . shaken. They don't understand why we appeared to turn tail and run. I know that probably isn't what actually happened, but—"

"We're needed elsewhere. At least it'll convince them the war's gone hot." More rough-edged than he'd meant, but he didn't soften it. Her eyes widened, then dropped to the gratings. He went on, "How much fuel did we get, before the breakaway? And how many Block 4s? Did we get all the missiles?"

"As you directed, they came over first," she said. "Making total aboard, eleven. We also got four Block 3s and two ASROCs." The Block 3s were the older, antiaircraft version of the missile. ASROCs were antisubmarine rounds, encapsulated torpedoes mounted on a rocket motor. "Fuel . . . I didn't get a final number yet, but CHENG said close to ninety percent."

"Okay, good. Get me a hard percentage soon as you can. Or have Bart give me a call. We'll need to watch consumption, now we don't have logistic support. Make sure the loadout board in

CIC gets updated. Remind Chief Quincoches how badly we need those rounds spun up, tested, and ready to fire. Also, schedule a live-fire exercise this afternoon. Five-inch and Phalanx."

Staurulakis was hitting keys on her BlackBerry, getting it down. Good.

He had the feeling that, in the next few days, they were all going to be tested.

The exec passed "lunch on station," which meant everyone stayed at his or her general-quarters station, and sent runners for sandwiches and coffee. Dan dithered over the need to establish the barrier and the fact that, now that their tanker was gone, he didn't know where his group's next drink was coming from. He compromised by not zigzagging. That upped the risk, should another sub lie doggo along their course, but he was used to the calculus. When you lessened one risk, you increased another. You could analyze it statistically, but an experienced skipper's guesstimate usually came out close to an optimal solution anyway. *Mitscher* reported no contact with the sub that had torpedoed the tanker. Dan checked his watch, and reluctantly ordered her to discontinue the search and head for her sector.

He was leaning back in his chair, rubbing burning eyes, when the covered phone beeped. The OOD held it out. "Captain Youngblood, sir."

CO of *Pittsburgh*. Dan grabbed it; like most

submariners, Youngblood hated to poke his radio mast up, to expose his boat even to send traffic. This close to their coast, the Chinese could probably triangulate any transmission within seconds. "Lonnie. This is Dan. Go ahead. Over."

"This is Polar Bear. On station." They discussed detection ranges briefly, then Youngblood said, *"Unless attacked myself, I plan to stay covert. Drop my sensor line, then hand tipoffs off to you. You skimmers can clobber the incomers once they hit your Red Zone. Over."*

"Concur, Lonnie. Reporting procedures?"

"One burst transmission on the ASW coordination frequency. I don't want to have to repeat myself, so maintain a close watch. Over."

"Got it. Stay deep and good hunting."

"Same to you, Dan. Polar Bear, out."

Dan handed the phone back to the OOD. "Log it. Tell Dave Branscombe what he said about contact reports."

Next up beside his chair was Ollie Uskavitch. The weapons officer was about the biggest man aboard. The chief engineer, a Harry Potter fan, had been known to address him as "Hagrid." But as he began to speak, Dan's Hydra beeped. He nodded to Uskavitch and unholstered the radio. "Captain."

"XO, sir. The NCIS agent is asking for a moment with you."

"Um, can't spare the time, Cheryl."

"This is important, Captain."

"I agree, but I really have to concentrate on operational issues right now. Take care of her. I'll break out a couple minutes soon as I can." He clicked off and glanced at the heavyset lieutenant. "What'cha got, Ollie? Can we get those missiles in the cells, like, yesterday?" He leaned to squint down on the forecastle. Gray-white weapons containers were ranged along the gunwales. The cell doors were open, and the loading crane, a complicated arrangement of beams and motors, was erected, with guys standing around it. But other than that, nothing much seemed to be happening.

Uskavitch blew out, looking harried. "Not gonna be that easy, Skipper. The one guy we sent to the training course rotated out before we left the States. I got the chief and first class reading the manual, and a guy with a grease gun getting everything unstuck."

Dan felt like jumping down his throat, but restrained himself. "You should have anticipated this, Ollie. We knew we were gonna have to rearm at sea. That crane should have been overhauled and ready before we went in for the unrep."

"Yessir." The long face grew even longer. "But it isn't that simple—"

It never is, Dan thought sourly. Uskavitch explained that both the forward and aft magazines had built-in cranes. They were designed to let the ship load its own replacement rounds, without having to depend on pierside equipment. But since no ship had ever expended its loadout before, the cranes had been officially deactivated.

"Right, I get it," Dan snapped. "And they dropped the parts from the supply system. I hope they saved a boatload of money. . . . But you've got the thing erected down there. So what's the goddamned problem now?"

Uskavitch swallowed. "Well, sir . . . First, we got to lift the canister, then get it lined up just exactly fucking right to slide down into the cell. We can't be rolling or pitching more than four degrees. If a round breaks loose, we don't want a warhead rolling around on deck."

Dan studied the horizon. "Seas aren't that bad. We can select the best course to minimize the roll."

Uskavitch swallowed again. Added, unwillingly, "Yeah, but see . . . even if we get it working, the main beam's aluminum. And the new Block 4s are way overweight. The manual says they're too heavy to reload at sea. At all. You got to load 'em pierside, with a heavy-lift."

Perched on his command chair, Dan was at just the right height to get both hands around Uskavitch's throat. Instead he dug the heels of his hands into his eye sockets. "So you're saying we can't load them."

"Well, sir, Quincoches thinks he might have a work-around."

"How's he gonna work around that?"

"He wants to weld a reinforcement on the top arm. Like a flange."

"There's got to be a downside."

"Well . . . we won't be able to retract the crane once that flange is sticking up. It's going to have to stay erect, in an open cell."

"Exposed to the weather?" Dan asked, and Uskavitch nodded unhappily. "And if we take a heavy sea over the bow? We're gonna flood that whole module. What else is in there?"

"Tomahawks."

Dan gritted his teeth. Decision time. "How long's it going to take to weld on this reinforcement?"

"They're cutting metal now, down in the machine shop. Weld it on . . . we might get it done before dark."

"Get it loaded, or get it rigged?"

"Get it rigged," the weapons officer said, not meeting Dan's gaze. "Then we have to load it, right. Sir."

Dan kneaded his eye sockets again. "So we're gonna steam around with all our lights on, on the forecastle, all night, lit up like a carnival? And have a hole in our foredeck, from then on?"

"Uh, yessir."

"And if that weld snaps? While you're loading a missile?"

"Then we're really fucked, I guess," Uskavitch offered helpfully. "Captain."

Dan sighed, then craned over the bulwark again. Chief Quincoches was gesticulating heatedly, pointing up at the crane, while Chief McMottie, the lead engineer, shook his head, arms folded. He closed his eyes. "Okay, here's what we're gonna do. Load all the other rounds, the ASROC and the regular Standards first. Get them in the cells and off the decks. Then weld up the fucking crane and give it a shot."

"One suggestion, sir."

"What, Ollie?"

"We hump all the regular-weight rounds aft, and load them in with the aft crane. Meanwhile we're welding on the forward one. We put all the new Block 4s up forward."

"Yeah, that'll speed it up. Good thinking. But you're still on my pad for not bringing me this a lot earlier, Weps."

"Aware of that, sir. Sorry."

"Reports every hour."

"Yessir," Uskavitch said miserably, saluting as he turned away. For a big guy, he seemed to fade from the bridge very suddenly.

Leaving Dan stewing in his chair. Ice picks were digging into his shoulders, his lower back. From the broken vertebra he'd gotten in the USS *Horn* explosion. Even if they could get everything loaded, that would leave him with only eleven ABM-capable rounds. Facing over a thousand Chinese intermediate-range warheads across the strait.

Cover Taipei? With eleven rounds of barely tested missile, running Beta-version software?

It sounded more like a bad joke than a wartime mission.

Dan was in Combat, monitoring a recon H-6 that had taken station in the strait, and watching the welding on the forward crane through the forecastle camera, when the daily HF update came in. Like most Ticonderogas, *Savo* had good topside coverage. The cameras for the forward and aft missile decks were controlled via a joystick from the command desk. The 25mm gun cameras, port and starboard on the aft missile deck, could move independently of the guns. Finally, he could look through the port or starboard Sea Whiz sights, though to do that he had to take control away from the weapons consoles, and move the guns as well as the cameras.

He also had surveillance in the passageways outside the main magazines, and a couple other spots within the skin of the ship. The chief master-at-arms had reviewed the tapes after each of the sexual assaults, but they'd never showed anyone suspicious. As if whoever had first fondled, then masturbated on, and finally raped his victims had known exactly where the cameras were pointed.

A disturbing thought . . . He read through the update. Vietnamese and U.S. forces had completed the occupation of the outlying atolls. Chinese reaction, press reports said, had been muted. But there was no mention of *Stuttgart*'s loss, or indeed of any activities in his theater. Had the lid clamped down already?

"The Chinese don't seem to want to venture out into the South China Sea," Lieutenant Singhe murmured, beside him.

Dan blinked up at the displays. The H-6 was in a slow orbit. Like the AWACS bird that was patrolling a similar racetrack east of Taiwan. He didn't have access to its data, since the satellite uplink was gone. Wenck was working on some kind of relay but wasn't there yet. There was more air activity over Taiwan, in response, apparently, to the steady buildup across the strait. "Probably wise," he told Singhe.

"Not to strike back?"

"Not in the Spratlys." The geographical plot for GCCS resided in the ship's computers. It was independent of satellites, unless you wanted real-time contact information. He typed, then spun the ball under his palm. Green land and blue sea jerked across the screen, updating in fits and starts, moving south, then west. Past the Philippines, out into the empty sea between

Palawan and the coast of Vietnam. "See how far from their home airfields they are? Six, seven hundred miles. They don't have that kind of reach. The next hop for the allies will probably be here." He aimed a movable callout.

"The Paracels." Singhe leaned closer. She didn't smell of sandalwood now, but of sweat and too-long-worn cotton. But it was still inviting, to a guy who hadn't been with his wife since Crete.

"Five hundred miles closer to the Chinese coast. After that, I'd guess, Woody Island. The airfield there can take fighters, and there's a major radar installation and antiship missiles. Past that, Hainan, and the sub base they built into the mountain."

Singhe brushed back dark glossy hair. When he stole a glance, her head was tilted back, eyes closed. "Then what? Hong Kong, or the Guangxi Autonomous Region? People think of China as this solid, homogeneous entity. But they have minorities, too. Ancient hatreds. Start an internal uprising, they'd be a lot easier to deal with."

"Come on, Amy. You're a student of Chinese politics, too?"

A smile curved full lips. "You'd be surprised, Captain."

A bell interrupted the moment, and Dan twisted in his seat. Chief Zotcher yelled from behind the dark blue canvas that curtained the sonar area, "*Chokai* reports contact. Range, twenty-two miles. Bearing, zero zero five. Vectoring helo for MAD run."

"Put it on the screen, Chief." He hitched forward, frowning. Strange that *Pittsburgh* hadn't picked it up. A premonitory foreboding prickled his shoulders. *Chokai* hadn't reported a course, speed, or depth yet, but it had to be headed for the barrier. Once they had a helo over it, with dipping sonar and magnetic-detection gear, they'd be able to identify class and nationality.

He tented his fingers, pondering. North Korean? The abortive attack on Pusan a few years before had reduced Pyongyang's fleet considerably. And the Chinese, if they were smart, would hold their older units close inshore for a last-ditch defense. Their nukes were much noisier than their conventional boats. So this was probably either a Kilo or a Song.

He pulled up the order of battle on his screen and studied the specs again. Both were well armed and capable, but a Song would be especially dangerous. The first class actually designed and built in China, it was estimated to carry wake-homing torpedoes, antiship cruise missiles, and the Russian-licensed, high-speed rocket torpedo called the Shkval-K.

A chill ran up Dan's back. He knew that weapon. If the Chinese could get close enough for a shot before they were detected, they could take out his blocking units. Turn the Sea of Japan, the

East and South China Seas, into strategic havens, then expand control outward. *Savo* herself had interim anti-Shkval spoofing gear installed, but it was untested against the real thing.

"Keep clear of the torpedo danger area. Pass that to both Japanese units." Singhe nodded. Dan hit the key on the 21MC, the "bitch box," by his elbow. "Sonar, Combat . . . Rit, you there?"

"Here, Skipper. I know what you're gonna say, and I'm on the net with the guy, okay?"

"What's he got? Anything identifiable?"

"I'm not making a lot of sense out of his return. Might be screw noises."

Dan double-clicked to sign off, and turned the dial on his own headset feed to catch the end of Singhe's transmission. Should he vector *Mitscher* closer to *Chokai*'s sector? But it could be a feint, to draw them north, while a larger force intruded from the west. He and Singhe discussed this, and she agreed.

Time stretched on. The gray-blue sea-line tilted slowly in the camera's view. The crane, a weird mechanical simulacrum of a human arm complete with elbow, rotated into position. Sparks cascaded as the welders went to work. Dan panned right and stepped up the magnification, but *Mitscher* was far over the curve of the horizon. Someone at the Aegis console put the output on audio, and the popcorn rattle of the outgoing pulses bounced off the overhead. He glanced over to see a familiar

93

brown-haired head, a round face lit green by the screen. He rose, patrolled the consoles, chatting or patting a shoulder. Ending up behind Petty Officer Beth Terranova. But just then a lean form sidled through the doorway: Bill Noblos. The civilian scientist folded his arms as Dan bent over the petty officer. "Terror, how we doing?"

"Our output parameters are within normal limits," she said softly to the screen.

"Great. But I meant, how are *you* doing."

"I'm here, sir. Personal . . . output parameters . . . are within normal limits."

He put out a hand to pat her shoulder, but lowered it without doing so. She might not appreciate a man's touch right now. He couldn't imagine what she was feeling, in the aftermath of rape. Surely, still afraid, since they hadn't caught her assailant. Probably angry, too. "Uh, have you . . . have you talked to the NCIS agent yet?"

"No sir. I know she's aboard. But I haven't seen her yet."

How could they expect her to keep working? But she had to. Chubby cheeks and all, she was their best Aegis operator. "We'll get this nailed down, Terror. I promise. And I really appreciate your sticking to your station right now. We need our best eyes on these screens."

"That's Petty Officer Terranova, all right," the civilian scientist said. "She's about the best you've got, Captain."

The way Noblos drawled it, it wasn't really a compliment. As if he'd meant to imply, *But best of a not very impressive team.* But she didn't respond to either man. Dan caught a warning shake of the head from Wenck. As he headed back for the command desk, Noblos took his place, and started discussing system calibration.

Back at the table, Dan took the clipboard a radioman held out. Scanned the message. Taiwan was sending a liaison. A Commander Fang, Republic of China Navy, would arrive by helicopter from Taipei no later than midnight. He passed the clipboard to Singhe. "ROC liaison. On his way."

"That's good. Link us up with their sensor network. Better access to air cover, maybe, too."

Dan nodded. "And a couple of their frigates? Perrys, or Knox-class—those are great ASW platforms. Some patrol missile boats, to screen us. And fuel—we could peel off one unit at a time for a run to port. Or even get a tanker out here."

He sucked air, heartened, then shook his head at himself. He must really be tired. His emotions were all over the place.

A clatter by the door. He glanced over to see Wenck and FC3 Eastwood setting down a gray container. The closures clacked as they opened it and began extracting components. He flinched at a sudden *pop pop pop*. Jesus! It was only bubble

95

wrap. He needed to untensify. Cut back on the coffee. Get more sleep. They could be out here for a long time. He needed to pace himself. And everyone else, too.

"Jeez, look at this shit." Wenck shook a switch tube, wincing as something rattled inside. "This is the best they could give us?"

"What's the problem, Donnie?"

"They're busted already. We're burning through these fuckers like crap through a goose, and they send us shit."

"Give me stock numbers. Hermelinda will put a top priority on it."

"She already did. This is what we got." Wenck pursed his lips as if to spit. "I'm not a fucking magician, Dan. I mean, Captain. We can't keep ALIS running if the fucking radar goes down."

Dan's earphones said, *TAO, ASW. Chokai reports negative MAD contact, negative screw noises on Datum Alfa.*

He hit the 21MC. "Sonar, CO. Hear that? What's your call?"

Zotcher: *"Sounds like a false contact. Whales?"*

"I'm thinking, classify with a Mark 46."

"Your call, Skipper. You da boss."

After *Stuttgart*, he didn't feel like taking any chances. Compared to losing another ship, a torpedo was cheap. "ASW: attack on last suspected datum."

"ASW, aye. Pass to Chokai, *carry out attack."*

96

Wenck stood over him, looking grim. Dan looked up. "Donnie. What we got?"

"Beth."

"She need a break?"

"The agent wants to meet with her. Can we spare her?"

"I guess," Dan said reluctantly. "For an hour. If you'll be on the console."

"Eastwood can take it. I gotta swap out these cards, get the system back up."

"I can take the console," Noblos offered, stepping out of the shadows. "One could argue I'm qualified."

Dan all but lifted his eyebrows—the civilian had never offered to help before, other than by offering condescending advice—but just said, "That'd be great, Bill. Yeah, if you could take a trick."

"I just can't do a fire order. Not being part of your command structure."

Yeah, that was more like the Noblos he knew. Dan said wearily, "The TAO will give any fire orders, Bill. Just run the radar for us. We'll take care of business from there."

"Coffee, Cap'n?" Longley, by his elbow with a carafe and a plate of cookies. What the hell time was it? He'd missed another meal. The thick black coffee steamed in the cold air. The cookies were chewy and dense, peanut butter, a meal in themselves. Make a note: compliment the bakers, next time he was on the mess decks. Food was a combat-readiness issue too.

He leaned back in his chair, watching the callouts click forward as *Chokai*'s helo headed in to the attack.

7

Aisha got up early the next morning. Spread out the little rug from her carpetbag, and did her morning *salat*, her prayers, in her stateroom. The girl she shared it with was gone, on watch, probably.

No one seemed to know who she was, to judge by reactions in the passageways. She got a couple of double takes, one from an attractive brother. He grinned, seemed about to say something, but then didn't.

This ship seemed more subdued than the carrier, where the passageways often rang with shouting and laughter. Or maybe this was simply a wartime atmosphere. She drifted down dead ends, trying to follow the scent of food. Not liking it when she was alone in a deserted passageway. But pressing on.

The grimy, crowded mess decks weren't all that different from the carrier's. Blue terrazzo decks. Glaring fluorescents. Overheated air. A stainless-steel mess line, with the servers in chef's caps behind Plexiglas sneeze shields. People coughing, clearing their throats, which reminded her of the "hajji cough" everyone seemed to get when she'd gone to Makkah. The smells of coffee, eggs, hot bread, the greasy sizzle of pig meat. She slid her tray along, picking and choosing. No way any of this was halal, but after seventeen years in, she was used to making do. The ship's roll was different from the carrier's, too. Faster, sharper, slightly sickening. She got hard-boiled eggs, toast, canned peaches, coffee. Was eating alone at one of the tables, when a dark-haired woman in the blue coveralls they all wore halted abruptly, hands on hips. "And who do we have here?"

"Special Agent Ar-Rahim."

"Oh—our investigator?"

"That's correct."

"They told me you didn't make it. Typical. Mind if I—"

The woman took a seat opposite without finishing her sentence. Toffee-skinned, with gleaming hair and a prominent nose. Like the Pakistanis who occasionally stopped by her home mosque in Harlem. They seldom returned. But even in the baggy uniform, she was striking. Twenty-five, twenty-six? "Amy Singhe," she said, extending a hand. No wedding ring. "Short for Amarpeet."

"Singhe. You are Indian, yes? Sikh?"

"A lot of Sikh Singhes, but my family's Hindu." She slid a notebook from a pocket. "You're here about the rapist? I want to help."

Over the years, Aisha had learned that the first people to approach you about a case were seldom the ones you really wanted to talk to. Those would be more reticent, erect barriers, hide behind the rules. She sipped coffee from a paper cup. "Lieutenant?"

"Strike officer. Tomahawk, Harpoon. Just recently, started to stand TAO watches."

"How are you involved? Did Miss Terranova work for you? Are you her division officer?"

Singhe leaned in, revealing a sparkle of gold at her cleavage. Aisha caught the scent of sandalwood on the heated air. Caught, too, the glances from the men around them. "I'm not her division officer. I'm involved because I'm in a navy, and aboard a ship, that doesn't welcome women. I've seen how the enlisted women are mistreated, and gone on record about it. I've written for *Navy Times* and the Naval Institute."

"So you're a . . . victim advocate? Self-appointed?" Aisha cut her eyes around. The nearest tables were emptying, but that could just be the abaya and head scarf. Though some of the crew wore scarves, too, all in olive and black.

"If we had one. Yeah."

"And you're telling me the command climate's hostile, even these days?"

Singhe said reluctantly, "I don't think the new CO's that hidebound. But he's fighting a middle management that hates change. You know what happened in Naples?"

Aisha nibbled on a hard-boiled egg. "No. What?"

"The old CO ran the ship aground. I was on the

101

bridge, trying to anchor. But he kept interfering. Then we had an engine casualty, and by the time that got straightened out we were aground."

"Was there a court-martial?"

"An admiral's mast. The old CO, the old command master chief, and some others went. Like I said, it's a little better . . . but the mind-set's still there. Women don't belong. A distraction. Never quite as good." Singhe sat back, a faint sheen of perspiration glittering on her forehead. "The rape was just the culmination of a lot of things. Verbal harassment. Groping. Exhibitionism. Those were never looked into. Papered over. And there's a lot more going on that nobody knows about."

Aisha kept her tone neutral. "That might be relevant, yes. Though sometimes it's hard to draw a causal line. I appreciate your introducing yourself, Lieutenant. May we talk in depth later? Once I've had a chance to get read on the facts of the case?"

"Whenever you want. I only want to help make things better." Singhe rose, stuck out her hand again, then flushed and withheld it. "You're Muslim, right? Aisha?"

"I do shake hands, Amy," Aisha said gently. She held the warm, slightly sweaty palm for just a moment before she nodded and let it go.

An hour later, she arranged a chair in the wardroom. Facing her was a seamed, leathery visage with deep grooves around the mouth. Hair was combed carefully across a bald spot. His name tag read TAUSENGELT. The largest hands she'd ever seen on a human being lay folded on the table.

"Basically, your investigation may have to wait," he said.

Tausengelt was the command master chief. The CO and XO were both too busy to see her, apparently. Well, she could understand that. A war, and a sinking . . . interesting that the CO, a Captain Lenson, hadn't seemed eager to stay around and help. In fact, they were steaming away now. Where, she wasn't quite certain.

She pulled her attention back as the senior enlisted explained that the ship had carried out its own investigations of the assaults. "I've called our chief master-at-arms, Chief Toan. Unfortunately, Hal's kind of tied up now too. Since we're still at general quarters and all."

"What happened to the tanker, Master Chief? To *Stuttgart*?"

He deliberated, as if pondering if she could be trusted. "She was torpedoed."

"I know that. I saw it, from the helo deck. But then what? She went down?"

"That's correct, she sank," Tausengelt said, gaze averted.

"What happened to the crew? Did you get the sub?"

103

"I can't discuss that."

"Master Chief, I hold a top secret clearance."

"That may be, ma'am, but with all due respect, you're here strictly on NCIS business. So, basically, you got no need to know operations, tactics, equipment." Tausengelt glanced at his watch. "We might be able to get you the victim now."

"I'd rather start with the scene," Aisha told him. "So I can make sense of what she tells me."

"All right then." Tausengelt got up. "I'll see if I can find you the chief master-at-arms."

"If, that is, he's not on watch?"

The heavy-lidded, seamed face of an old tortoise regarded her. "Yeah. If he's not on watch."

The crime scene was high in the ship, which left her puffing and dizzy after all the ladders. Hal Toan, the chief master-at-arms, was a slight Vietnamese. He smiled as he held a door for her, and as he updated her on the background of the case. Incongruous, but perhaps that was just his habitual expression. The space was lined with lockers, a work counter, neatly racked tools. The cold air smelled metallic. She unslung her camera. "Where, exactly?"

"Here. On the floor. On a blanket, the victim said."

"Where's the blanket now?"

"Didn't find one. Perp took it with him, I guess."

"Has the space been cleaned?"

"Um, yes . . . ma'am."

" 'Special Agent' will do."

"Yes, Special Agent. We cleaned it."

"Did you keep any dust, hairs, blood, fabric threads?"

"Put a fresh bag in the vacuum, then Baggie'd that. Special Agent."

"Okay, good." She went out in the corridor. Asked how many accesses there were, and made notes. Then went back in, closed the door, and turned the lights off. She took a flashlight from her purse and clicked the infrared LED on. Efflorescence glowed near the workbench, probably from whatever they used to clean the electronics. But nothing that looked like blood. She turned the overheads back on and inspected each sharp corner, where someone might hurt himself. If there was resistance, few assailants came away without some sort of damage. Scrapes, bruises, sprains. Facial scratches were common; women often went for the eyes.

She'd worked rapes before. The victim usually knew the perpetrator. Not surprising on a ship, but it held true even for air squadrons, Marine regiments. It was usually an acquaintance, not some stranger jumping out and dragging her (or, occasionally, him) into a dark passageway.

Most rapists weren't the knuckle-draggers you saw on television. They kept themselves well groomed. Knew how to present an attractive front. They lacked empathy or remorse, but could fake either. They were either openly or secretly contemptuous of women, viewing them as prey or scores. The profiles of sexual predators and acquaintance rapists overlapped. Some went back and forth, from using minimal force on women too intoxicated with drugs or alcohol to resist, to battery, then to torture, mutilation, and murder. It was a spectrum, and given time and opportunity, a perp tended to push his envelope. There were as many white players as black. Class mattered too: when an officer was involved, it was usually less the threat of physical force than of career intimidation—"Play along, or it'll impact your next evaluation."

Hardest of all to get a grip on was the guy who never left a mark, never crossed a line where he couldn't claim consent. She suspected there were a lot more of these crawling around than ever crossed the door of the criminal justice system. Most of their victims never reported it.

She blinked, running a finger along the edge of a cabinet. Remembering what the Indian lieutenant had said. *There's a lot more going on that nobody knows about.* It was true, some ships seemed to be rotten. It didn't always seep down from the top. Sometimes it seemed to bleed upward, from some mysterious cancer deep in the bowels of the ship, or its history, or some pivotal individual whose evil bore fruit years after he was gone.

But then, how did Singhe know?

A tap from the passageway. "Come in," she called.

"Need help?" Chief Toan said from the doorway. A slight white woman with blond hair stood behind him.

"I'm done for the moment. But please keep this space locked, in case we need to return."

"It's a repair space," the blonde said. "We may need to give the techs access from time to time. But other than that, we'll keep it sealed." She extended a hand. "Cheryl Staurulakis. Executive officer. Sorry we had to meet like this, Special Agent . . . Aisha?"

"Aisha works." She nodded to Toan. "The Chief's been very helpful. Right now, I'm just looking over the scene. Then I'll want to interview the victim. How is she?"

"The Terror . . . Petty Officer Terranova . . . she's shaken up. It's a blow."

"Is she medicated?"

"She had a sedative right after. That Army doc, Schell, gave it to her two days ago. Nothing since. That I know of." Staurulakis wrapped her arms around herself, peering past Aisha into the compartment. "Has the sheriff here told you this wasn't the only incident?"

"He said you had two previous. One, a groping up on the hangar deck. Is that an open case?"

"We handled that with our MA force. We never settled on a . . . specific suspect. Second, a near rape back in the supply spaces. Different woman. But the victim of the first groping was also Miss Terranova."

Aisha asked her, "Who was the second?"

"Storekeeper Seaman Celestina Colón. She was in the aft passageway, two level, when the lights went out. He shoved her into one of the spaces back there, then pushed her down onto something soft. Undressed her, threatened her with a knife, and used his fingers."

"They were interrupted? He would have gone on?"

"Doesn't seem to have been. You can ask, but what she told us was, he didn't actually attempt penetration. With his penis, I mean."

"Only with the fingers?" Staurulakis nodded. "This Terranova, Colón. Are they alike, physically? Build, hair color, ethnicity?"

The exec glanced at the chief. Toan shrugged. "I would say not. Terranova's kind of heavy. New Jersey Italian. Brown hair. Meek. Colón's Puerto Rican. Thin. Black hair. Built more like a boy. Kind of hard-looking, if you know what I mean."

"No, I don't," Aisha said. "Explain it to me."

"I mean . . . like not much is gonna make an

impression on her. That she's tougher than the average bear."

"We had our eyes on a suspect," Staurulakis said. "He kept trying to get her alone. A castaway we picked up. Claimed to be a religious refugee. Colón didn't think it was him, but he was on our short list."

"Where is he now?"

"We offloaded him in Singapore."

"Before the rape?"

"Correct."

"So he's off the board for that, but still a possibility for number two."

Toan said, "One more thing. Both guys turned off the lights. I mean, in all three incidents."

Aisha waited. "And?"

"The lights in the helo hangar passageway, in the supply storeroom, and in the radar equipment space."

"You're saying that's an MO? I'm afraid it doesn't give us much."

Toan said, "Actually, it might. See, there's no topside access from the interior passageway on the Supply Department level. So there's no darken-ship switch there. Somebody had to know how to turn them off back at the lighting panel."

Staurulakis nodded. "We thought, possibly an electrician. Or a compartment petty officer. The darken-ship switch up on the hangar-deck level was interfered with too. When the Terror was first groped."

"I see." Aisha filed this away. "Could we see the corpsman next? Again, except for operational needs, please keep this space locked."

"All right." Staurulakis hesitated. "What else can we do? To facilitate your investigation."

"I'll need a private space."

"I've set that up. Unit commander's stateroom. Main deck, starboard side, midships."

"And an assistant. Someone who knows his way around the ship."

The exec traded glances with the master-at-arms. "May take a little more doing. We're stretched pretty thin right now. Let us get back to you on that."

Savo's sick bay was well aft, a brightly lit, immaculate space that seemed almost new, in contrast with the rest of the ship, which looked worn at the edges. The deck shook, and the thrum of the screws imposed a constant, loud backdrop of ambient noise. The lead corpsman was named Grissett. "Hudson, Hud . . . most folks just call me Doc."

Aisha shook hands, looking around. Chairs, desk, examining table; a sink, a stool, white plastic jugs of saline and other compounds in racks. The containers shifted as the space rolled around them. Through a curtained door lay a dimly lit bunking area, apparently untenanted at the moment. The cool air was welcome after the stifling, close heat in the passageways.

Grissett introduced a petite strawberry blonde as Hospitalman Seaman Ryan. He said, "Grab a chair, ma'am. How can we help?"

"Well, so far I've spoken with the CMC, the CMAA, and the XO. I'd like your take on the Terranova rape."

Grissett pulled a file and took a seat. "Okay, where do you want to start?"

"Injuries."

"She wasn't significantly hurt. We took photos of some bruises."

"Under UV?"

"Actually, yes. I can provide JPEGs over the command LAN if you'll give me your shipboard address."

"I'm not plugged in yet, but should be shortly. Who conducted the examination?"

"Dr. Schell, assisted by myself and Duncanna here."

"Did you follow the protocol?"

"She was fragile. I kept the forensic examination short."

Aisha understood. Sexual assault forensics were intrusive and often humiliating for the victim. Yet they yielded the best evidence. "Are you SAP certified, Chief?"

Grissett made a wry face. "Unfortunately, no."

111

"Was the physician? This Dr. Schell."

"Not to my knowledge. We tried to contact squadron medical, get talked through it. But we're in River City."

"I've heard that expression, but what does it mean?"

"No Net. No e-mail. We looked up the requirements. Fortunately, we had fresh kits."

"So you took swabs, at least. Mouth, vagina, rectal?"

"Not mouth or rectal. She told us they weren't necessary. I took vaginal samples. Bagged, refrigerated, and sent 'em off on the helo. Scrapings from fingernails. The usual."

"Combed her pubic hair?"

Grissett nodded at the assistant. "Ryan here did the pubic inspection. And took all the photos."

"And you sent this all to *Stuttgart*."

"In the mailbag."

"So most likely, they went down with the tanker . . . which means, no forensic DNA."

Grissett said, "Not necessarily." He nodded to Ryan, who opened a small fridge bolted to the deck. Amid chilling soda cans and bottles of liquid medications slumped a small Baggie. When she held it up Aisha could make out the swab within, the carefully handprinted label. Ryan replaced it and sealed the door as Grissett said, "Sometimes official mail goes astray. Or takes too long to get there, and DNA degrades with heat. As you no doubt know. So I kept one sample."

Aisha nodded. "Good work, Doc. The question will be where to send it. Even in peacetime it takes six, eight weeks to get results back from the lab."

"Yeah, we're sort of hanging out here at the end of the pole." Grissett pointed to a ventilator fixture, which was buzzing in sympathetic vibration. "That thing only does that when we hit thirty knots plus. We're barreling the hell along to somewhere. Usually the CO comes up on the 1MC, gives us the rundown, but he's stopped doing that last couple days. You talked to the exec? She drop any hints where we're heading?"

"We didn't get into that. Just discussed the investigation." Aisha held out her hand for the folder. "May I?"

Grissett twisted in his chair. "You need a copy. Ryan, how about going over to ship's office. Clear the area around the copier. No one else looks at it."

When the girl left and the door was closed again Aisha said, "I'm told this was the third incident of sexual assault so far this cruise."

"That's right, but not the only incidence of sexual harassment."

"Really?"

"The XO had a man up for verbal harassment, too. Had him up to mast, I mean."

113

"Who was that?"

"A machinist's mate. He was accused under Article 134, indecent language. He called his female senior petty officer a 'hucking skunt.' The disciplinary review board kicked it up to the XO, who approved him for nonjudicial punishment."

"The CO punished him?"

"I don't remember exactly what he got, I wasn't there. Rumor has it, he got chewed out, then cracked down on pretty hard."

"Who was his petty officer?"

"An MM3 . . . Scharner. Patty, I think. No, Sherri Scharner."

"I'll want to talk to her."

"You can't." Grissett turned to pull another file out of the cabinet. "She's dead."

"Dead?"

"Natural causes. She was on the sick list. Malaise. Muscle aches. Dry, unproductive cough. Temperature, a hundred and one. Maybe a hundred and two. I issued ibuprofen, prescribed fluids and bed rest. The next morning, couple of her friends came down to check on her, take her to chow. But she was gone."

"Wait a minute. Leo Schell, right? He said something about legionellosis."

"Where did you see him?"

"On the tanker. For maybe two or three minutes, while we were hot decking."

"Uh-huh . . . well, that's what we had.

Legionnaires' disease. Maybe a third of the crew either got it, or had just gotten over it. That's why you'll see so many folks looking dragged out, like they haven't gotten any sleep. A lot haven't, but it's also the aftereffects of the Crud." Grissett held up a finger as she started to speak. "I wanted to pull us off the line, send us home. But the CO said we were on a national-security mission, we had to deal. Dr. Schell localized it to the forward hot-water heaters. We took all the freshwater systems down, tore the ship apart, and did a steam sterilization.

"I've been watching, and I haven't seen a case since. But it hasn't been that long. If you start feeling like you've got the flu, sore throat, see me at once. Most recover, but we had two who didn't. Scharner was one."

"You're absolutely certain it was simply the disease?"

"That's Dr. Schell's sign-off there, on the cause of death. Want a copy of that, too?"

Aisha handed the folder back. "I don't think so. Let's go back to the sexual assaults before the rape. From what the CMAA told me, you're not going to be holding any DNA from those."

"No. The first case was just a groping in the dark—"

"Petty Officer Terranova, back in the helo hangar—"

"Actually above it, the catwalk area. Coming

115

down from what we call the Iron Beach. No injury, except a slight abrasion to the neck. From a knife, we assume. No penetration, and no DNA recovery, though she did say he jerked off. But apparently into something he took with him.

"The second incident, Celestina Colón. That was in the aft passageway, next level down from here. The lights go out. Somebody grabs her from behind and shoves her into a fan room. He undresses and finger-fucks her, probably doing himself with the other hand. I took a rape kit, to be able to say we did, but no joy. He was rougher with her. She got bruised up some."

"Escalation." Aisha nodded.

"If it's the same guy, could be. They say they tend to go further each time—"

"It's in the literature. And borne out by my experience."

"I defer to you, Special Agent, on that."

Someone knocked. "It's open," Grissett called.

Ryan came in carrying two folders. She handed one to Aisha, who heaved herself reluctantly to her feet. "Thanks for the information, Chief Corpsman. Doc. I'll be back, I'm sure, as things develop."

A bulkhead phone buzzed. "Hold on," Grissett said. He listened with an abstracted air. "We got Seaman Ryan. Duncanna Ryan. She do? . . . Okay then. Yes ma'am, will do." He hung up. "XO wants to know if we had anyone you could keep

116

in your hip pocket. Help you out. Dunkie, can you take that? What're you doing right now?"

"Dusting the light fixtures, cleaning the head, back there. Then Beastie wanted me to inventory the dental tools—"

"Drop that, go with the special agent. Only come back here if we have a casualty drill or something. I'll tell Beaster. He's her petty officer," Grissett told Aisha.

"Shall we go? And maybe just stop topside for a couple of minutes, get some air—"

"Can't," Ryan said. "Not right now. They're running some kind of loading drill. Want everybody to stand clear."

"Then can you take me to the unit commander's stateroom? Petty Officer Ryan? I believe that's what the exec said."

"Seaman, ma'am. Yes ma'am—"

Aisha rearranged her cover-up, and reached for her purse. "It's time to meet Petty Officer Terranova."

For the first victim interview, it was important to pick somewhere neutral. If she'd been attacked in a work space, you didn't meet in a work space. If an officer was involved, you avoided the wardroom. In most cases, that boiled down to either Aisha's own cabin, or some semiprivate location like the library.

When Ryan tried the knob of the unit

commander's suite it was unlocked. Inside they found a large office space with a built-in desk, a blank computer screen, a coffee table, a settee, and two chairs. An open doorway showed the foot of a bunk next door. She had just time enough to use the little attached head before someone tapped at the door.

The chubby young white woman's brown-sugar hair was twisted back into a ponytail. She wore dark blue coveralls and heavy black steel-toe boots, and carried an issue of *Sea Technology* under her arm. Aisha estimated her at about five three, maybe 130, 140 pounds at the outside. Her exopthalmic, watery blue eyes blinked rapidly, gaze darting around the space. *This* was the woman they called the Terror?

"Beth?"

"Yes ma'am." Terranova came to attention.

"Please stand easy. I don't have a military rank, and you don't have to call me ma'am."

Ryan cleared her throat. "Um, do you want me to stay, Aisha?" She nodded to the girl. "Hi, Beth."

"Hi, Duncanna."

Of course they knew each other, in a complement as small as this. "Outside, please, um, Seaman. In the passageway. Don't let anyone in. Beth, is it all right if I lock this door?"

"Sure. I'd rather you did."

Her accent made it something like "Shueh, I'd

rada you did." Not to make fun, but she'd heard Joisey-speak from earliest childhood, from bus drivers, newsstand vendors, taxi drivers, cops roving the streets of the most polyglot city on earth. Working-class whites, most of whose gazes had slid past a little black girl in a modest dress.

"Beth—it *is* Beth? Yes, I see it is. From your file. Please sit. I'm Special Agent Aisha Ar-Rahim, Naval Criminal Investigative Service. I'm here to investigate the attack against you. Is it all right if I record this interview?"

Terranova nodded silently. Aisha set up the case cracker laptop and adjusted the camera so they were both within its field of view. "How are you doing? Holding up?"

"I'm doin' okay." But her tucked elbows, arms crossed over her chest, and hunched posture said otherwise. As did the dry white flecks around her lips, and the dull eyes.

"Are you still under sedation, Beth?"

"No."

"Sleeping okay?"

"No one's sleeping. We been goin' six on and six off, general quarters for missile defense."

"I understand you occupy a key position in the Weapons Department."

"Operations, not Weapons. I'm the lead Aegis petty officer. I run the SPY-1s. The radars. The big panels on the sides of the bridge."

"I see. That does sound important."

"It means that if we get attacked, we don't get sunk."

"I see." Aisha took a breath. "Well, Beth, most people in your situation experience mixed emotions. Generally, anger and shame. I understand, and I sympathize. But my job's to investigate a crime, and pass what I develop to the naval justice system. If everything works right, we catch the guy who raped you, and put him where he can't hurt you again, or anyone else.

"With that in mind, I need to take you step by step through what happened. Starting even before that—with anyone who expressed interest, asked for a date, said he wanted to hook up on liberty. Don't worry how trivial it seems. Just tell me who occurs to you first."

Terranova sat stoically silent for a while, then told her about the castaway. Aisha didn't object, or say he'd already left the ship before the rape; just noted it. "Good. Who else?"

A shrug. "Nobody."

"Really? You're an attractive girl. On a ship with three hundred guys. Nobody's hit on you? Not in the four months since the ship left home port?"

"I'm not that pretty." Terranova sounded sullen, head lowered. "The other girls, guys like them better."

All right . . . "How about your work center? Anyone you're close to there?"

"I work with the new chief . . . Chief Wenck. With Ginnie Redmond. And the other guys in the Aegis team."

"No close friendships? No enemies?"

A sigh, another shrug. "I'm the lead PO. It's like, an official relationship."

"All right, let's go on to the incident. Tell me what happened."

"I was down in female berthing. I got a shower. Then I remembered I left something in the Equipment Room. While we were looking at replacing one of the cards."

"What did you leave?"

"My, um, birth control pills."

Aisha carefully did not look surprised. "What were you doing with birth control pills in the Equipment Room?"

"I took them out of my pocket because I just had too much shit in there. The pockets on these coveralls are crap. Things fall out. If we lose those, the corpsmen give us a rough time. Like they cost the Navy all this money, or they have to account for each pill, or something . . . and some of the guys, they . . . like, think it's a joke, if they steal them and hide them. Then we have to go nuts and raise a stink, until they give them back. And they say things like—"

"Like, 'What do you need these for, you're not putting out for *me*,'" Aisha supplied. Nothing she hadn't heard aboard the carrier. "I realize this

121

is personal, Beth, and it will be off the record in any written report. But are you in a current relationship?"

"No," the petty officer murmured at last.

"Coming off one, maybe? With someone here?" Terranova shook her head again. "So, the samples the doctor took, those will tell us exactly who the rapist was? Once we can get them tested?"

". . . I guess so."

"Beth, it's very important we nail this down now so there are no gray areas later. Did you, or did you not, have sex in any form with anyone else, in the week before the crime?"

"No. I did not."

Aisha noted and underlined it. "All right. Thanks. So, you were taking the pills in case . . . ?"

"Yeah. In case. Anyhow, it's not good to stop them, start them, stop 'em again. The girls all say you can't depend on them to work if you start doing that."

"I've heard that."

Terranova murmured, "I was dating a guy for a while, back in Norfolk."

"From the ship?"

"No, he worked at a truck place in Virginia Beach. But I guess he didn't . . . wasn't . . . that interested after all. That was the last time I did it."

Aisha waited, but that seemed to be it. Too bad; the ex-boyfriend was always the number one suspect. Terranova added, "Then I heard somebody outside, in the passageway. I went out, but I didn't see anybody there.

"But when I went out again, the overhead lights outside were off. Somebody grabbed me from behind and stuck a knife in my neck. Then he pushed me back into the Equipment Room, made me take my coveralls off, and raped me."

Aisha cleared her throat. "I need you to go back a minute. You said, 'He made me take my coveralls off.' Tell me exactly how those came off."

The girl looked up, eyes suddenly blazing. "How they *came off*? I just told you, I fuckin' *took* them off. He had a knife to my throat!"

Aisha kept her eyes on her notepad. The cracker was recording the interview, but taking notes added a distance that interviewees seemed to appreciate. "You said it was dark when he grabbed you. From behind, right? So how do you know he had a knife?"

"I fucking felt it against my throat."

"Describe that, please."

"A knife . . . a point . . . a sharp pointed blade. Cold. Metal."

"Was the edge smoothly sharp, or serrated?"

"Smooth."

"Now secure from rearming. Secure from rearming. Now darken ship. Darken ship. Make all darken-ship reports to the officer of the deck

on the bridge. All hands stand clear of weather decks while transiting at high speeds. Stand clear of missile-launch areas. Now lay before the mast, all eight o'clock reports," the 1MC said, very loud, out in the passageway.

Aisha held her pen in the air. "Is that for you?"

"No. Chief Wenck'll take eight o'clock reports."

"Can you tell me how long the knife was? Or show me?"

The petty officer held up finger and thumb four inches apart. "That's a big blade," Aisha said. "It would certainly scare me. Did you feel the handle? Did it make a noise, a click or a springy sound? Folding, jackknife, switchblade, straight razor, dinner knife, commando-type knife?"

"I don't really remember. I was surprised. Scared."

"I understand, believe me. But we'll just go step by step and see what you can recall. When he held it to your throat, did you feel gloves, or bare hands?"

The corners of Terranova's eyes crinkled. "He wore gloves. Leather. *Soft* leather gloves."

"Okay, *very* good. Now, back to disrobing. Where were the two of you at that point?"

"The Equipment Room. He pushed me back in there."

"Did you take your boots off? Are those the boots you were wearing at the time?"

"Well, my boots—I never did take them off. I just unzipped and pulled the coveralls down."

"And then." Aisha made a note, kept her eyes lowered.

"Then . . . you want to know exactly what he did?"

"I'm sorry, but we need specifics. I know this isn't easy, but that's what's going to help us catch him."

"Well. Then he pulled my panties down. And then he got between my legs and—"

"You were where? On the floor? The deck, I mean?"

"I was bent over the work surface. The table."

"So he was behind you."

"I *told* you that . . . no . . . I guess I only said he grabbed me from behind. But he . . . fucked me from there, too. Only not in the, um, in where you might have thought. And, oh, he stood me over the work stool. So I was up higher. But he didn't take long, once he was in."

Patiently, going back again when she skipped ahead, Aisha drew it out. The mention of the work stool seemed significant. From the geometry, it meant her attacker was considerably taller. Did she feel a beard at any point, heavy stubble? Mustache? Glasses? What did his clothing feel like—was it cotton, like ship's coveralls, or the slick nylon of a flight suit, or the fine, snag-prone weave of twill polyester? Had she smelled anything? Terranova said she might have smelled something citrusy, like lemons. Aisha explored the voice. Rough, accented, high or low pitch? Terranova said it was pitched low, almost guttural, as if the rapist was disguising himself.

"So he was afraid you might recognize him," Aisha suggested. "Which means you know him. Which also means, maybe, you should be careful."

The young woman blinked. "Careful?"

"Not go anywhere without one of your girl-friends. Especially at night. Has anyone talked to you about that? Maybe Chief Toan?"

"No, but . . . you think I'm in danger?"

Aisha said she just meant to take reasonable precautions. "But if anyone threatens you, or harasses you for cooperating with me, tell me right away. Rape's serious enough, but there are additional penalties if someone tries to silence you. Do you need to change your work center? Or maybe take some time off?"

Terranova said she couldn't, the team depended on her, but that she'd report any harassment. She started to fidget, glancing at the bulkhead clock. "I should get goin' . . . need to get some sleep before I go on again."

Aisha frowned. "Surely they still don't have you on the watch bill?"

The frown lines deepened. Suddenly the girl looked older. More serious. "Do you got any idea what I do aboard here, Agent? Without my radar, we're fuckin' blind. I got a team to lead. They can't take me off the watch bill. Not now, at DEFCON Two."

"I'm not sure what that means, Beth."

Terranova stood. Her voice rose. Her fists clenched. "We're at war. Don't you get it? If I can't do my fuckin' job, my shipmates'll die. And it won't really matter then who raped me, will it? So I have to stay on duty, no matter how I feel, or how much I just wanta fuckin' *run!*"

Aisha kept her eyes on her notes. Victims often rode an emotional roller coaster. From stoic, to crying, to rage, to fear. It was hard not to ride it with them. "Beth, it's natural to be angry. Rape is a terrible crime. I know. It happened to me. As a child."

"Really?"

"Yes. And investigating it, this . . . *process,* well, it isn't exactly fun for me, either." She tried to steady her voice. "It's natural to be affected. You may have trouble concentrating. Feel overwhelmed. Night terrors, panic attacks. All those are normal.

"But if we do this right, we can bring this guy to justice. And that'll keep your friends safe too. Maybe not from a missile or a bomb. But so they can walk the passageways at night without being afraid."

Terranova looked down at her, face white.

"Without bein' *afraid*," she murmured. "Wow. Sorry it happened to you. I am. But you shueh make a lotta promises, don't cha, Special Agent?"

When the petty officer slammed out the door, Aisha turned off the case cracker. She whispered a *du'a*, asking for patience. For wisdom, to help those who were hurt. And for a little bit of luck. She asked for strength, and for Allah to stay in her heart.

Then she wiped her face with both hands and sat alone, listening to the throb of turbines, the rush of a speeding ship through a dark and trackless sea.

8
USS *Montpelier* (SSN 765)

The second day aboard the sub, in the cramped enlisted mess. Teddy was always taken aback by how tight it was. Every cubic foot was crammed with equipment, leaving only narrow vertical slots through which bodies could fit. The overhead was low, and there were only two dining tables, with bench seats; you had to pull your elbows in tight to your sides. You couldn't complain about the chow, though. He was digging in when Lieutenant Harch stopped to murmur, "How's the omelets, Master Chief?"

"Um, okay, sir." Teddy was reserved with Harch. The heavily mustached, dark-complected platoon commander was ex-enlisted. Good in one way, not so great in another. You didn't have to explain certain things, but he wasn't as ready to defer to his senior enlisted's advice. As to what kind of a leader he'd be when the chips were down . . . who the fuck knew.

"Bunkin' okay?"

"Tight, but we'll make it work. How is it up in officers' country?"

"Sweet. Especially the massage girls." Harch flashed a grin. "Let's pull the troops together after breakfast, Mast' Chief. 0830."

"Um, got it. Where?"

"XO said here is okay. Let 'em clean up, wipe down the tables. Then filter back in. Set us up for that big-screen TV."

Harch left and Teddy exchanged glances with Knobby Swager. Maybe they'd find out where they were going. "At long damn last," the first class muttered.

He passed the word along to Moogie, the other team leader—Swager was Team One, Moogie Team Two—and by 0820 everyone was mustered. He looked carefully at each man as they sat or leaned about. The platoon was embarked on two subs, as planned, but something had happened to the diver delivery vehicles en route. What, exactly, they had no need to know, apparently; but the DDVs were out of the picture for the operation.

Which would make it hairier. His guys were about as physically fit as a human body could get, but with all the gear they were towing and wearing, a five-mile swim was the absolute most you could expect and still leave them in shape to fight. The scooters would help, but they were range-limited too. The subs would have to crowd the beach. Which meant they'd be in shallow water, more vulnerable. . . .

And they had just fifteen operators, divided into two crews. There was a command and control element aboard the battle group flagship.

Commander Laughland, Teddy presumed, had briefed the best course of action to the group commander. He'd also have a quick-reaction force on a short leash, in case things went south.

True, one SEAL platoon wasn't that many men. But they weren't trying to occupy the island, just get in and out undetected. In action, an enemy often took a SEAL detachment for a much larger force anyway. They trained for superior firepower and extreme violence of action. Usually, that obscured their reliance on organic assets—what they carried in with them. They weren't the Army, with heavy artillery and unlimited logistics.

Teddy sighed and looked them over again. Echo Platoon, but not the old Echo. Only a few left from the White Mountains. Knobby Swager, yeah, and Moogie, and Mud Cat, his old 249 gunner. The rest were new. Swaggering young dicks, full of napalm and testosterone. But most seemed to have their shit wired. Any who hadn't, he'd bottom-blown before they deployed.

Seemed like not that many years ago he'd been one of them. Now he was the master chief. Supposed to teach them. Look out for them. Be an example.

That was a fucking laugh.

He was talking to Mud Cat, who was massaging his hand—he'd taken a bullet through his palm on the same godforsaken mountain Teddy had fallen down—when Harch charged in. "Attention on deck!" Teddy yelled, and those who weren't on their feet bolted up.

The lieutenant waved them down and handed Teddy a USB stick. "Seats, everyone. Jeezus! Okay, we got the PLO. Critical time frame, critical mission. We need to get in and take action."

Building on the warning order, the Patrol Leader's Order detailed both the mission and each team member's individual responsibilities. SEALs operated differently from more conventional units. In a way, Teddy thought, they were more like the Raiders had been, or at least the way Carlson had envisioned them. You told them what you wanted done, but not how to do it.

Harch stroked his mustache. "Time to let everybody in on where we're going. Not that I didn't want to before. One cell phone intercept, we can forget surprise. Everyone ready for a hairy-ass, balls-to-the-wall direct-action mission?"

When the hoo-ahs and whistles died down he said, "All right. Lights, please." Swager handed him the remote for the screen, and the first slide came up. The legend OPERATION WATCHTOWER was superimposed on a chart of the South China Sea.

"Within days, combined U.S. and Vietnamese forces will land on the Chinese-held Spratly

Islands, east of Vietnam. To cover them, act as a diversion, and prepare for the next step in an island-hopping campaign to the mainland coast, we will raid this objective."

An overhead shot, blue and white and green: a reef-fringed island, shaped like an off-center valentine. The tan oblong of an airstrip slanted across its eastern coast, jutting into reef at both ends. Squared-off jetties surrounded artificial boat basins. Someone had devoted years and millions of dollars into turning a few acres of scrub and shoal into a major military base.

Harch said, "Yongxing Island, also known as Woody Island. Roughly a mile by a mile. Population counts differ, but there's probably around fourteen hundred civilians, originally fishermen, servicing the military presence in one way or another. Military personnel: originally around three hundred, but since the start of the war, we expect they've been reinforced—probably an assault-slash-defense battalion of the 164th Marine Brigade. There's one runway, long enough to service the Sukhoi Su-30 multirole strike fighter. They've been observed operating here, but it's not clear whether they're permanently deployed. There's also a small naval base and refueling pier.

"Our object of interest, though, is this smaller island"—the image zoomed in, and the men around the room stirred and coughed "north of Woody. The old charts call it Rocky Island, but we're not sure of the Chinese name. It was recently connected to the main island by a concrete causeway.

"Formerly uninhabited, Rocky's been sealed off and turned into a signal and intelligence monitoring center. Note the antennas in this slant photo, and, near the edge, the tallest, the vertical ones. High-frequency monitoring arrays, for gathering radar and radio intel.

"From here, they can reach out a thousand miles in every direction, covering most of the South China Sea. Note also the dome-shaped, Quonset-type buildings. A common PLA prefab design, for barracks and other military functions."

Harch turned away to cough. "From these overheads, plus traffic analysis, Intel estimates the watchstanders and garrison numbers at at least two hundred, mostly sigint specialists. With both radar and elint capabilities, this is the enemy's main listening post on their south coast. Making it difficult, if not impossible, for any allied force to approach without being subject to detection, tracking, and air attack from fighters based at the strip."

Teddy raised a hand. "Master Chief," Harch said, not very eagerly.

"Sir, these antennas, plus the Quonsets—looks like they're spread out pretty far. How long is this island? The small one."

"About a quarter mile, Master Chief."

Teddy didn't like it. Over a thousand effectives, and the Chinese 164th Marines were an elite unit, trained in both assaulting and defending islands. But even assuming the SEALs could elude them, how were fifteen guys going to destroy all these structures, antennas, processing stations? They'd have to spend a full day just placing explosives. The garrison wouldn't think highly of that.

But the platoon commander had resumed. "We think these huts, here, and here, are where monitoring and processing take place. DIA suspects the data's transmitted direct to Beijing, via a submarine cable between Yongxing and the mainland."

Harch gave them a few seconds to contemplate the image. Despite his skepticism, Teddy found himself setting up a strategy. Land half the team on the causeway, with machine guns and light antitank capabilities. Once they lit up the night, both as a blocking force and a diversion, the rest of the platoon would insert over the northern beach, which looked like a steep gradient. They should be on top of the antennas and buildings in short order.

But seven hundred marines on the main island, three hundred more on Rocky itself . . . beside him Swager twisted his mouth, apparently coming to the same conclusion. "Not enough guys, not enough time," he muttered.

135

"No shit. Not with all those fucking antennas. Y'ever try to knock down an antenna?"

"It ain't easy."

"Excuse me, Master Chief," Harch said. "Did you have something to contribute?"

"Just eager to hear the plan, sir," Teddy said. "But I gotta say, I'm concerned about the force balance."

"Uh-huh. Well, I briefed three concepts of operation to the ops-o, then Commander L. Then the sub's CO . . . but he's not a happy camper about how close in we're asking him to go. He thought we'd be thirty miles out, riding the buses in . . . but here's the plan."

Harch stroked his mustache, talking to the screen. "We swim in submerged. I considered the rafts, but there's probably tactical radar protecting such a high-value target. As we proceed to target, a combined Tomahawk and standoff weapons strike will hit the airfield and the naval facility. Another salvo of precision-guided munitions will hit the repair shops and fuel bunkers.

"All in all, they'll lay down thirty tons of ordnance. Ten minutes later, we hit the beach at two points. Timing will be critical."

"No fucking shit," Swager muttered, elbowing Oberg.

The next slide showed two points of entry. Pretty much as Teddy'd already figured, one was at the causeway, the other at Rocky's northern beach.

Teddy leaned back, fingering his chin. Thinking again of Makin Atoll. You had only two choices in assaulting a beach. Pick hydrography with a shallow gradient . . . like Tarawa, where the enemy, if he was sighted in, could cut you to pieces as you waded ashore. Or a steep gradient, where the surf could tear you up almost as bad. Carlson's guys had come in over the open beach, and lost most of their weapons and gear in the surf.

Why not just chute in, do a HALO drop? But no, the radars made that impossible. No drop plane would get within a hundred miles before the Sukhois were on it.

Harch said, "Okay, we drilled with the Packages. I had one guy"—he glanced at Teddy—"ask me if they were radioactive. Well, they're not. And they're not bombs, either. If we had to just take out a sigint station, there are easier ways to do it than send us in." He gave it a beat, then said, "The Packages are EMP devices. They contain explosives, yeah, but the purpose isn't blast or fragmentation. They produce a super-powerful electromagnetic pulse. Enough to fry every radar and computer in a thousand-yard radius."

Harch edged past the table to the screen and pointed. "The first team, Echo One, lands here and moves out to the causeway. They set up a blocking position, isolating the island. The movement team, Echo Two, lands fifteen minutes

137

later. Exiting the beach, they head for the center of the island via this forested corridor." He circled a dark area on the slide. "It's mixed scrub, dune, and marsh; note what looks like a sewage pond to the northwest. Covert, in the dark, we should be able to traverse it without detection. At the centroid of the island, we emplace the Packages, on top of separate sand hills. The elevation will increase the effective radius of the pulse. Hit the timers, then link up."

The lieutenant pointed to Swager, who turned the screen off. "Give me the stick back. Okay, that's the plan. Maximum diversion. Minimum exposure. A lot of enemy, yeah, but if we do it right, nobody'll notice us. They'll be watching the fireworks down by the harbor. Both teams leapfrog back and retract from the north beach. Drägers and scooters. If we get contact, hose 'em down and withdraw. We'll have the F470s standing by, in case we need to take off wounded." The F470s were rigid-hulled inflatables, with inflation tanks and submersible outboards.

Teddy couldn't help shaking his head. Only slightly, but Harch caught it and frowned. "Obie? Are we not happy?"

"I'd rather not say, sir."

"Go ahead, Master Chief. If you have a better plan, I'm all ears."

Teddy considered not saying anything. Then

thought: Fuck that. "Well, sir, this might work against untrained troops. Militia. Draftees. But the first thing a sharp security force will do is look in the opposite direction from the first assault. Bomb the south coast, they'll look north. I'll also goddamn betcha that overhead doesn't show mines, wire, and listening devices on that northern beach, considering how golden an asset this is supposed to be."

He gave it a beat, then added, "Sir."

Harch's face hardened. "We discussed that at length, when we were going through the COAs. The first ordnance laid down on the south island will take out the marine barracks. In the middle of the night, that will cut down the number of effectives. The blocking force on the causeway will confine the remainder to the main island. Team Two should have a clear run."

Teddy found himself on his feet. He nodded toward the screen. "Granted, the strike will take out some of them, but how about the rest? They can flank the causeway. It looks shallow in there. Are we going in at low tide? Do they actually need the causeway? Are there boats?"

Swager nudged him. Mud Cat was shaking his head too. What the fuck? But he wasn't done. "And, what about our QRF? It's gonna be, what, two hundred miles away? And how's E&E going to work, on an atoll that small? It just seems like—"

Harch held up a palm. "All we have to do is

block, insert, and activate. A good mission doesn't make a ripple. If there should be trouble with elements on the north island, we cause maximum damage and extract. You're right, there's not much escape and evasion possible on an island that size. We'll have a Predator on call, and RHIBs holding five miles offshore. If we have wounded, need boats, the backup team inflates 'em, starts the motors, and runs in to the beach. Better?"

Teddy understood he'd been dismissed. He started to protest, then caught the glares of the younger men. Was he getting antsy? They were fucking SEALs, after all. The force ratios would always be against them. The QRFs were always going to be remote, the E&E plan hinky. What was the SEAL Creed . . . *I voluntarily accept the inherent hazards of my profession.*

"Any other questions, comments? All right then." Harch nodded curtly. "Dismissed."

"Attention on deck," Swager yelled. The men got to their feet again. Teddy turned away, headed back for the chief's quarters, where he was hot-bunked with a machinist's mate.

But Harch turned back, at the door. "Master Chief?"

Teddy wheeled round. "Sir?"

Harch jerked his head. "My stateroom. Now."

The junior officer staterooms were the size of porta-potties. When Harch slammed the door

140

and pointed to a bunk, Teddy had a moment of claustrophobia. The lieutenant took the single chair. Air-conditioning whooshed from a diffuser. Something whined on the far side of the bulkhead, stopped, whined again. "We got a problem, Master Chief?" the lieutenant opened. "You need to torque your shit together. Especially in front of the team."

Teddy grinned. "My shit's torqued tight, L-T. No problems on my end."

"You got a great record, Obie. A top-drawer operator. But sometimes I feel this pushback. Like maybe you resent I made it, and you didn't."

Actually, they'd offered him a commission after the White Mountains, but Teddy had turned it down. He decided to play it conciliatory. "Sorry if I give that impression, sir. I just want to make sure we're not sticking our dicks in any blenders. Which it sounds like we're getting ready to do."

"Well . . . maybe." Harch stared at his desk safe for a second, then coughed into his fist. "This is my first mission as a zero. Maybe I should confide in you more. And, I guess, you need to know this. In case I take a hit, or whatever . . . But nobody else does. Hoo-ah?"

"Hoo-ah, sir." Teddy sat straighter.

"What I just briefed is not the actual mission."

What the hell? "Not the *actual* mission, sir?"

Harch spun the dial. He unlocked the safe and took out an op plan.

141

Teddy looked it over. Destroying the sigint site was only the secondary objective. The primary . . . He looked up, frowning. "Want to give me the short squirt, sir? Or am I supposed to read this encyclopedia?"

"In words of one syllable, the true objective of Operation Watchtower is to plant an intel asset. Taking the site off-line temporarily is nice, it provides diversion for an invasion elsewhere, but more important, it gives us the excuse to get in and plant something for another government agency."

Teddy said, "I'm not sure I follow. Lieutenant."

"Think about it this way. Gear's easy to replace. Radars. Signal processors. Basically, computers and software. We could fry everything on the island and they'd be back online in a week.

"But if the mission looks like it's for something else, even if it seems like a failure, it can still accomplish the primary objective."

"So the Package isn't an EMP, uh, device? Like you said?"

"It *is* an EMP device," Harch said. "But it isn't going to work."

Teddy blinked. "Isn't going to—"

"Work."

Suddenly the already too-small room shrank even more. He half rose, wishing there was just a little more air. "We're putting the Team, all our guys, at risk for a *dud?*"

Harch waved him down. "Not a 'dud,' Master Chief. The first package will detonate. Sort of. Scatter pieces around. About the same order explosion as a mortar round. But the pulse will short-circuit. They put the fragments back together, they'll get an EMP bomb, all right. But an American round-eye foreign-devil fuckup.

"They'll snort and go back to operating. But now *we're looking over their shoulder.* We have our own eavesdropping capability, on their eavesdropping capability. They operate, but we see every keystroke. Know everything they know. Read their traffic. Messages. Data. Voice. Even video. See exactly what they see, on their radars. Total access, like we're inside their heads."

Teddy sat back, turning it over, trying to shake the feeling of being boxed in. "So where is this gizmo? Oh. That's Package number two."

"Correct. It's not a backup; it's the eaves-dropping device. They call it a QM-10, for whatever that's worth. Picks up anything, and I mean anything, on a radio frequency. We dig that in, and it self-activates. Transmits via a secure, highly directional uplink called 'ultrawideband.' Impossible to overhear. Or so they tell me."

Teddy rubbed his face. Swager might under-stand all this better, having been an electron pusher in a previous life. Pick up all this digital stuff, then send it someplace where they could study it, decode it, turn it into useful intel? Some arcane, supersecret CIA technology. Wouldn't it be simpler just to bomb the shit out of everything, then send in the Marines? But somebody upstairs had decided this was smarter. It was sure as hell more complicated. "Can I share this with my Team leaders?"

Harch grimaced. "No! Pass this to no one, Master Chief. I wouldn't have told you, except I had to. For the mission."

Mission first, last, and always. The Team credo. But none of this lessened his misgivings. If anything, they made them worse. He saw now why command wasn't obsessing about extract, or force ratios, or whether the QRF could get in fast enough to rescue the platoon. Total access to the enemy's secrets, day in and day out? Yeah. That was worth fifteen lives. As long as they planted this gizmo, maybe it didn't really matter, to whoever had designed the mission, if any of them made it out.

"Any more questions, Master Chief?" Harch said as Teddy stood. "Hoo-ah, right?"

But all he could do was shrug.

9

The next day *Savo Island* was still at Condition Three, wartime steaming. That made it hard to get around, even with Ryan's help undogging door after door, and dogging each again after them. The hatches that led from one deck to the next had also been secured; to climb up or down, Aisha had to wriggle through narrow scuttles. Sometimes the corpsman had to phone to get permission to open an access, and they had to wait in the stale hot air until a reluctant voice granted them passage.

But she persisted. After talking with the chief master-at-arms, the command master chief, and the exec, Staurulakis, she had a few possibilities.

The first was a damage controlman, one Petty Officer Third Class Benyamin. He was tall. He knew the lighting systems. The exec had earmarked him because of his attitude toward the females aboard, and his participation in some kind of computer game that involved rape. Aisha wanted to know more about this so-called game.

"Its name is *Gang Bang Molly*," Benyamin said reluctantly. They were sitting in the wardroom, which had been cleared; Ryan stood guard outside. The petty officer had a round, stubbly head. A hawkish nose. A gawky neck. Long fingers twisted as he glanced up at her.

"Tell me more," she said patiently.

"Well—it's sort of like *Grand Theft Auto*. Or *DayZ*. Or *Hitman*. Only kind of, you know, backstairs. You can't buy it at GameStop."

"I see. And it's about rape?"

"Hey, that's not *all*," Benyamin said defensively. "Also murder. Looting. Doing hits. Getting wasted."

"Sounds like fun."

"You should try it. Get inside the mind of the criminal."

"I spend enough time there, thanks. You can't get it at GameStop? So, where did *you* get it?"

"It was password protected, but you could play it on your workstation."

Aisha put down her pen, shocked. "It was on the *ship's network?*"

"On the LAN, yeah. Everybody played it. They took it down, though, when the brass heard about it. Actually, I think it was the CO figured it out."

She was still incredulous. "How exactly did you get it on the LAN?"

Benyamin sat up straight. "Huh? Not *me*. I played it a little, but I didn't put it up."

"Who did, then? Do you know?"

"Well, sort of. But, like, it's all scuttlebutt, what I'm sayin' here."

She told him scuttlebutt was worth checking

146

out, but he still seemed reluctant. Until she brought up the possibility of an official charge. He grimaced. "Carpenter. The old guy, who came aboard after the last captain run us aground and got shitcanned."

"Carpenter. What's his rate?"

"A ping jockey . . . sonarman. Stays in his own spaces most of the time, but you see him on the chat boards. Goes by . . . Poon Pinger, I think."

"How tall is he?"

"How . . . ? I'm not sure. Like I say, I don't see him that much. Just on the boards."

"What else do you know about him?"

The damage controlman said just that he was an older sailor, maybe even retired. Aisha wondered what a retiree was doing deployed, but made the note. She had to get on these boards, and meet this Carpenter. Maybe interview him in his native habitat.

Of course, he'd hear she was asking about him. So it would have to be now, before he had a chance to hide anything incriminating.

Ryan led her forward and down, cautioning her to hold tight to the handrails. They descended level by level, until the sides of the ship squeezed inward. The normal clanks and whirs grew distant. The air grew stale, uncirculated. They threaded storerooms and damage-control lockers walled with expanded metal in a labyrinthine underworld.

Ryan bent, and hauled up a scuttle. Aisha had to wriggle through feet first, groping with the toes of her Merrells for whatever lay below. Faded paint, a confined passageway.

Finally, so deep Aisha felt entombed, Ryan tapped on a door painted with earphones, a crossed torpedo, a lightning bolt. Beneath it someone had painted in flowing script, *Sonarmen do it aurally*.

"Yeah?" Whoever was in there sounded surprised. "Whatcha want?"

The door unclunked inward on a cramped wedge of space walled with electronics and piping. A paunchy middle-aged man turned up a startled face, then pushed back from a keyboard. "Hey, girls! Wow, two hotties. You here for the banana-eating contest?"

This had to be the guy. "Carpenter?"

"That's me." He patted a chair. "Park it, let's get acquainted. Nobody visits me down here anymore."

Close up, she revised her estimate of his age upward. Gray hair, thinning at the back. Sagging jowls. A gut straining the waist of his coveralls. His stubble was gray too. Black-and-white glossy eight-by-tens of old submarines and many-times-xeroxed cartoons were taped to the few open areas of white-insulation-sheathed bulkhead. He waved at them. "Used to have my babes up there. XO made me take 'em down. But hey, a guy can dream." He leered at Ryan. "I know you, right? You're one of the pecker-checkers . . . I mean, corpsmen. What's your name, sweetheart?"

Aisha plumped down into a chair, which creaked alarmingly and tilted as if to catapult her out backward. A strange smell lingered. Male sweat, ozone, acetone . . . and something else. "Petty Officer Reginald Carpenter?"

Carpenter winced. "It's *Rit,* honey, not 'Reginald.'" He reached for a thermos. "Want some bug juice? Where you from, brown sugar? That accent says . . . the Bronx?"

"Harlem."

"Uh-huh. Cute outfit. What are you, part of the sultan's harem?"

"I'm NCIS agent Aisha Ar-Rahim," she said. "I'm investigating a crime."

"NCIS. That's what used to be the NIS, right? They took down a ring of faggots on a boat I was on once. Let me guess, you want the dude who put the blocks to the Terror. Hey. Don't swing that way, kids." Carpenter lifted his hands. "Pubic Bay, Bang Cock, I paid for it fair and square. I could tell you some stories. Angles and dangles at the Anchor and Spur? The time I bought a puppy in Olongapo?"

"Let's stick to OS1 Bethany Terranova."

"Well, from what I hear, she was asking for it. The radarman, I mean."

By the door, Ryan huffed. "Really? That's very

149

interesting." Aisha shot a glance at her, warning her to keep out of it. "Why do you say that?"

Carpenter nodded and leaned forward, lowering blunt fingertips to the keyboard with a strangely delicate touch. "Want to see some pictures?"

"Photos, you mean?"

"Way I heard it, she was laying it out on the Iron Beach for everybody to see. Topless. Kind of an open invite, don't you think? Let's be reasonable. Me, I'm just a dirty old man. But you got young guys here, away from home four, six months, ain't had a decent liberty since Rota. Ever tried to get laid in Jebel Ali? Ain't gonna happen, Ahmed. They lock 'em up tight. And you know what else they do to their women? Cut off their—"

"That's not done anymore," Aisha said.

"Ain't what I hear. But don't blow your shitter, girl. They like boys better anyway." The sonarman swiveled the monitor toward them. "Grab a gander."

The color still showed women on blankets and beach towels, in colorful swimsuits, lying on gray nonskid in bright sunlight. Over it, a gunsight reticle. The aiming dot in the center was centered on the crotch of a bikinied woman, chunky pale thighs spread, arm over her eyes. Her top was pulled down to show white skin. At the top of the photo, the sea was a creamy wake stretching out behind the ship.

Carpenter smacked his lips. "Whaddya think? Nice little rack of lamb, or what?"

"Where is this?"

"The Iron Beach, they call it. Top of the hangar. Girls only up there." Carpenter winked. "Maybe a little blue-on-blue action? Back out of camera range."

"This photo's on the ship's LAN?"

"Just cutie pies on a beach. Harmless fun."

Aisha said, "I hear something else on the LAN is fun too."

Carpenter tensed, then chuckled. "Oh—*Molly?* Shit. Nobody has a sense of fucking humor anymore. It's a *game.*"

"That involves rape."

"Yeah, you ever seen the other shit the guys play? The magazines they pass around? The fucking Navy's getting as PC as Berkeley. I mean, this used to be a fun organization. You turned to at sea, but when the anchor went down, you cut loose. Now it's just work, work, work, and when you do pull a little liberty, they expect you to paint an orphanage."

"I'd like to see this game. Who are your high scorers?"

The sonarman hacked out a smoker's laugh and rocked back. His duct-taped chair creaked and almost pitched him out, but he rode it down and back up like a mechanical bull. "Let's make it easy. *I'm* the high scorer. 'Thug Numba One.' "

"How about Petty Officer Benyamin?"

"He's not in my league. And no, you can't see the game, because the skipper himself shut us down and confiscated my boot copy."

"Lenson did that?"

Carpenter shrugged, obviously conflicted. "Him and me got history. Some high-pucker-factor situations. Along with Donnie Wenck. Lenson's solid. But also, like, this uptight Annapolis ring-knocker type. He listened too much in Sunday school, or something. No offense."

"Wenck." The name sounded familiar. She made a note, with a question mark. "Who's he, again?"

"OS chief. The Terror works for him."

"Oh. Right." Aisha sighed. Thought of asking if Carpenter owned a knife, but didn't. This guy wasn't tall enough, and with his paunch and age, she couldn't seriously make him for the assault. Just an overage, loudmouthed holdover from the Jurassic. "Are you married, Petty Officer Carpenter?"

"Haven't met the right girl yet. She's deaf and dumb, with no teeth, and a flat head to set your beer on."

Ryan chuckled, and Carpenter shared a grin with her. Aisha said, "Let's get back on track. You could be helpful, you know. Any ideas? Somebody who talks about rough trade, a woman hater. Knife fetish, talks about teaching the sluts a lesson? Trigger any thoughts?"

152

The sonarman shrugged again. "I'd like to. I really would. But, see, everybody gets weird, this long at sea. It's the DSB."

Beside her Ryan sniggered. "The what?" Aisha said. "This is the legionello—?"

"Deadly sperm buildup. Drives guys over the edge. To where they get their rocks off taking pictures through the Sea Whiz cameras." Looking at the screen, he sobered. "Hey, I come across flip, I know. But maybe it wasn't exactly like she said. You think there's no guy-girl hanky-panky going on in this ship, you're just closing your eyes. She gets it on with some swingin' dick, he dumps her, she blows the whistle. Only makes it like, she didn't know who it was, so you have to nail him for her. Whaddya think, corpsperson? Am I blowin' smoke through my asshole, or what?"

Ryan didn't answer, arms folded as she leaned against a rack of amplifiers. Her expression said it all. Amused disgust. Aisha cleared her throat, then got up. The chair creaked and flipped forward as her weight came off it, almost propelling her into Carpenter. "Please keep this talk between us. If a name, or a conversation, occurs to you later, let me know."

"Feel free to come back and visit," Carpenter told Ryan. "I'm down here alone most of the time. Or, we could *arrange* to be alone." He winked at Aisha. "Goes for you too, honey. We can keep it *all* between us. You bet."

• • •

Aisha felt like taking a shower, but put it aside. She'd had her own problems as a new female agent, not to mention being a Muslima, but nothing like what the first women aboard ship must have had to put up with. With three hundred, five hundred sailors with Carpenter's mouth and mind-set. Ryan had seemed to find him cute, or at least amusing. Maybe he was, but she didn't see it. If he'd been younger, he'd have been on her short list, based just on that last talk.

She was squirming up through the last scuttle, into the main deck passageway, when it connected in her mind. She snorted. "What?" said Ryan.

"Never mind."

"Where you want to go next? It's almost noon. Mess line's open."

She usually ate in the wardroom, but sitting down with the crew now and then both increased your visibility and, in apparent contradiction, helped you fit in. Her tray followed Ryan's down the stainless rails. She had to keep her diet in mind. Vegetables. Fruit. Protein kept you filled up. . . . She followed her white shadow out into the crowded messroom. Not as noisy as some she'd seen, with flying food and pushing. In fact, it seemed subdued. The lingering effects of the shipwide illness? Or simply the weight of war? Ryan wended toward a table of women, who shoved over to accommodate them. "Guys, this's Aisha. She's looking for whoever did the Terror."

"Hi, Aisha. Ginnie."

"Celestina."

"Maie."

"That's a pretty wrap, Aisha. I like the—dogwood flowers? Is that Chinese?"

"I think that's what they are. Got it in New York. Could be Chinese." She sipped the sweet colored fluid the Navy called bug juice, noting the dark-haired woman with the mole. Celestina. Could this be Colón, the victim of the second incident, the one that might have been intended as a rape—but was aborted at the last moment by some failure of will or resolve?

"Any progress, uh, Aisha? I work with Beth. She's really taking this hard."

Aisha dissected a chicken breast and set aside the greasy brown delicious-looking crackling. She yearned for a taste, but it was pure fat. "I can't comment on an ongoing investigation. But you could all help me."

"Tell us." Colón, if it was her, leaned forward. "Next time, he's going to cut whoever he drags off."

She gave them the litany she'd just given the sonarman. "Guys who harass women. Who talk rough. Or the other extreme—women haters. Somebody weird, with a knife fetish. Who says stuff like 'teach the cunts a lesson.' Or 'You

155

won't hook up with me, you'll be sorry.' Sound like anybody you know?"

Furrowed brows. Slow chewing. "There's a snipe, this asshole in Engineering, used to bad-mouth his petty officer like that. Just skating what he could get away with."

"This wouldn't be . . ."

"Peeples. Art Peeples."

"On my list. Who else?"

But they couldn't come up with any others. Aisha frowned. Either this ship's company was composed of total gentlemen, or the girls were already wary of her. Of "ratting out" shipmates. "Well, that's all right," she said at last. "I'm in the unit commander's stateroom, if anyone wants to come and see me. On the QT." They looked puzzled. "Totally confidential. Your name will never be mentioned."

They nodded. Then Maie asked Ginnie, who worked in CIC with Terranova, where they were. Ginnie said, "We're headed for Taiwan. To take station there, defend the islands. The captain thinks the Chinese may try to break through there."

"Which means we'll be up to our asses in torpedoes and missiles. Air attacks, too." Colón fingered the dark mole on her cheek.

Ryan shoved her tray away, muttering, "You all better make damn sure your ee-beedies work, you have to get out in a smoke-filled environment."

The girls moved on to their home lives. They

complained about not being able to check their bank accounts, e-mail their parents, log on to Facebook. "I just know he's seeing her again," Colón murmured, pushing pudding around on her tray. "It's real simple. She's there, I'm out here. And I can't even Skype with him."

Aisha finished her meal and looked at the soft-ice-cream machine. Started to leave, but found herself mesmerized by the thick chocolate and creamy white, light and dark, intertwined and braiding endlessly as they oozed from the angled nozzles. She got in line.

CIC was smaller than she remembered from the cruisers she'd been on before. Or maybe, just more crowded. Icy cold. The ice cream rumbled uneasily in her stomach. The screens up front were milling, contacts being tracked to the accompaniment of a susurration of muttered conversation. A white officer was hunched at the front table, a red-bound binder open. He was rubbing his chin as he glanced from it to the screens. Eagles glittered on the points of his collar. The CO, Lenson. He was tall, all right. Sandy hair, graying at the temples. Lean. Fit-looking. She started to approach, but he looked too busy to interrupt. So she asked a woman at a console, "Is there a CIC officer here?"

"Uh, the CIC watch officer? Over in that right-hand seat."

The chief she pointed to was facing the displays too. His name tag read SLAUGHENHAUPT. He listened stone-faced as she explained who she was and what she wanted. He pondered, blinking at the rapidly changing symbology on the screens. Finally he grunted, "Let's go over by the scuttlebutt."

In a dark corner, he leaned in. "We're in Condition Three, Agent. Might have to launch ordnance at any time. Do you really need to be here right now?"

"I have a job to do, Chief."

"Well, so do we, ya know? Like, executing an operational mission. You got any idea what's going on?"

She said she didn't, and that it was outside her need to know. This halted him; he'd been going to pull that card himself, but having it thrown down on him took him aback. "Uh, okay. Yeah, so you see."

"But can you just tell me about the cameras. They're gun cameras, I think."

Slaughenhaupt coughed into a fist, squinting past her as the mingled soft voices grew momentarily louder. "Uh . . . there aren't any 'gun cameras' on a CG. Not for the forward or aft five-inches, if that's what you mean. There are cameras that survey the fore and aft missile decks. You can pivot those with that black joystick, between me and where the TAO sits.

But they're not stabilized. They're mainly to be able to monitor the hatches, the launch cells."

"I don't think that's what I was asking about. These have sights on them. Like gunsights."

"Like . . . ? Oh. You mean the 25mm video sights. Port and starboard on the aft missile deck. They're gyroed. Or, from here, you could look through the port or starboard Phalanx camera at the RCS. But keep in mind, the Phoenix mount has to move in train and elevation to point the lens." He hesitated. "Any of that help you out? What, you're trying to find some kind of recordings?"

"I'd rather not discuss why. But since you mention it, those are videotaped, right? How long are the recordings kept?"

"I'm not sure. If it's during an engagement, we keep those forever. Upload the video via the uplink, and file backups. But day to day . . . I doubt we keep those long. I'll have to check, get back to you on that."

"Please do. I'd be particularly interested in anything about one month ago." It had crossed her mind that if she had video, or even stills, before or after that shot of a reclining, relaxed Terranova, she might glimpse whoever had fondled her in the vestibule. The very first incident. Slaughenhaupt was eyeing her suspiciously, when someone called him from the desk. "Chief? Let's get eyes on around two six

159

five. Make sure the EWs are listening on that bearing."

Past him, she caught the gaze of the captain. Gray eyes fixed on her, a faint frown, a doubtful look. Then it vanished, absorbed back into that intense concentration as he pressed a mike button and, looking up at the screen, began to speak.

She called it a day after that. A decent start on the investigation. It didn't look as if there was any particular hurry. From what the girls had said at lunch, she wouldn't be getting off the ship anytime soon. And whoever had attacked Terranova, and Colón, then Terranova again, wouldn't be leaving either. They were locked down together.

And maybe headed into combat . . . She'd been shot at and car-bombed in Yemen. Never yet been in an all-out war, though. NCIS wasn't supposed to be aboard ship in wartime. Their wartime missions mostly had to be done from shore bases. But they didn't want her. They said they wanted to understand the Faithful, yet had no use for her? Well, it was all Allah's will. Or, the Navy way of saying it, she guessed, "It all counts on twenty."

"Want me to stick around?" Ryan leaned in, holding the door open.

"No, thanks. I appreciate your helping out today, Duncanna."

"The guys call me Dunk."

"Thanks, Dunk. Maybe meet up again tomorrow, after breakfast?"

The corpsman said she had sick call early, plus there might be GQ again. If there wasn't, she'd try to meet her around 07. Then eased the door closed.

Aisha made sure it was locked. It wasn't unknown for someone feeling unjustly suspected, or threatened for other reasons, to barge in.

The case had been a two-victim shooting at Parris Island, the Marine boot camp in South Carolina. Two bodies had been found at the BEQ, one the senior sergeant major, the other a female drill instructor. Both had been shot with a target-grade .45 registered to the drill sergeant, which had been found on the bed.

At first, it had been unclear if the sergeant major's wounds had been self-inflicted, or if a third party had been involved in the shooting. Spatter patterns on the cinder-block walls had been inconclusive. No one had seen anyone enter or exit the BEQ during the early-morning hours the autopsy indicated had been the time of death. But traffic was sparse then, and the night desk clerks watched movies in the back office. The local resident's preliminary investigation hadn't cleared the air, leaving the possibility of a double murder instead of a murder-suicide. The pistol was very oily, which made the absence of fingerprints explainable two ways: either all had been dissolved by the military-issue preservative, or it was a murder weapon, wiped down by the killer.

Aisha had interviewed the sergeant major's wife, the other decedent's husband, an air side chief on active duty aboard USS *Essex*, and six of the female victim's male workmates, almost all of whom she'd apparently slept with at one time or another. She'd suspected one, a base armorer with a history of violence and jealousy. He could have had access to the sergeant major's private weapon, or known where it was kept. But she'd never been able to link him to the scene. His wife, a cowed first-generation Filipina, had sworn he was with her that night. The case had finally cleared as murder-suicide, but she'd never felt comfortable with that conclusion.

She'd been staying at that same quarters, to get a sense of the nighttime traffic, when the armorer had knocked on her door, and forced his way in when she'd opened it. Drunk, of course. He felt she needed to hear more, as a black sister. She'd managed to get him out, but ever since had locked her door.

She changed and showered in the bare cold WC off the little bedroom. Everything looked unused. She couldn't find any soap, and had to use her shampoo to shower with.

Toweled off, in bathrobe and flip-flops, she parked herself in front of the desk. First, she updated her notes, on her laptop. This was a running diary of the investigation: a messy collection of documents, interview notes, and affidavits that by the end of a case sometimes stretched for hundreds of pages. She recapped hints, links from the victim to others. Usually she tried to assign a percentage of suspicion to each suspect, ranking them, but it was too early yet to do that.

Notes completed, she turned the ship's computer on. Booted up, logged on, and accessed the LAN.

There, though, she found her access restricted. No personnel files. Just the plan of the day and an e-mail account blazoned with a warning about discussing classified information. When she went to e-mail, a popup informed her the ship was in River City: no Internet access unless cleared in advance by the CO or his designated representative.

Her mother was digitally challenged, but she'd managed to set up a Skype account. She'd Skyped with Tashaara from the carrier, logging on during the 0100–0200 time frame so as not to overload the broadband. It wasn't like the old days, when all you had was a letter every week or so. But then this had all started, the mess with China. Her family was still safe, though. She felt sure of that. Whatever happened in the Pacific, they'd be all right, back in New York.

A chill wormed up her spine. Unless . . . but no. The United States still held the advantage, in nuclear weapons.

She looked at the photo in the little gold frame,

propped by her bed with her clock and the cup her bridge went in at night. She rubbed her face, exhausted. Climbing ladders, wriggling through scuttles. She was getting too old for this. No . . . not too old . . . just too damn fat.

She laid the rug she'd bought in Makkah on the tiled deck, guessing at the direction, and knelt and did her *salat.* She said an extra *du'a,* asking for strength to resist temptation, in the form of ice cream and other forbidden lusts.

Then sat back on her heels, looking up at the photo.

She'd wanted to save just one child from drought-stricken, war-torn Ashaara. The Consular Report of Birth Abroad had documented the out-of-wedlock birth of one female child, Tashaara Ar-Rahim, to one Aisha Ar-Rahim, U.S. federal employee on duty abroad.

The thump of a rubber stamp, and an orphan had become a U.S. citizen.

She touched the photo, smiling back at the little girl's happy grin. Then set it down gently, and crawled into bed. Said the Talbiyah quietly, the prayer pilgrims said on the hajj, giving herself to sleep.

Here I am at your service, O Lord, here I am.

Here I am, no partner do you have, here I am.

Truly all the praise and goodness is yours, and the kingdom.

Amin. . . .

10

The helicopter came in fast out of the night, braking mere feet from *Savo*'s upperworks. It flared out with a shrieking whine and planted itself with a thump that Dan, on the bridge wing looking aft, could hear even this far away.

The next morning, but barely. 0100. Outside, the sea was dead black, the windows fathomless mirrors that returned only the firefly glows of pilot lamps and nav screens.

Cheryl was back there to welcome the liaison. Dan had wavered on where to receive him. Asians liked ceremonial welcomes. Finally, he'd decided on the bridge. He made sure they had hot coffee. A plate of fresh *Savo* cookies teetered on one of the radar repeaters, where an exhaust fan blasted warm air into the chill.

A rising clatter again from aft. Both *Savo* and the aircraft were running darkened, though Dan had ordered the deck-edge lights turned on for the last seconds of the approach. The flare of the turbine exhaust burned in the near infrared, lifting as it veered off to starboard, then winked out.

Dan's Hydra crackled. *"Skipper? Captain Fang is aboard."*

Captain? The messages had said he was a commander. Dan nodded to the boatswain, hidden in the darkness. "Hangar area only," he cautioned.

The 1MC crackled, then intoned, *"Commander, Korean navy, arriving."*

The angry murmur of someone recalibrating the boatswain was followed by, *"Belay my last. Captain, Republic of China Navy, arriving."* Dan counted the muffled bells that followed. Six. Good.

Minutes later the door creaked open. Bodies filed into the darkened space. Dan led them into the nav room and closed the door.

When the deep red lights blinked on he faced a tall, thin Asian with a jutting chin. "I am Captain Fang," he murmured, gripping Dan's hand with more than the usual strength one got in this part of the world. Some kind of birthmark, or rash, on either side of his nose appeared black in the scarlet light. He looked as tired as Dan felt.

"Dan Lenson. Commanding Task Group 779.1. How was your flight, um, Captain? Where'd you fly out of, anyway?"

"Hualien Naval Airfield. We went fast and low," Fang said. "It was . . . exciting. In the dark." He looked pale. His insignia sparkled. Still new. The guy had just been fleeted up, to match Dan's rank as his opposite number.

"Well, I'm glad you're with us. Coffee?

Cookies? They're a little sweet, but they're good."

Fang nervously pulled out a cigarette. "These are permitted?"

"Looks like you might need one right now . . . so go ahead. But after this, only outside the skin of the ship. If you go out on deck after dark, though, be careful. We don't want to lose anybody overboard." As the guy stroked an enameled Zippo, shielding his eyes, Dan nodded to Cheryl. "You've met my XO?"

"I have met Commander Star-Lakis." Fang sucked the smoke deep, held it, let it out with a sigh. The tobacco smell was pungent in the little space.

"Have we got the captain's luggage taken care of, XO?"

"Longley's got it, sir."

"We're putting you in my inport cabin. I'd have made it the unit commander's stateroom, but we didn't know you were coming and we have another rider in there already."

"I will be happy anywhere you think suitable. Sir."

Dan gripped his shoulder. "Call me Dan, okay? And what do I call you?"

"My name is Chih-Pei. When I was at Monterey they called me Chip."

"Oh, you went to NPS?" The Naval Post-graduate School was the Navy's technical grad school. "What discipline?"

167

"Meteorology," Fang muttered reluctantly. "But I have put in most of my time in frigates."

"Me too." Dan clapped him on the back, then regretted it as the thin shoulder flinched under his blow. "Look, we can either brief now, uh, Chip, or let you crash for a couple of hours and get to it first thing in the morning. Your call."

"I would begin our cooperation now, if that is all right."

Dan nodded, reluctantly parting with his own hope of getting his head down for a few hours. "Okay, let's do this in Combat. Cheryl, round up the team."

Mills, Singhe, Staurulakis; the command master chief, Sid Tausengelt; Wenck, Zotcher, and the other div-o's and chiefs in the Operations Department gathered in front of the large-screen displays. Dave Branscombe, *Savo*'s comm officer, was holding down the TAO seat.

Dan paced back and forth as Mills began pulling up slides, feeling like a game show host. In short sentences, to make sure it made sense to a non-native speaker, he gave the liaison the high-level overview of what the task group brought to the table, and how he planned to hold the Miyako Strait. The last screen showed the zones, Yellow, Orange, and Red. He finished, "Our left flank's anchored on Miyako Jima. Japanese territory. Can I ask, how are you covering the sea gap

168

between there and Taiwan? It's not much good holding the center if they can end-around to the south or the north."

"May I have a chart of that area?" Fang asked quietly.

When it came up, he aimed the red dot of a laser pointer at a point between Miyako and Taiwan. "This is Yonaguni Shima. Japanese, but we have arranged for an antisubmarine helicopter squadron to operate from there. So the Japanese may focus their efforts on the northern Ryukyus. We have bottom sensors in place. And two of our quietest submarines are stationed behind the island.

"Thus, we feel confident we have a secure barrier between Miyako and Taiwan." Fang paused. "Do you want our overall force laydown? Our deployments to the south, and in the straits?"

"Maybe later. Right now, could we focus on the threat, our op area, and how we can work together?"

"All right, then. The threat." Fang smoothed the front of his uniform shirt, coughed, and hooked his fingers under his belt. He glanced at Singhe, then dropped his gaze. "After many years' buildup, we believe the mainland actually intends an invasion this time. We base this on human intelligence. In fact, we have copy of their plan. The mainland calls it Operation Sheng Chi. This can mean something like 'Breath of the Dragon.'

But can also read ideographs as 'Overthrow of Ruling Dynasty.' It will be an even bigger cross-water invasion than Normandy."

He let them ponder that, then went on. "Their success depends on our air force and navy being defeated first. But we are witnessing building up of air forces. Gathering of invasion craft. More and more troop units reporting to ports. And increased reconnaissance."

"How soon?" said Staurulakis. She looked worried. Or maybe just tired.

"Our sources could not provide that. It could be only days. Apparently, General Zhang will give the 'go' order personally."

"How do your guys see it playing out?" Amy Singhe asked. Staurulakis gave her a sharp glance, but Dan waved a soothing gesture. It was a fair question.

Fang compressed his lips. "Whether they come by sea or air, they must cross two hundred miles of kill zone. The question will be whether we can keep enough attack aircraft operational to attrite forces, as they cross, down to a level our army can cope with.

"We are very strong on the ground. Fifteen active divisions, with another million and a half reservists. Artillery. Armor. Thus, landings must be made with five divisions, at the very least. They must take a major port, to resupply and reinforce.

"Thus, we expect the first phase of the campaign to be air and missile strikes against our air forces."

"Like the Battle of Britain," Dan said.

Fang faced him. "Very much so, Captain. Without ruling the air, Hitler could not succeed. The British took heavy losses, but they continued to defend. Eventually the Germans gave up."

"Can you do that?" Wenck insisted.

"That will be the point of the war," Fang deadpanned. "To answer that question."

Dan cleared his throat. "Okay . . . granted. But that's out of our hands. Our task group has three missions. Shield the population of Taipei against ballistic missiles, hold the line Miyako-Okinawa, and maintain a credible strike capability on call.

"First, the ABM mission. Donnie, when we were operating in the East Med, we had a problem coordinating with the Patriot battery at Ben-Gurion. I'd like you and Commander . . . sorry, Captain Fang to work out arrangements with the batteries at the north end of Taiwan. Deconflict the radar spectrum. And arrange air asset forwarding, so we can Link-16 between us and the ROC air-defense system.

"Second, we could be here a while. You may have heard of the loss of *Stuttgart*, Captain. Our logistics tail."

Fang inclined his head. "What would you need

to stay on station, Captain? Or should I address you as Commodore?"

"Captain's fine. Or just Dan—like I said. We need three Fs: fuel, food, and frigates. We burn marine distillate. JP-5, JP-8, JP-4, NATO F-34, commercial Jet A-1. Or plain kerosene if that's more plentiful. If you could arrange for a tanker or yard oiler to keep the task group topped off, that would extend our stay time."

"I can promise fuel. We have stockpiles. Food may be a more difficult problem. We are already rationing, for the population. What else? Water?"

"We can make our own. Given fuel."

"Very good. Then—frigates, you said?"

Dan nodded. "Perrys or Knoxes, with towed sonar arrays. I'd place them here"—he swept a hand behind the Red Zone—"to catch any leakers. A final line of defense. Also, to watch our backs. We're going to be tunnel-visioned to the west."

Fang looked doubtful. "I will inquire, but both the navy and air force are concentrating all our resources on the strait. Given the importance of that mission."

Dan blew out. "I can understand that."

"Air cover," Staurulakis murmured.

"Uh, yeah. In case there's a major air threat, who can we call on?" Dan asked. "You have F-16s at Chiashan, right? Any possibility we could get a combat air patrol, or at least, designated responders on strip alert?"

Fang looked away. "Our aircraft locations are classified. Also, we have dispersed them, for operations from highways."

Dan frowned. "Highways?"

"Instead of runways," Fang explained. "We have built many of our highways to be usable as airstrips. About air cover: again, the requirements of homeland defense may prevent us from offering the support we would like to provide."

Dan nodded again. To an island facing invasion, even the defense of the northern and southern sea passages might have to play second fiddle. "All right. See what you can do."

Branscombe tensed, bending into his earphones. He held up a hand. A moment later a voice called from the ASW consoles, *"Panther, panther! From Polar Bear."*

Dan lifted his head, jerked alert. "Polar Bear" was *Pittsburgh*, running covert deep in the Yellow Zone. And "panther" was the proword for a hostile nuclear submarine. "Excuse me, Captain." He dropped into the command seat, reached for his headphones, snapped the selector to the ASW circuit. To hear, *"Panther Alfa, bearing from* Pittsburgh, *zero three five, estimated range twenty-eight thousand yards, estimated demons one hundred, estimated speed five knots, right bearing rate. Classified as Han-class nuke. Also, Goblin Bravo, bearing zero four zero, estimated range thirty-two*

173

thousand yards, estimated speed five knots, hot piping, right bearing rate. Polar Bear will maintain contact at scope depth and pass data."

Not one, but two subs making for their barrier. One nuclear, though an older class. The other, conventional, and snorkeling. Most likely, sucking down a full charge before going deep for an outbound transit, through either TG 779.1's area or that of the Japanese straits to the northeast.

Another voice, from the air console. *"Bandit, bandit! Multiple hostile tracks. Bearing two niner zero, angels three. One hundred forty miles. Course one seven zero. Three hundred knots. Angels decimal five. No squawk. Naked."*

"I'm on it." Wenck nudged Eastwood out of his seat and slid into the Aegis operator's position.

The contacts came up, with course, speed, and altitude readouts. Dan clicked his keyboard, zooming in. A flight of five aircraft had popped up on the mainland. Crossing the shoreline at near-wavetop height. And traveling with both IFF and other electronics off, which pretty much meant hostile, by definition.

"Attack aircraft," Branscombe muttered in an aside to Dan, off the net.

"Yeah, but headed where?" A minute passed. Dan stretched, trying to relieve the bowstrings winding taut in his back. "Chip. What's going on here? Could they be headed for us?"

"I'm not sure," the liaison muttered, blinking up at the screen. Dan blinked too, eyes stinging from cigarette smoke. Hadn't he asked the guy to . . .

"Could be headed for the Senkakus," Branscombe muttered. "We'll see in a couple of minutes, I guess."

"Set up a solution." Dan noted the time. Was startled to see it was close to dawn. Though here, in the timeless no-time of CIC, there was no way to tell light was creeping up from the east. "Mongoose that to *Chokai*, to pass to the Japanese warning net."

Fang blinked. "Are they within Standard range?"

"Not just yet. But I need to see where they're headed first. At a hundred and forty miles, they could drop a zombie and scoot. Like the Argentines did in the Falklands. Or they could be headed for the islands. Air support, to back up their troops."

"Spoke, bearing three one zero," the EW operator said in his phones. *"Racket, racket. R band. Also, we got another ferret."*

Dan coughed into his fist. A "ferret" was an electronic warfare aircraft. The rackets and spokes were jamming, again from the mainland. Good: The EWs would plot each jammer and fire-control radar that brushed its fingers over them. These would go into *Savo*'s target set, to be dialed into her Tomahawks in case they got called away on the strike mission.

175

The situation was developing . . . A dawn raid, coordinated with a submerged attempt to run the blockade. Dan snapped, "I know *Wilbur* has Force Air Defense, but put out a 'condition hairy' to all TG units. Tell *Kurama* I want dippers out along their extended track. Fish in the water as soon as they have a solid contact. The faster we deal with these guys, the more reluctant they'll be to test us again. They'll probably designate this bogey gaggle to *Mitscher*, but confirm weapons tight for now. TAO: Go out to all Steeplechase, from Ringmaster: Go to Condition One. Pass that to Dreadnought."

Beside him, Branscombe put out the warning over the task group command net. The symbology on the screen winked and changed. The flight from the mainland clicked ahead, definitely, now, aimed for the Senkaku Islands. Their ID came up as Q-5s, NATO designation "Fantan."

Fighter-bombers, attack types, just as Branscombe had guessed. But whom were they attacking? As far as he'd heard, the Japanese weren't defending the islands.

The Aegis system painted a second flight of Fantans rising from another airfield. Then, a third. This was building into a major strike package. Voices began to rise, along with the clatter of keyboards. Fang was still standing to the side with arms folded, the cigarette smoke blowing off him like fog. Dan nodded to the embarked commander's seat to his own left.

"You can park it here, okay, Chip? We'll get you up on a terminal. But for now, observe, all right? Any input you may have, advice, lean over and let me know." He almost added, "And put out that fucking cigarette," but no sense humiliating the guy in public.

The air side: *"CO: Three fighters banzai from Naha. Squawking as JDF F-2s. Vectoring two four zero."*

"All *right*," Dan said. At last, Tokyo was responding to the intrusion. F-2s were heavied-up, longer-range F-16s, more than capable of taking on the slower, less agile Fantans. The Japanese took a while to get everybody on board with a policy decision. But once made, they tended to stick with it.

"Coffee, Captain?" Longley, at his elbow. Dan nodded, and glanced over to the Aegis console. A childlike face bent over the keyboard. The Terror was on the job.

He straightened in his chair, eyes stinging anew as a wave of sheer fucking pride washed over him. Not just for her. For the whole team. Maybe this was what *Savo*'s factionalized, demoralized crew had always needed, since the day hc'd comc aboard. To face the elephant together.

Over the next minutes the flights converged, the attackers from the mainland, the defenders from Okinawa. Branscombc sct up a rcmotc on a voice channel for Fang to try to contact the ROC air net, see if they could get a data handoff from the islanders. Their picture had to include the AWACS data, and the ROC had an AWACS of their own, too. He needed a theaterwide picture, but GCCS was still down and they were still struggling with the fucking line-of-sight problem.

"Hey, Skipper." Wenck, beside him, waved a hand. "Is the smoking lamp lit in here?"

"Not for you, Donnie."

"Oh. I get it. . . . Look, we got something up in the black. Same weird shit we saw in Hormuz."

Dan snapped, "What're you talking about, Donnie?"

"Up around a hundred thousand feet. Radar return. A transient. A ghost. It's there, then it ain't. The cross section's gotta be super small. Golf-ball size."

Dan sighed. "You saw this in Hormuz, too, Donnie, but there's never anything there. It's some kind of atmospheric phenomenon."

"I thought so too. Maybe a sprite. But those only happen in thunderstorms."

"Then it's intrinsic to the radar. A lensing effect. An artifact. You run it past Noblos?"

"He doesn't believe it's real."

"Then get him up here to see it. Or quit bothering me about it already."

"Yeah, right. Billy Goat doesn't like getting woken up at oh fuck thirty."

Dan twisted in his chair, abruptly enraged. "Get him here before it disappears. And don't keep nagging me unless there's really something there!"

"Jesus," Wenck mumbled, pushing hair out of his eyes. "I really . . . sorry, Cap'n." He retreated into the darkness by the tactical data coordinator's console.

Dan's earphones said, *"Silver Tiger flight leader reports Judy, Judy."* The leader of the F-2s was taking control from ground-based intercept. Which meant he had radar or visual contact with the incoming strike. The callouts showed he had ten-thousand-feet height advantage. Dan was no fighter pilot, but it looked like a short engagement.

Branscombe, beside him: *"Kurama* reports, they have contact on the panther. Dipping sonar. Solid datum. They call it as a Han class. Standing by to drop bloodhound."

Dan nodded. Hans were first-generation attack boats, roughly comparable to the old U.S. Skipjack class. They were fast, but notoriously noisy. Why would they send a Han to try to penetrate an ASW barrier? It didn't make sense.

Unless all their newer boats had already sortied, and this was the last nag out of the gate.

Incomplete and contradictory information, that he had to fill out by guesswork and instinct . . . in other words, the way most battles began. He didn't, couldn't, tear his gaze from the screen.

Until something sharp nudged his elbow. The corner of a clipboard. Held by the duty radioman. "Flash message, Captain."

Dan ran his eyes down it, then again, disbelieving. "You're shitting me."

"What is it?" Branscombe said.

"It's from PaCom, via Seventh Fleet." He blew out and leaned back, trying to get his head around it. "It reads: 'Though we stand with allies, U.S. is not yet at war in the Pacific. No hostile acts are authorized unless in response to active maneuvering or weapons employment. Forces in forward positions are specifically prohibited from initiating combat, or warlike acts unless in response to live fire, or as cleared on a case-by-case basis.'"

The TAO hissed through his teeth. "We're here to block passage, but we can't fire on anyone unless he fires first? That's nuts."

Dan chewed his lip, running the pros and cons. This was a very specific warning, practically by name, or as close as the writers could come without actually saying *This applies specifically to Dan Lenson.* On the other hand, wasn't a nuclear submarine coming at you a hostile act? After one of the units under his tactical control had already been torpedoed?

The ASW air controller reported, and a moment later Branscombe repeated, "Silver Tiger flight leader reports contact."

"That's the Japanese? From Okinawa?"

The answer was yes. Dan zoomed on the gaggle south of the islands, but they were maneuvering too fast to make sense of. The altitude and heading callouts spun dizzily. "Sheez . . . can you declutter this furball, Terror?"

"I'll try, Captain, but between the jamming and all the tinsel both sides are kicking out—"

"I understand. The best you can."

The picture shifted. A lot of the ground return dropped out, but it was still too fast-paced for him to make sense of. Someone put a tactical voice circuit on an overhead speaker, but it was in Japanese. Slow, belly-grunted Japanese: the pilot was pulling a lot of Gs.

"I think he just said: Splash one Fan Tan."

"EW: Birds away. Multiple birds away."

A burst of excited Japanese from above his head. "Turn that down," Dan snapped. The swarm settled into a swirling maelstrom. A typical fighter furball. EW reported more air-to-air missile seekers and jammers.

"Going to initial that, sir?" The messenger held out a pen.

"Fuck," Dan sighed. Washington was backing away.

On the other hand, the Japanese seemed to have made up their minds to fight. And the fact that those had been ground-attack aircraft, in the Chinese strike, meant there'd been someone on the islands to bomb. He scribbled *DL* and tried to hand the board back, but the messenger lifted his palms. "Another one under that, sir," he said.

It was a protest from Berlin over Dan's handling of the sinking of *Stuttgart*. A request that the U.S. convene a court of inquiry. That if found guilty of neglecting his duty to protect, of abandoning castaways, the commander of USS *Savo Island* be disciplined to the fullest extent of the law.

He initialed this with a wry smile. About the least of his worries right now. "Anything else?"

"Things aren't going so well back in the States, sir. We overheard a MARS guy from Guam. One of those ham radio dudes."

"Why, what's going on?"

"Basically everything from the banking system to the Internet crashed. Rioting in LA and DC. Fires. National Guard."

The air controller came on his headset. *"CO, Air: Tiger flight leader reports dropping contact."* The gaggle began to disperse. On the screen, the blue symbols of friendly aircraft began to exit the furball. They rejoined in a loose V and headed for home. The red symbols of hostile aircraft, noticeably fewer, departed to the west, two at lower altitude and reduced airspeed. Damaged, or low on fuel and bingoing for the nearest friendly strip.

"Kurama reports: Panther in a port turn. Standing by on bloodhound."

"Copy." Dan reoriented his logy brain to the subsurface picture. The Han-class might be refusing combat. Or, possibly, had just been sent to see whether it would be detected. Her CO must have brass balls indeed. Or maybe they just hadn't told the poor schmuck what he was facing. "How about number two? The snorkeler?"

"*Kurama* reports: Lost contact on Goblin Charlie. Ceased snorkeling, went sinker, below thermocline, lost contact."

"Shit," Branscombe muttered. Dan sagged back into his chair. Even Fang looked dismayed. "Tell *Kurama:* we need to regain contact. That Han could just be to distract us. Or put so much noise into the water, we drop track on his buddy."

"*From* Kurama: *request permission to drop bloodhound on datum, Goblin Charlie.*"

He almost granted it, then remembered: He didn't have authority to. Was specifically *prohibited*.

On the other hand, *Kurama* wasn't a U.S. national unit.

On yet another hand, Dan *was* her tactical commander.

The Japanese didn't seem to have any doubt they were at war. But the U.S. was wavering. What the fuck? Branscombe eyed him; so did Fang. He caught Wenck's and Terranova's worried glances from the Aegis area. Crunch time.

"Chip, any input?" He was playing for time to

think, but maybe the Taiwanese could contribute something.

"You should attack," Fang murmured, in a voice pitched for Dan only. "Send them the message. America will stand by its allies."

Dan nodded. About what he'd expected. And the guy was right. With every passing moment, the second sub was moving farther from its last confirmed location, lessening the probability a torpedo could acquire. If it evaded them, the next indication they could have of its existence might be a torpedo in their hull, or an antiship missile breaking the surface, too close and fast to react to.

On the other hand, wasn't it in Taiwan's interest to have him pull the trigger? Maybe Fang had another purpose than simple liaison. Such as, force a commitment. Get Washington off the dime.

But . . . Higher knew better. At least that's what Admiral Barry "Nick" Niles had told him once. In the Navy Command Center, deep in the Pentagon. "You're down at level four, second-guessing what's happening on level one. Second-guessing *us*," Niles had said.

The CNO had given him another chance. Trusted him.

How many more chances did he have left?

More to the point . . . was Niles right?

He cleared his throat, shifting under their gazes. Right or wrong, he had to decide, *now*.

But then came realization. He had to admit, he might not be fully in the picture. Not out here, at the end of a tenuous comm link, face-to-face with the putative enemy. There might be a deal in the works. Some way both sides could save face. A diplomatic solution.

Maybe they could still defuse this. The allies would have the Spratlys soon, as a bargaining chip. To balance against Quemoy and Matsu. No American unit had been lost yet, after all. Just one German tanker . . . a country that wouldn't be directly involved, even if things went hot.

If a compromise was possible, he didn't want to be the guy who derailed it. He clicked to the tactical circuit. "*Kurama,* this is Ringmaster actual," he said reluctantly.

"*This is* Kurama. *Go ahead. Over.*"

"This is Ringmaster. Weapons tight. Continue efforts to reacquire, but I say again, weapons tight, on direction from Higher. *Kurama,* confirm."

The disappointment in the voice was almost palpable. "*This is* Kurama. *Confirm weapons tight.*"

The helo searched for the next half hour without regaining contact. A second bird vectored to relieve it, refreshing the sonobuoy barrier between the lost-contact position and the Red Zone on the way.

Finally Fang sighed and stood. "I will try to

185

find my stateroom," he murmured. "A long day." Dark circles outlined his eyes, a counterpoint to the birthmarks on either side of his nose. Dan nodded, and gave directions: down two decks, and head aft; ask someone if he got lost.

When the Chinese had gone he hoisted himself up too, but staggered and nearly fell. Branscombe gripped his arm, steadying him. "Y'okay, Skipper?"

"Yeah. Yeah. Fine." But his legs felt weak. The aftereffects of *Legionella savoiensis*, no doubt. Plus having had practically no sleep for the last three days.

Maybe some fresh air. Out in the passageway, he undogged a door and stepped out.

Suddenly he was alone, forty feet above the undulating sea. They were lazying along, with one shaft powered while the other idled, to stretch fuel and limit own-ship self-noise. The bridge wing cantilevered out above him. The sun, a thumb's width above the horizon, sparkled off the nearly colorless water.

Was it dawn, or sundown? He wasn't sure. He leaned over the rail, suddenly nauseated. Acid burned his throat. Fatigue dragged at his bones, as if they'd turned to depleted uranium. Small sprigs of what looked like naked grape stems floated here and there on the surface, then rolled apart, vanishing in the churn of *Savo*'s wake. A sea dragon, inhaling air, breathing out fire.

He leaned there, rubbing the corded muscles in his neck, wondering dizzily if he'd made the right decision. Praying others would not pay the price, if he'd screwed up.

Then he went back inside, and resumed the climb to the bridge.

11

The store was as crowded as if it were Black Friday. Shoppers pushed loaded carts, looking harried and desperate. Queekie Titus's motorized chair whined ahead, wobbling down the baking-supply aisle. Blair's mother wielded her little silver laser like a fairy queen's wand, pointing the beam at what she wanted, and clicking the red vibrating spot to signal the number of units. Blair trailed her on foot, pulling things down into her quickly filling cart. The last one left; it was crippled with a squeaky, nutating wheel that locked and skidded, constantly jerking her to one side.

"Walnuts, they'll keep, five pounds. Sugar, that's going fast, get ten pounds. Not that brand, Blair. General Sugar. We should ask the Holders for a contribution to your campaign, honey. King Arthur Flour. Baking powder. Yeast."

They were in a Harris Teeter not far from her parents' home. Queekie had insisted they go, citing what her mother had told her about rationing in World War II. Her dad was at Sears buying oil, transmission fluid, wiper blades, plugs, and spare tires.

As they were leaving the big house, he'd taken

her aside, dropped something heavy into her purse, and snapped it closed. "Take care of your mom," he'd muttered. "She tires easy these days. Keep her off her feet."

"Checkie . . . what the hell was that?"

"Your .38. The one I bought you."

"Good Lord. It's not loaded, is it?"

"Damn straight it is. All that cash you're carrying? The Galens' daughter got robbed on the street. Broad daylight. The lowlifes know people are carrying real money again. . . . Remember what I said. But get whatever she says we need."

Now the red spot searched trembling along rows of cans. "Condensed milk, grab a dozen . . . no . . . take all that's left. Cocoa powder. Baking chocolate. Raisins, the golden ones. All right, let's do meats next."

Blair's cell went off as she rounded the turn, into a jam-packed aisle. For a moment she couldn't identify the ring tone. People were clawing down the last cans of Spam and tuna and corned beef and canned chicken. The store manager was waving her hands, stuttering as she explained to a growling ring of red-faced housewives that yes, everything in the store was out on the shelves. A siren howled outside, and the women quieted for a moment, then turned back to their surrounded, sweating scapegoat. The manager shook off the beseeching hands. "Shut up. Shut *up!* Yes, everything's marked up. Fifty percent. It wasn't my decision! Higher management! Cash only. No checks. I'll close this store, I swear I will—"

A heavyset woman in a track suit growled, "Just *try* to close, bitch. We'll break the windows and take what we want."

Blair considered trying to make peace, but decided to finish shopping before the manager made good on her threat. She followed her mother's whirring whine down the paper goods aisle while trying to answer her cell. The first call in days; maybe the network was coming back. Dan? But the number said it wasn't. A 410 number, local. "Blair here," she said, shielding the phone from the pandemonium with a cupped hand.

It was her campaign manager, Jessica. *"Blair, where are you? What's all that screaming?"*

"At the grocery. They're cleaning the place out."

"Yeah, my husband's out buying stuff too. Can you talk? I'm here with the guy from the billboard company. Clear Channel. He's telling me, we buy twelve, we get a break."

"We want twenty at the price of twelve. And they all have to go up by the end of the week."

A pause, then, *"He's not liking that."*

"Tough shit, Jessica. Nobody else is buying. He's going to have blank billboards if he doesn't work with us. Tell him that. 'Bye."

Her mother was grabbing her hand, moaning. "Oh God, Blair—the toilet paper's all gone. My mother said there was never any during the war. They had to use newspapers—"

"Some wet wipes—" No, those shelves were empty too.

They loaded up with Bounty paper towels instead. Her mom powered her chair, motors whining, toward the beer aisle next. "Some of that brown ale your stepdad likes. And maybe some dry whites—"

But their way was blocked by carts being loaded. The smell of fermented yeast filled the air. Glass littered the tile. Burly men stood with arms folded, blocking Blair's way, as other tattooed men emptied the refrigerated section. "All taken, blondie," one growled at her.

"We just need a couple of those brown ales—"

"All taken, lady. Sorry." He shrugged, and swigged from his can of Bud.

Again she debated making a scene; again, thought better of it. *Congressional candidate arrested in fracas at grocery store.* Queekie made a dash for the pet food aisle, but Blair headed her off. "Get in line at the checkout, Mom. I'll get the Purina."

"And food for your cat. Don't forget your cat. Jimbo won't eat the dry—"

"I won't. Relax, Mother." She tucked the last two battered boxes of off-brand laundry detergent under her arm. "You've got the money, right? You didn't leave it in the car?"

Age-spotted hands clutched a purse. "Right here. Hurry, Blair. Things are getting ugly. And we need to go to Walgreens, get our prescriptions refilled."

A security guard stood by the checkout line, fingering a holstered Taser as women pushed and shoved, ramming carts, wedging them ahead of one another. A slow, bitter struggle, fought with all the determination of Antietam. But they made their way ahead, inch by inch.

They were almost at the register when the lights went out. The conveyor whirred to a halt. Silence flooded in from wherever the hum of refrigerators and the unnoticed background music had penned it. An excited gabble rose.

"We're going to have to close," the manager announced over the din. "I'm sorry, but please cooperate. We'll open again as soon as we have power back."

The hubbub died down. But only for a moment. Then, into the appalled hush, one raw-edged voice broke. Outraged. Strident. "You don't need them registers. You said, cash only. Here it is. Take it!" Hands waved fistfuls of bills, pulled from purses, pockets, billfolds.

The manager shrank back, exchanging terrified glances with the checkout clerks. "I can't, we don't have any way to . . . We're closing. That's final."

Another voice yelled, "Hell with this. We're takin' out what we bought."

"Shit yeah."

"We offered to buy it. You don't want to take our money—"

The burly men with the carts piled with beer, ale, wine, were circling the guard, glaring him down. He hesitated, hand on his stun weapon, looking to the manager. Then backed away. Held up both hands. "Don't want no trouble," he said.

The queue broke, men and women pushing and shoving. They grabbed the counter displays bare, then kicked them over. The burly men went for the cash in the register. Candy and convenience items skittered across the tile. Queekie screamed and clung to Blair, who bent over her, cradling her mother's blue-haired head. Other customers, thronging in from outside, began looting the fruits and vegetables.

Falling glass crashed in the manager's office, followed by a throat-ripping scream. "Let's get out of here," Blair shouted, clutching her purse. She groped for the revolver, but it was hooked on something, snagged in the silk lining at the bottom. The people thronging inside were beginning to loot the carts of those going out, and men and women shouted in one another's faces, exchanged clumsy punches, wrestling over yellow cans of Chock Full o' Nuts, tearing apart Wonder loaves, snatching cans of tinned salmon.

Her mother aimed her chair at the doors and hit the yellow button on the handle. The motors whined as she bulldozed through the melee, knocking a fat woman down. Muttering apologies, Blair pushed her own crippled, wobbling cart rapidly after her, elbowing off jackals until they reached the lot, where torn packaging and broken glass littered the asphalt. A siren wailed and she tensed—they hadn't paid, no more than had the brawling others—but it was a fire truck, speeding past on the main road.

"Are we looters now, honey?" her mother muttered distractedly, smoothing down disheveled hair. "Is that what the world is coming to?"

Hitting the hatch button for the Subaru, Blair looked back over the trash-strewn pavement, at the horde streaming out of the grocery. Along the mall other storefronts were smashing outward in crystalline explosions, boiling with people who leaped or lunged through, lugging boxes and cartons. Some had blood streaming down their faces. "I guess so, Mom. Get in, all right? We'd better get out of here."

She had to be back in DC that afternoon. But her tank was empty. Home again, her mother and the groceries unloaded and put away, she talked her stepfather out of a five-gallon can he'd squirreled away for the lawn tractor. "You're going to have to replace it," he warned her, gurgling it into her sedan through a funnel. "Go to a military base. I hear they still have gas. If they have transmission fluid, get some of that, too. Sears was out, NAPA was out—"

"I don't have a . . . wait a minute. I guess I do." She'd never really had a use for the dependent's ID they'd issued her as a Navy wife. "I'll . . . try, Dad."

The Bay Bridge was nearly deserted. The E-Z Pass booths were closed. Cops waved her through. Amazing, how dependent the economy had become on the Web. Without connectivity, commerce had returned to cash on the barrelhead. The valuations of huge firms, worth billions weeks before, had dropped to zero. Except for occasional interruptions, the massive blackouts that had rolled over the West Coast and the heartland seemed to have missed the older, more densely knitted networks of Maryland and Virginia. But she couldn't help dreading what the outages must mean to the defense industries. Aircraft. Missiles. Drones. Those plants were almost all out west.

Rolling on down a nearly empty Route 50, she listened to NPR discussing the cyberattacks that had taken down cable networks, commercial air traffic control, and the Cloud. For decades, experts had predicted that doom would come in the form of nuclear weapons. Or, failing that, biologicals. But instead of mushroom clouds or the plague, Americans faced blank screens. Silent power stations. Dead phones, and no e-mail. A sobering return to 1950, for a lot of people who'd never in their lives written a paper check, mailed a letter, or read a newspaper. On the radio, a Homeland Security official was saying not all the attacks carried Chinese fingerprints, but enough did that it was clear what was happening. *"We thought we were ready. We thought we had protection, firewalls, compartmentation. But every system they attacked, they've penetrated."*

"Are we striking back?" Diane Rehm pressed.

"I can confirm that we are. Beyond that, I can't comment."

"You can't because we aren't," Blair told the radio. Every attempt by Congress to police the private sector, even get them to share information about cyberattacks, had been defeated by an unholy alliance of industry lobbyists and NSA-haters. Americans had believed their government was spying on every e-mail, every cell conversation. Not only that, but "countervalue cyberwar," as it was called at DoD, was illegal under international treaty . . . so the U.S. had been restricted to defensive measures. There were probably contingency plans for taking down an enemy's military networks, but that would be all.

Unless, of course, some secret order had been

issued. Which, with this administration, wouldn't surprise her.

The next segment was from Taipei, man-on-the-streets about how the confrontation with the mainland was affecting life there. An interview in a noodle shop. At a shrine. With an academic, who'd spent his life studying the PRC-Taiwan relationship. Turning up the volume, she listened carefully, brow furrowed.

Jessica Kirschorn had come highly recommended. "The best," everyone said. "Young. Hungry. Smart. You want to win, hire her." But facing her across the table at the Silver Diner, Blair had to admit that the principal at Kirschorn Associates didn't look the part. Corkscrewed ringlets of lavender-dyed hair cascaded onto a soft-looking pink sweater. Rocket-and-planet earrings dangled from multiple piercings. Her nose, too, sported several perforations, each marked with a silver ball. Her makeup was heavy on the purple and black. They discussed the service on the Metro, which Kirschorn had taken in, and ordered— avocado turkey burgers. Then Kirschorn flipped open a binder. "Know you're busy, but we gotta cover several issues. The campaign's up and running, but we need to discuss strategy. First, the voter aspects. Then I'll go over fundraising, advertising, and message development. Finally, we need to talk about your debate schedule.

197

Okay, before I start, anything on your mind?"

"Just that I don't think I'll have much spare time."

A flash of widened green eyes. The same trick, Blair reflected, she herself used to convey that she was giving someone her full attention. "Ms. Titus, you can't phone in a campaign these days. Unless you're, like, a six-term incumbent. Beiderbaum's showing unexpected strength. This will not be a shoo-in."

"I know that, I'm sorry. . . . What have you got for me?"

Kirschorn started with the "ground game," as she called it: how she and her assistants, along with the local party, were targeting voters, where the databases came from, how the door-to-door, phone, and direct-mail canvassing was going. "In general, voters are reacting with interest, but also with a level of anxiety I've never seen before."

"No wonder." Blair told her about the riot at the mall. "Full-blown looting. The police arrived just as we were leaving. But I know what you mean. When people can't access their accounts, they can't buy food. Or pay bills. When they can't buy gas, they can't drive to work. And when the power goes out too—"

"They *panic.*" Kirschorn bit voraciously into her burger. Chewed.

"Correct."

"Oh yeah . . . We picked up a volunteer who says she knows you. A marine, I believe. Wants in. Margaret Shingler? Sound familiar?"

Blair's heart sank. "Um, yes. She's . . . well organized."

"Seems devoted to you."

"Maybe too much so."

"Oh." Kirschorn widened her eyes again. "Don't tell me any more."

"There *isn't* any more. She was my aide at DoD. That's all."

"Well, that's good . . . we can play to this, Blair. A ten-second ad targeting that free-floating fear. Tying the war to the administration, and painting Beiderbaum as a tool of the president. A *warmonger*."

Blair touched her ear, then forced her hand away to the sweet potato fries. "I'm not coming out against the war. I told you that. This president's as big an idiot as they say, but I don't believe it's in our best interest to show weakness now. Not to the Zhang regime."

"It closes off a good avenue of attack."

"Nevertheless, I don't want to go there," Blair said again, more firmly this time.

Kirschorn made a note. "Okay, but you're taking away my ammo—"

How many times did this woman need to hear no? "No, I said!"

The girl shrugged, the mauve curls bouncing.

"I *getcha*. But in that case, I'm gonna propose something you may not like."

"Go ahead."

"Your opponent came out last year. Out of the closet, I mean. But Beiderbaum's party base isn't exactly gay-friendly. It'd have to be done with a light touch. Maybe by someone else, not you. But there's yardage to be gained."

Blair loathed football metaphors, but they seemed as unavoidable in politics as in the military. "You're right, I don't feel good about it. How would we approach that, without losing votes on our own side?"

"The spin? That's easy. As a state legislator, he voted against gay marriage. Four times. At the least, that shows he's untrustworthy."

"That was years ago, right? The numbers were against it then. He was just voting his constituency."

Kirschorn blinked, regarding her over her burger as if encountering some alien life-form. "Blair? We don't have to *believe* any of this. These are his *weak points*. You don't think, any dirt he can dig up on you, or even *make up,* he's not gonna use it? We peel five percent of his base away on any of these issues, you win."

Blair picked at her fries. The meat in the burger looked underdone, revolting. Her hip hurt. She checked her watch. She needed to wrap this up and get over to SAIC. Maybe the kid was right.

She said reluctantly, "See what you can develop. But I want approval before we release it."

"Thatsa girl." Kirschorn grinned. "Okay, next. Your debates. Everybody I know is cutting thcm. People aren't going to drive to see them. We can do a radio thing."

"We had a commitment. At the junior college."

"We had *four* commitments. I recommend canceling them all."

"I promised Heather at the League we'd make it."

"Unpromise her."

Blair threw down her napkin. "Jessica, let's get something straight. You're my manager. But I'm still the candidate. I don't want to have to tell you everything three times to make it stick. I believe we have to win this war. Or at least, fight. And I'm going to do a debate at the community college! Set it up with Beiderbaum's people."

Kirschorn tilted her head. The rockets tinkled to a microscopic shrug. "You da boss. But if you want my advice, Blair, better get a lot more flexible, if you really want to win this thing."

The headquarters was in Tysons Corner, on Leesburg Pike. Fourteen floors of colorless concrete, with the white-and-blue corporate logo out front. She turned into the garage, found her spot, slipped on her heels, and clicked toward the elevator.

In the twenty-first century, with the exception of the Congressional Research Service, the U.S. government did little policy research. Science Applications International was one of the largest and most influential think tanks. Founded during the Nixon administration, it specialized in analysis and recommendations to policymakers, mainly in defense, intelligence, homeland security, and energy. A lot went on in the building she didn't know about—it was huge, and there were scores of satellite offices around the world—but she knew the company as almost a shadow government.

Seen in retrospect, this hadn't been an unremarkable step in her career. From the staff of the CRS, to adviser to Bankey Talmadge; eventually, adviser to the chairman of the Senate Armed Services Committee. The last president had met her at a speech to the National Guard Association, invited her to serve on his transition team, then appointed her undersecretary of defense for personnel and readiness. But then they'd lost the election.

She'd been at home, in Maryland, sleeping late. Queekie had brought in the phone. "This sounds important," she'd said.

"*Oh, hi. Blair? Chagall Henri here. We worked together on Albania. On their force restructuring?*"

Blair had blinked, trying to keep from sounding

sleepy. "Oh . . . Hello, Shaggy. Yes, of course I . . . I remember you. RAND, right?"

"Close. SAIC."

"I'm sorry, I—"

"That's all right. Hope you don't mind me calling. Bill Galina mentioned you might be looking for a position. Until the next election."

He mentioned a number that made her stifle a gasp. Three times what she'd been making as undersecretary.

"Plus fringes, and a percentage of any contracts you bring in. Are you there, Blair?"

"Oh yes, sorry . . . Chagall . . . I'm right here." She sipped water. "That's a generous offer. Though I really am not actively looking, but . . . what precisely did you have in mind?"

"Well, Blair, as you know, unlike some of the other folks in the field—Cato, Heritage, Center for Progress—we've always been nonpolitical. Or maybe a better word, bipartisan. The most effective solutions, regardless of party. You struck me as one of the more pragmatic, knowledgeable people I've worked with.

"Think you'd like to come in, see what we're doing? You'd be advising on the highest-level issues. Most of the folks who cover these areas, here, came from senior positions—the Hill, the Joint Chiefs, the White House. We could really use someone who has her fingers in personnel and readiness policy. There's a manpower

crunch coming our way. We have to figure out how to meet it. Without going to the draft, which we're hearing is a possibility, and you have a background in technology development, too."

"They can't be serious. It'd take months even to scrub down the rosters—"

"See, that's why we need you. We have plenty of generals, retired congressmen, but nobody who can put their finger on recruitment through retirement, force levels, skill sets, expansion. We'd start you as a business unit general manager. In a year or two, we can discuss a vice presidency. And think about anybody you'd like to bring with you."

The road led the other way, too. People went from SAIC to principal undersecretaries, secretaries of the services, other senior positions. A motorized revolving door between it and the government proper.

"Give me a week or two, Shaggy," she'd said at last. "I'll come in, and we'll talk."

The typical meeting room, though larger than she'd expected, with a three-color projector jutting from the overhead and a staffer fussing with a laptop. Two dozen attendees, by the time a uniformed guard drew the doors closed. Blair found a chair that reclined, so she could ease her hip; sitting for long periods quickly became excruciating.

They went around the table, introducing themselves. A lot of heavy hitters, including a retired chairman of the House Ways and Means Committee. The only other woman besides Blair was a smooth-faced, petite Asian of perhaps a well-preserved sixty, with short, blunt-cut black hair. She wore a tailored blue suit and heavy gold bracelets and earrings. Blair knew most of them by reputation, and had met many with Talmadge or during her time at the Pentagon. There were generals, of course, and intelligence analysts. Foreign Service experts, a political science professor from Stanford, and executives from Boeing and Google. The last-named was younger than the rest and seemed nervous, fiddling with his cell. She leaned over and whispered, "You need to turn that off during classified briefings."

"Sorry," he muttered. "It's not working, anyway. My first time at one of these things."

A small, balding, gray-suited man stood, taking charge with a glance around the room. He supported himself with a cane. "Good afternoon. I'm Haverford Tomlin. Some of you know me as the former head of StratCom—Strategic Command. Up to now, I've been working with the targeting folks, but I've been asked to chair this committee as well.

"Today we're discussing an emergent tasking for SAIC Strategic Plans and Policy Division. Of course, our discussions here, and even *what* we're discussing, will be top secret, special access. That includes any notes you may take, which will stay here. Along with the Air Force, we'll be working with StratCom, the Joint Chiefs J-5 shop, the policy shop—maybe some interaction with the operational shop, too. But as you can imagine, they're tied up with current developments right now. Our job is to look further ahead.

"But first, a history lesson."

A slide, in old-fashioned Courier font, headed **WAR PLAN ORANGE** in all caps and underlined. "In 1941, we had a clear plan as to how we'd win the next war." The next slide showed arrows marching across the Pacific. But the photo after that showed burning battleships. Columns of smoke. Rows of wrecked, shot-up bombers. "God laughed. We lost most of the Army Air Forces and the Pacific Fleet in the Philippines and at Pearl Harbor. It took months to decide on a new strategy"—more arrows, curving this time, and flashes indicating battles—"and years to regenerate forces to implement it. Meanwhile, thousands of Americans suffered and died in prison camps when we had to leave them behind.

"We'd like to fast-track that process this time.

"Our forces are now facing a holding action in the inner island ring. Prior to the commencement of actual hostilities, we drew down Chinese surveillance systems, sensors, and computer networks. That's where our cyberwar efforts were targeted too. So far, we seem to have been reasonably effective in degrading their air defenses and over-the-horizon targeting."

Tomlin looked toward the window, which was covered with a pinholed, silvery anti-eavesdropping screen. "Despite calls from Taiwan and Korea, we've not yet attacked the People's Republic land-based ballistic or cruise missile infrastructure. In fact, we haven't laid a single warhead or bomb on the mainland."

"The counterpunch through the South China Sea? Taking out the fortified islands, Fiery Cross Reef, the Spratlys?" One of the admirals, Blair guessed, though no one was in uniform.

"Ongoing, but we're not seeing a force shift to counteract it. It's as if they think it's a distraction.

"Unfortunately, our strategic options are limited. Obviously, we're never going to conquer mainland China. They fought us to a standstill in Korea, and Zhang has a huge demographic advantage now. Specifically, almost two million more young men than the country has young women for—probably one driver for his expansionist policy."

The next slide read

Briefing Is Classified
(TOP SECRET/SACHEL
ADVANTAGE/IRON NOOSE)
OPLAN 5081
CHINA

Tomlin cleared his throat, glanced at some notes, then went on. "JCS Op Plan 5081 reflected the conventional view of how this would play out. We would neutralize assets that threatened the inner island chain, while our allies mobilized and we brought up additional battle groups and air assets from the States and Mideast.

"After slamming the gates, we'd wait. When they came out, we'd have the buildup in place to make the East and South China Seas and the Sea of Japan into kill zones. Meanwhile, the U.S. is self-sufficient in both food and energy. But China has to import both. We estimated they'd run out of oil in three months and food in six. That would add rationing and spot starvation onto inflation, unemployment, and heavy force attrition. The regime would either fall, or be forced to the conference table."

Tomlin looked down. "What did Napoleon say? 'No plan survives contact with the enemy.' We did break the kill chain, degrading space and cyberspace assets. We're also undertaking some major intelligence initiatives, which I can't discuss. And we have succeeded, largely, in penning in their sub force, while ours is taking down any warships that venture out. But the deep strikes in the initial plan have been canceled.

"Meanwhile, the enemy's pursued an asymmetrical strategy. This included major efforts in anti-access and area denial, along with degrading and compromising our own C4I. In addition, you know about the cyberattacks and other sabotage against the continental U.S. They've crippled our economy and struck at civilian morale, as well as industry.

"But their major effort has been focused on the battlespace around and above Taiwan, and the Japanese waters and airspace flanking it. They've managed to degrade U.S. forces there, with mines, runway accidents, and sabotage. Our air assets have been particularly overloaded. We're burning fuel and crew hours conducting a mission we haven't done for a long time—basic overwater reconnaissance.

"The Navy's trying to hold against over-whelming force, conduct barrier operations to prevent a breakout into the Pacific, and deter any invasion of Taiwan. The Army's preparing, if necessary, to withdraw those U.S. force elements that still retain their mobility in Korea."

Tomlin straightened. "Now—Ms. Clayton. What do we have on our enemy?"

The Asian stood, and finally Blair recognized her: a senior member of the De Bari admin-istration; Dan had worked under her in the West Wing. Clayton gave a passionless briefing in a High Boston accent. "The plan for a cross-strait invasion is called Operation Breath of the Dragon. They're prepared for heavy losses. Success would depend on the Taiwanese air force and navy being heavily degraded first.

"That is, assuming that the Republic of China decides to fight, rather than arrive at some more or less disguised capitulation. Which is a possibility, especially if they lose confidence in our ability to support them."

Tomlin thanked her. "Now, if this happens . . . if they come across the strait . . . what do we have to meet it with?"

A force-balance slide gave the answer. Blair shook her head as she added the numbers.

Clayton said, "Not enough. Our single carrier in the region was immobilized by mines. We have a makeshift surface task group more or less plugging the gap until the *Franklin Roosevelt* battle group gets there. But we're also facing a North Korean threat. If the PRC crosses the strait, well . . . leaving aside whether we're obligated to intervene, there seems little available to respond with at the moment, aside from long-range B-2 strikes from Guam."

Blair began to feel uncomfortable, and not just from the hot needles of pain being driven into her hip. She raised a hand. Tomlin nodded. "Blair Titus, correct? Question?"

"Correct. You're saying, we expect to lose this battle?"

Tomlin made a face. "I wouldn't put it that way. But . . . J-3's fully occupied fighting the current campaign. They can't plan for what happens if they lose. Not at the same time. Also, there are political implications in having the combat commanders plan for downside possibilities. It's more palatable if that takes place outside the DoD structure. At least we can start to formulate options the National Security Council can consider, if the eventuality arises." He paused, then added, "Ultimately, too, we must establish phase lines beyond which our national interests demand an escalatory response."

"We're going to try to contain this war," someone said, and Blair flinched at a familiar voice. "But not too hard."

Dr. Edward Szerenci was in a light gray suit and pale blue tie, with an American flag pin in the lapel. His hair had gone platinum at the temples; his eyes, behind professorial horn-rims, were a hunting hawk's. Two men in dark suits stood behind him, arms folded, gazes roving the room. The national security adviser had come in quietly, at the back, while Tomlin was speaking. Blair tensed, remembering the last time they'd met. In an elevator in the Russell Building, on the way to her husband's testimony before the Armed Services Committee.

Szerenci had said then, "War now could be better than later, with a more powerful adversary."

Now he came forward, and handed a memory stick to the aide at the computer.

Two jagged lines, red and blue, with an intersection point. Along the bottom, decades, from the 1980s to the 2030s. The blue line dropped steadily, decade after decade. The red line climbed, its slope slowing from time to time, but always rising.

"This shows the nuclear force balance, in total warhead megatonnage. As you can see, the recent breakout, if continued, will shortly place us in an inferior position. Our antiballistic capabilities may push that into the out years—I emphasize the word *may*—but I do not intend the United States ever to be in an inferior position. Therefore, our major goal in this conflict has to be to restrain, cap, and if possible, eliminate Chinese nuclear strike capabilities." He let that hang, then added softly, "We have to set clear red lines, and enforce them. If they want to test our resolve, we're ready."

Someone breathed, " 'Red lines'—'test our resolve'—you're talking about a nuclear ultimatum."

Szerenci said gravely, "Let's not cherish illusions. No weapon's ever been invented that wasn't eventually used. This conflict may be lethal. Resource intensive. And bloody. But if the unthinkable should happen on our watch, I want us to be ready for it, survive it, and win it." He nodded. "This isn't a disaster. It's a historic opportunity." He looked to Tomlin. "I've got to get back to the Eighteen Acres. We need your output fast, General."

"Within the week, Doctor."

Tomlin waited until the Secret Service men closed the door. "So, there you have it. If Zhang invades, there's a good chance Taiwan will fall. Some of that's out of our hands—it depends on the fighting efficiency of the army, the resolve of the government. And so forth.

"But the question we need to focus on is, if the worst happens, where and how can we seize the initiative again, and sustain that effort to end the conflict on acceptable terms?" Tomlin nodded at the professor. "Dr. Glancey happens to be an expert on war termination. We need to think ahead of the current hostilities, and envision a postwar settlement both sides can live with."

"Which is probably not going to satisfy anyone," Glancey put in.

After a moment, an older man, probably one of the retired generals, said, "We're being asked to plan how best to surrender?"

Tomlin said quietly, "If you see an open discussion that way, sir, maybe this isn't the right committee for you."

"I don't see why not. If you're discussing options, isn't that one?"

A murmur ran around the room. Hands shot up. Blair raised hers too and, when Tomlin nodded, stood. "What about the forces currently in theater? If as you say we can't hold. We do . . . what? Write them off?"

Tomlin made a wry face. "Unfortunately, that may be forced on us. We had to write off the Asiatic Fleet, and the garrisons on Bataan and Corregidor, early in the last major war. The distances are too great. Our reserves, too thin. We need time for regeneration, resupply, rebuilding a logistics chain. And the other side's going to do everything they can to slow us up, deny us bases, deny parts and fuel and access. How do we shore up the breach? Or, failing that, how do we come back?"

He looked at his watch. "You heard Dr. Szerenci; the pressure's on. We'll split into subcommittees—strategic, logistics, information warfare, diplomatic, cyberwar. A Red Team, to game enemy countermoves. First session will be eight to noon. Staff will research the issues you surface and work up the notes in the afternoons. We'll do a night session from six to ten.

"I want to wrap and deliver by the end of the week. A reminder: please sign your SF 312s in the back before going to your subcommittee. Again, nothing can be removed from the working areas. If you want to keep notes, mark them as 'working papers,' date them, and hand them to a staffer for secure storage between sessions.

"All right—let's get to work."

Thunder rumbled outside. She sat hunched as

the meeting broke up, as a staffer announced room assignments for the subcommittee deliberations. Wincing at the hot pain in her hip, as rain clattered against electromagnetically shielded glass, and the sky darkened with an advancing storm.

12
USS *Savo Island*

The master-at-arms brought Peeples to Aisha's cabin after noon meal. The Engineering Department chief, McMottie, had told her he couldn't break him out till then, not with the ship at Condition Three.

The girls on the mess decks, as well as the exec, had mentioned Peeples as the guy who liked to flip off women in authority. Which put him on Aisha's short list for the rape. He must have sensed this, since he was sweating even before she sat him down and introduced herself. Toan, the master-at-arms, leaned against a bulkhead, seeming to melt against the steel. Peeples was white, with concrete-gray hair, heavy stubble, and hooded eyelids. He wore blue camo utilities instead of coveralls. His knee jiggled. His nails were dark with dirt or grease. He reeked of the fuel these smaller ships ran on.

Aisha leaned back, pretending to review his record, though she already had. Machinist's mate seaman. Sometimes rowdy on liberty, but basically a solid sailor. Supervisors' testimonials always read the same. As far as shipboard justice went, having a rep as a hard worker went a long way, whatever you were up for. In the most recent incident, he'd called his female petty officer a "hucking skunt." They'd charged him under Article 134: using indecent language to a senior, to the prejudice of good order and discipline.

She glanced up from the file. "Don't be nervous."

"I'm not." The leg stopped jiggling.

"Good. Please tell me what happened with Petty Officer Scharner. In your own words."

The tremor resumed as he wiped his face. "Well, she . . . she always gave me the shittiest jobs. Down in the fu . . . down in the bilges. Cleanin' out the head. Chipping voids. I just lost it. Just once. Never meant nothing by it. I was sorry when they found her dead. From the Crud, I mean."

"I'm sure you were. It sounds like that took quite a toll. Did you get it too?"

"Shit yeah. Fucked me up royal. Still got to drag myself around."

"What exactly is a 'skunt,' Peeples?"

He sucked air. "They ain't no such word. I made it up. Told the chief that. Told the skipper, too. He understood. Reamed me out, but hey. I get it, you gotta go through the motions."

"What was the punishment?"

"Sixty days' hack, half pay for three months, suspended for six months."

"That seems . . . light. Since there's no liberty anyway."

"It did to that lieutenant too."

217

Aisha frowned. "What lieutenant?"

"The Indian. 'Armpit' Singhe." He grinned, showing scraggly teeth.

"She was at your mast? She's not in your chain of command, is she?"

"Duh, no! She just showed up, out of the blue, and tried to argue the CO into upping my punishment."

"Why do you think she'd do that?"

"Fuck if I know. She's got a hard-on for the enlisted girls, what I think." He started to say more, but halted, squinting up at the overhead. "I said enough. Ain't my fuckin' business, izzit? But it ain't fuckin' fair, z'all I'm sayin'."

"I see." She glanced down at her notes, wrote *Singhe+enlisted women?* "You're a machinist. Ever go down to the supply spaces? Or up around the bridge area?"

"I pretty much stay down in the hole."

"How about electrical work? Do much of that?"

"Machinist's mates don't do electrons. Atoms, that's us." He grinned. For a moment the hooded eyes danced, and he was almost attractive. The bad-boy type . . .

"Do you have a girlfriend, Seaman?"

"Back home. On and off."

"Where's home?"

"West Texas."

"A long way from Texas."

"You're a long way from Harlem."

218

Scuttlebutt traveled. She should've remembered; nothing that happened on a ship stayed secret long. Which usually helped an investigation, but so far it hadn't aboard *Savo Island*. She consulted her file again. "Ever played *Gang Bang Molly*?"

"Heard about it. Never played. We got real work to do, down in the black gang. Especially, long's we been out. We're trying to rebuild pumps, valves, should be done in the yard."

She squinted at him. Was he . . . No, "black gang" was just what snipes called themselves. From the days when coal dust had covered everything. She asked a few more questions, about where he stood watch and when, then nodded to Toan that he could go.

In a little space off CIC, a chief in coveralls positioned a chair in front of a screen. He was blond, with an unruly cowlick and an infectious, slightly mad grin. Younger than the other chiefs. Wenck. Terranova's supervisor, whom the new CO had brought with him when he'd taken over. Like Carpenter . . . She sighed and dropped into the seat. "These are the gun camera tapes?"

"Well, what we got. For that date. Red said you wanted to review them."

"Red?"

"Chief Slaughenhaupt."

To her surprise, Slaughenhaupt had sent her a

message. He'd located the tapes for the day she wanted, and would make them available when she had time to go over them. "They're from the aft Phalanx," Wenck said, leaning past her to press keys. She smelled something spicy, and a memory suddenly lit. She said, too sharply, "What's that you're wearing?"

"Huh? Just some aftershave."

In her first interview, Terranova had said she'd noticed a smell like lemons. This wasn't exactly lemon, more like cinnamon, but . . . "Where did you get it? Ship's store?"

"Had it for a while. Bought it back when I was at TAG."

"TAG?"

"The Tactical Analysis Group. Little Creek. Must've been, at the exchange. Why?"

"No reason, I just like it. Maybe you could tell me the brand?"

"Sure, I'll look." He bent over her again, and brought up a screen.

She recognized it at once. The same circular reticle as the old sonarman had shown her. The same field of view, looking out over the hangar onto the flight deck. Only this was no still. The horizon slanted up and down. A blue, brilliant day. Sun flashed off the wake. A time/date readout pulsed. She checked the date, but it was clear from the way people were strolling back and forth that this was a day off. Steel Beach

Picnic, someone had called it. The Iron Beach was the next level up. They lined up before grills, cradled paper plates, sat around in groups. Some sprawled in the lowered nets. A shoving match broke out, horseplay, guys grab-assing around. An older man moved in and broke it up.

"Want me to fast-forward?" Wenck hovered behind her. Another hint of the scent. Not Old Spice, but like it. "What are you looking for?"

To see you, climbing the ladder to the top of the hangar, she thought but didn't say. "Were you there? At the picnic."

"Me? No. Crappy ship's hamburgers and GSA chips. We're pretty much full-time trying to keep Alice happy."

Aisha frowned, trying to place the name. Did he mean the exec? Wasn't her name Carol? No, *Cheryl*. "Who's Alice?"

"Not Alice, ALIS . . . used to mean Aegis Leap Intercept, but now it's the software that drives the TBMD programming. CFA's hinky, and we got issues with the switch tubes. Signal rate return's below par. Doc Noblos is always riding our asses about performance against benchmarks."

Too technical. "Noblos is the civilian scientist? I met him briefly."

"You won't see him much. He's helping us tune, but we never had the training the follow-on ships in the pipeline are getting. *Hampton Roads* and *Monocacy*."

221

During this she'd been watching the screen. Someone was obviously on the controls of the camera. It zoomed out as if looking for something. It stayed there for some minutes, panning back and forth along the horizon line, jagged, distant. The back of her neck prickled. If it was Wenck behind the assaults, she was alone here with him. She twisted. He lingered in the doorway, studying her. "Yes?" she asked. "You wanted something?"

"Got any idea who did this yet? I really hate to think of bad shit happening to the Terror. She's good people."

The words were right, but those pale eyes didn't meet hers. Someday NCIS would issue them a computer that would read voices, or eyes. Be able to tell a lie from the truth, a half lie from an evasion. Until then, though, she needed hard evidence. Such as an image caught on magnetic tape . . .

As she glanced back at the screen the field of view shifted suddenly, jerked, then dropped. To the scene she'd already glimpsed.

The crosshairs pointed aft now, at women on blankets and bright beach towels. In colorful swimsuits, they lay on a dark gray deck in bright sunlight. The aiming dot hunted restlessly. Her skin crawled; it was so much like Hollywood depictions of a sniper's field of view, before taking out the victim at long range. The dot searched out splayed thighs here, a slick curve of oiled buttock, a deep V of cleavage. One woman sat up, tossing her hair back, shaking it out. The unobserved grace reminding her of a Degas painting she'd been riveted by at the Met. The lens dropped to search again. This time it found a pale heavy girl in a bright green bikini. The top was pulled down, half exposing her breasts. The white bulge of her belly looked sad, vulnerable. The dot explored her intimately, lubriciously, almost a rape in itself. She recognized Carpenter's screen shot.

She was inspecting the edges of the frame again, for a lurker, a shadow, when she winced. How could she miss something so obvious? "Um, who recorded this?"

"That's after Phalanx camera."

"I mean, who was at the joystick? Someone was moving it in train and elevation, staring at these women. And enjoying the hell out of it. Chief Slaughenhaupt told me that. So, who was pointing the camera just then?"

Wenck shook his head, came back to peer over her shoulder. "No way to tell. There's three different places you can control those cameras from. Local, remote, CIC. Oh . . . you also got access from the LAN. I'd have to look into it, but you got somebody digital-savvy, he could probably figure out how to control them from his own terminal."

"Really. Anyone who had access to the LAN?"

"Maybe," Wenck said, gaze distant, as if processing his own software behind those opaque eyes. *Like you?* she wanted to ask, but didn't.

She watched for another half hour. Saw Petty Officer Terranova finally pull up her top, rise, shake herself, wrap up in a towel with a beach scene. The girl stared out at the wake, holding the towel to her chest. The plowed trail of disturbed sea unrolled behind the ship, glittering in the bright sun, so that now and then the pixels blanked, fried by the glare.

Then the young woman turned, and picked her way among the other bodies, toward her appointment inside the hangar.

Ryan seemed to be unavailable. Aisha could find her way to the wardroom by now, to CIC and the bridge, but she needed a guide to get any-where else. Plus, she wasn't supposed to wander unescorted. She typed up her interview, and thought about revisiting the scene of the rape. Something could jog her memory. But it would be smarter to do so at night. As close as she could get to when the crime had occurred. Make notes on who used the passageway, went up and down the ladder. See who was around, who had access.

The corpsman finally came by to pick her up for dinner. "Sorry, they got us crazy busy down there getting set up for mass casualties."

Aisha tensed. *"Mass casualties?"*

The girl's eyebrows lifted. "You know where we are, right? The Chinese are attacking Taiwan with missiles. Invading the islands north of it. We've got to be ready to take a major hit, and care for casualties."

Aisha fidgeted with her head scarf. "I've been focusing on the investigation."

"That's fine, but the rest of us got other priorities, you know?" Ryan waited for an answer, but when Aisha had none, said, "Okay, let's go get you something to eat."

The girls at the mess table looked tired. The ship leaned alarmingly, and a tremor ran through the decks. It sounded like a bus on a gravel road. They discussed the war in worried voices. Colón asked Aisha if she was making any progress. She said, "I'm still investigating."

"I'd look at that fucking Peeples again," said one of the women. "He gives me the creepy-crawlies."

"Or it could be three *separate* guys," another said, tearing apart a dinner roll.

Aisha smiled. "It's possible, but the modus is so much the same, I'm pretty sure there's one actor."

"Actor?" Colón said irritably. *"Actor?"*

"Perpetrator, if you prefer. I think we're dealing with one man, with a grudge against women."

"Every guy on this fucking ship has a fucking *grudge*," one of the other girls said. "Either somebody slept with him and dumped him, or she wouldn't sleep with him, or she wanted to sleep with him and she wasn't hot enough." Snickers ran around the table.

Aisha looked at her watch. "Dunk, if you don't mind—"

More snickers. "You let her call you *Dunk?*"

"Dunkie's got a new girlfriend," singsonged around the table.

"Shut the fuck up, you whores." The slight redhead grabbed her tray, but there was no real anger in her voice. Just fatigue. "You wanted to go down to the Goat Locker? They'll be on their desserts now. Probably the best time to step into the den."

"Goat Locker" was Navy slang for the chief's mess and berthing area. Ryan tapped on a door. "It's fuckin' open," a gruff voice yelled from inside.

Middle-aged men in coveralls and faded khakis surrounded a picnic-bench-style table crowded with plates. Another room, probably a bunking area, was screened off by a faded curtain. They blinked up at Aisha. "Oh," one said, and she recognized the leathery visage: Tausengelt, the command master chief. He rose so quickly a half-gnawed ear of corn leapt off his plate to land on the deck; a much younger man went after it, trapped its roll with a boot. Tausengelt muttered, "It's the custom, Special Agent, to call before you come down here. Basically, get an invite. You didn't know that?"

"Like you said, it's a custom. Not a regulation. The XO gave me access throughout the ship. I go where I have to."

His beaky face crimped like a discontented tortoise's, but he just waved at the others. She noted that, unlike on the carrier, there were no female senior enlisted here. "Who exactly you looking for?" Tausengelt murmured, not meeting her gaze.

"I'd like to address you all, if I may."

"Address us all. Here? Now?"

"If that's all right."

He held up both hands. "Guys! Listen up. The agent here wants a word."

They fell silent, but it didn't feel like an attentive silence. More like a resentful, even hostile one. She cleared her throat. "As you all know, I'm here to investigate a rape. Petty Officer Beth Terranova. It took place up in the Equipment Room, third deck. But previous incidents of sexual assault have taken place elsewhere: in the aviation area, the supply spaces. We have DNA evidence collected from the . . . victim, but we need to narrow down the pool we'll take samples from.

"So I'm assembling a short list.

"What I'd like from you, as the leaders aboard ship, is to let me know, in confidence, if you know any individuals who fit a certain profile."

They'd stopped eating, and stared up. She crossed her arms and paced between the bug juice machine and the door. "We've dealt with crimes like this before. By 'we' I mean the federal investigative agencies—FBI, NCIS, Army Criminal Investigation, Secret Service. We've built up a list of characteristics, a profile, if you will, of serial rapists—which is how I'm classifying our suspect."

She began with the typical rapist. Most usually attempted to lure the victim into a remote location using verbal blandishments, though sometimes force was used. Threats and often a weapon were used to maintain control. "Many of the offenders display sexual dysfunction during the crime. We think this might have occurred during the attack on Seaman Colón, in the supply spaces. It doesn't mean the rapist is impotent, just that he's building up to the full display or enactment he ultimately has in mind. Or was interrupted, or feared interruption.

"Some don't seem concerned with protecting their identities or preventing apprehension. But every rapist's different. Their motives, fantasies, the ways they try to satisfy drives.

"The one we're dealing with here appears

228

smarter than those I've investigated before. The crimes were preplanned, with the locations set up in advance. He brings certain objects to the scene and removes them afterward. He seems to pick venues that are heavily trafficked but deserted at the moment he needs them. I suspect, to lower the possibility of leaving personal traces, such as fingerprints. This leads me toward a further insight—"

A chief lifted a finger. "So we're looking for a single guy, somebody oversexed and—"

"Rape isn't about virility, or lack of available sex outlets," she put in. "It's about control. Deep down, rapists hate women. Their relationships are based on dominance. They show histories of conflict and stalking, and an inability to relate to women as human beings rather than objects."

The chiefs looked uneasy. Probably reviewing their own relationships, she thought. "That's pretty goddamn general," one finally grunted. "Can you lay a few more groups on us, about that?"

"We know a little more, but I'd rather not reveal all those details now."

"So you're saying, you got nothing right now," another said. "Just comin' to us to . . . give up whoever we think might have done it."

"You know the crew better than anyone else. Certainly better than the wardroom."

"Okay. What, exactly, are we looking for?" said a small white man. He seemed familiar, in a weaselly way. She couldn't recall his name, but had seen him checking her out furtively in CIC.

"Okay, as I was saying, we can subclassify this guy. We call it the Ted Bundy type, because this brand of serial rapist and the serial killer are very similar in personality.

"This man is highly organized. Even anal. He likes everything in its place, everything just right. Often, a loner. He doesn't identify with others. He feels he's superior, with higher standards. For exactly those reasons, he may be a good military man, if you will. Because those characteristics, in moderation, aren't bad. Until they get twisted around and attached to violence against women."

"Sounds like a nuke," one of the chiefs said. The others chuckled.

"Since he plans ahead, covers his tracks, we're going to have to dig deep, and think the way he does, to catch him.

"I would say this: We're looking for someone who obsessively stalks and eavesdrops on certain women. He may have their pictures up at his workstation, or hidden near his bunk. He may keep a 'rape diary,' a score sheet, or souvenirs. We think he's taller than average. We also have reason to believe he has electrical expertise, and owns a knife.

"Please search your minds. If you have anyone who fits this profile, bring him to my attention. In total confidence."

She paced again. "But don't fool yourselves. You already had trouble aboard this ship. Lieutenant Singhe probably strikes you as a pain, but she has a legitimate grievance about the work environment for your enlisted women. I'm not here to investigate that. But the longer this guy runs loose, the more frightened and unsure your women are going to be."

She halted and took a breath, gazed at the bubbling purple fluid in the drink machine. Not wanting to say this, but they had to be warned. "Also . . . these type of crimes tend to escalate. Especially with the structured guys. Since it's about control and anger, they need to push harder each time to get their high. So things progress from simple rape . . . to darker acts. Beating. Cutting. Torture. Then, finally, murder.

"I want to catch him before he gets to that stage."

The chiefs glanced at one another. One held up a hand. "Yes," she said.

"I think you know we're with you. We want to get this guy too."

They stirred, some glancing at watches, or at a bulkhead clock. "But we got a bigger problem, you know," another said. "Not to say this isn't important, but we're in a freakin' war zone. Any day, the Chinese could come through our operating area. This is important to you, and, yeah, to the girls. But we got a fight to concentrate on."

She nodded. "I understand. And I'm trying not to disrupt operations. But the rule of law, protecting the innocent—that's part of what we're fighting for. Isn't it?"

Their expressions didn't give her a very positive answer.

She climbed the ladder slowly, fatigued, heavy. Her ankles were swelling. The food was so salty. She needed to cut down on eggs, cheese, milk. But there were no fresh vegetables. Everything was frozen or canned. Well, they'd been out a while. She patted her purse, which also weighed heavy. Camera? Yes. Flashlight? Yes. SIG? In the side pocket.

She halted outside the Equipment Room. Yes, this was the right time. Night. The ladderwell echoed with distant creaks and groans. She was fifty, sixty feet above the sea, but the passageway felt like some buried tomb, Pharaonic. She rubbed a finger on a stain on the bulkhead. Something oily . . . Yellow tape still blocked the door. She ducked under it.

The lights came on when she entered. Cold air streamed from the overhead diffusers. The walls were stark white, lined with electronic gear in steel racks, thick cables twisting away behind them. Tools, racked parts, and binders of schematics waited as if abandoned by some vanished civilization. The wordless patience of things . . . A soldering gun in a tabletop holder teetered uneasily as the ship rolled. A clock ticked above a maintenance chart.

So far, the short list included Benyamin, Peeples, and now Wenck. Carpenter she could probably cross off. A dirty old man, a peeper, but no rapist. All talk. But she still needed to develop the case. Fortunately they had DNA. And she'd put the word out, to the women, the officers, the chiefs. Someone would come in with something.

Something outside creaked, popped, reverberated. A ship could be spooky. She patted her mouth, shoulders tensed. Something about the silence . . . Why was she so tense?

Then she had it.

It was like the Stairwell.

The stairs outside her friend Rina's apartment always smelled like pee, or worse. Men from the street would come in to go to the bathroom. It was painted lime green, or had been once; now brown stains ran up above her head. A fruit shop out front, run by Koreans or Chinese. They shouted and jabbered above her, ignoring a small black girl with her library books hugged to her chest. And the boys, on the benches, the bikes. Weaving out into traffic to make a delivery, pedaling the money back to the sharp-eyed, gold-chained man on the corner. Never talk to the dope man, her mother told her. Stay away from those bad boys. But she had to walk between them every day to school. Carefully not looking up. Just recently, they'd started to notice her. "Wear your long skirt, your hijab," her mother told her. "Then they won't bother you."

No one had answered at Rina's apartment. She'd waited, and knocked again.

The man had gone by her, then, on his way down the stairs from somewhere in the dark floors above. "Lookin' for that li'l Reena? She gone," he'd said. "They done moved up to 125th."

"Thank you," she'd whispered.

He'd clattered down a few steps, then stopped. Climbed slowly back, looking around at the empty landing, the echoing silence, broken only by the far-off noise of the street three floors down.

"You a pretty little thing," he'd said, smiling.

She collapsed on the work stool lashed to the work table. Not wanting to remember. Unable not to.

Then she frowned.

Voices echoed down the ladderway, with the dead clunks of watertight doors behind them. They were coming down, from the bridge, probably. She went into the passageway and stood working her BlackBerry as if not wanting to be interrupted. No signal, of course, but the best way to avoid being noticed was to act as if *you* didn't notice anything. In reality, she was noting each face, each slouch or start of surprise as the offcoming watchstanders straggled past, rounded the landing, and descended, boots scuffling, the heavy cast-aluminum ladders clanking under their weight. No one on her list, so far.

Then, a face she knew. Worried. Withdrawn. Preoccupied, and deeply tired.

The commanding officer paused across from the Equipment Room. He was in ship's coveralls. Heavy black boots. Cold gray eyes examined her. "Agent Ar-Rahim."

"Captain Lenson." Right, that was his at-sea cabin. Where he slept when they were underway.

Right across from the crime scene.

Lenson looked down at his fingers, where they gripped the knob of the door to his cabin, the skin pale white. He seemed to sigh, though she didn't hear a sound. "We haven't had a chance to talk yet. Stateroom okay? You're in unit commander's, right?"

"Yes, Captain. It's very comfortable. Thank you."

"We got you off *Stuttgart* just in time." He blinked. The skin under his eyes sagged. She noticed that, along with the fact that he was not heavily muscled, but looked strong. A little gray around the ears, but still fit. "How's it going? The investigation?"

"I've kept Commander Staurulakis informed,"

she said. "I hope she's sharing that with you."

"Yeah, yeah, we've got a lot on our plates right now but . . ." He coughed, as if he too had suffered from what everyone referred to as the Crud. "I've had experiences with NIS in the past."

"We're a different agency now, Captain. Even got different initials."

"I hope so. I hear you're being very thorough."

"I try to be."

"I want this asshole. But I also don't want this investigation to hurt my ship, Special Agent."

"I appreciate your position, Captain."

He gritted his teeth. "Do you? I have a leading Aegis petty officer who's on the verge of a breakdown. The chiefs distrust the JOs. The women have to go buddy-system after lights-out. There was supposed to be a battle group here. Instead we've got cruisers and destroyers to hold the line. My gut feeling, the enemy won't wait. They'll try to punch through while we're still flailing around.

"Close this case, Special Agent. Wrap it up. So we can concentrate on what we're here for."

"I understand. Investigations can be disruptive. I want to close. But in the right way. With solid evidence. We really don't want to nail the wrong guy."

"Well . . . no. Who've you got so far? Any opinions, guesses?"

She half smiled. They always asked that. And she always gave the same answer. "I don't have *opinions,* Captain. Only facts."

"You must suspect somebody. Cheryl says you've been interviewing."

"Sir, we're the Investigative Service, not the Judging Service. Yes, I've been interviewing. And gathering physical evidence."

"We sent DNA to the . . . oh, shit." His face fell. "*Stuttgart.*"

"Your corpsman kept backups."

"Grissett did? Excellent. That's great." Lenson glanced at the doorknob again. He sighed and scrubbed his face with flattened palms. "But we can't send it back until we get a logistics linkup. So, what next?"

"I'm trying to narrow the suspect pool. Once I have a small number of potentials, ideally no more than three or four, I'll ask you for what's called a 'command authorization for search and seizure.' We'll take swabs from each suspect, and forward them along with the remaining samples from the rape kit. Hopefully, that'll solve our case."

"Meanwhile, he's loose?"

"Meanwhile, we take precautions."

"Which you've discussed with the chief master-at-arms?"

"Yes sir."

"All right, keep Cheryl informed. Tell her if

you need anything. If she can't make you happy, come see me."

He nodded, once, slid inside, and closed the door. The lock snicked. So he too locked himself in.

Leaving her standing again alone in the leaning, creaking passageway, looking at the spot where the commanding officer of USS *Savo Island* had ducked his head slightly, to avoid the low jamb.

13

It was going for his throat. Dan tried to fend it off with bare hands, but its black, slavering muzzle kept coming in. He threw an elbow into its jaws, but it evaded him. And darted in again, growling.

Sinking its teeth into his throat—

He woke, heart hammering, flinching and struggling. To catch Singhe's astonished look, her hand on his shoulder. "Captain! You okay?"

"Yeah. What—"

"You were having a bad dream, I guess."

Dan blinked at the time readout above the main displays. Stretched, until the vertebrae in his neck cracked. He rubbed grit and crap from his eyes. God. Had he been drooling on the command desk?

Suddenly he was terrifically hungry.

Pancakes, coffee, and sausage in the wardroom fixed that. In his sea cabin, he shaved, showered, and changed into fresh coveralls. He showed his face on the bridge, and went over the nav plot with Van Gogh. The navigator was also on as OOD. They were getting half-hourly radar fixes off three distinctive land features on Miyako Shima. Dan nodded, satisfied they didn't have to rely on celestials anymore. But glad he had them in reserve, in case the radar went down.

When he clattered down the ladder back to Combat, a bearlike man-shape waited at the command desk. Bart Danenhower, chief engineer, complete with striped locomotive-driver's cap. After discussing the rotating assembly on fire pump number four, the CHENG threw down a clipboard of graphs.

"We're burning more than usual," Dan noted.

"Been under way a long time, Captain, and in warm water—the Med, Arabian Sea, the IO, WestPac. Crap builds up. On the bottom. The screws. Heat exchangers. Over time, it takes a toll."

Dan rubbed his mouth, not liking how fast the fuel percentages dropped toward the trigger point for an off-station call. Usually cruisers were refueled every three to four days, to maintain above 50 percent. But as far as he'd heard, the nearest resupply was still back at Guam, waiting for the *Roosevelt* battle group. "Maybe we'd better plan on reducing speed even further."

Danenhower shook his head. "Long as we're keeping fire in the turbines, there isn't any regime below what we're doing. Aside from going dead in the water. And I don't think you want that."

Dan was studying the displays over the engineer's shoulder. A lot of activity around the Senkakus. Traffic to and from the coast,

240

some high-speed: hovercraft or patrol boats. Transporting troops? Reinforcing?

Danenhower cleared his throat, and Dan grimaced. No, he didn't want to be dead in the water. Not with a hostile sub somewhere around. "And we can't reduce generator load?"

"Not if you still want radars, sonars."

"Hotel load? Cut back on that?"

"Cut back on hot water, you're gonna risk regrowth of that Crud. Boxed in, we are."

"Okay, Yoda." At least it was a change from Harry Potter.

The 21MC, at his elbow. *"Combat, Radio. Flash incoming. Want it on your screens?"*

Dan hit the lever. "Put it on the LAN. 'Scuse me, Bart. Might be important."

Taipei was reporting early warnings of ballistic missiles being prepared for launch along the coast. PacFleet wanted *Savo* on ABM alert, positioned to cover the capital and population center at the north end of Taiwan.

He looked from the terminal to the Aegis console, but neither Wenck nor Terranova was there. "Petty Officer Eastwood. Chief Wenck on deck?"

"Turned in a couple hours ago, sir."

"Get him up again." Dan passed the word to the XO over his Hydra, then dialed the J-phone for Noblos's stateroom. The scientist didn't answer, though Dan let it ring. He tried the wardroom next, and caught him there. "Bill, we're getting

241

early warnings on launch preps. Can you double-check that we're in the best intercept position?"

"We already did those calculations, Captain Lenson." Noblos sounded annoyed. *"I gave you my recommendation. You chose to ignore it."*

"I didn't *ignore* it, Bill. We had to compromise, for the barrier mission."

"Anyone can do ASW. You're the only ABM-capable unit out here. Though calling us 'capable' is a stretch."

Dan reflected sourly that at least he'd used "us" this time, instead of "you" or "your team." "Well, look, we're going to full-on ABM mode. I could use your help here."

Noblos agreed, but irritably. Dan hung up and massaged his brow. Talking to the guy always gave him a headache. But he'd helped design ALIS. They were lucky to have him aboard. It would help, though, if the bastard were less of a pain in the ass to deal with.

He propped chin on fists, pondering the screen. The SPY-1 picture extended out over two hundred nautical miles, but from their current position, that didn't reach the mainland. It covered the northern tip of Taiwan; to the north, Okinawa; to the west, about halfway across the strait. But not to the coast. Unless, as in the case of the recon aircraft, their target was above the radar horizon.

With no satellite cuing either, he was blind, as far as the ABM mission went.

The TAO, beside him, murmured that the EWs were reporting test emissions from a Ku-band radar on Uotsuri, largest of the Senkaku Islands. "Correlates with NATO Tin Shield radar. We call it as an S-300. Surface-to-air missile."

A heavy, advanced antiair missile. Fifty miles' range. Multiple target tracking and engagement. The next time the Japanese sent fighters to the Senkakus, they'd lose some.

The Chinese were digging in. Probably already starting on piers, a port, an airfield. Turning the islands into another forward base, like they had in the South China Sea. Creeping around Taiwan's northern flank, and less than a hundred miles away.

Not for the first time, he cursed the Navy's reliance on satellites for over-the-horizon reconnaissance and targeting. The Chinese were actually in better shape, with their legacy squadrons of H-6s and shore-based radars . . . like the ones that had been scanning the task group since they arrived on station. The missing piece was high-altitude ISR—intelligence, surveillance, and reconnaissance. If the carrier had made it out of port, it would have supplied it. The Navy's E-2s, their eyes in the sky, provided a long reach, along with the new UAVs. The Air Force was probably running drones and U-2s out of Kadena, but their output was stovepiped; he couldn't get his hands on it.

Leaving him groping, able to see only a little way around him. Like lighting a match in Carlsbad Caverns.

The allies had lost information dominance. They'd lost the strategic initiative. Now they were losing territory, too.

Fang might be the answer. If the Taiwanese liaison could link them up, get the ROC air-defense network to share real-time data, he'd no longer be nearsighted. Taiwan had just built a massive new surveillance radar on Leshan Mountain. Dan twisted in his seat, but Fang wasn't in CIC. He tried his stateroom on the J-phone. No answer.

Donnie Wenck, hair on end, eyelids swollen, cheeks blotchy. "Y'wanted me, Skipper?"

Dan outlined the situation. Wenck nodded halfway through and began backing toward his console. "I'll get us a reposition. But, you know, we're gonna lose our air picture when ALIS boots up."

Operating in BMD mode, the SPY-1 dropped its 360-degree search function and focused a much narrower beam far into space. The mission took so much bandwidth, *Savo* basically lost all her self-defense but the Sea Whiz and the five-inch guns. Instead of a godlike overview, he would be reduced to peeking through a telescope. High magnification, but leaving himself open to getting clobbered from behind. "I'm familiar with the problem, Donnie. We've dealt before."

"Yeah, but we had somebody riding shotgun then. Who we gonna have watching our butt this time?"

Dan didn't have an answer, which irritated him. "Just get me the position, Donnie. Can you do that for me, without—ah, never mind."

Silence descended around the command table, and he realized he'd probably snapped that out louder than he'd meant to. Short temper was a human failing. But not a good trait in a CO. He added, loud enough that the others could hear, "Sorry, didn't mean to go ballistic on you. But I'm working that issue, all right?"

They worked it through the morning. Fang came in and got on the horn to his opposite numbers in the air-defense network. Noblos and Wenck argued, debating geometries and probabilities.

It wasn't a simple problem. A modified anti-aircraft missile, the Block 4 Standard had limited range, limited speed, and a low-altitude envelope. It could intercept an incoming terminal vehicle only near the end of its trajectory, from shortly before to the beginning of atmospheric reentry. Also, tests had confirmed that the meeting angle was critical. The Block 4 didn't do well against crossing targets.

Thus, probability of kill depended on four variables: the type of warhead, its launch point, its target coordinates, and *Savo*'s position. The calculation was complicated even more by the fact that they knew neither where the Chinese launchers would be located, nor their intended impact points.

On the other hand, his orders weren't to defend everything on the island. Only Taipei, the capital and major population center.

Around eleven, they came to him with a result. Assuming the TBMs were fired from somewhere around Fujian, opposite the island, *Savo* should position fifty miles northeast of the tip of Taiwan. That placed the oval-shaped intercept envelope over the city.

"That puts me pretty far from the ASW barrier," Dan observed, running both hands through his hair as he looked down at Noblos's laptop. It would also, though he didn't say this, put *Savo*'s back to the newly established Chinese position in the Senkakus.

"You asked us for the optimal positioning, Captain," Noblos said stiffly.

"Thank you, Doctor. I did." Dan sighed. "Okay, make it so. I'll move *Curtis Wilbur* up to take our place. That leaves us without a second line of defense, unless Fang can break us loose those frigates."

"Are you continuing that fight, Captain? Seems to me we're getting very isolated out here."

"Well, this is where our orders put us, Doctor."

246

Dan debated his next offer, but made it anyway. "You're not ship's company, Bill. We can still airlift you out. Put you on a helo, lily-pad you to Okinawa."

"You need me too much, Captain." Noblos looked down a long nose at Wenck and Terranova, at the console. "We've discussed the shortcomings of your team before."

"At length. Yes."

"I'm afraid I owe it to you to stay."

"Well," Dan said, very reluctantly, "we're glad you're here." He felt like a hypocrite, but if it would help mission effectiveness, he was willing to soft-pedal his personal feelings.

The deck slanted. A buzzing vibration wormed through steel and aluminum and Kevlar. *Savo*'s turbines, spinning up. "Coming to course two niner zero," the TAO called.

Dan nodded; they would dogleg around Miyako Jima, then alter course west, toward Taiwan. "Time to station?"

"Five hours, twenty minutes."

When everyone was working he stood irresolute for a few moments. Started for his stateroom. Hesitated outside its door.

Then kept on, climbing the next ladder, too, until he reached the bridge.

Hermelinda Garfinkle-Henriques was on watch. He returned her salute, and told the boatswain to stand by for an announcement.

The earsplitting whistle echoed over the weather decks. He took a couple of deep breaths, and accepted the mike.

"This is the captain speaking."

The echos were disorienting. He took another breath, trying to ignore them.

"A couple of issues, to keep everyone updated.

"We are proceeding to a location north of Taipei, to defend the population of that city should the mainland Chinese carry out their threat of a missile strike.

"I know we're all short on sleep. So am I. But we may be called on to save thousands of innocent lives in the next few hours. Or defend ourselves from cruise-missile, air, or torpedo attack.

"All gun crews, self-defense teams, Weapons Department, and Ops Department personnel, make final preparations to fight the ship. Engineering, Damage Control, and Firefighting: we have to be ready to take a hit and keep steaming. I depend on you to keep us able to do that.

"We've trained for this. Now it's time to earn our pay.

"You're the best crew in the Navy, and I'm proud to serve with you. Proud to lead you. And confident in your abilities. Savo Island. *'Hard Blows.'*

"That is all." He clicked off the 1MC and

looked at the faces around him on the bridge. They looked impressed. Good.

If only he himself could muster more enthusiasm for what was looking more and more like a long, bitter struggle.

After lunch he did a walk-through, stopping at every work center. At each, he emphasized focus. They could skate on admin requirements, but not on safety or operability. The crew seemed upbeat. Everyone wanted to shake his hand, for some reason. He was in the forward passageway when Sid Tausengelt pulled him aside. The lean, leathery senior enlisted adviser looked either deeply worried or extremely angry. "Captain. A word."

"How's the crew holding up, Master Chief?"

"Basically, they're gonna do, sir. Good talk on the 1MC, by the way. And that part about the best crew in the Navy—they ate that up."

"You said I needed to get on the horn more. Keep everybody in the picture."

"Yessir, I did. A CO that listens to the chief of the boat, that's a good thing."

"We talked about healing this crew," Dan murmured. "Are we on our way?"

"Basically, this is gonna help, sir. Combat, it's a self-licking ice-cream cone, where your basic morale's concerned. But we got another problem." Tausengelt glanced around, then led them into a quieter nook. "It's that Ar-Rahim."

"What about her?"

"You talk to her, sir? Last couple days, I mean."

"We had a short conversation," Dan said cautiously. He didn't want to blurt out anything that might compromise the investigation. "Why?"

"Well, sir, it's like . . . basically, she suspects all of us. Barged her way into the Goat Locker. Now she wants tapes from the cameras. DNA from everybody."

"Not *everybody,* Master Chief. She's going to narrow down her list, then subpoena, I guess is the word, samples from the suspects."

"You want to know what I hear, well, a lot of people aren't happy." The old chief hesitated, then added, "She suspects you, too, Skipper."

Hmm. Dan ran that through his circuits. "Why do you say that?"

"I got my sources. And I didn't want to bring this up, but—that head scarf—"

"What about it? The crew wears *savo* shemaghs. What's the difference?"

"Nothing," Tausengelt said, but the reluctant tone made it significant.

"Look, Master Chief. You and I remember how weird the NIS used to be. But they're more professional now. I trust her. She just seems really intent on getting this guy. And you got to admit, having a rapist loose is not helping the women focus."

"Basically, I got no beef with that. It's the way she's doing it," Tausengelt insisted.

Dan patted his shoulder. "I'm taking what you said aboard, all right? Keep an eye on her. Let me know if she really goes off the rails. Now, let's get back to making sure we're ready to go into harm's way."

The grizzled master chief nodded and left. Dan looked after him, wondering who was in the right here.

Later that afternoon he was up on the forecastle with Chief Quincoches and Noah Pardees, the first lieutenant, inspecting the wood-and-canvas deckhouse the hull techs had built over the exposed crane, when his Hydra beeped. He snatched it off his belt. "Captain."

"Sir, TAO. Link 16's up with ROC air defense."

"Great news, Matt." With access to data from Taiwan's radars, he could get advance keying on any missile launch, too. "Was that Chip's doing? Captain Fang?"

"Yessir, he worked that magic. Some not so good news, too, though."

"Hit me." Dan halted at the deck edge, looking out over the sea. Wind from the north, about ten knots. Low overcast. He smiled at Pardees and mouthed *Good work* as he strolled aft.

Mills said that a second Japanese air strike

was headed for the Senkakus. Also, a force of marines had landed on one of the smaller islands.

Dan halted inside the break, startled. "U.S. Marines?"

"No sir, not U.S. Japanese Maritime Self-Defense Force."

"Oh." He turned that over as he undogged the door, nodding to a sailor who came to attention. "I wonder how they got there. We never saw them. So they're gonna fight?"

"Looks like it, sir."

"Anything on size of the troop commitment?"

Mills said there wasn't, just a short press release from Tokyo that their forces had been engaged on the islands for three days now. The Western Amphibious Regiment had been mentioned, out of Nagasaki.

"Okay. But why is that bad news?"

"That's not it, sir. The Philippines are reporting an invasion of the island of Itbayat."

Dan started climbing the ladder. "Itbayat . . . which is where?"

"South of Taiwan. Also, Captain Fang says the cross-channel assault's still building. They've identified the amphib fleet loading out in Ningbo. And a lot of small boats clustering opposite the strait."

Ningbo, near Shanghai, was the base for the Eastern Fleet, a huge complex of military bases and airfields. A concentration of small craft had been the classic signature of an impending assault, from Napoleonic times to 1940.

CIC was dark, the air at sixty degrees of chill. "Captain's in Combat!" someone yelled. The word passed down the ranked consoles, and faded into the hiss of air-conditioning, the murmur of circuits, as he headed for the command desk. Everyone had coverall pants tucked into socks, with gas mask, helmet, flash gloves, and emergency escape breathing device handy. Flash hoods draped their necks. He bent and tucked his own cuffs. In a flash fire, something that simple could save a life.

Their renewed access to data was evident with his first glance at the displays. The air and surface picture, fed from the ROC network, teemed with contacts. Now he could look deep into eastern China, too.

He sagged into his chair like a man with sight restored. He'd dreaded going into missile-defense mode without situational awareness. Now, added to the coverage he was getting via his drones and task force units, he could see all the way from Okinawa to the Babuyan Channel, north of the Philippines.

Heavy air and surface activity to the south drew his attention. The screen flickered, then suddenly zoomed in.

"That's Itbayat," said Mills, from his keyboard. "Eighty-six miles south of Taiwan. Commands the southern approaches the same way the Senkakus do the north. There's an airfield. Single strip, but big enough for fighters. Which the Chinese have apparently already captured."

"Already? How the hell did they get ashore?"

"Landed on the airstrip. The Filipinos never garrisoned it."

Dan reflected grimly on how history repeated itself. How could Manila have overlooked a garrison? Even as he wondered, he knew. They'd feared to anger the dragon. But an undefended island, in such a strategically important position, must have looked like unguarded chocolate to Zhang Zurong. "Anything from Manila? Do they plan to recapture it?"

Cheryl Staurulakis said from another console, "They're filing a diplomatic protest."

Dan nodded. He huddled with the exec for a few minutes, discussed messing on station, getting everyone fed during Condition Three ABM. Then went back to the command desk, and settled in as Fang let himself in the aft door. "Captain. I was about to call for you."

"I was looking for you, too."

"Let's put our heads together." He called Staurulakis over too. "Okay, Chip, want to kick off? Oh, by the way—great work getting us linked in. This is really going to help."

Fang half-smiled thanks, then went sober again. Looking at a black wheelbook, he laid out the situation in dry sentences. The ROC Navy wanted to take action to break up the invasion force while it was loading in mainland ports. The Republic of Korea might be offering a surface task group to help.

Dan blinked. This was gutsy. Maybe seeing how Zhang had kicked the acquiescent and pacifistic Filipinos in the teeth was wising up the other regional allies.

Fang said, "For obvious reasons, even if it is a combined force, a Taiwanese admiral must be in command. Admiral Hsu has been nominated to lead the raid. His Korean counterpart would be Admiral Jung."

"Just a sec," Dan said. "That wouldn't be Jung *Mun Jun,* would it?"

"I believe that is his full name. You know him?"

"I do. From an exercise that . . . got complicated."

"I see. However, the Koreans have received a note from Beijing. Their participation will be regarded as an act of war. So it is up in the air as to whether we will actually see reinforcements."

Dan nodded. The artichoke strategy. Peel off allies one by one. Hitler had employed it, with stunning success . . . until he bit off more leaves than he could chew. "Okay, we're en route to defend Taipei. But I don't want to sit on my thumbs waiting to be attacked. Chip, can we organize some form of interoperability training with your submarine and air?"

"I can look into it."

"Please. Cheryl, Matt, see if you can staple together an emergency plan, at least, for how the task group can help in case China actually tries to invade. No point guarding the Miyako Strait if we lose Taiwan. Make sense?"

Fang looked doubtful. "You have orders to do this, Captain? So far, the United States has avoided any overt help to the Republic of China."

"No, and I don't plan to ask permission. I'll beg forgiveness afterward."

He eyed the screen. Operation Sheng Chi was rolling out. Years in the preparation. A skillful game of Go that blended military moves, diplomatic bullying, and China's overwhelming land army. And once again, the democracies—optimistic, hedonistic, all too ready to look away from any threat—were going to have to play catch up.

How long had the Peloponnesian War lasted, between Athens and Sparta? Twenty-seven years. This wouldn't run nearly as long. Not with modern armaments. But it could change the course of history just as much.

The first missile rose at 1610, 4:10 P.M. local. *Savo* was still an hour from station, but the missile warning buzzered as ALIS locked on.

Dan was by the scuttlebutt, eyeing a patch on the black-painted bulkhead where a 9mm bullet had punched into the spall liner. Where his first exec had threatened everyone in CIC but, in the end, shot himself. Intentionally or not, they'd never know.

He jerked his mind back. Mills had taken over TAO. He ran his eyes over the bent heads along the consoles. Yeah. Noblos might not think so, but he thought he had the first team on deck.

Someone had turned on the audio from the SPY-1; a familiar crackle, like popping popcorn. The beam going out, five times a second.

"Sir, cuing from ROC air defense," the Terror called. "Suspected launch. Vicinity of Fujian."

Mills bent to the keyboard and put the raw radar output up on the rightmost display. The spoke-like beam was locked on the Chinese coast, its amber rays shifting back and forth along the narrow arc of the antimissile coverage.

A glowing dot blinked on above a scatter of mountain return. Terranova dragged in the designation hook to snag it. "Profile plot, Meteor Alfa. Altitude, angels twenty . . . twenty-five . . . angels thirty. Very fast climbout . . . first-stage separation."

"Classifies as a DF-11," Mills murmured. "Solid-fueled. Two-stage. Designate hostile."

Dan nodded. "Concur." The rapid climbout gave them even less time to plot an intercept. But Fujian was far south of *Savo*'s coverage. Given the DF-11's limited range . . . He said into

257

his mike, "I doubt that one's gonna be IPP'd at Taipei."

"Concur with that, Skip," said Wenck.

The horizontal velocity callouts began to flicker. Nosing over already. Yeah, aimed at Taiwan's west coast. Dan checked the gun radar. Shorter range than the massive phased arrays, but he hated not being able to see behind him. He clicked to another circuit and checked that the antitorpedo gear was in self-defense mode, just to be sure. In case one of those missing Songs tried to clobber him from behind.

A second buzzer sounded. Then a third. More contacts winked on, near where the first had appeared.

Then, suddenly, many more. Eight. Nine . . . He sucked a breath and hit the lever on the 21MC. "Bridge, we have TBM attacks starting on Taiwan. This thing's going hot. Pass to all units Steeplechase. We're gonna be busy in Combat."

"Bridge aye."

He tensed, but after ten pips, they stopped appearing. Just the first salvo? One battery's missiles being fired, from TELs?

The ovals of the IPPs, the predicted impact points, blinked into existence as the seconds crawled by. More or less as he'd expected, they overlay the early-warning radar site at Leshan Mountain and the military airfields on Penghu Island. Mills kept passing information to the task group, but Dan tried to hover above the action. Time to start letting go, allow Cheryl to run the ship while he monitored the big picture.

Which reminded him . . . "Bridge, CO; XO up there?"

"Yessir, Captain, standing by. Want her on the bitch box . . . I mean, the 21MC?"

"No, just hadn't heard from her for a while." He double-clicked off.

Fifteen minutes into the attack, a single missile came up north of the previous launching points. Terranova designated it Meteor Kilo. It climbed as fast as the others, but the horizontal vector was different. Angled, possibly, toward Taipei.

Dan clicked to the Combat circuit. "Set Circle William. Launch-warning bell." He reached for the covered voice net, then saw Mills was already passing it to the rest of the task group. He snapped to the Weapons circuit, and got the chaff and decoys ready to deploy.

"IPP coming up!" Terranova yelled. Dan squinted at the screen. It wasn't a point yet, of course. Only an oval overlay on the geo plot. With each recomputation, it shifted. Clicking east, then south. But contracting with each sweep.

More and more clearly, centered on the capital.

Over the next minute, Terranova refined the solution and designated the target to two Block 4s in the forward magazine. Dan groped into the neckline of his coveralls for the firing key. "Stand by to take Kilo. Two-round salvo."

Beside him Matt Mills was going through the checklist, listening to responses. "Launchers to 'operate' . . . Set up to take Meteor Kilo. Two-round salvo. Sound warning bell forward. Deselect safeties and interlocks. Enable battle short. Stand by to fire, on TAO's command."

Dan pushed back from the table, letting Mills run it. Bumping what was happening against his ROEs, his other guidance, and the common sense a commander was supposed to have. As well as trying to guess what the other side had in mind.

For just once, the situation seemed clear, which in itself was enough to set off his own personal alarm. The oval of the IPP kept shrinking. It was definitely aimed at the city.

But why had they only fired *one* missile?

That couldn't be a serious attack. Unless Meteor Kilo was nuclear-tipped, which seemed unlikely. The enemy must know *Savo* was on station here. That she could intercept a single-round attack. And that if she didn't, the city's own, closer-range Patriot batteries would.

Obviously, it was either some kind of message, or a bid to deplete their magazines before the real attack started.

But just as obviously, whatever the enemy's aim, his own response was clear. And for once, his orders and his personal druthers coincided.

260

He couldn't let a missile fall on a city.

He fitted the key into position as he reported the launch and his intentions to Fleet, tersely, not waiting for a response. He flicked up the clear plastic switch cover. Snapped the toggle to the FIRE position. "Authorized," he announced.

Next came the same long, seemingly endless pause endured at every firing. No more than three seconds, yet feeling eternal.

The vent dampers *whunked* shut. The ventilation sighed to a stop.

A rumble built, growing until it shook the steel around them. Hot gas flared incandescent in the forward deck camera.

"Bird one away. Stand by . . . bird two away."

The symbols left *Savo*'s circle-and-cross, blinking into blue semicircles as they gained speed. Dan said, "TAO, inform PacFleet, two Block 4s fired against a presumed DF-11 or DF-15 with IPP on Taipei."

Terranova chanted, "Stand by for intercept, Meteor Kilo . . . stand by. . . ."

"Intercept . . . *now*," called Wenck.

Dan squinted up at the display as the blue and the red callouts merged. The brackets jerked off the hurtling missile. Tracked back. Then hunted back and forth, as if unclear what they were supposed to be looking for.

"Return's going mushy."

"Ionization trail. Missile breakup."

Sighs around the space. Dan checked with Slaughenhaupt again, ensuring that the chief was keeping a weather eye around them. When he tuned back in, the last traces of the hot, electrified gas that marked the reentry of the warhead were fading from the screen. "Our first round connected," Mills said.

"Good work," Dan said, but thinking, We expended two rounds against one of theirs. They've got over a thousand of the things, plus hundreds more in their production lines, probably.

Not a reassuring exchange ratio.

Over the next hours they stayed on alert, but although warheads continued to fall on air bases, communication nodes, artillery parks, and the radar and Patriot sites that lined the west coast, no more came their way. The buzzer went off for outgoing missiles, too. The island was retaliating with a strike on the mainland's signal intelligence station at Dongjing Shan. Taiwan's missiles were smaller than the main-landers', but Dan had no doubt they'd be more accurate. One by one, radars went down as they hit.

But the air was boiling behind the coast. Scores of aircraft were rising from fields, joining up into flights, orbiting just out of range of the Taiwanese defenses.

"They're generating a major air campaign," Amy Singhe noted, behind him.

He glanced up at her profile. Dark-haired, dark-eyed, she reminded him more than ever of Kali, the avenging Hindu goddess. All she needed was a necklace of skulls. "Looks like it," he allowed. "You passed that to Fleet, correct?"

"Yes sir. We going to take them on?"

"Not in our guidance, Strike Officer. Hold the strait, defend the city. That's the mission, so far."

"The time to strike was before they attacked."

"No argument, Amy. Maybe the thinking is, see how they do on their own before we get involved."

On the screen, the multiples of red carets—hostile aircraft—had merged into distinct groups. Now they began tracking east. "One headed for Penghu Island," Mills muttered beside him. "One for, looks like, the south aircase cluster. One for the middle of the west coast. That northern gaggle's for the airfields west of Taipei."

Dan rubbed his face. His eyes hurt, but he couldn't pull his gaze from the events unfolding on the screen. As the red carets crossed the coast, blue semicircles winked on above the mainland. The defenders' numbers seemed pitifully few, considering what was coming at them.

"Never have so many," Mills muttered.

"Yeah. The Battle of Britain all over again. On the other side of the world."

"And both sides speaking Chinese."

More blue contacts popped into existence. These did not orbit, but tracked quickly west. They didn't seem directed against the incomers. "Zoom in on one of those," Dan called to Terranova. "Get an altitude readout."

"Altitude, angels decimal three."

Three hundred feet . . . "Cruises," Mills stated. "Deep counterstrike. Gonna hit their airfields. Cratering munitions, I'll bet."

Dan reflected that they might have been more effective *before* the attackers rose from those strips. But the ROC obviously hadn't wanted to get ahead of the escalation curve. Make it clear to everyone who was the aggressor; not a bad tactic in the opening hours of a war. From the diplomatic point of view, at least.

Suddenly half the world died. At least, on their screens. "Data's down, from ROC air defense," Wenck called.

"I see," Dan said quietly. The feed had gone out. No telling why, but their remaining contacts were from the task force's own sensors. Which severely cut down their information on what was happening west of the island.

"Alert on bogey pack three," Terranova announced.

Halfway across the strait, one of the flights from Fuzhou broke off the main body. Six aircraft swerved and tacked east. Toward *Savo*? Mills assigned weapons. Dan had to consider, quickly, whether his orders would require them to act against not a missile strike on a city, but an air attack on it. But after several tense minutes, it became evident that the flight was headed for neither *Savo* nor the capital, but for the Senkakus. "Putting more ordnance on the Japanese," Wenck observed.

"There can't be that much more to bomb."

"Unless they're reinforcing."

Dan frowned. Tokyo was being closemouthed about its long-range intent. Granted, these small islands were national territory. But they were unpopulated, and much closer to the Chinese homeland than to the Japanese home islands.

In the deck cameras, their only reminder a world existed outside this air-conditioned, flicker-lit cave, the sun was setting. He reminded Wenck and Terranova to watch for launches against *Savo*. Intel had reported ship-killing missiles being deployed in China. But though more missiles rose, and curved, then plunged down onto the embattled island, none seemed to be aimed at them. The sheets of scratch paper taped to the diffusers fluttered. Only clicking keyboards interrupted the hiss of air-conditioning, and the occasional discordant howl of the buzzer as the red and blue symbols closed, and merged, and flared. And, many of them, disappeared.

A silent holocaust, mediated by digital

electronics from hundreds of miles distant. Dan watched, rubbing stubbled cheeks. Wondering how long the embattled island, steadily being denuded of defenses, could hold out.

And when *Savo*'s turn would come.

14

The 1MC woke Aisha early. The exec's terse tones exhorted everyone to maintain material condition, uphold normal maintenance standards, and remain alert on watch. *"I know we're all getting tired. It's stressful, plus we're worried about what's happening at home. But we have to maintain situational awareness and readiness for battle. We could be in contact with major Chinese forces at any time."* Then Staurulakis reminded everyone to schedule proper periods of sleep and rest.

Aisha shook her head, lying in her bunk. Obviously no one could. Other than herself, that is. But she had only one job aboard here, and no watches to stand.

After making morning *salat,* she decided to get on with it. She went to the wardroom, but no one was there. The mess decks too were all but deserted. Only a few steam tables were lit off. But there was coffee, and paper cups. She got scrambled eggs again, and toast, and canned peaches in sweet syrup.

When she carried her tray out, the only woman there was Terranova. Alone, her back to a faux-wood divider bulkhead. Aisha hesitated. Then gripped her tray more firmly, carried it over, and set it down. "Beth. All right if I—?"

A reluctant nod. The girl's round face looked drawn. Mulberry stains underlined the protuberant eyes. Her fingers trembled. The gutted remains of several pastries, cored with cherry or strawberry jam, littered her tray. Her fingers were stained red too, and there was some around her mouth. Aisha resisted the temptation to pick up a paper napkin and dab it off, as she would have for Tashaara. "Are those good? I might have one."

"They're awful sticky. But sweet."

"Everything going okay up in CIC, Beth?"

"Um, not really. Dr. Noblos keeps saying we're screwing up, we're stupid and we don't tune right. It's true, our numbers aren't great, but—" She halted, obviously remembering she shouldn't discuss a readiness issue. "Don't tell anyone I said that."

"I won't." Aisha started on her eggs, and they didn't speak for a few minutes. Men glanced over, then altered their courses to sit at other tables. A shrimpy messman with a face like a capuchin monkey's leered from where he was swabbing up a spill.

Terranova picked at her sleeve. She mumbled, "How *you* doing? Where they got you staying? With the officers?"

"In the unit commander's stateroom."

"Nice. I was in there once. Your own cabin and head and everything. We gotta share, twenty girls in one room, one head with three stalls. It's a zoo." She hesitated, then added, "How's it going? Your investigation, I mean. Did you figure out who . . . Maybe I shouldn't be asking, I don't know. . . ."

She suddenly seemed close to weeping. Aisha covered her hand with her own. Terranova's felt sticky. "I can't give details, Beth. But we're making progress. I've done several suspect interviews—"

"The chiefs. They're okay with this?"

"They're not enthusiastic, but they're cooperating. We just have trouble getting to certain people; they seem to be on watch all the time."

"Well, right now we have to be ready to launch in like fifteen seconds. Everyone's wound tight up in CIC. They keep saying we're going to be in a fight soon." She shot Aisha a frown. "If we get hit, what do you do? Got an eebie? A fire-party assignment? An abandon-ship station?"

"An eebie . . . an emergency breathing device? There's one in my cabin. They trained me on it, on the carrier. The exec told me to report to her boat amidships, she'd make sure I got taken care of. Fire party . . . I'm not assigned to anything like that, I don't think."

"No, I guess not," the petty officer said. The

way she glanced at Aisha's middle didn't make it a compliment.

Aisha sipped from the paper cup. The coffee was bitter, burnt, but hot. "Beth, we'll nail this guy. Remember those swabs they took? Most went down with the tanker. But the chief corpsman kept some. Enough, I think, to make a positive identification. Once we narrow the list, we'll take samples. We send those back along with your swabs, and that gives us grounds for a court-martial."

Of course, it was more complicated. If there was a match, and that was a pretty big if, the case would first go to an Article 32 hearing—like a grand jury. Only if the "32 officer" decided there was enough evidence to move forward would they get a recommendation for a general court-martial.

But she didn't feel like explaining, and anyway, the young woman didn't look as thrilled with the news as Aisha had expected. "You'll take him off the ship?"

"In this case, yes, I'm going to recommend he be removed and kept in custody until the trial. To protect you."

"To protect me," Terranova whispered. She was shielding her face, and it took a moment before Aisha understood she was crying. Holding it in, shoulders jerking, but wiping her eyes with the back of her hand. "I didn't deserve any of this.

Why the fuck me? I asked God. He doesn't answer."

Aisha took her hand again, murmuring, "Evil hurts. But sometimes it makes us stronger. Maybe that's what's happening to you. Don't doubt God, whatever name you call Him by. He blesses us with strength when we need it. Do you pray?"

Terranova shook her head. "Maybe you should try it," Aisha said.

"Aw, fuck it . . . forget it. Forget I said anything! Jersey girls're tough. You were telling me about the trial. Once you catch him."

"Well . . . it could be delayed. I've never tried to do this in wartime. But we'll get him off the ship, away from you." She set her silverware down with a clatter. Then flinched back as the monkey-like man in the paper cap reached past her and whisked it away, grinning. A dirty rag slapped down, rastered the tabletop, and whisked away.

"Fuck you, Troll!" Terranova shouted after him. "She wasn't even done!"

Aisha sat back. The girl shifted gears in seconds. Well, that could be both the strain of imminent combat and sheer fatigue. It didn't mean she wasn't a victim. But it might hurt her credibility as a witness, if a defense lawyer rattled her cage. She looked after the attendant. "Who *was* that?"

"We call him the Troll. Used to be the

271

compartment cleaner, up forward. Guess he got a promotion."

"He ever hit on you? Annoy you?"

"Hey, he fucking annoys *everybody*. Forget him." Terranova flicked her fingers, and a bit of red jelly flew off and stuck to Aisha's shirt. "Oh, sorry . . . let me get that off ya. . . . Look, I got to get back to CIC. There's only Chief Wenck and me can run ALIS."

"Wenck. He's an interesting guy. He ever make a move? Try to force his attentions?"

"Donnie?" Terranova frowned. "He's more like a big brother. Kind of nuts, but not *weird* nuts. Just, his mind's going a million miles an hour. Look, gotta go. Really." She rose, picking up her tray, and vanished in the direction of the scullery.

Too late, Aisha remembered what she'd wanted to ask. In the first two incidents, there'd been a blanket. Presumably, that the attacker had brought with him, since there were no blankets in fan rooms or darken-ship vestibules. But none had been mentioned in Terranova's account of the rape itself. She resolved to ask the next time she saw her.

She'd meant to do another interview that morning, but the ship went into lockdown, "Circle William," which apparently meant she was confined to her cabin. The 1MC kept saying things about biocontamination stations and water

272

washdown. Apparently they expected a chemical or biological attack. If that happened . . . she might never see her daughter, or her mother, again. She shuddered. But why worry? She couldn't do anything. There wasn't that much to occupy herself with, though. They were still in River City, so she still couldn't send e-mails off the ship. She read her hadith for a while. Said the noon prayers. Shaved her legs, wondering, as she did every time, why she bothered.

Then, sitting at the big desk made for an admiral, she booted up her notebook and read over her notes. She drew a grid on paper and tried to assign a percentage to each suspect. Who was around, who was on watch, who had motive, opportunity. Who just plain raised her hackles.

Carpenter was too old, and too short. Benyamin was tall enough, and seemed to have the predilections, but his berthing assignment and work center were far from the 03 level. Peeples, too, worked far from where Terranova stood watch. Especially if a blanket was involved. Anyone carrying one through the passageways would stick in someone's mind. And so far, no one had mentioned it. That didn't rule them out— they could have stashed a "rape kit" in advance— but it lowered their percentages.

In terms of propinquity, Wenck was in the lead. They were together every day. Like boyfriends, work mates were natural suspects. He had the height. And someone with his training would find it simple to take an automatic overhead light out of operation, as the perp apparently had in both the first and second incidents, though it hadn't been necessary in the radar-maintenance space.

She tapped her pencil, staring at Tashaara's picture. Bright black eyes, a smiling face, pig-tailed black hair.

Then there was Lenson. *Savo Island*'s commanding officer.

Also tall. Also working closely with the victim, or at least in CIC with her. And his stateroom was right across from the Equipment Room.

He could rove around the ship at will, *anywhere,* day or night, without anyone thinking it odd.

She tapped the paper again, but didn't put his name on it. And at last shoved the matrix away. The shredder whined, scissor-like teeth slicing suspicions and prejudices into ragged ribbons. Maybe she hadn't cast the net widely enough. Should she do a SCAN process? That might pull in more suspects. But the ship was already on edge. An agent had to think about that, too. Especially in wartime.

Or could Lenson's warning have been to restrict her from inquiring as deeply as she should?

"Now secure from Circle William. Secure from decontamination drills. Set modified material condition Zebra throughout the ship," the 1MC

274

announced. *"Open Circle Zebra fittings must be guarded. On deck, Condition Three, watch section one. All hands stand clear aft of frame one hundred and fifty two for live fire."*

She turned her computer off. Picked up her carpetbag purse, heavy with camera and notes and pistol, and went out again.

She climbed laboriously all the way to the bridge. The watchstanders were in life jackets and had gas masks strapped to their thighs. Along with the checkered shemaghs, some wore flash gear. She got passing glances, nothing more, until a gnarled little man with a silver pipe hanging around his neck asked what she was doing up there. "Getting a breath of air," she said. "All right if I go out on the side there?"

"On the wing?" The man glanced out to where the CO and XO were standing, heads together. Lenson had to stoop, he was so much taller than Staurulakis. Past them another gray ship hovered on the horizon, and beyond that, far off, a mountainous land. "No. You can go out on the other side, for a few minutes. But we can't let extraneous personnel hang around up here, understand?"

Outside, the wind was warm. A seaman in a bulky flak jacket leaned into binoculars, elbows planted on a varnished wooden rail. A heavy black headphone trailed a wire to his feet. Aisha looked out over a flattish sea. Another island

275

floated far off beneath a woolly piling of clouds. A staccato blatting clattered from aft: machine-gun fire. Red comets hovered, then descended. White geysers burst up in a dotted line across the blue. She edged to her left, until she was almost touching the lookout. A brother, younger than she, solidly built, with a heavy, stubbled chin. A strong face, and the smooth caramel skin she'd always thought looked so good on a man.

"What land is that?" she muttered. "Out there?"

He didn't take his eyes out of the glasses, but lifted one of the earpieces. "Don't know. Japan, I think."

"What are you watching for?"

"Missiles. Periscopes. Planes. Small boats. Other ships."

"You can see missiles?"

"Cruise missiles, yeah. They'll be little dots with smoke behind them. Better hope I don't see any." He spared her a side glance. "You the detective?"

"Detective? I guess so."

"Where you from?"

"New York. Harlem. Aisha."

"Mycus. I see you wearing the head scarf. What, you in the Nation?"

"My family was. Not now. All races are the *masjid,* not just us. You?"

His lips barely moved. "How would you like to go to heaven? Instead of hell."

Oh help me, Allah. "I hope I'm on my way."

"Not if you deny Jesus. He said, 'Anyone who rejects me is rejecting God, who sent me.'"

"Islam doesn't reject Jesus, upon him be peace. We respect him as a prophet and messenger—"

"There's only one God, and one truth. That's Christ Jesus, declared in the written Word, the Bible."

She tried hard not to grit her teeth. "Allah isn't another god. 'Al—Lah' *means* 'the God.' it's the same word Arab Christians use. We just—"

"What the hell's going on out here?"

It was the captain, not looking pleased. "Ar-Rahim. This lookout has a job out here. A very important one. He doesn't need to be arguing religion with you."

"I'm sorry. I didn't start—"

"I don't think you have a reason to be up here. Do you?"

"Um, not really." She backed away. "All right. Again, sorry. I'm leaving."

He seemed to unbend, but only slightly. "I can't have any interference with operations. Wartime, Agent. Could be in combat at any time." He put a hand on the lookout's shoulder. "Ammo here could save all our . . . uh, backsides. Don't talk to the lookouts, or anybody on watch, okay? Actually, the best place for you would be in your stateroom."

She kept her eyes lowered before that fierce

277

gray gaze. "Not to contradict you, Captain. But I can't carry out an investigation from there."

"Ammo, get your head back in those glasses," snapped the little man with the silver pipe, from beside the captain. He took her elbow. "I'll escort the lady off the bridge, Skipper."

He was leading her to the door she'd come out of when another officer called from across the pilothouse, "Is that the special agent?"

"Yeah, why?" said the boatswain.

"Chief corpsman wants her down in sick bay, ASAP."

"What for?"

"Won't say. Just needs her down there right away."

The last thing she heard before the door sealed behind her was "Cheryl, keep tabs on what that woman's doing." It seemed to be the captain's voice, Lenson's. But she had to admit, she wasn't absolutely sure.

Ryan opened the door to sick bay. The lights glared off scrubbed and waxed tile. The little redhead's face was so pale the freckles stood out. "I meant to get up with you this morning, but—"

"No problem. What do you need me for?"

Past the seaman hospitalman, Grissett rose from a chair. "Special Agent. Not good news, I'm afraid." He nodded to the side.

A padlock and a hasp lay on the gleaming tile.

278

Metal shone ragged where rivets had torn free of the refrigerator door. A dogging wrench, a heavy steel pipe, lay nearby.

"We didn't touch anything," Ryan said. "Just called you."

"A break-in? When did it happen?"

"Last night sometime," Grissett said. "We didn't open for sick call this morning because of the decon drills."

"Those were yesterday."

"We had to restow and re-inventory. We were back in Medical Supply. When we came in, we saw it." Grissett cleared his throat. He too seemed run-down. Had he had the Crud too?

"You don't lock medical spaces?"

"Not this outer office, not in wartime steaming—repair parties have to have access. The controlled medications are back in my private office, in the safe. That area, yes, that's always locked."

"Is that standard procedure? That these spaces are unlocked?"

"Not much is standard in wartime, Agent. XO told me to leave the outer door cracked. In case we get hit, take casualties, there'll be no delays getting them taken care of. So I did."

"I see. So what's missing?"

"Actually, nothing. That is, it's all accounted for." She frowned, puzzled, until he added, "Look in the microwave."

She reached for it, then stopped herself and pulled a disposable tissue from a dispenser. Touching only the tip of the handle, she unlatched the oven door.

The ziplock had four long wooden-handled swabs sealed inside. The plastic was partially melted, lying in flattened puddles where the contents had heated, then cooled.

"Terranova's samples," Grissett added. Unnecessarily, since her name was printed in green Magic Marker on the outside.

Aisha fished the bag out, still using the tissue, and dangled it before her eyes. A tablespoon of clear liquid pooled in the bottom corner. "The heat?"

"Destroys DNA. Actually, denatures it, breaks the hydrogen bonds. If it's hot enough."

"Was this hot enough?"

"We don't know what temperature it was set at, or for how long. But I think we can assume these are history." Grissett paused, lips compressed.

"So you're saying we just lost the last physical evidence?" She slapped the tabletop, hissing as her fingers stung. "Because you left the door unlocked? Let him in here?"

"You're accusing us?" Ryan said.

"Not you, Dunk. But maybe someone else." She glared at the corpsman. "One of the chiefs. Who don't think I should be investigating this crime. Who might even be colluding, to protect whoever's assaulting women."

"Whoa there." Grissett didn't seem upset at the accusation, though. "I don't mind personal attacks, but leave the other khaki out of it, okay? Saying stuff like that is not gonna help you with anybody aboard."

"Oh, right. The all-powerful Goat Locker."

"They *could* help you, Special Agent. Accuse me if you want, but don't make enemies, is my advice." He hesitated, then added, "But that's not what really is surprising about this. Anybody could have grabbed a dogging wrench, pried open the fridge, nuked the sample. It's what else is in that bag that worries me."

She looked at it again. "Water?"

"That's not water. Or, it is now. It *was* hydrogen peroxide." Grissett nodded at a brown plastic bottle beside the oven.

Aisha looked around for a chair, feeling the onset of some dark cold cloud. "What are you telling me, Doctor?"

"Not a doctor. But they do teach us this." He sat back, tenting fingertips. "DNA's made up of two linked strands of amino acids. The famous double helix. Above a certain temperature, around a hundred degrees centigrade, boiling water, it unzips. Heat breaks the hydrogen bonds that link the two strands.

"But when it cools, it can zip up again,

281

reconstitute itself. Unless either the heat is high and long enough to completely destroy the nucleotides, or there's acid present . . . or lots of oxygen."

He nodded at the brown bottle again. "Hydrogen peroxide gives off oxygen when heated. Excess oxygen plus high temperature guarantees degradation of DNA."

Aisha pursed her lips. "So whoever did this knows chemistry? Or biochemistry?"

"Well, I guess at one time they would have. Actually, all you'd need now would be to Google it."

"But we don't have an Internet connection."

"River City doesn't mean all connectivity is gone. Only that certain individuals still have access."

"Who determines that?"

Grissett eyed her as if guessing her weight. "The CO."

"So he—"

"They could have looked it up before," Ryan put in. "We weren't in EMCON for quite a few days after the sample was taken. They could've researched it then, but only acted on it now. Or, like you said, Aisha, they could already know."

She stroked the bridge of her nose, glancing from the oven to the ripped-off handle. Who would know that obscure tidbit of organic chemistry? The chief corpsman. Maybe Ryan.

But who else? Then she realized that was the wrong question. "What I don't understand . . . why bother to microwave the stuff at all? Walk off with it. Throw it overboard, we'd never see it again. Why something this elaborate? Just to wave it in our faces?"

"Exactly." Grissett nodded somberly. " 'I'm smarter than all of you put together'—that's what he's saying here."

"Giving us the finger," Ryan said.

Aisha bent, examining the broken lock. The bright edges of ragged metal. "I doubt we'll get any prints. I'll try. But I'd be very surprised."

"We didn't touch anything," Ryan said.

"I believe you . . . but this guy's too smart to leave prints. He's probably wearing soft leather gloves."

Grissett said, "Gloves?"

"Terranova mentioned them. So did Colón. He leaves no prints. Erases physical evidence." She took a breath, studying a colorful print on the bulkhead. A human form, flayed of flesh and muscle until only nerves, veins, arteries, guts, remained. Painfully, unnaturally exposed.

"Then how are you going to find him?" Ryan asked.

Aisha stood. Gathered up the hasp, the ziplock, and the plastic bottle. Ryan held out a larger bag, and she dropped them in.

She murmured, "I'm going to cast a wider net."

15
Tysons Corner, Virginia

Y es, I'll hold for the General." Blair shifted in her chair, and gasped as pain stabbed her pelvis. It had been years since the injury, but it still hurt. There didn't seem to be much the doctors could suggest. She swiveled angrily, and cursed under her breath at another, even more intense pang.

A Chinese-accented voice came on the line. *"Blair?"*

"Good morning." She was in her office on the third floor, on the noon break between committee sessions. So far, in two days, they'd nailed down little in the way of consensus. CNN stayed on in the conference room 24/7, and the news from the Pacific grew worse each hour. "General Shucheng?"

"How are you, Blair? Still well?"

She got the small talk over as soon as decently possible. Shucheng was one of the highest-ranking officers in the Army of the Republic of China. She and the deputy chief of staff had met on a fact-finding mission to the Ministry of National Defense two years before. They'd shared a mat at an official dinner, during which Shucheng had gotten drunk enough on Taiwanese single malt to try for a feel. It had made things awkward for a moment, before they'd both decided to roar with laughter.

He was still in office. And apparently under the impression she was still in DoD—a misconception she had no plans to disabuse him of. "Luong, I'm calling on a sensitive matter. We're trying to sketch out our options in the Pacific. Could I ask a couple of questions, off the record?"

The distant voice fell. *"Your* options. *I believe those are already spelled out in our treaty."*

"I understand. And you can depend on us. But I need to know *your* intentions."

Shucheng seemed to turn away from the receiver, to answer someone else in rapid Chinese. When he came back on he sounded angry. *"You know about the missile strikes on our airfields. And on our antiaircraft sites, radars, command nodes."*

"How heavy is the damage? I know you carried out that hardening program—"

"Unfortunately, only half completed. And, you know, this is just the beginning."

"Go on."

"The mainlanders are opening a drive to expand their foothold on the Diaoyus. If they succeed, they will outflank us. But our Japanese allies are fighting there."

She chewed her lip, swiveled the chair again, and almost cried out at the wrench in her hip.

285

Concentrate! Setting aside that he'd used not the Japanese name for the Senkakus, but the same one Beijing used in putting forth their claim, what she was getting from Defense Intelligence was less rosy. According to them, the battle in the Five Islands was degenerating into a hand-to-hand struggle between Japanese and Chinese marines. The advantage depended less on maneuver or superior weapons, or even numbers, than on the struggle for air supremacy and the capacities of the resupply pipelines, one from the mainland across the East China Sea, the other south from Japan.

Both sides were feeding in men, and taking heavy casualties. So far the Japanese were holding, but neither their manpower reserves nor their air force could stand high rates of attrition for long. "And your own intentions, General? If the conflict broadens geographically? I think—"

Shucheng interrupted: *"You mean, if they invade? That I can tell you. We will resist. Even if they land armor, we have good weapons. The terrain favors us. We've had sixty years to get ready. They have no idea what our artillery can do. We'll cut them down like ripe wheat. Then, declare full independence."*

It sounded good. But what else could you expect a general to say? The double beep on her line said another call was waiting. "Luong, can you hold briefly?"

"Only for a moment, Blair."

"This is Blair Titus."

"Blair? It's Jessica."

Her campaign manager. "I'm on another call, Jessica. Asia. So make it fast."

"We've got a problem. Mr. Blaisdell called—he can't follow through on his commitment."

"How much was that?"

"Significant. A quarter million."

Blaisdell, a friend of her stepfather's, had been an early supporter. Her finger hovered over the button for the other call. "What can I do?"

"It doesn't sound like anything we did, just that the market's wiped out his 'me' money for this election cycle. People are worried, Blair. The purse strings are tightening."

"I'll call you back."

"If you want to try to get him back on board, I wouldn't wait."

"I said I'll get back to you, Jessica." She hung up before the other could answer.

To her relief, the general was still on the line, but he didn't sound happy at being put on hold. After apologizing, she said, "Our intel warns that a major cross-channel assault is building."

"We are watching the far side very closely, believe me. Yes, they are concentrating their amphibious fleet in the ports of eastern China." His tone went bitter. *"We should be attacking them in the staging areas. But your secretary of*

state is advising us to take no action. He does not want us to 'antagonize' Premier Zhang.

"Believe me, what we do, or don't do, won't affect his decision. The man is an insane tyrant. To throw away all those years of industrial development? Attack India, Vietnam, even antagonize the Russians in the north? Unfortunately, it is our troops who will die. But we will fight. We will meet them on the beaches, and throw them back into the sea."

Blair nodded into the phone. "How about your own force dispositions? Specifically, if an invasion attempt really is the follow-on to these attacks?"

"I cannot discuss our plans. As I said, we will fight on. Even if we have to retreat to the Chingyan Shan, and guerrilla from there."

The Chingyan Shan were the mountains of Taiwan. She'd flown over them on her visit. Unpopulated, rugged, densely forested, no doubt they could be defended. If you were willing to dig in, endure privation, hold or die. She glanced across the desk as a staffer dropped a folder on it. The notes from this morning. "Um, this is a secure line, General."

"There is no such thing anymore. There may even be officers in our own army . . ." His voice trailed off. *"Are you at the Pentagon, Blair?"*

"Actually, no."

"Where precisely are you?"

288

Time to come clean. "I'm at SAIC. I thought you knew. I work here now."

"You are no longer—oh—I did not . . . Dear Madam Titus, I must go. I am called away. It was very good to speak with you."

The line beeped and went dead.

Convened once more, the China Emergency Group nearly ended with a shouting session between a retired three-star general, who accused them of planning for surrender, and the young man from Google, who refused to believe changing this or that border in the Pacific would make any difference. "As long as trade and data flow freely, national borders no longer matter."

Blair and the general exchanged furious, weary glances. "Let me explain this again," she said, putting her hand on the lad's arm. It felt warm, and for a moment, her fingers resting lightly on his skin, sensing his pulse beneath it, she flashed a sudden picture of how his chest would look under that loose shirt. She shoved the image aside; she was almost old enough to be his mother, for heaven's sake. "Trade and data flow freely only between *free* countries. Zhang's building a zone of hegemony. Once it's fenced off, outsiders won't be welcome.

"We also have responsibilities to our allies. Some are formal, like those to Japan. Others are understood, or implied, as with Taiwan." She tightened her grip, trying to come up with a simile he'd identify with. "If we break our promises, it's like breaking a contract. Who would deal with your company after that?"

"Contracts get renegotiated all the time." The executive took out his cell, looked at it, realized the screen was blank, and reddened. "What about this peace feeler I saw on the news? We should at least talk."

Ms. Clayton, the former national security adviser, observed in a precise voice that the 'peace through unification" proposal the Chinese had put forward at the UN was simply a proposal for Taiwan to allow free entry of mainland troops. "Beijing would gain full control, with all that implies. Including basing rights. The guarantees of elections and a separate democratic process are paper promises. There's no mechanism for inspection, and the lethal way Zhang put down the riots in Hong Kong gives us no assurance he'll be less repressive in Taiwan.

"In essence, he's saying surrender, and he'll run Asia from here on in." She blinked across the table. "Blair, you were going to sound out your contact at the Ministry of National Defense?"

"General Shucheng sounds determined to resist. But less positive about their ability to repel a full-scale invasion."

Clayton inclined that bobbed head. "I've sounded out my counterparts in Hanoi and the

Philippines. They have long memories. Even if we're pushed back, as long as we're still fighting, they understand it's not over. We've already started building the coalition to prosecute a protracted war. With blockade and exhaustion, that's how China will be defeated."

Blair smiled. The little woman was so crisp. Determined. Clayton beckoned briskly to a staffer. "Let's have that map again."

The map . . . they'd pored over it hour after hour. Since the first question was whether Taiwan could be held, they'd invited a historian in from the Joint Staff College to give an overview of Operation Causeway.

The Army-Marine assault on Formosa planned for late 1945 would have been the largest landing of World War II. Half a million troops would have landed on four beaches. Heavily supported by naval gunfire and air, they would have established airfields on the southern third of the island before fighting north along the west coast, toward Taipei.

"It would have been a bloody campaign," the historian had said. "After the way the Japanese resisted on Tarawa, Saipan, and Tinian, we expected heavy casualties. But we would've taken the island. Eventually."

After him, a DIA staffer had briefed on where a present-day Red Chinese landing would probably take place, and how likely it was that ROC forces could throw it back. Blair had noted that the landing beaches in his analysis were the same the U.S. had planned to use in 1945, with the addition of airborne descents to seize the airfields.

The outcome, DIA predicted, would hinge on two issues: first, how stoutly the islanders resisted; second, whether the mainlanders could maintain a supply and reinforcement link across the strait. He'd presented comparative buildup rates. "The initial landing is only the start of what could be a long, intense campaign. The PLA can probably get a foothold on a small scale. Overall success will depend on how quickly they can build up that initial force. So ports and airfields are the second key issue.

"Next, if the island holds out, will we be landing U.S. troops? Or, possibly, Japanese? Tokyo has a valid security concern if Taiwan falls. If Japan feels threatened, and if they see the U.S. is determined to hold the inner island chain, they could step in, whatever a treaty says or doesn't say." He'd pressed his lips into a thin, bitter line. "Zhang's not exactly observing the letter of the law either. After all."

Now, as they came to the end of the session, Tomlin said, "A war without a strategy is just random slaughter. A breakthrough has to be contained at the flanks."

Somehow the four of them, Clayton, Blair,

Tomlin, and the Stanford professor, Glancey, had ended up at the head of the table. Clayton nodded. "As we've heard. Even if a beachhead were established, it would take time to gain full control. Especially if sizable remnants continued to fight in the mountainous spine of the island."

"The Chingyan Shan," Blair said. The range Shucheng had mentioned.

Tomlin nodded. "Correct. And if we could isolate the invasion force, cut it off on Taiwan, we could engineer an encirclement of enormous proportions." They all looked at the committee's staff director, a white-haired yet young Marine reservist who sat farther down the table, taking notes. "Let's work that up overnight. Get whatever help you need."

Blair asked, "What about forces currently in theater?"

Ms. Clayton shared a glance with the general. Who murmured, "Assume the worst. Plan for none of them to survive."

At the Metro she was surprised to see troops posted at each exit. The Monocle was on D Street, across from the Library of Congress, where she'd worked before crossing to the Senate offices. She spared the great green dome an affectionate glance. The cold air smelled like rain, but so far it was only sprinkling. This restaurant was one of Bankey's favorites, handy for meeting attorneys, high-level officials, and lobbyists. Just the place for quiet conferences over excellent steaks or succulent crab cakes, without fear of reading about it in the *Post* the next morning.

"Good evening, Ms. Titus. The senator's at his usual table." The chubby, mustached maitre d' bowed her into a small room with dozens of autographed photographs on the walls.

"Thanks, Carley."

An ascetic-looking face glanced up from one of the tables as she passed. "Senator Glenn," she said, nodding.

"Hey, Blair."

Bankey Talmadge lumbered to his feet as she approached. "Missy! You look younger every time I see ya."

She submitted smiling to a pat rather too low on her back, accompanied by the scent of good bourbon. "Great to see you too, Bankey. You saw Senator Glenn was here, right?"

"Yeah, we said hey." Talmadge waved at the other senator. "I ordered for you. And gin-tonic, right?"

"Maybe just one."

"I know you like the filet mignon, medium rare." He laid a worn, faded manila folder on the table. "How's it going, that thing you said you were on now, over at those bandits—"

"SAIC. We're not supposed to talk about it."

"You know I'm silent as the grave," he said.

Not perfectly accurate, but as the committee chairman, he was cleared. She compromised with "We're discussing alternate strategies. In response to possible Chinese moves."

"That ain't JCS business? Ops and Plans?"

"They've got their hands full just now. We've got a lot of their ex-membership, though."

"I get the picture." Talmadge nodded. "SecDef wants to look at what happens if we get knocked on our keisters. Like Korea, in 1950."

She just smiled. On the nose, as usual. He went on, "And I gotta say, it could happen. The Chinese, I mean *our* Chinese, they're tellin' me they can't hold."

"Really? Who told you that?"

"Frank Fabricatore. You remember, he was helping them out on that F-16 sale a couple years ago. From the horse's mouth." Talmadge winced, and pulled out a cell phone. Frowned at the screen. "Service! I better take this while it's workin'. Hold on a sec, okay?"

She nodded. He murmured for a few minutes, then put the phone away. "Okay, sorry, where were we?"

"Whether the Taiwancsc will fight. Who exactly is the horse's mouth, Bankey? I talked to one of their top generals. He said the exact opposite."

The big hoary head waggled. "They pulled out of Quemoy and Matsu without a shot. Military can't fight if the civilian leadership goes weak at the knees, Blair. Hey, here's your gin-tonic."

She kept poking around, trying to get some feel for who'd fed him that information, but he just grunted. She went to her second issue. "Bankey, forgive me for bringing this up again, but the last time we met, over at the Russell with Hu and Mindy, you mentioned funds you could bring to the table for my House run. You even mentioned a figure."

"Five," the senator mumbled, examining the drinks menu.

"Correct. Is there any way we can move that forward? I'm running out of credit with my campaign manager. Not to mention the ad agency."

Talmadge glanced away and sighed. "Well, here's how it is. I really would like to help you. We been together a good many years. But sometimes I want to help somebody, and sort of get ahead of myself. Fact is, I'm not the only one with his hand on that spigot, d'you see? And the others, *they* want to see which way the party's gonna jump on this vote. Authorizing use of force to defend Taiwan."

"Well, pardon me, Bankey, but I don't see what that has to do with your promise to me."

"It wasn't a *promise,* Missy. Just said I'd try to get it for you. But there's something else."

"What's that?"

Talmadge muttered, again not meeting her gaze, "Here's the thing. We just gotta figure out, as a party, if we're going to go in for another war. This president's already got us up to our eyeballs in Iraq. Syria. Yemen. And maybe Iran, too, if he gets his way. Are we going along?"

"Well, you're the chairman, Bankey."

A rueful smile. "The Senate isn't the British Parliament, Missy. You know that."

Their food arrived. She draped the napkin across her lap carefully. "So, what are you saying?"

Talmadge coughed out half-sentences punctuated by forkfuls of steak. "Here's . . . goddamn problem. First off, this whole thing reminds me of Guadalcanal. Remember Guadalcanal?"

"You go back longer than I do, Bankey."

"Well, I was a kid, but I remember it. We were fighting the Japs up and down that island chain for I think well over a year. Not just on land, either. In the air, and we lost a hell of a lot of ships in Iron Bottom Sound.

"Now, certain members are afraid that's what we're looking at again. A weird combination— our left wing, plus Tea Party types, and the libertarians—they're all sayin' we'd be better off abandoning the Pacific. Leave the Japs and Chinese to sort it out."

Blair lifted her eyebrows. "Abandon our allies, and we're finished as a superpower. Speaking of history, remember the Copperheads?"

A quick glance, a grin. "Yeah—*Copperheads.* Only this president's no Abe Lincoln. The manufacturers, the Chamber, are saying that if we go to war, the economy will crash. Hey, that was the call I just took. Know who it was?" He snorted. "You wouldn't believe me if I told you.

"Anyway, that's why we're stalled on this goddamned resolution. Nobody can agree about what happens if it goes to shit, so we can't decide on the legal language. What it would say, when we consider it, and who brings it forward."

She sliced steak carefully, took a small bite. "As to the business base, I can interject a little history there, too. The Civil War, World War I, World War II—the Cold War—we came out of each with a roaring economy. I don't like saying this, but historically, war's *good* for domestic business. But . . . back to my campaign . . . this impacts it how?"

"Well, until we make up our minds, there are certain people who don't want to back a hawk for the House."

She gave him a grim ironic smile. "So I'm a hawk now?"

"Not my words." Talmadge spread his hands. "But you were in Defense. And married to a fuckin' war hero. Pardon my French."

"All right, this authorization. No points of agreement?"

"Just that everybody agrees there has to be an

authorization. But what's gonna be in it, that's the problem. Maybe . . . air and sea power, with a restriction on commitment of ground troops. Others say no, this time it's gotta be a full-fledged declaration of war. The administration's saying the Hill just can butt out, it's within executive purview. Then there's this idea all we need is time for the sanctions and blockade to work. That we don't actually have to *do* anything."

He banged the table suddenly, violently; Blair grabbed for a toppling glass. "Well, shit fire, if we let this goddamned White House make war on his own say-so, we might as well call the son of a bitch Julius Caesar and have done with it! We can't sit around with our thumbs up our collective asses any longer. I'm gonna bring it up in Armed Services."

"They'll tear you down. Whatever it is."

"Well, maybe it'll get 'em off the dime." He opened the worn manila folder, and she smiled. Vintage Talmadge: he reused everything. Even his letters to constituents were written on the backs of discarded government documents, all part of the "help your dollar make it across the Potomac" shtick he wheeled out at each Rotary meeting, union meeting, and VFW hall during campaigns. Pinching pennies in the office, while disbursing billions in the defense budget . . . "I'm gonna do it tomorrow."

"That's . . . sudden."

"I had Missy, goddamn it, I mean *Mindy,* take a stab at it. This is what she got, but goddamn it if I'm real happy with it. Take a look."

Blair leafed through three drafts, the latest stapled on top. Even with a quick scan . . . "This might have some holes," she observed.

"No shit! 'As necessary and appropriate,' but 'will prohibit ground combat operations.' Now, how in the hell can you run a war without ground operations? Even if it's just flyin' airplanes, somebody gotta guard 'em. That's how Westy got the Marines for Da Nang in '65. Base protection."

"Um, I'm not clear yet, Bankey . . . are you favoring use of ground troops or not?"

"You can't fight without 'em."

"So that's a yes." She made a note in the margin. "And this one-year limit—do we want to keep this, for a major war?"

"Goddamn right. That's so if it does look like Guadalcanal, or Vietnam, we get a chance to debate it. No blank checks, not to that Szerenci fellow. He'll have us in an atomic war before you can say Jack Straw." He snorted, drained the glass, flourished it for a refill. "Missy, be a darlin'. Take this draft home. Write it up the way it should go. Then come sit beside me tomorrow."

"Bankey, really, this is Mindy's—"

The big head wagged. "Little girl's cute as a button, Missy, but she can't write legislative the way you can."

In all modesty, she had to admit it was true. Drafting legislation demanded a suspicious brain, precise language, a lawyer's eye for loopholes, and a comprehensive grasp of how the proposed policy solution would impact other players in the political arena, any of whom could knock the marble out of the ring.

Leverage? Maybe she had a little. "Um, I appreciate the compliment, Bankey. Really. But there's this strategy committee, and I have to try to run my own campaign in between. . . . Oh, and back to my funding. I appreciate that you're not the only one who has to sign off. And I might not be the candidate everybody wants. But, Jesus, you're senior to all those other guys. And I need your support right now."

Talmadge made a production of rolled eyes. "Squeeze my balls, why don't you? Okay. Do this for me, and I'll try to get that on the fast track. Small bills in a briefcase, that work?"

She almost laughed, then sobered; with the banking system choking, he might well be serious. "I don't care. We just need the funding."

Talmadge mumbled something, then tilted his head. "You mentioned Lincoln."

"I think *you* mentioned him, Bankey."

"Uh-huh, maybe so. But if we do get sucked into this thing in a big way . . . I just want to mention a possibility. Maybe a distant one. But I'll mention it."

"What 'distant possibility,' Bankey?"

Glancing away from her again, he said, "Remember what he said about public sentiment?"

"Who, Lincoln? Not exactly."

"He said, 'Public sentiment is everything. With public sentiment, nothing can fail; without it nothing can succeed.' If we do really go to war . . . to sustain the effort . . . we're going to need public support. Which means, victories. Or if we don't . . ."

She laid down knife and fork. Touched her lips with the napkin, frowning. "I'm not sure I understand what you're driving at, Bankey. If we don't have victories, what?"

"Just sayin' . . . remember Colin Kelly? Howard Gilmore? Guess you don't. Well, how about Corregidor then?"

"I'm still lost. In plain English?"

"All right." He was looking away again, never a good sign. "If we don't have victories, at the very least, we gotta give the folks a hero. Even better . . . a heroic sacrifice."

She was about to ask again what he meant, when the maitre d' was beside them, wringing his hands. "Yeah?" said Bankey.

"Excuse me, Senator, but in case either of you arrived via the Metro—"

"I did," said Blair.

"Well, it's closed. Some kind of accident on the Red Line."

"Accident?" another diner said, from a side table.

"Actually, a collision. Two trains, at Metro Center. Sounds bad."

Blair frowned. Related to the troops she'd seen? "A terrorist attack? So the whole Metro's—"

"Shut down. Sorry, ma'am."

"We'll get you a taxi," Talmadge rumbled.

"How about you, Bankey?"

"Oh, I'll just . . . Mindy's got an apartment over by Stanton Park. Maybe she can put me on the sofa." His eyelid twitched, as if he'd only just suppressed a wink. "Anyway, get me a Missy-draft of that resolution tomorrow. And I'll see about getting you what you need. All right? Never mind what else I said. It's all just Bankey Talmadge bloviating, right? Now, how 'bout some of that creme brûlée?"

The credit card reader was down, of course. But the maitre d' waved them off; the senator was an old customer; they'd take care of it later.

Outside, in a cold drizzle, waiting beneath the Monocle's green awning, she found herself worrying again. Wherever Dan was, she doubted he'd be able to stay out of the thick of the action. Not with *Savo* the only missile-defense-capable ship in the Pacific. Wait. No, there was one other. But that still didn't make good odds. And his fucking Naval Academy sense of duty . . . she still wasn't sure if she admired it or not.

Good God. Could that be what Talmadge had been hinting at? About 'a heroic sacrifice'? A cold edge, like steel, touched her spine. She shivered.

But some things were bigger than relationships. And, trembling in the cold rain, she could sense them on their way.

16
USS *Savo Island*

Yeah. It's coming," Cheryl Staurulakis said late the next morning. "We just have to be ready. Unfortunately, it won't be easy."

Slumped in his command chair in CIC, Dan rubbed the top of his head. Was he starting to go thin up there? Ha. The least of his fucking worries . . . His mouth tasted like stale coffee— he'd been up all night, expecting the cross-strait assault. Instead, air activity had ebbed after midnight. This morning an occasional track glowed over the mainland, but almost none over the strait, except for shore-hugging patrols a few miles off both coasts.

"What exactly are you people putting together?" he grunted, pushing back from the command table.

"Sorry, Captain?"

"Never mind, XO. Talking to myself. I mean, sort of, talking to Beijing."

Someone coughed discreetly. Dan looked up to a hovering Captain Fang. "Unfortunate news, I'm afraid," the Taiwanese murmured.

"Hit us, Chip. Is it about the interoperability training we requested?"

Fang looked unhappy. "That does not seem

possible to arrange. I suspect we are trying to catch our breath before the next development. I asked about antisubmarine training, but they tell me our subs are fully tasked. No aircraft are available either."

"Well, damn it—"

"There is worse news." The Taiwanese went on stiffly, as if delivering a memorized speech. "This morning, the Republic of China officially informed Washington it may not be possible to hold the island against a major attack. They request American air reinforcements, and American troops, under provisions of the Taiwan Relations Act and numerous presidential assurances of support."

Dan started to rub his head again, but made his hand stop. He felt like a chocolate bar left on a hot dashboard. Sagging. Melting. Had to get some sleep soon, or he'd be worthless in the crunch. "And if we don't reinforce you? What's the plan then?"

"I don't know that, sir."

Dan stroked his chin, sensing a cliff edge crumbling beneath him. Korea News said the Philippines was debating its response to the Chinese landing on Itbayat. The piece speculated that China had warned Manila not to interfere with the occupation of the island, which commanded the sea and air-space south of Taiwan. If the Filipinos acquiesced, though,

Beijing had promised that Itbayat would be returned at the close of hostilities.

But it might all be academic: Manila had no military to speak of, either to resist the occupation or to force the island's return. Meanwhile, ROC air defense showed transports shuttling between China and Itbayat, no doubt bringing in more troops, construction equipment, and heavy weapons. The reality: Taiwan had been outflanked to the south, and the allies surprised and outmaneuvered once more. He tented his fingers. "I understand, Chip. Your backs are against the wall. But what if the U.S. doesn't step up? Does your government plan to fight?"

Fang hesitated. "I possess little insight into the political realm, Captain Lenson. I personally believe we will fight. But if things get too bloody, well, it's possible the government might consider asking for terms." He smiled apologetically. "The one area where I made a little progress, I'm happy to report, is fuel."

"Oh, good." Staurulakis brushed a lank curl off her face and sagged against the Tomahawk console, every line of her body suggesting fatigue.

Fang turned to her. "Yes, ma'am. Our only true tanker is tasked with supporting our destroyer fleet. But a civilian ship will be here tomorrow. We will have to discuss how the fuel will be charged off—"

"I'm not talking billing," Dan cut in. "We're here to protect your country."

"Um, Captain, with due respect, Washington has yet to make that decision."

"Funny. Explain to me, then, why I just shot down a missile aimed at your capital."

Fang seemed about to argue, but looked away instead. He blinked up at the rightmost screen, which showed, at the moment, empty sea. *Savo* was still steaming slow racetracks in her defense-of-Taipei station. "I acknowledge your point. And we are grateful for that assistance."

"You're welcome. But is that from you, or your government?"

"Both, Captain. And we will make that plain to Washington as well."

Dan rocked back, sighing. Personally, he didn't care one way or the other about kudos for the shootdown, but it would give the crew a boost. He should get on the 1MC again, bring everyone up to date.

But first . . . "XO, a couple of days ago I asked for an emergency action plan on what we do if this, uh, Breath of the Dragon,"—He almost chuckled; it sounded like a bad mouthwash commercial. But it wouldn't be funny, face-to-face with the dragon itself. "If they actually roll across the strait in force. What we can do to help." He nodded toward Fang. "I know, but this is just me, not Washington. How 'bout it, XO?"

"Sir, that was only yesterday you asked." Cheryl dug fists into her lower back, wincing. "We . . .

to be honest, I haven't had time to look at it yet."

"Then put Amy on it. The strike officer. Mills. Win Farmer. Van Gogh, for navigational resources. Captain Fang, will you chair? It'll give our second string a chance to do some operational thinking." He glanced at his watch, and swung down. Even fifteen minutes in his bunk . . . or a shower . . . no, the bunk. "Let's make it tomorrow, right after morning chow. 0700, here in Combat. I'm crashing, Cheryl, Chip. Unless it's red hot, I'm getting my head down."

He left them staring after him.

But the chief master-at-arms was waiting at his at-sea cabin. Behind him lurked the rotund, well-draped figure of the NCIS agent, expression hostile under her flower-embroidered head covering. He sighed. The passageway tilted as *Savo* leaned. "Sheriff. Special Agent," he muttered reluctantly.

He half-reclined against the bulkhead as they brought him up to date. The reefer in sick bay broken into. The last shred of evidence destroyed. He closed his eyes and massaged his brow. "When?"

"During the night."

"It wasn't locked?"

"Doc said the outer office isn't secured during wartime steaming," Chief Toan said. "Just the back area, where he stores the controlled meds, and his records."

"So anybody at all could have busted the padlock on the reefer and destroyed the swabbings. Or whatever you call them."

Toan looked at the deck. "Essentially, yes sir."

"Okay, it's a blow, but spilt milk now, I guess. Special Agent? Anything to add?"

Ar-Rahim pursed her lips. "It's what we found with the ruined sample, Captain. Your chief corpsman assures me very few people would know hydrogen peroxide decomposes the DNA in a sperm sample. That presupposes either medical knowledge, or access to medical books or online resources."

Dan said, "Books, then? Because we've been in River City for quite a while."

"Actually, a few people still have access," she said.

"Who?" he asked, then answered the question himself. "You mean me. Correct? You mean me, Special Agent?"

She met his eye. "I didn't make that accusation, Captain."

He gripped the knob to his cabin. "Well, let me know when you need an alibi." He couldn't help making it sarcastic; he was just too fucking angry. "I'm sure between the bridge and CIC, my time has been pretty well accounted for over the last forty-eight hours. So, what now?"

Ar-Rahim cleared her throat. "With your permission, I'd like to cast a wider net."

She explained the technique. He wasn't sure he followed it all, but waved off her offer of a fuller explanation. "A questionnaire? If you think it'll help. But, please, steer clear of the Chief's Mess. Your accusations aren't helping you with them."

"I'm accusing no one, Captain. Just trying to ascertain the facts."

"Right." He pushed past them. Got the door closed, nearly on Toan's boot.

Alone at last. He sagged into the chair. His upper arms, neck, and back felt as if he'd been beaten with sticks by the entire Army lacrosse team. He eyed the bunk, but couldn't muster the energy even to get up again and roll into it.

The dread had been growing all day, since the missile attack. The battle for the Senkakus was heating up now that the Japanese had landed. He wasn't getting anything through official channels, but Aegis gave him the air picture, and he could eavesdrop on the electronic emissions.

A grim and grinding action, if limited in scope, seemed to be developing on those unpopulated islands. The Chinese had landed on the largest, Uotsuri. The Japanese had established toeholds on the smaller islets, to the southeast. Throughout the night, high-speed surface contacts had run in toward the respective lodgements from both directions. Low-level air activity had been almost continuous. Dan had no doubt there were corpses in the surf, small craft sunk or shot up as they tried to run men ashore.

A battle like that could flicker and smoke for a long time. Could kill a lot of good men, fed into the grinder a hundred at a time. But it wouldn't decide anything.

He dragged himself up at last. Threw water on his face, and made a stab at brushing his teeth. His mouth tasted like the Dumpster behind a Starbucks. He pulled off his coveralls and collapsed into the long-desired haven. Stared up at a picture of Blair taped above his face.

So the war was on. At least China, Taiwan, and Japan thought so. But where was the American response? The dagger-thrust into the "soft underbelly" of the South China Sea that Op Plan 5081 had described? Surely the Chiefs wouldn't hold *that* up for authorization by Congress. He covered his face with his hands, pleading with his brain: Stop, stop, go into sleep mode. . . . An attack in the Paracels might distract Zhang from the eastern island chain, confusing and short-circuiting his offensive.

He lay listening to the creak and sway of a ship in a seaway, both longing for and dreading the oblivion of sleep.

Which he must have achieved at some point, because when he woke someone was tapping at his door. The phosphorescent numerals of his

Seiko swam like bioluminescent dinoflagellates. Seven. He'd managed a couple hours. Unless it was 07, the next morning . . . that didn't seem possible . . . no, that was evening blue leaking around the porthole cover. But a little bag time just made you want more. "Yeah!" he yelled. A fit of coughing doubled him. "Come in," he called, when he could breathe.

The message board pulsed before his eyes. The messenger waited, hands clasped, as Dan groped for the reading glasses.

The People's Republic of China had issued an ultimatum to the "renegade province" of Taiwan. The island could either submit to "peace through unification" or be destroyed.

General Zhang Zurong was now elevated to Party general secretary and state president. The three leading titles in the state. There were rumors of executions of more leading Party members in Beijing.

The United States and China were both going to heightened nuclear-defense conditions. The Senate was debating a resolution to support Taiwan, but the voting lineup was shifting. There was a real possibility the force-authorization resolution would fail.

USS *Monocacy* had reached station south of Taiwan, to defend that end of the island. CTG 779.1, the Ryukyus Maritime Defense Coalition Task Group, was directed to coordinate air and missile defenses with CTG 779.2, the Luzon Channel Task Group, with separate orders to follow.

A U.S. fast logistics ship had been sunk in the Arabian Sea, apparently by a submarine.

"Need a pen, sir?" The messenger offered a Skilcraft.

Dan initialed the messages without answering. His brain teemed and crawled with thoughts, interpolations, apprehensions, breeding like maggots in rotten meat.

The second ABM cruiser was on station. Good, they could link data, hand off targets to each other.

But he'd tipped his hand during the single-warhead strike on Taipei. He'd wondered why only one missile had arched over from the mainland. Somehow, during the night, his unconscious had figured it out.

It had been a probe. A test of the U.S. and ROC intercept cuing and ABM capabilities. Now Beijing knew exactly where and who *Savo* was, and how she responded to an incoming missile.

Now that they had him targeted, he could expect to head the next strike list.

His consciousness clicked to the next line of code. The sunken tanker, in the western Indian Ocean. Obviously, part of the enemy's anti-access strategy, to slice off the Navy's logistical tail. But how had they known where it was, to vector a sub against it? Could the Chinese still have some over-the-horizon targeting capability?

Or—an even more chilling possibility—had they penetrated U.S. codes? Was that what the repeated cautions not to trust voice messages were about?

And Congress. Could they really be wavering on defending Taiwan? What did they think would happen to South Korea and Japan, if the keystone of the island chain fell to the enemy?

The messenger. "You all right, Captain? Look a little bit under the weather."

"Yeah. Thanks," he mumbled. Breathed hard for a couple of seconds, then handed the clipboard back. As the door closed, he reached the J-phone off the bulkhead.

CIC answered on the first squeal. *"TAO here, Captain. Lieutenant Mills."*

"Matt? How we coming on the plan to intercept an invasion? Oh, and we really need a name for that—"

"The CHENG suggested 'Dragonglass.' "

Dan felt guilty. Danenhower had been obsessing about their dwindling fuel state, but he'd forgotten to tell the engineer he didn't have to worry; the Taiwanese were sending a tanker. "Bart did? Okay. Dragonglass it is. Did you see these latest messages? The invasion may be starting. When can I get a brief?" Too late, he recalled they'd already set a time. But based on

315

the news . . . "I, uh, know I said tomorrow. But we're getting overtaken by events. Even if all you have's a concept—"

Mills sounded resigned. *"Yessir. Haven't got much. But we can brief what we have. In CIC? In an hour?"*

"That'll work. Uh, ring me back when everyone's assembled."

He sank back and closed his eyes. But even as his mind rotated and vibrated, his lids drifted closed again.

Sprawled in his bunk, alone, the captain snored, writhing uneasily from time to time. Until, once more, the J-phone chirped.

17

The South China Sea

Sixty feet below the surface, in darkness, rebreathing his own exhaled air, Master Chief Teddy Oberg was focused on the faint lime illumination of his instruments. A compass. A charge indicator, dropping faster than he liked. A tachometer. And a depth gauge. The grips of the underwater scooter vibrated in his fists, dragging his gear- and weapon-burdened carcass through the water. The shrouded prop drummed in his ears.

Two miles to the beach.

The sea was icy. Some bitter current, snaking beneath the warmer surface. Ominously, even down here he could feel the sucking as waves passed overhead. Heavier than Fleet Weather had predicted. The shallowing gradient had stopped *Montpelier* miles short of the planned launch point. Her skipper had refused to close farther. They were at the outer limit of the scooters' ranges, with barely enough battery power to get there and back.

Lieutenant Harch's scooter was an occasional dim green flash to his right. The flank guards were V'd to left and right, invisible in the night sea, but now and then a single flashlight-flicker signaled they were still there. They weren't in the plan, but Teddy had argued the lieutenant into them. If word of the raid had leaked, they could be whirring into an ambush.

He drew breath after breath. Slow. Easy. Breath control was mind control. The rest of Echo trailed them, two abreast.

This was R-day. If every Team guy around him was alive at the end of it, it'd be a miracle. They were facing over a thousand troops, and seven hundred were elite marines. The 164th Brigade were armed with light tanks and heavy weapons, and the Chinese had had years to plant beach obstacles, mines, sensor networks. Echo Platoon's best defense was stealth. Get ashore, execute, and retreat. Like Harch had said, a good mission didn't make a ripple.

But he had a bad feeling about this one. To forestall detection via acoustic sensors, Harch wanted them to swim the last mile. This heavily burdened, towing the Packages, they'd be exhausted when they hit the beach. Then there'd be a long crawl-and-drag inland, to the vicinity of the treatment plant.

Still, it could work, he told himself. Actually, Obie, it's your job to make it work. So turn that frown upside down. He twisted and caught a flash off to starboard. Moogie, leading Two.

Minutes later, the *chuk-chuk-chuk* of Harch's scooter slowed. Teddy twisted his own throttle and the drag of the sea lessened. He sank, checking watch and depth gauge. Yeah, a mile off the coast. Something brushed the tips of his fins. He twisted the throttle grip back more, and his machine settled.

Into coarse grainy sand. Excellent; he hated mud. Coated you all over and stank. But sometimes you had to make love to it, like they probably would in the marshy areas past the dunes. Around him, like settling bats, the other scooters dropped from the dark. He groped in his pack for a pinger. Harch would be setting one too, but SEAL wisdom was "Two is one, one is none." They wouldn't want to be hunting around for these things once the clock was ticking on the Packages.

The Packages. One primed to look like a failure. The other, a Trojan horse burrowing into the enemy's communications. If it worked, yeah, this was the kind of thing that could determine the course of a war.

Harch's light, up and down; the guide-on-me signal. Though actually he'd told Teddy to swim point. Teddy's legs felt creaky. Pain ignited in his calf as he pushed off the sand and forced his fins into motion. Shit, at BUD/S a mile swim had been nothing. But that'd been fifteen years ago. . . .

Maybe it was time to think about easing off. Make this the last mission. Once you were past it for direct action, there were still places for you on the Teams. Training. Intel. The Pool, for shore duty.

But did he really want to be the Old Man, the has-been, the ghost?

He pumped along, settling into the rhythm. Watching the fat glowing needle of the wrist compass, keeping up twenty beats a minute with his fins. Fifteen more minutes to the beach. But his ears kept popping. The turbulence sucked his whole body up and down. Which meant heavy surf topside. Good; a lot harder to see a swimmer. But he'd better slow as they came in . . . check the flank guards, make sure there were no surprises. Hitting the beach, that awkward transition from sea creature to land soldier, was when they were at their most vulnerable. He and Knobby would go first. Then the command element, Lieutenant Harch and his radioman, "Snake Eyes" Jamison. Once ashore, they'd signal the rest, who would emerge, dripping, to shed gear for the push inland.

Dragging the mass and weight of the Packages behind them.

His head broke water. Fins pumping, he spat out his mouthpiece and sucked sweet air. Then bobbed there, carbine in one hand, peering shoreward for any activity. Fires. Lights.

Nothing yet . . . Next, he considered the way the seas were battering him around. A *lot* bigger than Weather had predicted. You could sort of bodysurf, but they were eight, nine feet out here, and judging by the glimmer of foam at the surf line, they were gonna get knocked around no matter how they went in. He ducked his head again and got right down on the sand, made about fifty yards in, until his knees hit, and resurfaced. Tucking his fins under him, he reached down and shucked them.

Not soon enough. The wave knocked him off his feet. He rolled over and over, facemask grinding into the coarse sand. His rebreather whacked him in the back of the head. His M4 got away. He was a black blob in somebody's gunsights, rolling over and over in the white of the breaking surf . . . He fought vertical, got his booties rooted in the wet, giving sand this time. Hauled in on the tether line, and got his weapon back. With the butt to his shoulder, he took another five crouched wading strides up the beach, till the retreating waves splashed ankle-deep. Then dropped to a knee, to minimize his silhouette. Swept the muzzle right, then left.

No moon. But the stars shed enough light to see. The beach stretched east and west, with a peninsula off to his left. He flipped down the NVGs and powered them up, making sure the Illumination button was off. In their green, distorted radiance, the shore was still empty. If the wind had been more easterly, that peninsula might have given them some shelter. As it was, they'd just have to suck it up.

A pop and hiss beside him, almost lost in the crash of the surf. Swager. They didn't speak; Team One just pointed. Teddy nodded and bent into the water's resistance, slogging forward. Another wave knocked him to his knees again, shooting agony through the bad leg, but he got up once more and slogged on, sweeping the shoreline with the muzzle of his Colt. If anybody was here, he wanted them to fire now, not when the rest of the Team was coming out of the surf.

But no one did. His booties crunched on dry sand at last and he sank to a knee, wheezing and panting. Fighting surf took a lot out of you. He checked his watch again. Pretty much on time so far, though. In fact, shit, *right* on time. 0135.

Cue the fireworks . . . and when he lifted his head there was the first white flash of high explosive. A couple miles away, on the far side of the island, so he didn't hear anything yet, though a second or two later orange flame pushed up, laced with black. Ack-ack started flying up, tracers probing the dark like incandescent catheters.

Beside him Swager dropped, sucking air. Good, it wasn't just Teddy. The crack-BOOM reached them then, quaking the air like a lightning bolt, and built to a rumbling series of thunderclaps. The Tomahawks would land first, hitting radars and missile batteries. Following them would come the standoff munitions, from the carrier air, and Stealths out of Diego Garcia. A huge fireball climbed like the rising sun. The shock wave rippled through the scrub and slapped their faces, even this far away. Birds pierced the night air with startled cries, rising, flapping away out to sea. Teddy drooled out grit, and spat. "Must of whacked the fuel piers with that one," Swager muttered. "Got some bad news."

"Hit me."

"Lost one of the weapons cases. We're down one pig."

The "pig" was the M240. They'd gone in gun-heavy, with three heavy machine guns for Echo One, on the causeway, and two with Two. They still had their personal weapons, but nothing equaled the pig for keeping an enemy many yards from your ass. "Christ. What happened?"

"Tether broke. We searched, but it's fuckin' gone."

"Fuck. What else we lose?"

"Masks, sidearms, couple primary weapons . . . Some of the guys got beat up coming in."

"Anybody hurt bad? Where's Doc?"

"Right here," said a form tumbling into the pit with them. Anderson. "Scrapes and bruises."

He hadn't expected to lose an MG. Not yet in contact, and their suppressive fire was down. Well, they'd just have to stay covert. Which was the idea, after all. Teddy spat more grit, lifted an arm, and signaled the advance.

He and Swager, opening to five yards in case of mines, jogged heavily up the beach. He kept looking for wire, obstacles, some sign of observation, but made out only some kind of vertical posts, a good distance away. Hard to tell, but they might just be fish weirs. He couldn't believe the Chinese would leave the beach undefended. Not with a major signals intelligence station here. The imagery had shown a curving line where the scrub started. Intel had interpreted this as a seawall—

Four troops, in dark clothing, in a scalloped concrete trench about two meters deep, with a fire step facing the beach and netting over them. Which was why the overhead hadn't shown it. Fortunately, they were looking toward the fading fireballs, not in his direction, and a shape that bulked like a heavy machine gun had a tarp over it. He and Swager double-tapped them, putting two in their backs before they realized they were being shot. The last one standing tried to draw a sidearm, but Harch, behind Teddy, nailed him, the silenced report only a pop, lost in the din from the south. Teddy jumped heavily down, cursing as he stumbled, and went through the trench looking for comms. Found a radio, and put a bullet through it.

He scrambled up out of the reverse slope and

oriented inland. Harch was crouched, pointing an infrared beam out to sea for the rest of the team to guide in on. With a clear path inland, no point risking mines along the rest of the beach. "Cache the gear here. Make this the first rally point," the lieutenant muttered. "Get your war paint on, we're in Indian country now." Teddy passed it on, reminding Knobby to post guys to guard their rebreathers and other wet gear. If they hit resistance, had to split up, they'd circle back and meet again here. As he smeared on camo paint, Jamison was muttering into the squirt radio in muted tones. Teddy laid a hand on his shoulder. "Keep it short, Snake Eyes," he breathed into his ear.

"Wasn't actually transmitting, Master Chief."

"Don't. Remember, this whole fucking island is a listening site. They could catch a sidelobe, or something."

All right, orient. The map in his head: A coast road somewhere to their right. Probably just over that dune. Yeah, a prickle against the sky in his goggles: poles, a power line. Stay clear of that. Another road to the left, crossing the smaller island, heading for the causeway south. Steer away from that, too, though they might have to close it, farther on, to get to the island's high point. The wavy line that was probably the seawall: to their left.

"Obie? Mast' Chief?"

325

It was his radioman-grenadier. "Loopy" Wasiakowsky carried a PRC-117 manpack intersquad radio. It could back up the heavier radio Jamison carried, but he reminded Wasiakowsky, too, not to transmit if he could help it. Teddy started to whisper, Stay with me and the lieutenant, then didn't. Loopy knew what to do.

A dune hillocked behind the trench. Usually you wanted to lay up awhile after insertion, make sure everything was quiet, but now that they'd had to take down the OP, they couldn't waste time. A relief could be on its way. He passed that to his squad leaders and scrambled up the hill, booties sliding in the sand. At the top he dropped to his belly, staying beneath the salt scrub. Trees loomed dark ahead. Cover, but a couple hundred yards to get to it. He slid down into a hollow. Then up again. The rumble of ordnance ahead was fading. Tracers were still arching, fired blind, but the next troops they ran into might not be ogling them.

Fifty yards on he took a knee again atop another sand hill, wheezing and sweating, screened by prickly, brittle brush, and waited for the guys hauling the first Package to catch up. He'd picked the huskiest, Moonie and Butt Plug, but even they were puffing as they sledged the burden up and braked it down the hills, which grew steeper as they pushed inland. A little overhead cover now, a little tree action. Which was good, though it would also screen them from the drone. The crackling and snapping as they yanked their load through the bushes seemed to be getting louder as the detonations died down, though.

He shot a line with the compass, then realized they could steer by the Dipper. It glittered above them. He muttered as the racket approached. "A little to the left. And fucking keep it down! I can hear you twenty yards away."

No answer. He checked his watch. Ten minutes to get to the target hill. Basically, he could leave the first Package, the dud bomb or whatever it was, atop any of the dunes. But the O-10 had to be buried, carefully camouflaged, on the west slope of the highest dune he could find. Only there, Harch had said, would it be able to pick up signals from the west, where the major listening post was.

He was scrambling up the next dune when somebody stumbled behind him and slammed into his back. He started to resist, then went down with him as he caught it too.

The *whack-whack* of blades. Did the Chinese have gunships? No one had briefed gunships.

The helo burst up with all its lights on, blinding beams backlighting every bush with shafts of probing glare that haloed every branch and leaf. He tucked his rifle under him and buried his face. Froze as all around scrub, hills, the glittery quartz facets of the sand in front of his eyes, lit with the brilliance of a noonday sun. The chopper hurtled over so low the rotorwash whipped the bushes back and forth, kicking up a tornado of loose leaves and sand. For a second he thought it was going to land. But it passed over, very low, and the lights receded. He couldn't make out the type, or whether it was a gunship or just a recon bird.

He breathed out. And was beginning to rise when the distant *whack-whack* wheeled and came back.

This time it passed over higher, maybe two hundred feet, and faster, turbines whining. At the same moment other engines, diesels, growled to the south.

Then, the chatter of automatic fire.

Harch, above him. "Y'okay, Master Chief?"

Surely the idiot hadn't been on his feet when the chopper had gone over? The lieutenant stood taller than any bush. Even motionless, he'd cast a long shadow. But here he was, still talking, grabbing Teddy's arm as if to yank him to his feet. . . . He shook him off as the lieutenant muttered, "That's some kind of reaction force hitting Team Two. Hear that? That's an M240. And that—" A deeper, slower *tap-tap-tap* that seemed to echo in a way the lighter fire didn't.

"A DshK," Teddy supplied.

"Probably light armor. And troops on trucks.

Get 'em moving, Master Chief. Another hundred meters, and let's lay that egg."

Teddy didn't like armor. Not since a BMP had busted through the wall of a mud house at a Taliban ops center north of Kandahar. They'd almost got wiped out before catching a lucky break: the driver had never qualified on the main gun. They'd finally got a Spectre gunship to lay a round on it. The high-explosive 155 had split the night open like one of Jove's thunderbolts.

Carlson's Raiders had had the submarines, with six-inch guns. Harch didn't have six-inch guns, or Air Force gunships, on call. And Moogie only had seven guys out on the causeway. They'd probably blown it by now, although the noise and flashes of the air strike made it impossible to be sure. They had mines and light antitank weapons.

But if the Chinese got through them, with light armor and seven hundred marines, Echo was gonna be the filling in the biggest shit sandwich in SEAL history. He craned around for Wasiakowsky, Jamison, Harch, but didn't see them. He lifted his voice. "Suck it up, SEALs." Labored forward, and seized the line. Put his weight on it. Halfway up the hill he glimpsed Harch again, huddled with the radioman down in defilade.

As they hit the top, incoming started. Green tracers, from their right. Sounded like 5.8s. Not close, but aimed in their direction. He could still hear motors from the causeway, but Harch would have told him if Moogie had reported a breakthrough. Bent double, he put all his strength into getting the burden through a clump of scrub.

Okay, far enough. This was a vantage spot: he could see almost back to the beach. He dropped to a knee and signaled for a perimeter. Shadows settled into defensive positions. "Designate Rally Two. Down in this hollow. Bury the fucker here," he croaked, and the others dropped the tow lines and unsheathed entrenching tools.

Package One was going in, but the instructions for the O-10 had been more exacting. The three-foot discoid, weighing 310 pounds, had to be at least a hundred yards from the EMP device. Even if it only partially exploded, the pulse would fry it any closer than that. Package Two had to be buried on the western slope of the highest dune, no less than two feet and no more than four feet deep. Level, with the indentation on the side aimed due west. It also had a photosensitive booby trap. After five hours, if light hit it, a shaped charge would destroy it, and probably also the poor bastards digging it out. Finally, of course, all signs that anything had been buried there had to be erased.

But where was its team? They'd been behind One back at the beach. He almost pressed Transmit on his bone phone, but didn't. So far, no one knew Echo Two was here.

Shadows, slipping and cursing. Swager's voice. "Obie? Master Chief?"

They bumped heads. Knobby muttered, "We got hung up. Had to chop down a couple of bushes to get through."

That wasn't good. "The bushes—"

"We buried 'em. Smoothed the sand. Jockstrap's making sure we're not leaving any traces."

Teddy nodded. They both shot bearings, and came up with a hillock fifty yards away. He did the math to make sure that would be at least a hundred yards from the first burial, and came up safe. He looked up into the dark sky. There was supposed to be a drone up there, observing. But who? The CIA? The Navy? Air Force? He coughed, muffling it with a fist. "Okay, see that hill out at two six zero? Move out."

Swager passed it on in a whisper. Obie looked around for Harch, then remembered: he hadn't seen him since down in the hollow. He stood, slowly, and peered south. Fires still flickered, but the rattle of small arms had ebbed. Not a good sign. "I can give One a call," Wasiakowsky muttered, hunkered beside him.

"No comms."

"Then why'd we bring the fucking 117, Master Chief?"

"Receive only, Loopy. And cut the crap." Teddy rotated again, slowly, with the night-vision goggles on. Where the fuck was Harch? He dropped and slithered down the dune, following Knobby's guys.

When he got to the dune they were digging like mad. He could see why: the dune stood right on a small east-west road whose empty concrete shone in the starlight. The poles he'd seen earlier marched along the shoulder. Windows glowed on the far side, a couple hundred meters away. A generator throbbed. The air strike must have taken out the power station. And was that a fence? Too far away to see. Even as he watched, shouts bounced across the sand. "They're deploying," he murmured to Knobby.

Swager was knee-deep in the hole. Each SEAL stepped in, shoveled furiously for sixty seconds, then broke off, to be relieved by the next. A tarp lay to one side. When you built a hide site, you kept the topsoil separate from the stuff lower down. You spread it on top again when you were done. Teddy stepped in and took a turn. Then lay on his belly catching his breath, listening to the shouting. Chinese. It was clear what was happening. A line, a perimeter, anchored on the road. After they got set up, they'd sweep out from it. Which made his position dangerously exposed. On the other hand, if the idea was to orient the eavesdropping device toward the installation, he could hardly do better. The CIA would have a direct line of sight from here. "How deep?" he grunted.

"Three feet," someone said, not Swager.

"Deep enough. Get it in the fucking hole. Make sure that nipple's pointed west. Knobby, soon as you get it dug in, pull your guys over the crest. Run a gear check, make sure we're not leaving anything." He chanced another brief stand-up, cranking his height up centimeter by centimeter, so as not to present a sudden motion to anyone watching through a riflescope. Where the fuck was the lieutenant? They'd drilled this, and so far it was going reasonably according to plan, but it would be nice to have leadership in sight.

A whisper came up, but he didn't catch it. "Say again?"

"R-T says they got through Echo One. A hundred effectives, on foot over the causeway. Echo One, four wounded, one KIA. Starbursting and rallying on you."

That changed things. "Got it. Knobby, take the rest of your guys. Spread out along this dune line and get ready to suppress these hostiles on the other side. One's headed back to us, probably down the main road."

Swager shook his head. "They wouldn't take the main street, Obie."

"If Moogie's still in charge, he'll take speed over concealment. Trust me, they're gonna hammer down that north-south road. Put the 240 on the left."

He rolled over and checked on the burial party.

The last guy was finishing up, hand-sprinkling the top sand over the disturbed area, then bending to whisk out any remaining bootprints with a branch. He rolled back and checked his weapon, made sure his magazines were loose in the pouch, and focused on the far side of the road. The first responders would be base security. Drilled to set up a perimeter and hold it against an assault. The bushes rustled and crackled as the team took overwatch. Teddy backed up, making sure to smooth the sand as he retreated, then low-crawled up the road, staying behind the dune.

A hundred yards on, he scrambled down to the pavement and dropped flat in the drainage ditch, looking south. Chance it? The MX-300s were scrambled, but the enemy could still pick up the location of a transmission. He decided, and hit the bone mike. "Moogie, you there?"

No answer. He tried once more, then let it alone. Stared into the dark, hoping he wasn't screwing up. If Two was working back through the dunes, it would take them an hour to reach him. And he didn't have an hour. They'd get pinched from two sides, with the sea at their backs. Worst case, the marines were loading into boats, to hit them from seaward as well. Then they'd really be in the shit. Time to wrap this up! He tried the MX again. No answer. He clicked the NVGs on, staring down the road.

Was that motion? A glint? A shadow?

Men running, doubled over, on both sides of the pavement, half hidden by the ditches?

And if it was . . . was it Moogie's guys, or Chinese? He laid his sights on the lead shape's chest.

Until the man halted, then dropped. His MX hissed. *"Team Two, Team One."*

"This is Obie. Moog?"

"That you up ahead? In the ditch?"

"Giving you an IR flash . . . now." He hit the button, got a double flash back. "Guide in on me, but keep to your right. Hostiles on the other side."

At that moment, at least three automatic weapons opened up from the woods on the far side, from the direction of the windows. Tracers. Most too high, over their heads, but some digging into the dunes. Didn't sound like either AKs or M4s, the report was sort of in between in timbre, but whoever was blasting away, it was spray 'n' pray time. A lone sniper with an IR scope would've been more dangerous, but a random bullet could kill you just as dead. Teddy lined up and fired out a magazine in single shot, putting each round as close to the muzzle flashes as he could. The weapon quit firing, but he couldn't tell if he'd hit anything or it was just a mag-change-and-shift.

A blundering shadow. Moogie, whooping air and stumbling under the weight of another

335

man. They dropped alongside him as the SEALs opened up. "Get your dudes over the dune," Teddy told him. "How many?"

"Five. Two WIA."

"Who'd you lose? Never mind, let's get you into cover." He grabbed one of the wounded guy's arms, and slipping and sliding they climbed the dune, bullets popping into the sand around them. The roar of counterfire from Echo Two was nearly continuous; under it the fire from across the road slackened, especially when several rifle grenades went off over there. He got to the top, and they handed the wounded guy down to the radiomen. "Anybody see the L-T?" Teddy asked them. They shook their heads.

Okay, well. Forget running covert. He keyed his MX. "Echo, this is Oberg. You on the net, sir?"

"This is Echo actual. Where the hell'd you go, Obie?"

"We got separated, I guess. On the road now. Where you hear the fire. Where are you?"

"Rally Two. Over."

"Echo One just came in. Three effectives, two wounded, one unaccounted for."

"We don't leave men behind, Obie."

Moogie came up on the net. *"We had to star-burst, sir. They were pincering around behind us, over the reef. Hundreds of 'em. I got one guy down hard. JC. The other's either still on his way, or the Chinese've got him. That's Sapperdoo."*

"SEALs don't leave SEALs, Kaster."

Kaster was Moogie's last name. Teddy wanted to say, SEALs don't use real names in radio comms, either, but didn't. "Sir, we've gotta leapfrog back to Rally One and get off this island. Or we're all gonna get encircled and either captured or wiped out." Even at their best, a platoon wasn't up to a lengthy engagement. SEALs had a saying, "The fight doesn't start until you're wounded," but one by one, they'd be cut down, till they were overrun. "Sir, you got comms with Higher? We can probably hold off these local guys, but if those marines get across in force . . . Can they call in a strike on the causeway, something to keep 'em occupied while we extract?"

Silence. Then, *"I'm trying to get through. Rally on me, Master Chief."*

The words sounded right, but Teddy didn't like the tone. Or that he'd apparently had to remind the L-T they had Higher on the line. Fuck, they could argue later. He hit the intrasquad again. "Knobby, Moogie's guys are coming back. Moogie, guide on Two. All hands: Fall back to Rally Two."

Retracting off a hot beach was about the sketchiest maneuver imaginable. SEALs did contact drills, retreats under fire, until no one had to think what to do. Each squad split into two

337

fire teams. Constantly looking for safe escape routes, they leapfrogged back, each putting out horrendous volumes of fire as the other gave ground. The Teams had developed the tactic in the jungles of Vietnam.

Unfortunately, there wasn't as much conceal-ment here on the dunes as there was in a tropical environment, and one of those fire teams was now without its pig. His job, aside from helping Harch coordinate, was to make sure nobody got left behind. He popped his head up, to see muzzle flashes closer in. Whoever was out there, they were working their way forward. "Okay, move."

Their single 240 would be the key. He slid in beside it. The gunner was taking it slow, working one set of muzzle flashes at a time. Like stamping out a grass fire. A burst was supposed to last only three or four seconds. Long enough to mutter, "Die, asshole, just fucking die." The assistant gunner, an arm's reach to the side, was shooting too, and the riflemen were laying down grenades. Behind them shadows loped over the dunes, running and dropping, staying low.

The first shot from the other team cracked over their heads. The gunner jerked the bipod out of the sand. Teddy grabbed the ammo box and followed them down, then uphill, then down again. His goddamned leg was really hurting now, but he didn't have time to favor it.

They set up and started hosing again. But this time, the muzzle flashes were from atop the dune they'd just left. Not good. Whoever was out there was on their heels. Firing and moving, too, almost in step with them, rushing hard as the SEALs pulled back. Teddy fired out two more magazines. "Get the ammo off the wounded," he put out over the MX. "We're gonna run dry if they keep pushing like this. Echo? Echo on the line?"

"Echo actual."

"We're falling back on you, L-T. We're gonna—"

His mouth was still open when the lights came on. White hot, brighter than a thousand suns, they rose from above the dune behind them. Accompanied by the *whock* of blades, and followed by a ripping fire that blew off the top of the hillock in a million stinging splinters of sand and lead.

The gunner bucked and fell over onto him. The corpse shuddered as more bullets plowed into it. Explosions quaked the dune as if it were made out of Jell-O. Teddy moled into the sand, fingernails snapping off, digging his face in. *Miniguns*, someone back in his brain said. *Rockets. You saw the Taliban getting worked over. Now it's your turn.* But there didn't seem to be anyone listening, just a terrified reptilian body digging for a safety that didn't exist.

The firing stopped, leaving his ears ringing. The black massive fuselage of the gunship helicopter moved over him, blasting down the brush and trees with its rotorwash. He could have reached up and grabbed its skids. He dug for his rifle, but couldn't find it. He pulled his SIG and pumped round after round after the pterodactyl shadow, knowing the full metal jackets would just bounce off the bottom armor of a battle copter. The miniguns blazed again, a white-hot stream of incandescence searching here and there in the dunes. A second pod of rockets blazed, and the blasts rocked the air.

Teddy heaved the gunner off his back and checked him. Not much he could do; the guy was bleeding out from four or five heavy-caliber wounds. The pig was wreckage. A "hurrah!" from behind jerked him around.

When he turned, they were running down the slope of the dune, running and firing from the hip. His fingers found his rifle at last and he turned the IR illumination on and took down one after the other, rapid fire, prone, just like at the 300 yard line at Camp Perry. Only at Perry he wasn't deafened and seeing double from concussion, and the targets weren't dropping and firing back, at his flashes, the way he was at theirs.

Some time later, he must have blanked out there, because he was down behind a different dune, not the one that had been rocketed, and somebody was helping him drag a body. They were making heavy weather of it, and bullets kept cracking into the sand and spraying grit. A conviction of disaster rode his shoulders, though he somehow couldn't quite recover what was going on or where they were. Still, he knew they had to press on. Something dangerous was on their tails. Echo Two, second fire team—it was coming back now, and he waggled his head and more rushed back, all at once—was laying down cover as they dragged the limp weight toward a clump of trees. But there was light back there, too, too much of it, as if the beach was on fire. Someone was yelling at him. *"Master Chief. Master Chief! You copying me? Answer up!"* He looked around blankly, then remembered: the bone phone. "Here."

"Where are you? Wait. I got you in sight. We're back at the rally. The emplacement. See my strobe? Guide in on me."

A strobe. An IR strobe . . . He shouted, "Turn it off, L-T. Turn it the fuck off!"

"Marking our position, Master Chief. Guided munitions coming in. Don't want to land them on us."

A distant growl. The *whock-whock* of blades, behind them. The realization they'd just blown it, blown it all. Harch had fought in Afghanistan. In Iraq. But the hajjis didn't have IR imaging.

341

Teddy screamed, "Turn it off, Harch! Gunships incoming!"

He dropped to a knee, racked and tapped, and lifted his weapon. The thousand suns rose again. Two helos lifted over the dune, coming directly at him. Even in the dark he could make out the pilots' faces behind the windshields, their eyes masked by some sort of point-and-shoot headset. The muzzles of the miniguns, like red flashing eyes. The last thing so many insurgents, Taliban, al-Qaeda, ISIS fighters, must have seen.

Above him, fire from the sky . . .

The helicopters disintegrated before his eyes. Torn apart from inside by massive detonations that turned them into flaming fireballs out of which subassemblies fell in slow motion, still-spinning rotors, tailplanes, gun pods, masses of exploding ordnance in firework cascades that bounced and burned across the dunes.

He cowered, shielding his face. *"Hellfires, from the drone,"* Harch said in his ear. *"Get back here, Master Chief. That won't hold 'em for long."*

When he half fell, half crawled into the emplacement, it was burning. The last helo pass had turned the north end of the island into an inferno. Napalm and rockets. The gunships were off the board, but the infantry, marines, were still pressing hard. They'd stayed too long, that was all, and the response had been faster than expected. What was left of the platoon lay flat or crouched in the emplacements, pulling on gear. Their single remaining 240 was firing without pause. Time to ruin the barrel; they weren't going to be able to extract it anyway. You could always buy more gear.

A stocky silhouette in the firelight. Harch beckoned him over. "Master Chief. This is a clusterfuck. RHIBs are offshore, coming in to extract. Where've you been? Need a muster, fast. Who's missing. Where they were last seen."

Teddy looked around for his squad leaders. Knobby and Moogie were both hauling wounded. Moogie had reported one MIA, back at the causeway. All they could do was hope he was dead. Anyway, even if he was captured, he wouldn't know about the O-10. Only he and Harch knew that.

The lieutenant accepted Teddy's verbal summary with grimly set lips. "All right, retract," he snapped. "Into the water. One goes first. Echo Two, hold the perimeter. Than FT one covers when two withdraws. Hoo-ah?"

"Hoo-ah," Teddy muttered. He passed that on, and dragged himself to where he'd left his wet gear. The dirt had fallen in, or been blown in, and he started digging, with bare hands.

The Chinese came down a gully between the dunes in a scrambling sliding charge that carried them into the midst of the SEALs before either side could react. Not just in contact, but face-to-face. A point squad, led by some glory-hungry hard charger. They hit the trench and split up, half to his end, half to the other, firing and moving. He had to admit, they were good. His SIG was in his hand. Shooter House time. He fired and moved, using what little cover the trench offered. Fired the mag out and changed it, looking over the weapon at two Chinese with rifles at close range. One had the sights on him, but seemed hesitant. He knew that feeling. First time in combat, he'd been the same. He shot the boy twice in the face, wheeled, pumped two more into the other. Head shots, since they were wearing Russian-style body armor. Which left only one more at his end of the trench. The guy kept coming, though, over his buddies' bodies. Teddy pulled the trigger, but the chamber was empty. The Chinese pulled his too.

Click.

They stood face-to-face, both with empty magazines.

The Chinese, younger than Teddy, but not much smaller, went for a knife. A quarter of a second slower, Obie went for his thin-blade. They circled, feinting, feet getting tangled in loose dirt and gear and dropped weapons at the bottom of the trench. The thin-blade wasn't steel, it was some kind of ceramic that never got dull and never broke. He'd put in a lot of hours with it, now and then for real.

But he wasn't as young now. On the other hand, the other guy's OMON vest, though decent—aramid fiber, with steel plates—was cut out under the armpits, to allow free movement. A right-hand uppercut would put the blade right in the heart.

Before he could, the Chinese lunged. Teddy blocked, knocking the blade down and backing a step. On his bad leg, which almost buckled. Fuck! Something moved at the corner of his vision, but he didn't dare take his eyes off his opponent's boots. The feet signaled the next move. The trick was, react faster than the other could change his footing. But the guy was watching *his* feet, too. Uppercut, uppercut, wait till he sets himself for his attack, *now*—

A flash, a bang, and the side of the marine's head flew off. His eyes locked on Teddy's for a fraction of a second. Then he buckled like a falling building. Teddy started to step over him, then stopped himself and climbed partway up the collapsed side of the trench to get around him. He blew out and sheathed his knife. "Thanks, Knobby."

"What swim buddies are for, asshole."

The firing grew to a crescendo as the remaining SEALs, spread out along the dune line, fired full auto to cover the withdrawal into the surf. Teddy picked up an M4 and joined in. The trouble was, the fire coming back was at least as intense, and growing. The whole dune line around them was one undulating line of muzzle flashes, along with the deeper bark of crew-served weapons. How had they gotten heavy MGs over the dunes? This was where they could have used a sniper weapon. Put a Barrett or a .300 Winchester Magnum out there and take the crews out one by one. But there wasn't enough cover, really, for a sniper.

A hand on his shoulder: Harch, kneeling beside him. "Time to boogie, Obie."

"You first, Lieutenant."

"No, Master Chief. After you." Harch waved an exaggerated invitation, like a drunken maitre d' ushering him toward a table. For the first time, Teddy noticed the field dressing under his arm.

"Sir, I'm gonna bring up the rear. Like we briefed. You're wounded. Uh, where's the radio?"

Harch pointed inland. "Up there, with an IM in it. First guy lifts it, gets a surprise."

Booby traps were another Team specialty. His regard for Harch clicked up a notch. He'd dropped out of sight during the cross-country, but apparently to coordinate the drone strike. Which had saved their bones, all right. "You go ahead, sir."

White teeth in a grin. "Let's go together, Master Chief."

They turned as one, fired out their magazines, and rolled over the lip of the trench.

Oberg froze, crouched low. A shape, out in the dark.

A boat.

Only they didn't have any boats. Not like that. With the goggles down, he made out a profile. A patrol craft. Fifty, sixty feet long. Cruising down the beach. With some kind of gun on the stern. Automatic grenade launcher, probably. Enough firepower to saturate a beach, cut down anyone trying to make it into the surf. A starburst of brilliant green burst out. It swung like a lighthouse beam, then steadied. They were illuminating Echo with IR, as they tried to extract.

He turned, and stumbled over Harch. "See it?" the lieutenant breathed.

"Hoo-ah."

"Gonna cut us to pieces. Pin us on the beach and chum us up."

They were unslinging their rifles—you didn't make much of an impression on a patrol craft with a 5.56 round, but it would at least warn the others—when Teddy thought of something better. He grabbed Harch. "Fuck, that's my goddamned shoulder," the lieutenant grunted.

"Ever crew on a Dash-K?"

A hesitation, then: "Yeah, in Iraq. Good idea, Obie."

It took only seconds to kick the dirt off the heavy machine gun. Teddy got under it and nearly cried out at the boiling bolt of pain in his leg. Something was tearing loose. But he got the piece hauled back up, pointing to seaward. They stamped the tripod legs into the sand. The lieutenant snapped open the lid on the feed tray and blew out the dirt. Latches clacked on an ammo box, and he hefted a belt of cartridges, each big as a Coney Island hot dog.

The Chinese Type 54 was a modified DashK. The upper feed was the same, and it fired the same round—a 12.7mm, roughly a U.S. .50 caliber. Fuzzy as his head was getting, Teddy's memory of the weapon was clear; he'd used these in Afghanistan. They fed from the left. Open bolt. Full auto only. Charging handle on the right. He nestled into the shoulder brace and found the sight. Harch snapped down the feed tray and clapped him on the back. Teddy racked the charger and let it fly forward. He thumbed the dual triggers—Jesus, that was a heavy pull—but got only a click.

"Crap in the chamber," Harch said, but Teddy was already jerking the handle all the way back. Something heavy flew down and thudded into the dirt. Harch whacked the belt feed lid hard and Teddy let the charger go. He bent into the brace again, acquired, estimated range, corrected for wind, elevated for drop, and mashed the dual triggers, hard.

The muzzle flash was huge, blasting sand up in front of the muzzle. He fired two-second bursts, with Harch slamming the feed module open and closed whenever the belt hung up. The night lit. Bright green tracers hung like flares, then plunged over and past the boat. He aimed lower. Another burst. The MG jammed, and Harch cleared it once more. Teddy worked the charger and fired again.

The patrol boat seemed to hesitate. Then it shortened. A roostertail spurted up. She was coming around, putting her stern to the beach. Teddy elevated and fired a long burst, four seconds, ten rounds a second, until the belt ran out, holding the crosshairs above the boat as it retreated. It felt good, felt right on. He was hitting it, all right.

"Nice shooting, Master Chief," Harch said. Then a shot cracked and he fell silent, slumping over the feed tray.

Teddy had time to half turn as the Chinese surged down the dune behind them. Something punched him, hard. He tried to swing the gun around but it wouldn't go. He went for his SIG but something punched again, even harder, and he couldn't see who it was. Then the darkness came up, cold as the sea.

18
USS *Savo Island*

A isha stood by the rail as the sea rushed past. The warm wind tore at her head scarf and flapped the legs of her cargo pants. The waves were almost black. It was a long way down. She hugged herself as the mustering petty officer went down his clipboard, matching each name against the grease-penciled placard on the bulkhead.

"Okay, all present and accounted for who's already signed up. So who's not? Who here's not on the watch, quarter, and station bill?"

She raised her hand, and so did the scientist. "Okay, names?"

"Aisha Ar-Rahim."

"William Noblos."

The mustering officer penciled them in. "You shoulda been on here long before this, Doc."

"I thought I was. I mustered here before." Past the petty officer, he winked at Aisha. Sharing the joke.

"Then Gussy didn't log you in. He's the mustering PO when I can't make it." The petty officer raised his voice into the wind, looking around at the gaggle of bodies on the starboard side, frame fifty-five abandon-ship station. "Okay, listen up! The following will be a brief on procedures to be followed in the event of abandon ship."

He read from the clipboard. " 'The first indication is the general alarm, followed by the command "Now all hands, abandon ship" passed over the 1MC. If the 1MC is out of commission, word will be passed verbally. The order must come from the bridge or the senior living command authority.

" 'When preparing to abandon ship, wear a full set of clothing including shoes and a soft cap or head covering as protection from exposure. Do not wear a helmet or plastic hard hat when going over the side. Life preservers shall be securely fastened. When distance to the surface is over thirty feet or there is burning oil on the water, throw the life preserver over the side first. Inflatable preservers shall not be inflated until wearer is in the water. The life preserver shall be inflated as soon as wearer is in the water and/or clear of flames.

" 'Go over the side by means of a line, ladder, or debarkation net if time permits. If it is necessary to jump, look first to be sure that water below is clear of personnel or floating gear or wreckage. Do not dive! Always jump feetfirst, with feet and legs together and arms crossed over the chest holding on to the life preserver.

" 'Abandon ship as far away from damaged areas as possible. Check the direction of the wind and go over on the windward side, if possible, to avoid flames, oil, and downwind drift of ship.

" 'Once in the water, stay calm and avoid panic. Obey the following rules: One, conserve energy by moving as little as possible. Two, keep clear of oil slicks. Protect eyes and breathing passages by keeping head high or swimming underwater. If swimming underwater, prior to coming up, put hands above head and splash the water surface to disperse oil, debris, or flames. Three, if there is danger of underwater explosion, float or swim on the back as near the surface as possible. Four, stay with other persons in the water to reduce danger of sharks and make rescue easier. In cold water, forming close circles with others will preserve heat.

" 'Five, if ship is sinking rapidly, swim clear promptly, and tow injured persons clear, to avoid suction effect.' " He looked up. "Any questions?"

Aisha hoped she didn't look as apprehensive as she felt. She raised a hand. "I have one. Where's our lifeboat?"

"You're looking at it." The petty officer nodded at the gray fiberglass barrel. "The twenty-five-man encapsulated life raft. The ship has fifteen. We also got the two RHIBs, port and starboard. Total capacity, four hundred and fifteen. So even if some don't inflate, or get shot up, we got plenty of rafts. Get over the side, swim to a raft, hole up, wait for rescue."

"Now secure from abandon-ship stations, once training is complete," said the 1MC. *"Secure from abandon-ship stations, once training is complete."*

He looked around. "Any more questions? No? Then go ahead and secure."

She stood there for a while after the others left, a hand on the lifeline, staring down at the passing sea. From the sound of things, it could be an all-out war out here. Was it possible that this immense ship could go down? Disappear beneath the waves forever?

Leaving them floating, like debris, alone under the burning sky?

Dunk Ryan was waiting when she got to her cabin, cradling the last accordion folder to her chest. She wore the ship's black-and-olive head scarf gathered around her neck. Aisha unlocked the door. "That's all? All the files?"

"The last ones. From Lieutenant Garfinkle-Henriques. Supply Department."

"On the table, with the rest."

The SCAN process was a deceptively simple but analytically powerful tool for screening a large group of suspects. She and Ryan had sat down with the questions she'd used in previous cases, and come up with ten for this one. Some were easy-peasy, just to get people writing. But buried in with them were others that she'd look at closely.

The key was the essay. She'd asked: How did you first hear about the attack on Petty Officer Beth Terranova? Where were you the night and time she was attacked? What should happen to the person who did this?

Working around their watches and maintenance, every man on the ship had filled one out. Though not without grumbling. Complaints that they were wasting valuable time in the middle of a war. But with the exec's support, she'd rammed it through.

"Printout from ship's office?"

"Here." The corpsman laid it beside the stacks. Aisha had asked the exec to generate an Excel printout listing all male crew members over five feet ten inches. Based on Terranova's height, five four, she'd guessed at that as a cutoff point for "tall." That left thirty-three individuals. Ryan went through the last batch from the accordion file, adding them to a smaller pile separate from the others.

"How many's that make?"

"Thirty-five, total. Out of the whole crew."

Aisha seated herself with a sharpened pencil and a lined tablet, prepared for some puzzling. Just since she'd joned the NCIS, she'd noted a marked decay in naval penmanship. A lot of her entries were hand printed, in varying degrees of neatness. A few were decently handwritten, but many were in some peculiar scrawl halfway between script and shorthand. Of course, the quality of the writing wasn't germane. In fact, given the level of intellectual accomplishment she was gradually assigning to this perp, an illegible, nearly illiterate scrawl might even help cross a candidate off the list.

This guy was definitely full of himself. He'd defied them, "flipped them off" as Duncanna had said, with the DNA samples. Not just in the destroying of the only shred of hard evidence, but in the way he'd done it. Flaunting his intellectual superiority.

But that pride was also a weakness. A flaw she planned to home in on.

She picked up the first statement. How did you first hear about the attack on Petty Officer Beth Terranova?

I did yes it was scuttlebutt in the shop.

Where were you the night and time she was attacked?

In the shop, trying to make deckplate screw because were out of them and the supply system is two years backlog. All our deckplates in Aux 2 are loose or riveted down with copper wire. Chief McMottie was there he will back me up on this.

What should happen to the person who did this?

Naval justice court-martial go to prison if he is gilty—but got to have fair trial as some girl will say yes and then say they say no to get back at you.

Nothing stood out about this one except the brevity of the answers. Sometimes terseness was a sign of withholding, but in this case, from the laborious writing, she got the feeling it was simply economy of effort. A hint of misogyny in the last answer, but she couldn't disagree with it as a statement of fact. Revenge, jealousy . . . occasionally a false accusation was wielded as a weapon, but usually all it took was a sit-down with the complainant and a heart-to-heart to clarify things. This response got a yellow sticky note reminding her to check with McMottie and see if the alibi held up. "Next," she muttered, then noticed Ryan was reading ahead of her. "Don't read those!"

"Why not? I just want to help—"

She explained gently but firmly that aside from the CMA, she couldn't let ship's company help with investigative steps. "Not that you'd knowingly do anything wrong, but an untrained assistant just doesn't know what *not* to do. In your off time, who do you talk to about the case? Are you friends with any of my potential suspects? Everything we do, we might have to testify about. A defense attorney would crucify you on the stand, and we'd get hammered for allowing someone without law-enforcement training to conduct investigative steps."

The girl made a face but turned the paper over. Aisha went back to the questionnaire.

How did you first hear about the attack on Petty Officer Beth Terranova?

From the chief of my division during quarters.

Where were you the night and time she was attacked?

No real alibi. I was turned into my bunk that night as I was off watch bill due to migraine headache.

What should happen to the person who did this?

People like this animal should be strapped down and let the women cut his nuts off. That's what they do in Arabia and it sounds good to me. You wouldn't have rapists then or at least only once.

She puzzled over this one and at last set it aside. Better spelling, better handwriting, and a touch of overeagerness on the punishment angle, combined with a hint of imagination.

The next statement was two pages long. It seemed to have been written by someone in a fever, or with severe attention deficiency. She puzzled over it for some minutes. This guy wasn't into impressing anyone. "Who's R. M. Downie?"

"You know him. The weird little guy on the mess decks. The Troll," Ryan added.

"Oh. Right, right." Aisha nodded and put it on the reject pile.

Half an hour later she had six prospectives and twenty-nine rejects. Some of the latter she

357

wasn't certain about, but a SCAN didn't give you absolutes, only leads that had to be followed up the good old-fashioned way: bootsoles in the passageways. Two of the names were familiar. Benyamin and Peeples. Both rated high on the misogyny factor and neither had much of an alibi yet, even after having been interviewed, knowing they were suspects. A third was the same Mycus Ammons who'd advised her, on the bridge wing, that being a Muslim condemned her to hell. She didn't think that was why she'd felt moved to put his name in the suspect pile. It was his raving about how shameless the women were on board ship. His answer had been, *I heard about it from one of the ops specs. Wasn't surprised when I heard. I knew her and she was always asking for it.*

But two names were new to her. One was a Kaghazchi, first name Bozorgmehr, storekeeper third class. Ryan said he was Iranian. Along with being a storekeeper, he was often up on the bridge helping with translation, or talking to foreign ships when a Parsi speaker was needed.

"So he'd be familiar with that passageway, and had access," Aisha murmured.

"Could be." Ryan nodded. "And you know, there were three other Iranians aboard back when we were in the Indian Ocean. Guys we picked up at sea. That was the first time Beth got groped."

Aisha reread what the storekeeper had written.

I will speak here as I always do, the absolute truth without attempting to think what anyone will find acceptable or correct. Both the evil man who had sex intercourse with her and the evil woman who consented should be whipped first, then stoned. A woman is as guilty as the man she lies with. No one can thread a moving needle. There is a reason God made marriage. American women tempt men and seduce them, drive them from reason. They have no shame. But they will learn one day.

Hard-core all right. The old line: it was the woman's fault. "You're saying one of them might have started it, and he got the idea from them? You know him?"

"Just to say hi. When he comes in for sick call, or we have to update his shot record. Like, when we did the anthrax series."

Aisha pondered that, rereading the last sentences. *They have no shame. But they will learn one day.*

It was a threat, all right.

She set the page aside for the next, and cleared her throat. "What about this other guy? Jeffrey Differey?"

"Jeffrey?" Ryan briefly looked confused; then her brow cleared. "You mean Storm?"

"His name's Storm?"

"I mean that's his flying name. He's not really shipboard complement. He's air side."

359

"One of the helo crewmen?"

"Usually he flies as copilot for Mr. Wilker. Strafer and Storm, they like to use the names together."

She nodded. Certainly a pilot would have reason to be back in the hangar area, where the first groping had taken place. "Do the pilots spend a lot of time on the bridge?"

"Sometimes, yeah. Talking with the CO or the navigator. About the weather, usually. And in CIC, too, with the air controllers."

Aisha quizzed her, but she didn't know any more about Storm Differey other than that he wore his hair super short, smiled at all the female crew, and was cute. "He's married, though."

"Believe me, that doesn't mean he can't be a rapist, honey." She flipped through her case notes, looking for a printout of the player names for the *Gang Bang* game. Sure enough, there it was. Storm, points 367, player rating Gangsta.

The fifth paper she'd selected out was one Daniel V. Lenson. The commanding officer. His answers read:

How did you first hear about the attack on Petty Officer Beth Terranova?

Notified by CMAA and XO.

Where were you the night and time she was attacked?

Most likely either on the bridge or in CIC.

What should happen to the person who did this?

Once a suspect is identified, punishment will be determined by a court-martial. My personal opinion is that the most appropriate punishment would be imprisonment for a term of ten to fifteen years.

She lifted her head and blew out. Brief but thoughtful answers. Hewing to the requirements of legal procedure and the Uniform Code of Military Justice. Just what you'd expect from a senior officer.

Then why did they sound evasive, like words mouthed behind a screen?

"So what do we do now?" The corpsman hovered by the door, cupping her elbows.

"Carry on with the investigation. What else? We have a couple of new people to interview."

"You know what's going on, right?"

She got up and went to the mirror. Checked her appearance. "What do you mean? In the investigation?"

"No. That China issued an ultimatum to Taiwan."

"I didn't hear that."

"They said, surrender or be invaded. It's going to be a real war now. Not all this dancing around we've been doing out here."

"That doesn't affect my mission."

"It affects mine, Special Agent. I want to help you find this guy. But we've got to be ready to treat mass casualties. If we go to Condition One,

GQ, that's where I'll be. If we get attacked, it might not matter if we catch him. If we all, like, die together."

Aisha turned her head slightly, evaluating her eyelids. "Is that likely?"

"The girls say it could happen. A missile. A torpedo." She hugged herself more tightly.

Aisha nodded, still looking at her own hooded dark eyes. The too-round face, the sagging chin line. She looked tired too, the way everyone on the ship did. "What will you do then?" the corpsman added.

She smiled sadly at herself. "I believe I will trust in God."

"That's all you've got to say? Trust in God?"

"Who else is there?"

The corpsman didn't answer. A moment later, the door clicked behind her.

19

The second wave of missiles hit just after midnight. And along with it, a contact report arrived from *Pittsburgh*. Two Song-class boats, at the midpoint of the strait. The data link with the ROC defense network came up sporadically, along with the relayed picture from the AWACS orbiting east of the island. During the times it was up, it showed dozens of warheads rising from the mainland, turning east, and accelerating. Donnie and the Terror concentrated on any that might be targeted on the capital. But Beijing seemed to be consciously avoiding the city, or indeed, any heavily populated region.

Which might not be as good a sign as it seemed . . . Chip Fang, looking ragged, slumped next to Dan at the command desk in CIC. His thin chest was wrapped in a *Savo Island* foul-weather jacket. And under that . . . Dan did a double take. "Where'd you pick that up, Chip?"

The Taiwanese patted the olive-and-black shemagh tucked ascot-like into his collar. "I had to buy it. Expensive, too."

"I thought we were out, in the ship's store."

"You are." Fang smirked. "A private transaction. Where'd you get them?"

"Jebel Ali. Should have bought an extra hundred. I didn't know they'd be this popular."

"My uncle has a textile mill. We can run you off a few thousand. For less than you would expect." Fang sobered. "But they're probably shut down now. Our whole workforce is in the reserves. They're mobilized, I'm sure."

Dan nodded, eyeing the weapons inventory tote. Worrying over how few rounds he had left. Especially the Block 4s. But help was on the way. USS *Franklin D. Roosevelt*, with a full strike group, would be on scene in two days.

At that point, Dan and *Savo* would have done their job, and TF 779.1 would most likely be relieved. They'd head for Guam to rearm and resupply, prior to being folded in with units currently finishing hasty overhauls in West Coast ports.

At least that was what he hoped for.

Fang bent into his earphones. He spoke rapidly in Chinese, then listened again.

The 21MC lit. *"TAO, Engineering. CO there?"*

Dan hit the lever. "Go ahead, Bart."

"Sir, that tanker refuel, got a time and rendezvous yet?"

"Thought XO passed that to you. Early tomorrow. Five thousand tons, out of Hualien. Comms on channel 22. He does us, then *Mitscher, Curtis Wilbur, Chokai, Kurama*. In that order."

"Copy. Does Noah know that? First Division's

gonna have to set up if we're doing an astern fueling."

Dan scratched his head. "Can you make sure they do? A lot's cooking up here. We'll need to hook up, top off, and return freedom to maneuver as quickly as we can."

Danenhower signed off as Fang laid down his earphones. "What's the news?" Dan asked.

"Not good. The mainland's announced this latest barrage is retaliation for a raid on their base on Yongxing. Woody Island, you might know it as."

"Woody . . . that's in the Paracels?" As the liaison nodded, Dan did too, but for a different reason. The left hook he'd expected. But not as a raid . . . A raid, though, would be how Beijing would present it. . . . Doubtless the full might of Strike One and the Vietnamese were surging over the islands at this very moment. And each time the Chinese tried to reinforce, they'd have to do so under U.S. air out of Cam Ranh Bay and the old airfield at Da Nang.

He put that aside. "How's the population taking it?"

Fang said the Republic of China had prepared for this for generations. The reserves were mobilized. "Almost two million men. They can shell us, bomb us all they like. But they will have to conquer us one by one. And to do that, they will have to cross the strait, put their boots on our sand, and kill us all."

Dan pushed back from the command desk, hoping the civilian leadership was as determined.

If they weren't, his task group could be caught in a nutcracker. Pinched between the lodgment in the Senkakus, and a newly "reunited" Taiwan, there was no way the Navy could hold the Miyako Strait. Or the Bashi Channel and Luzon Strait, either. Would that satisfy General Zhang—no, President Zhang now—and a triumphant China? Or would it be only the first step on a career of conquest?

He felt pretty sure he knew the answer to that one.

By dawn over two hundred warheads had fallen. Fang reported Leshan Mountain had been hit again and was no longer operational. The airfields had been sledgehammered, with both cratering and cluster antipersonnel ordnance, to discourage runway repair. Special operations forces had been reported landing on Penghu Island, in the middle of the strait. The ROC Army was counterattacking, attempting to drive them back into the sea.

Then, for two hours, a massive, obviously carefully planned air blitz, comprising nearly two full wings of bombers covered by fighters and jammers, had worked over Hengshan and Chiashan, the major air-defense headquarters near Taipei, with earth-penetrating bombs.

Only a few interceptors rose to challenge them. Fang said they were being husbanded, to unleash against the invasion fleet. Amy Singhe had pleaded with Dan to take them out with Standards. He'd weighed the decision. And said, finally, that the situation lay outside his rules of engagement. They weren't attacking the civilian population.

Now it was 0800. He paced the bridge, trying to conceal impatience and apprehension. Puffy white clouds grazed across a pale sky. Wind eight knots, from 120 true. One- to two-foot seas.

"Now secure from flight quarters," Nuckols announced over the 1MC. Red Hawk 202 was laying a trail of brownish-gray exhaust, heading north. Dan wanted "Strafer" Wilker, loaded with flares and chaff, between him and Uotsuri. Both Ku-band radars were radiating now, so he assumed both triple-A batteries were active.

"Right rudder, come to course 130. Make pitch and turns for ten knots," Ensign Mytsalo murmured.

All but nodding off, Dan leaned on the bulwark of the bridge wing as Mytsalo carefully chiseled the bow in behind a surprisingly small, blue-hulled, white-superstructured products tanker. *Bao Shan III.* A puke-green wake unrolled from her stern. A drogue porpoised, throwing spray as it bounded. Sea sparrows darted above the rocking foam. Dan remembered the old seamen's

367

lore: Low-flying birds meant a storm on its way. Though these were probably just skimming the churned-up wake in hopes of an early lunch.

He blew out, impatient, but kept his expression mild. Better too slow than too fast; an overshoot could plow them into the other's stern. USS *Curtis Wilbur*'s low gray outline rode off to the west, placed to intercept any surprises from the direction of the mainland. Even farther out, *Pittsburgh* lay in wait for subsurface intruders.

But so far, aside from the test probe by the Song-class and the old nuke boat, no Chinese subs had tried to pierce their barrier. Which was puzzling. Were they sneaking through so covertly he just hadn't detected them? But *Pittsburgh*, *Wilbur*, and *Mitscher* all had their tails streamed, and *Kurama*'s helos had laid sonobuoys. Had the whole sub fleet made it through before he'd latched the gate?

Or were they holding back, waiting for the allies and their carrier groups to move in close enough for a crushing, overwhelming right cross?

The fog of uncertainty had descended on the battlefield, thickened by jamming, distance, and the lack of recon. All he could do was execute his last orders . . . and maybe, if he had to, look past their wording, to what Seventh Fleet and PaCom *would have* ordered, if they'd seen the situation up close. The way the U.S. Navy had always operated.

Always bearing in mind that whoever stepped over the line had better turn out to be right.

"Put the eye of the ship right beside it. Which side doesn't matter," he told Mytsalo. "But crowd in close, to make it easy for the folks on deck. They have to get that grapnel on it, and that won't be easy."

"Captain. Good morning." At the doorway to the pilothouse, Dave Branscombe held his salute. Dan beckoned the comm officer onto the wing with a crooked finger.

"Skipper, we have the response to your message to the Korean task force commander. Admiral Jung. We've set you up HF voice. Just remember, it's an uncovered net."

Dan nodded. Min Jun Jung was a savvy officer, and the Koreans were good seamen, aggressive and tough. Their ships were short on creature comforts, but fast and heavily armed. Just now, Jung's force was at sea, covering the Korea Strait. Dan checked his watch. "Remote to the bridge? . . . Good. Call sign?"

"You're still 'Ringmaster.' Admiral Jung is 'War Drums.' "

"JOOD . . . range and bearing to *Mitscher*."

Dan listened with half an ear, eyeing the drogue, which Pardees's and Chief Anschutz's boatswains were manhandling up to the break in the forecastle. It was lashed to a cable, which was in turn made fast to a five-inch refueling hose, unreeling off the tanker's stern. The engineers were standing by an already-connected feeder stub. Make the hose up, signal the tanker to start pumping, and they'd be sucking aboard Jet A1 at a thousand gallons a minute. It would take half an hour to top off *Savo*'s tanks. By noon he wanted everyone fully refueled and on their way to the outer limit of the Orange Zone.

Time to see if he could get some help. Taking a last glance down at the forecastle, where the engineers were gathered, he went into the pilothouse. Unsocketed the red phone, reminded himself he was on a nonsecure net, and hit the Transmit button. "War Drums, this is Ringmaster actual. Over."

The answer came back at once, and surprisingly clear for an over-the-horizon high-frequency message. *"This is War Drums actual. Good to talk to you, Dan. I always thought we'd meet again."*

Dan pictured him. Oversized hands, small dark eyes, the scent of expensive mentholated cigarettes and too-sweet cologne. His English was almost perfect, with a touch of California. "Hello, Min. Congrats on the promotion. Over."

"Same to you. Good to have you back. Just wish it wasn't for the current reason. Over."

"This is Ringmaster. Understand. Uh, is Commander Hwang still with you?"

"He commands Jeonnam, *one of my units of the Third Fleet."*

370

Okay, they were getting into classified territory. But he had to know one fact. "This is Ringmaster. Interrogative. Are you under command of combined, uh, authorities? Or national authorities?" In wartime, the entire South Korean navy came under U.S. Navy command, so operations could be coordinated.

"This is War Drums. Command has not yet been transferred."

Okay, which meant he and Jung didn't have to ask permission from Fleet. "Roger that. Are you in receipt of our message of 0220 local? Outlining Operation Dragonglass."

"War Drums. We have your message, and clearance from Seoul. I believe this move should have been made earlier. However, I am eager to participate. Have hopscotched several units toward you in anticipation. Including flagship. We will come up on the frequencies specified. Over."

Dan blew out again, stymied by the insecure net. He wanted to discuss deployment. The last readouts, before the satellites had gone down, had shown ten South Korean units in the Tsushima/ Korea Strait area, including *Sejong The Great*, Jung's flagship, two destroyers, two submarines, and seven Ulsan-class frigates. They were heavy on ASW and surface armament, but light on antiair defenses, though the flagship had a full Aegis radar and combat system. The smaller corvettes and patrol boats had hung back in the Tsushima Strait.

But he had to assume the enemy was listening to each word they exchanged. He fingered his chin. There'd been a way, once, to get over-the-horizon data link without satellites. "Slow Lead" wasn't fast, and using HF to communicate had other limitations. But if Jung had KG-84A crypto equipment, they could link. Once they got close enough for covered VHF, they could even coordinate their attack by voice, in real time.

He glanced down at the forecastle, then out at the stern of the tanker. Was it closer? Chief Van Gogh was aiming a laser range finder. He was relieved to see Cheryl Staurulakis standing by the OOD. "Uh, this is Ringmaster. Excellent. If the balloon goes up, we'll need to move fast. If you would like to move farther in my direction, that will reduce the time necessary to join up. Over."

Jung acknowledged, and Dan signed off. He resocketed the handset and stood watching as, down on the deck, an engineer twirled a finger in the "start pumping" signal.

Over the next few hours he shifted *Savo* to 25 degrees 36 minutes north, 121 degrees 30 minutes east, twenty miles off Taipei. Close enough to keep a decent angle on any incomers, but nearer to the strait at its narrowest point. As each screen unit reported "fueling complete," he assigned it to a new station farther west.

Once *Kurama* had completed fueling, and the tanker had disappeared over the horizon back to Hualien, he repositioned the helicopter carrier to the center of the strait. She would goalie. Unless the Chinese mounted a major push right there, right then, she and the fixed-wing ASW assets should cover his temporary absence.

After lunch from a tray at his command seat, he went over the plan once more with a fatigued-looking Mills and a very wilted Staurulakis.

Then they waited.

He managed to squirrel away in his cabin for a nap, and fell asleep almost instantly. Into a dreamless, black void.

And woke, to his surprise, several hours later, almost refreshed. No one had called. He checked with CIC and the bridge on the phone. Then stepped into the shower.

He had a hand on the control before he noticed the tag-out. Only certain systems had been cooked with saturated steam. *Legionella savoiensis* might even yet be lingering. He pulled on gym shorts and a T-shirt. Got his Hydra from the charging station. Toed into flip-flops, and carried soap dish, shampoo, a towel, and a change of underwear, socks, and coveralls down to officers' country. Showered, shampooed, shaved, he let himself out into the passageway feeling freshly issued.

To nearly collide with a short, rotund black woman in a flowered dashiki. Aisha Ar-Rahim was toting a bundle of papers locked to a clipboard. She clutched them to her chest, as if protecting them from him. She looked drawn, cheeks puffy. Behind her was a slight strawberry-blond woman he recognized after a moment. "Special Agent," he said. "Petty Officer Ryan."

"Good afternoon, Captain."

No mistaking it, she was avoiding his gaze. The woman seemed to nurse some concealed dislike. For him? For white men? Christians? For *all* men? He cleared his throat, and dabbed at a trickle with the towel. "How's it going? Any progress?"

"We're narrowing down our list." Ar-Rahim made as if to slide past.

He took her elbow to detain her. Big mistake. She flinched away, eyes blazing. "Don't touch, Captain!"

"I wasn't—sorry. Just wanted to ask if there was anything else I could do to help."

"The investigation is proceeding, Captain Lenson. When I have a conclusion, I'll let you know." She grimaced, apparently catching Ryan's horrified look, and backtracked. "Your people are being helpful."

"Even the chiefs?"

"We're making progress. Unfortunately, with the DNA gone, it will be more difficult to make a charge stick."

"Well, I meant what I said. If you can narrow down to three, four suspects, we'll lock them down. I don't want this guy walking around. If I have to restrict the suspects to their battle stations, so be it."

"Very well." She started away, Ryan at her heel like an obedient Labrador, then wheeled back, loose robe swishing out around her ankles. "One question."

"Shoot." He evened the ends of the towel; he needed to get back to CIC.

"These drills, repair, flooding, abandon ship—even at night—your crew seems very tired. As, if you will excuse me, do you."

"We exercise all the time, Special Agent. SOP."

"I've ridden a lot of ships, Captain. They don't drill like you do. And the chief corpsman. Grissett. Do you know he's worried about you? Your exhaustion. Your mental state."

"News to me, Special Agent."

"He's afraid to tell you."

"But asked you to mention it?"

"No. He didn't. Still, you're pushing too hard. Your crew. And yourself."

"Maybe because I've seen what happens to a ship that wasn't ready."

"You mean *Horn*?"

So she'd read his record. He said evenly, "Yes. I don't plan ever to go into harm's way without being fully prepared. If that means I have to 'push too hard,' so be it."

She met his eye at last. "You seem tense to me too, Captain. Do you expect a battle?"

"This *is* a warship, Special Agent. And we're in a war zone. So, yes, we could see action." He took a deep breath. "If you hear general quarters, lay to your cabin. If things go really bad, it might not matter if you catch this guy. We'll all go down together."

"That's what Corpsman Ryan here was saying."

"Well, she's right. But until then, yeah, by all means, pursue your investigation."

He evened the ends of the towel one last time, and turned away. But he could feel her gaze on his back.

The hours oozed by. EW reported jammers going active, then shutting down, on the mainland. Like an orchestra tuning up. He considered going back to his cabin, but instead reclined his seat in CIC and tried to relax. Until, around 1700, strikes began lifting from the military airstrips. He still didn't have linkage with ROC air defense, so all he had was *Savo*'s own Aegis. Still, it lit dozens of contacts. A swarm of hornets milled, coalescing, then turning east. They ate up the hundred-mile crossing minute by minute. More contacts winked on over the island. ROC fighters, dispersed, concealed, but rising now to intercept. He admired their courage. But there were so few. So very few.

Blue semicircles met red carets. Flickered, and went out. Red symbols vanished too. But the swarms inched onward, clicking closer to the island with every sweep of *Savo*'s SPY-1.

"We're seeing a lot of surface radars coming on," the EW petty officer called. Dan got up, back creaking, and went to stand behind him as he called out various commercial and military ship radars. Dan sent a Flash reporting the beginning of the invasion. He got an acknowledgment but nothing more.

Matt Mills and Chip Fang started a plot. By local dusk, putting together what Mills observed with the intel on the Chinese op plan Fang had brought with him, they were able to brief him. Two transit lanes were being set up, out of Fuzhou and Quanzhou. Fang suspected there might be more farther south, out of radar range. "The lead units are emerging," he murmured. "A powerful force. Not just amphibious units. Also commercial transports. Hydrofoils. Surface effect craft."

Dan braced with legs apart as *Savo* rolled. As the birds had predicted, the wind was rising. Which would pitch up the seas, but probably not enough to discommode a cross-channel movement. "Is it possible this is a feint?"

"Not with this level of effort, Captain. And not with the submarine pre-positioning *Pittsburgh* reported this morning." Fang eyed the pencil sketch of the transit channels he'd laid out on the command desk. "This will be at least two divisions. Most likely, four. The northern elements are stronger than we anticipated. Which means the landing may not be on the southern beaches."

"Okay, then what's the landing point?"

Fang ran his fingers along the coastline. "Taiwan is mountainous. We have always considered there are only a few possible places they could come ashore. That, of course, is where we have concentrated our defenses. It does seem, so far, as if their analysis is the same as our own. With a significant exception. We expected several landing points. Instead, they are concentrating their preparatory bombing on one. On the military airfield and air-defense battery just south of Hsinchu."

Dan peered at the map. A city. The mouth of a river. But the hydrography didn't look all that promising. "Uh—where's the beach?"

"You're right. It is not great terrain. Mudflats, mostly. But, as you recall, Inchon had mudflats. It does offers advantages to a small force with heavy air support. Which they have, from the Putian complex, across the strait." Fang looked sober. "Our army will inflict heavy losses. But if they can take the airfield, and cut the main north-south road, they will isolate Taipei. It also gives them a small port. We will mine it, but they can send their air-cushion vehicles up the river to destroy the bridges. Again, reducing north-south movement and our ability to reinforce."

A silence went around the table. Finally Fang murmured, "If America truly wished to help . . . Once the mainlanders are ashore, it will be difficult to dislodge them."

Dan took a deep breath. The Koreans were on board. Enthusiastically, but that was Min Jun Jung's way. The Japanese had made it clear they would follow Dan in, if he went. The only thing he was missing was Fleet authorization. And they'd be waiting on PaCom, who would be waiting on the Joint Chiefs. "I'm going to need a few minutes," he muttered. The others looked down at the maps, or up at the displays. Where the first wave was setting out into the open sea.

It meant men would die. Chinese, yes. Americans, possibly. Koreans and Japanese, too, probably.

"I'm going outside the skin of the ship for a minute," he told Mills. The operations officer nodded.

When he let himself out the sky was orange, peach-blossom, lavender. The colors burned like soundless fire under the high, fluffy, beautiful clouds common to the Western Pacific. Each detached from its peers, like them, yet separate, they skated past overhead. With a steady humming whoosh *Savo* churned through three-foot seas the color of burnt glass. Leaning over the lifelines, he tracked tiny sprigs of algae, no, some kind of weed passing down the side. They bobbed serenely, each, no doubt, freighted with its own tiny creatures. Until *Savo*'s bow wave creamed over them, tearing those universes apart.

War would tear many universes apart.

He lifted his face to a gleaming Venus low in the west. China had perceived weakness, friction, and opportunity. A tyrant had grabbed the levers of power, and steered her toward war.

But now was no time for regrets. It was a time for warriors. Not that he thought of himself as one, precisely. But ready or not, he seemed to be the guy on the spot.

He strolled aft, hands locked behind him, toward the boat deck. The whalelike bulk of the hoisted inflatable.

The Navy hadn't carried out a night surface attack since 1945. He could lose a ship. Hell, facing the waves of aircraft, not to mention the bristling guard-line of destroyers and frigates, he could lose *all* his ships.

He had two choices. One: stay in position and request orders. Which obviously weren't going to come until it was too late. It would be safer. Stay put. Wait.

Two: make the decision himself. Grasp the nettle. Strike when the invaders were at sea.

Savo's motto. He'd never liked it, but it sounded right just now. *Hard blows.*

The sun glowered with a last despairing flash, heatless and sullen scarlet. The sea burned gold. Then, somehow, it sucked the sun down into it, the deep red orb shimmering like a stranded jellyfish on a brazen beach.

Dan stood watching, fingers tucked into the belt loops of his coveralls. Hoping they all would see it rise again tomorrow.

Then turned away, and let himself back into Combat.

20

The word had gone out.

Dragonglass.

Dan sat back in his command chair, flash hood pushed back over his collar, and wondered if it might not be wisest to unsay it. Except for the rush of air-conditioning and the tremor of the deckplates beneath his boots, Combat was dead still. Everyone was already in flash gear, socks pulled over pants cuffs, sleeves rolled down. Not that it would do much good in the case of a direct hit. The Chinese, following their Russian mentors, believed in *big* missiles.

On the display, the blue circles denoting friendly ships were moving into position, kicked up to flank speed, running all out. He was taking his ships south in the classic night-attack formation. Line ahead, but in two separate columns. *Mitscher* led. The Burke-class, with its all-steel superstructure, Dan judged more survivable than *Savo. Savo* came next, though, at an interval of three nautical miles. Then the Japanese destroyer, *Chokai. Curtis Wilbur,* another Burke-class, brought up the rear now, but during the withdrawal, she'd face the enemy last.

If they actually got to withdraw.

The second line, ten miles to the west, was Korean. Dan had left its disposition to Jung. He had no doubt the Koreans would fight. Extricating them might be more difficult.

In general, U.S. sensors outranged those of the Chinese. Which meant he'd have a slight advantage as he closed. That would vanish as he came within range of the ships and aircraft guarding the northern invasion lane. He'd thought about going in silent, radars off, but the risks were too great. They would go in radiating. Able to see, but also, unfortunately, losing surprise.

Next to him, Fang spoke urgently into the red phone. He was trying to arrange a coordinated attack. If the still-considerable ROC surface forces could pincer from the south as Dan closed from the north, maybe they could cut the lane entirely. And air cover, of course, would help immensely.

It hadn't been gamed. But it was all he could come up with to give himself an advantage.

Someone cleared his throat behind him. Dan twisted, to confront Wenck's blue eyes. "What you got, Donnie? I mean, Chief?"

"An anomaly. SPY-1's picking up one of those funny high-altitude contacts again."

Dan frowned. They'd seen them before in the Strait of Hormuz, then again in the Indian Ocean. Always close to land, but very high, very small, and moving so slowly and with such a small radar cross section that they couldn't be aircraft. "How high?"

"This one, eighty thousand feet."

"We gotta figure out what these are, Donnie. You report them, right?"

"Every time. But, you know, now I got an idea what to do about it."

"Yeah? Well, look, can we discuss it later? This isn't really the time. Okay?" He looked to Fang as the liaison hung up, muttering. "Any joy?"

"They will see if it can be done. You might have two F-16s."

"Only two . . . How about jamming?"

"I don't think you will have to worry about that. We've invested heavily." Fang grinned. "And we have a few other surprises for them too."

"Not mines," Dan said, tensing.

"Oh, certainly. But not in your path. No. I have also checked that none of our submarines will be in the sector. Any you detect, you may attack."

He couldn't help blowing out. A relief . . . *Pittsburgh* already had two Chinese boats localized. He wanted to keep her covert as long as possible, though, so Red Hawk and *Chokai*'s helos were vectoring out. In a few minutes . . .

The ASW controller: *"Fish away, Red Hawk 202."*

In Dan's own headphones, tuned to the command net: *"Ringmaster, this is* Mount Shiomi. *Torpedo away."*

A minute passed another. Then, a yell from behind the curtain to Sonar. "Detonation, bearing two two five. Range indeterminate."

"Very well."

"Breaking up noises, bearing two two five."

He cradled his head in his hands, trying not to think about what was happening to the men in that crushing shell of steel. One sub down, but where was the other? Another minute ticked by. At last he clicked to Red Hawk's frequency. "Stafer, this is the captain. We're not hearing a detonation on your drop. Refire."

"Red Hawk. Refiring." The pilot's laconic drawl.

From the Aegis console, Donnie Wenck: "Skipper, we got trouble. Four air hostiles, breaking off from that strike group I'm high-lighting."

"TAO: Tracking 0817, 0818."

Dan blinked up at red carets. Each H-6D carried two C-601 antishipping missiles. Obviously positioned to orbit over the invasion lanes, in case of just such an attack as he was carrying out. Fortunately, his crew had encountered this missile before. The Chinese had sold them to Syria and Iran, and Wenck had ginned up a way of hijacking the altimeters that made them plunge into the sea. Still, he couldn't assume the Chinese hadn't updated the range gate circuitry. "Uh, Captain Fang . . . those F-16s you mentioned anywhere in range?"

"Not launched yet. Available in fifteen."

"Uh, that's gonna be too late, Chip. I'm going to have to take these guys." Dan reached out to the Fire Auth switch. He flicked the protective cover up and snapped it to ON.

He said quietly, "Designate to Standard, TAO. Take 'em."

Beside him, Mills repeated the command for two two-round salvos. He backed it up with the click of his keyboard.

With a thudding *whunk,* the vent dampers clamped closed. The ventilation died, the rush of cold air bleeding to a halt.

The roar penetrated the deckplates, the stringers, the hull. A white burning like an ascending saint climbed skyward in the aft display, illuminating everything around it with brilliant light and stark shadow.

"Bird one away," the 1MC announced.

Dan eased a breath out. "Time to let everybody know what's going on. Matt, inform Fleet we're entering the strait to take on the invasion fleet, in support of our commitments to the Republic of China. We've opened fire on two Chinese aircraft who were in attack profiles. That's within our self-defense ROEs. They're not going to say anything, but get a roger, so they can't say we never informed them."

The ship's fabric shuddered again. *"Bird two away,"* Nuckols said over the announcing system.

Eleven seconds between each launch, to prevent buildup of exhaust and clear the guidance for the succeeding round. Two. Three. Four.

Three blue semicircles clicked into existence and began tracking outward from the circle-in-a-cross that was Own Ship. Dan frowned. He had a radar return from the last round, but the track data looked different. He gave it five seconds, then swiveled in his seat. "Status on Standards."

"Round Four's not responding to semiactive guidance." The console operator lifted her head. "Permission to abort and destroy."

"Matt?"

"It's out there seekering on its own, Captain. If it misses the H-6s, it'll cross the air transport corridor. Recommend we let it go."

"Uh . . . okay. I guess."

The EW operator called across the space, voice going high, "Vampire, vampire, vampire! Missile seeker. X-band. Bearing . . . two four zero. Correlates with C-601 terminal radar seeker. Designate Vampire Alfa."

Dan nodded grimly. The H-6s were launching before his weapons reached them. Might even have detected them on their way. Muffled thuds came from outside. In the cameras, smoke trails smcarcd thc sky, tipped with flame-hot pinpoints. "Chaff away," Wenck murmured. "Deploy rubber duckies?"

Inflatable decoys, released from aft. "Let's hold

off on them," Dan said. "Donnie, can you spoof these guys off us? I hate to waste more birds on them. Range to the nearest picket?"

"Vampire, vampire—"

"Belay verbal reports, got 'em on the screen. Unless they get within twenty miles."

"Range to picket, thirty-two miles, Captain. Classify as Type 054 frigate."

Hunched, staring up at the diplays, he was running the numbers in his head. As, no doubt, Mills and Fang were too. Dependent for so many years on carrier aircraft for sea control, the Navy had neglected long-range missiles. Resulting in his main antiship weapon being the Harpoon, with both a shorter range—only around seventy miles—and a lighter warhead than those of comparable Chinese weapons. On the other hand, long-range missiles were useless without targeting information. And both sides had destroyed the others' recon satellites.

Unfortunately, the H-6s orbiting behind the Chinese coast were probably feeding targeting on him at that very moment. It would take time to percolate up and then down again. But that time might be measured in minutes, or mere seconds.

"Surface contact, designate Skunk Alfa. Looks like that Type 054. Designate to track . . . lock on."

"He's a shooter. Soon as you have a firm lock, bust him and the guys with him. Coordinate with

Mitscher. Simultaneous launch. Bust 'em hard."

Mills passed that over the net, then clicked back to Weps Control circuit. "Stand by on 'Poon. Four engagement, salvo fire . . . batteries released."

Again the ship vibrated to the rumble of outgoing freight. That was half his Harpoons gone. Only four left, in the slanted racks on his fantail. *Savo* just hadn't been loaded out for surface action. "Stand by for intercept, tracks 0207, 0208," Terranova said, voice soft, but carrying.

Dan glanced over, gauging her expression. Bland. "Roger, Petty Officer Terranova," he said, and got a level look back from the Terror.

He was back on the display when the friendly-missile and hostile-aircraft callouts merged. At the same time, the EW stack operator called, "Vampire, vampire close! CSSC-2 seeker, locked on."

"Taking for action," Wenck muttered, head down.

Dan risked a glance. He didn't like the chief's expression. "Can you fox it?"

"Don't know—trying to take control now."

"If you can't, crash it. We've got other problems."

From EW: "Launch indications, Skunk Bravo, Skunk Delta, Skunk Kilo. Multiple fire-control radar lock-ons. Noise jamming from two six five.

Correlates with Heart Ache. Commencing ECM."

"Shifting to antijam waveform," Terranova called over the console.

A separate battle was taking place in the radio spectrum. Along with warning and threat identification, *Savo*'s suite could jam, degrade, and blind the enemy's radars, including the seekers on the incoming missiles. The cruiser didn't have to disappear from their screens, just break its track, or present an electronic doppelganger in a different location. A second's, two seconds', delay could send a missile zipping harmlessly past, or force it to pop up and dive toward where the ship wasn't.

An arcane art, highly classified and only partially computerized. Unfortunately, the more radars their suite had to work against, the less bandwidth and power it could spare for each one. Power density, bandwidth of the victim receiver, antenna factors, propagation losses, environmental effects—he couldn't get down in those weeds. But in high-signal-emitter environments, they could be overwhelmed.

He just had to trust that his guys knew their business.

He tore his gaze away. "Shift Aegis to self-defense. Sea Whiz released. Standard released. Shift chaff and decoys to slick-32 control."

Mills passed the commands. Voices rose behind them. The displays flickered, afflicted with some digital palsy that made the hostile symbols stutter and jump. The enemy was degrading him as well. With the A/C off, the air was growing stuffy. A nitrate stench of solid-fuel smoke penetrated. A tickle grew in his throat; he hacked out a cough. The space leaned as *Savo* angled herself, presenting a smaller target to the artificial intelligences her own computers were matching themselves against. He hunched over the desk, blotting sweat off his forehead with the sleeve of his coveralls.

Over the next fifteen minutes, still tearing south at thirty-three knots, *Savo* fielded six incoming Silkworms and two newer C-803s, taking the last under fire with five-inch guns and Phalanx as they shook off attempts to hijack their guidance. Red Hawk reported in and asked for orders. Dan vectored the helo to set sonobuoys to the northeast, to make sure their route out would be clear. The flat slams of the guns vibrated the stringers more sharply than the longer-drawn-out roars of departing missiles. More missiles homed in on the other ships in his battle line, and on the Koreans, miles to starboard. The bass drone of the full-auto 20mms shook dust out of the overhead. Dan stayed on the command net, counting down the miles as more and more contacts speckled the radars. Ships, aircraft, more bombers, turning toward him like T-cells targeting a dangerous microbe as whoever controlled the invasion realized the threat developing to the north.

"We have a problem, Captain," Fang muttered,

"I see that." Dan eyed a new swarm lifting from Fuzhou. Some were no doubt H-6Gs, which the red book said could remotely cue land-launched missiles onto his location.

A shiver ran up his back. He'd expected a reaction, but not in this strength. He needed the Air Force. Needed penetrating stealth bombers, to take out the jammers and coast defense batteries that were spitting missiles like olive pits at a Greek dinner. He clicked the IC dial to the Aegis circuit. "Donnie? We're gonna get blitzed here pretty damn soon. What've you got for range to the nearest fat, dumb troop transport?"

"Roughly seventy miles. But we're degrading. Somebody out there's good. He's freq-hopping about two milliseconds behind us. So we get one good return, then garbage."

"What are you calling it as? Amphib, commercial?"

"Got a group of five at 138,000 yards, bearing two two five. See it up there? Four solid contacts, a smaller one that might be an escort."

"Rice Lamp fire control and Racal nav radar on that bearing. Correlates with Jiangkai I frigate," the EW petty officer put in.

The Jiangkais carried C-803s, a high-subsonic cruise with a jamproof homer. "He might have fired those last two we had to take with Sea Whiz," Mills muttered. In the blue glow of the screens, his face gleamed with sweat too.

"All right, we're in range." He scanned the weapons-inventory screen. "How many Harpoons left . . . oh yeah. Program all four rounds for simultaneous TOT. Then let's crank the fuck out of here." Mills nodded, murmuring into his mike, and Dan clicked back to the command net. "All units Dragonglass, this is Ringmaster. Weapons free. I say again, weapons free. On my command, turn away. Starboard column turn starboard, port column turn port. Chaff and decoys. Retire on course zero five zero. Flank speed. Acknowledge."

The responses came back fuzzed by a buzzsaw wail of noise jamming. *"This is Mount Shiomi, roger, out."*

"This is Steel Hammer, roger, out."

"Cannoneer, roger, out."

He gave it a beat. Then, "War Drums, War Drums—did you copy my last? Over."

Jung's drawl was casual. *"This is War Drums. One swing of my sword, and blood will fly."*

"Oh, fuck me," Dan muttered. He exchanged a horrified glance with Fang. Said, into the mike, "This is Ringmaster actual. Admiral, we have at least twelve inbound aircraft, loaded with vampires. Recommend you expend Harpoons and turn away."

"This is War Drums. We will press the attack home. Do you see the larger group behind the one you just fired on? We're taking them. First with Harpoon. Then with guns and torpedoes. Over."

"Fuck me," Dan muttered again, disbelieving what he was hearing. On the screen, yes, though it wavered and blanked, a second gaggle of transports was taking shape behind the one *Savo*'s Harpoons were jumping toward each quarter of a second. Unescorted, as far as he could make out. On a course for Hsinchu. Five of them. No, six.

You could put a division on six transports. Half the first wave. He couldn't believe it wasn't escorted. But even the PLAN didn't have infinite numbers of cans. They'd probably front-loaded them, first across the strait, to clear any resistance and have them on station to provide gunfire support during the landing. And cover the beach assault of the air cushion craft, if Fang was right about using them to push up the riverbed.

But there was no way Jung was getting into gun range. Not with the avalanche headed their way.

In his ears: *"Ringmaster, this is Cannoneer."* "Stony" Stonecipher, on *Mitscher.* Two miles ahead, four thousand yards closer to the enemy. *"All ordnance expended. Interrogative execute turn away. Over."*

"Uh, stand by . . . break. War Drums, this is Ringmaster. Major air reaction headed our way. Imperative we break off action now. Over."

"This is War Drums. You may break away, by all means. We are heading in."

"He's not turning back," Mills muttered. "We need to give *Mitscher* the okay. Turn away in column? Or corpen?"

Two ways existed for a formation in line ahead to turn in the face of the enemy. To "corpen" away meant ships turned in succession, one after the other, each unit putting its rudder over in the same patch of sea as the ship in front. In classical tactics, this had meant that an enemy line could concentrate its fire on each ship in turn, "crossing the T"—a recipe for heavy damage. A "turn together" meant every unit put its wheel over at once to a common course. Resulting, if the turn away was 90 degrees, in a line abreast, or if 180 degrees, in a fast, neat, orderly reversal of direction, with the unit formerly bringing up the tail now in the lead.

Dan had envisioned two course changes of 90 degrees, to lessen the confusion—always a good thing in battle—and reduce the possibility of collision, while allowing full play of train-limited launchers and jamming systems.

Now Jung was refusing to break off at all. He wanted to charge for the guns.

Just like the Light Brigade.

Just like Pickett's Charge.

He gripped the edge of the table, caught in the

toothed jaws of a dilemma. Joining Jung might mean their own destruction. Turning away meant leaving him to disaster.

"Maintain course and speed," he forced through numb lips.

"Captain. You serious?" Mills had gone white. "This is suicide."

His own mouth had gone dry. "I know. But we have to do it, Matt. Close up the lines. Tighten the interval. Mutual support. I'll try to reason with him. Meanwhile . . ." He reviewed the formation in his mind. . . . "Release *Chokai*. Give her a turn two seven, ninety degrees to port, so she clears *Curtis Wilbur.*"

Mills rogered. Dan cased the displays again, noting yet more air contacts blinking into existence above the mainland. Once they hit angels ten, they turned toward him. For the first time, he wished *Savo* were a submarine. He wanted to pull the sea over him. Go deep, go silent, vanish under the opaque solidity of salt water. On the other hand, two of the five surface skunks he and *Mitscher* had chosen for the brunt of their attack had vanished from the screen. If *Savo* had to go down fighting, she wouldn't perish alone.

"Vampire, vampire. Multiple seekers, X-band, correlate with C-802 terminal homers, bearings two seven eight through two eight zero. Inbound."

He was rogering when the 21MC clicked on. Cheryl, from the bridge. *"TAO, CO: Are you hearing Dreadnought on Navy Red?"*

"Dreadnought" was Seventh Fleet. His immediate superior. "Uh, this is CO. I guess I turned that remote down . . . a lot going on here right now. . . . What are you hearing, XO?"

"Denial of permission to enter the strait. Denial of permission to attack."

He couldn't suppress an ironic smile. "A little late, Exec. Seems like we're already here."

Savo leaned into a turn. Closing the files, as he'd ordered. Beside him Mills put his hand on his arm. *"Chokai* refuses order to turn away."

Staurulakis: *"I passed that information. Fleet orders you to break contact and extract."*

So there'd be hell to pay. "Uh, that's my intent, but I seem to be having problems getting it through to everybody. Put it to 'em again, Matt. There's no point everybody riding into the jaws of death here." He coughed again, couldn't seem to stop this time. Someone slapped his back, pounding hard.

He caught his breath and straightened, to another thunder-clamor as more missiles departed *Savo's* forward and aft magazines. Aegis was in full auto mode now. Evaluating the incoming threats. Running the detect-to-engage sequence, calculating probabilities, assigning weapons, and taking the shot, faster than any human brain could follow.

But at the same time, depleting ordnance much faster than he liked. He could almost feel her floating lighter in the water. The weapon-inventory numbers were dropping. At this rate, his magazines would be empty in minutes.

Someone had put the forward camera on the leftmost display. They zoomed in on a tiny glow, like a hot star, low to the horizon. Other than that, the screen was dark. He'd almost forgotten, it was night up there. The thud of the chaff mortars made him flinch. The star brightened, glowing, began to rise, then angled off to starboard. An incoming Silkworm or C-803. Following the bright infrared beacons of the burning flares.

Then, suddenly, a reddish flash on the horizon. Not too far ahead. "What the hell was that?" Fang muttered, frowning up at it.

Dan reached for his terminal and keyed, not trusting memory. Searching for ship class, then weaponry, then specifications. Ulsan-class frigates carried the Blue Shark. Basically a light anti-submarine torpedo, but with a surface attack mode, too. Range, about fifteen miles. At forty-five knots. But . . .

"This is Cannoneer," Stonecipher's voice came over the tac net. Enunciating slowly. "Missile hit forward."

"Mitscher's hit," Mills announced, getting it by some other channel, apparently.

Dan asked for damage reports. This was

looking more and more like the battle *Savo Island* had been named after. That had been a night action too. The Imperial Fleet had surprised, outnumbered, and outfought the overconfident, badly coordinated U.S. and Australian tin cans and cruisers.

He couldn't keep plowing ahead, into the dragon's yawning jaws. But neither could he pull out, and let the Koreans throw away their lives.

Only one possibility suggested itself. He leaned to hit the 21MC. "CO, Sonar. Carpenter, you there?"

"Hey, yeah, Cap'n. What'cha need?"

"Blue Shark, Rit. Korean torp. Know it?"

"Oh yeah. Worked with 'em at TAG."

"Tell me it has a loiter mode. Circular cruise at low speeds until it picks something up."

"Like a Mark 46? Yeah, it does. I'm pretty sure."

"What'd be the range, running that fish out in cruise mode? A lot farther than the rated high-speed range, right?"

"Yeah, hell of a lot. Based on how we used to tinker with the old Mark 35 on Pargo. *Drop speed by a third, we'd double the range. And, hey, don't forget ASROC. We don't carry 'em, but some of the guys in company do."*

The old sonarman meant the rocket-launched torpedoes some of the ships without organic helicopters carried, to extend standoff distance.

"Good reminder, Rit. Yeah, that would reach out." He eyed the screen as the bombers clicked closer. They were nearly in launch range.

Carpenter added, *"But don't forget, if you can get to them, they can give you a dose too. We sold 'em all our torpedo know-how. Now we're gonna pay for it."*

Dan double-clicked off. Carpenter was right, but then, the other side didn't know where USS *Savo Island* and her consorts would be in an hour. Whereas he knew pretty much exactly where they were headed. "Matt. Range to the main transport group?"

"I'm getting . . . thirty-two miles."

He stared up at the display, visualizing the vectors, solving them in his head. If they aimed where the transports would be in fifty minutes, straight run would be less than thirty miles. He clicked to the Weps Control circuit. "CO, Torpedo Control. Mark 46, surface mode, extended range?"

A hesitation; then a taken-aback voice said, *"Uh, we can set that anywhere from twelve to thirty miles, Captain. If you really want it to go slow."*

"How fast is slow?"

"Twenty knots?"

"Set it up," Dan told Mills. And clicked to VHF. Mustering all his persuasiveness, he said, "War Drums, this is Ringmaster actual. Over."

"War Drums actual, over. Hello, Dan. Side by side we ride into battle."

"Uh, right. About a torpedo attack. Excellent idea. Propose we execute coordinated torpedo attack at time thirteen. All units. Then execute simultaneous turnaway, time one five. Over."

"This is War Drums. That's extreme range."

"We'll put ASROCs out there first, to slow them down and sow confusion. At low speed, our regular fish will arrive just as they're milling around. While we're withdrawing to fight another day."

He waited, fidgeting with the headset. "Think he'll go for it?" Mills muttered. Dan shrugged. Rolled his eyes. Caught everyone in the space staring at him. He forced a confident smile, but he didn't feel like smiling.

"This is War Drums. You don't want to close to gun range?" The Korean sounded doubtful, as if Dan proposed taking away something he'd long dreamed of.

"Can't risk it, Min. I can gamble with my force, but your ships are too important to Korea. We need you out of here in one piece."

Another too-long pause. Then, *"War Drums. Agreed. Fish in the water at time thirteen. Turn away together at time fifteen. Out."*

"Vampire, vampire . . . multiple seekers, bearings two four zero to two eight zero," the EW petty officer announced. "Eight, ten . . . sixteen

. . . too many to count. TAO, EW: exceeding jamming, spoofing capability."

"Time on target," Mills muttered, bent over the keyboard. "Roughly . . . ten minutes."

"On the ASROC—"

"*Curtis Wilbur, Chokai, Mitscher*. Total round count, twenty-one. How many of them do we hold back?"

"None," Dan said. "This is our chance to inflict serious damage. Pass range, bearing, course, and speed on the formation."

The TAO looked uncertain. But just said, "Setting up to fire."

Dan pushed both hands over his hair. The palms came away cold and wet. He wouldn't be within range, for the surface-launched torps, for another five minutes. The incoming wave of sea-skimmers would hit them in the middle of their turn away. According to his inventory board, he had eight evolved Sea Sparrows and four SM-2s left. He could expend them all, and still not . . . but wait . . . the incoming missiles would see, not one, but eight different targets.

Unfortunately, the first line they'd hit, coming from the west, would be the Koreans. And they had little more than point defense. He'd have to cover them. He passed a warning to Jung, brought Mills up to date on his intent, then checked the clock again. Four more minutes. He clicked to Weps Control, confirmed that they were prepared to fire, and that all the fish were set to minimum depth. There wasn't a discrete antisurface mode on the 46, but he had to believe they'd attack a ship. Otherwise all a sub would have to do was surface, and the torp would ignore it.

Then he sat back, trying to pull his head out of the now and look down from ten thousand feet. If they could extricate . . . return to barrier patrol? But what good would it be holding the sea north and south of Taiwan if the island itself fell?

"It's up to us now," Fang said softly, as if reading his thoughts. "But, like I said. It is a battle we have been preparing for for a long time. They will not find it easy."

"*Mitscher,* damage report . . . stand by . . . *Mitscher* reports another hit. Midships this time. Warhead failed to detonate, but they've got a fuel fire—"

"TAO: tracking 0823, 0824, 0825, 0826—"

"Take the ones vectoring for the starboard line with Standard. The ones coming for us, with Sea Sparrow," Dan told Mills. He reached out and kneaded his shoulder. "Keep cool, Matt. We're gonna pull through this."

"Think so, Skipper?"

"Leaker, leaker!"

They both jerked their heads up to see, in the aft camera, a scarlet pinpoint, terrifyingly close. The camera jerked up, following it, as a solid stream of white-hot light reached up. The bass

403

BRR BRR BRRRP of the Phalanx shuddered from aft, along with the thuds of IR flares. A pop-up, Dan thought in that frozen second. A low, fast, possibly supersonic missile attacking from astern. Neither Aegis nor the EWs had picked it up until its final maneuver. The hot red star of its exhaust drifted downward, past and through the white-hot beam of 20mm shells, and passed out of the field of view.

"That goddamned second submarine," Mills muttered. "The bastard's *behind* us."

The whole ship shivered to a violent detonation. The lights flickered, screens flickered. Alarms began to beep and whine.

"Missile hit forward," the 1MC announced. *"Repair Two provide."*

The CIC officer pulled up the forecastle camera. Smoke was blowing aft. For a couple of seconds they couldn't see anything. Then they could: the bright orange flicker of a major fire. Off on the horizon, more flashes and tracers where *Mitscher* was blazing away.

"Don't lose focus, Matt. We're gonna have to buckle down if we want to get our cans out of here in one piece."

Mills looked puzzled. Then he smiled, reluctantly. "Nice pun there, Captain. You're a cool one, aren't you?"

"It wasn't a pun," Dan said. "Oh. Yeah. I guess it was."

"Two minutes to torpedo launch. Stand by for hard left turn."

The EW operator called, inflection near despair, "Vampire, vampire. Tracks . . . too many tracks to count. And more behind them."

A hatch popped open in the light of the flames. The ship shuddered, and the camera went blank with the white blast of booster rockets. Answering roars growled from aft, and the five-inch guns began to bang. *Savo* leaned hard as the screen blanked again. Alarms beeped and whined, a deafening, pulse-racing chorus. On the rightmost display, the red carets of incoming missiles converged. Dan stared, entranced, horrified, and carefully lifted his hands from the keyboard.

In full automatic mode, USS *Savo Island* fought on, for all their lives.

21

Aisha lay staring at the overhead, blanket pulled close. Her daughter's picture was wedged where she could see it in the half-light from the porthole. A distant bell rang on and on. She squeezed her eyelids shut, waiting for another explosion. The first had shaken the bulkhead, made the picture jump and fall. After it, a stampede of feet, and frantic, uninterpretable announcements over the 1MC.

For the past day, she'd been all but locked in here. Ryan had said she could wait with them in sick bay, help out, if they took casualties. She'd spent a couple of tense hours there, but at last had returned to her cabin. And cowered here since, hugging the curved yellow plastic of the emergency breathing device. As embarked staff, agents had been trained on what to do during emergencies. Unlatch the top, pull out the hood, bite on the mouthpiece. The oxygen flow started by itself. If she had to get out, she needed to be able to breathe. "Just remember, topside, fast as you can," Differey had told her. "Get to the open air. There might not be a lot of time."

She'd interviewed the helo copilot the day before, in a makeshift ready room off the hangar.

406

Though the term "hangar" was a joke here after the yawning, blocks-long cavern that went by that name on the carrier. Here it was just adequate to squeeze a helicopter into with its blades folded. Jeffrey Differey was tall, all right, with close-cropped sandy hair, bright green eyes, and a disarming smile. Yeah, she could agree with Ryan. He *was* cute.

She'd begun, "You seem to be cutting quite a swath through the female crew, Mr. Differey."

"Call me Storm." A disarming grin. "Hey, if anything's happening, and I'm not admitting a thing, it's consensual."

"I'm sure. Is that why you're ranking number three on *Gang Bang Molly*?"

A frown. "I don't know what you're talking about." He leaned back. "I'm at sea here, Special Agent. So to speak."

"I have the rankings of the players, off the records Mr. Carpenter maintained, down in his little dirty sonar room. Number three, ranking Gangsta, name Storm."

"Sorry. Check my flight schedule against when this other guy was playing. You'll see."

She'd actually thought of bumping the online time against watch schedules, but Carpenter had insisted that data had vanished when the CO had ordered the game scrubbed. "So you're saying whoever used the player name Storm wasn't you?"

"Could be anybody. The Barfin' Bears, our squadron, we got a tradition. Putting stuff over on each other. Could be the crew chief, one of the guys. Or anybody, really."

They'd stared at each other until she'd drawn breath, glancing down again. "This questionnaire. 'What should happen to the person who did this?' You write, 'Tie him down and let the girls have him.' What exactly do you mean by that?"

Differey had bared his teeth, a little-boy-caught-out expression. "Guess I didn't take it seriously."

"I see. So what *do* you think, seriously?"

"Rape's a crime. If it was rape."

"If?"

"That's what I said. Word is, the Terror was pretty much green-decked for anybody."

"Green-decked?"

"Cleared for landing. Ready to hook up."

"And you decided to give her a try?"

The pilot had lifted his hands and winked. "Not me, Special Agent. Got other arrangements, if you know what I mean."

The ship had gone to general quarters shortly thereafter. But later that day she'd managed one more short interview, with the Iranian, Kaghazchi, in one of the supply offices.

The minute he'd come in, she'd felt it. Maybe it was her head scarf. Or just her color: Iranians

408

weren't the most racially tolerant people around. But he'd seated himself without a word, folded his arms, and stared over her shoulder. Not at her, past her.

"Storekeeper Third Kaghazchi."

He inclined his head regally, gaze nailed to the bulkhead.

"You're a storekeeper. With access to the storerooms."

"Correct." A bass rumble deep in his chest.

"D'you know Seaman Colón?"

"I know her." Guardedly.

Colón had been attacked in one of the supply spaces. Aisha looked over his questionnaire. "You say here, 'I write the absolute truth.' I respect that."

He nodded, and she went on, "You say both the man who had intercourse with Petty Officer Terranova, and Terranova herself, should be whipped, then killed."

He nodded. "That is correct."

"I understand you're Iranian. But you know we're in the United States now?"

"Of course. But you didn't ask, what should happen according to the law. You asked what I thought. A woman cannot be forced to submit unless she is unconscious. The women on this ship are whores." Dark eyes burned under beetled brows.

"That's . . . a strong opinion, Bozorgmehr."

"You ask me, I tell." He shifted on the chair. "But I didn't rape. Captain Lenson calls me to CIC, to speak on the radio. I don't tell him what I think. Only translate what I hear. Say what I am told to say."

"And to the bridge? Sometimes?"

"Yes. I speak on the radio from there."

"Where were you the night Terranova was attacked? On the bridge then?"

"Working, doing inventory, back in the dry stores."

"Are you Saturn? Or Storm?"

A moment's hesitation. Then a lofty, "I have no idea what you are talking about."

"You don't play *Gang Bang*?"

"If you mean a game, I play chess sometimes. That is the only one."

She couldn't shake his lofty rectitude. Which left her, when she finally let him go, deeply suspicious. The most outwardly sanctimonious were often the most depraved in private. And the ones who urged the harshest sanctions, oddly, were often those who deserved to have punishment visited on them.

It seemed to be human nature.

So she'd spent the rest of the day waiting for the shell or torpedo that would end everything, while bells rang, guns banged, and several times a hoarse roar shook everything, knocking her phone off the charger stand. The ship kept tilting and rattling, like a bus going over cobblestones at seventy miles an hour. The PA system kept warning people to stand clear of the main deck, or called so and so to lay to here or there on the double. Then the explosion had shaken the bulkheads, knocked the picture down.

But gradually, as the hours wore on, the fear wore off. Or maybe she was just getting numb. And hungry, she'd had nothing to eat since morning. Eventually she turned on the desk light and started going over her notes. Sooner or later, if they didn't get sunk, she'd have to report on the investigation.

What did she have? Not much. No hard evidence. No eyewitnesses. She'd gone over the tapes from the flight deck cameras, with no real progress. Maybe eliminated a couple of possibilities . . . Carpenter, for instance. And the pilot, Differey. She'd looked at the flight logs, maintained by the air boss in CIC, and his alibi checked out; he could hardly have assaulted anyone if he was in the air.

But what did that leave her with? The SCAN had netted more suspects, not winnowed them down. If there were two suspects, an Article 32 could be convened, with the covering Region Legal Service Office having buy-in. But she still had four or five. Benyamin, Peeples, Kaghazchi, Wenck. Lenson? She couldn't rule him out. He certainly had access.

Coming to the ship, she'd counted on the DNA. Maybe too much. A comfortable backstop that had all but assured she'd clear the case, given time for forensics in San Diego. But it had disappeared in the microwave.

If she came up with no clear suspect, the case would go cold . . . meaning the file would stay open, but all investigative steps had been exhausted. That was the trouble with modern forensics. They made you lazy. She'd been around long enough to remember when they hadn't had DNA profiling, or IR imagery, or even reliable testing, really, for blood type. Back then you depended on confessions. Sweating the truth out of scared men. Now, the new agents, coming in . . . if they didn't have fingernail scrapings and hair samples, semen or blood, they hardly knew where to start.

But she didn't want to walk away. Not leaving a three-time offender loose aboard ship.

Like the man in the stairwell . . .

The harsh keen of a boatswain's whistle. *"Now secure from general quarters. Set the Condition Three underway watch. On deck watch section two. Battle messing will be available on the mess decks and in the wardroom until twenty hundred."*

She lay for several more seconds, staring at the picture of her little girl. Then rolled out and headed for the wardroom.

• • •

There were only a few officers at evening meal. The darken-ship curtains were drawn. Plates of cold cuts, sandwich makings, a tureen of chili on the sideboard. The CO was nowhere to be seen. Aisha joined the line, and found herself behind the exec. "Commander."

"Special Agent." Staurulakis looked haggard, pasty. She kept sighing, as if she couldn't get enough air.

"What's happening?" Aisha asked. "All I hear is guns going off, and the engines. It's sort of . . . terrifying?"

The exec told her, in a monotone, that the Chinese had carried out a second major bombardment. The Taiwanese were fighting back, but no one knew how long they could keep it up. "You know we lost *Mitscher*, right? Hit by three missiles. Heavy damage. The captain ordered her to withdraw."

"I heard an explosion—"

"A sea skimmer hit us. We're still isolating damage, bridging the electrical power and firefighting loop, but it wasn't as bad as it could have been. Minor casualties, no dead, thank God."

"Yes, thank God." They got to the tureen. Aisha hoped it was beef chili. "Are we winning?"

A shadow crossed the exec's face. "Hard to tell when you're down in the trenches. The

Chinese are taking losses. But they started with more pieces on the board. We're almost out of ordnance. We lost a Japanese destroyer, too. Torpedoed. *Roosevelt* strike group's on the way, but if the enemy can hold the flanks, isolate the battlefield, they can come across the strait in force. And they'll probably win a land battle."

Aisha sucked a breath. "I wish there was something I could do."

"I know, it's hard being an extra wheel. Did Grissett talk to you about lending a hand in sick bay?"

"Ryan will call if they need me. For . . . mass casualties."

Staurulakis started for the table, carrying her bowl, but stopped. "So where are we on the investigation? Have the questionnaires narrowed it down?"

"Actually, they produced two fresh suspects. I eliminated one, but the other's still viable."

"If I asked who the front-runners are—"

"I couldn't tell you."

Staurulakis nodded heavily. "We can't let a monster like this make the ship his hunting ground. The best thing you can do for us right now is nail him. And give everyone a sense of hope."

Aisha followed her to the table. Looked at her bowl. Then pushed it away, and reached for the sandwich makings.

· · ·

The passageways were rolling violently. She started down to sick bay, but a damage-control team was busy at the bottom of the ladderway. She didn't feel like picking her way through the hoses and cables snaked across the filthy deck. Instead, she backed away, irresolute. What now? Differey had suggested she cross-check watch bills with her suspects.

She could do that. But suddenly she didn't want to. She sighed, just as Staurulakis had, and turned and climbed the ladder again. Went aft, through empty passageways, dogging and undogging doors behind her, until she got to her cabin.

She was reaching for the light switch before she realized her door hadn't been locked.

When she clicked the switch, nothing happened.

He came out of the dark fast, swinging something, but she'd already crouched and as he stumbled over her she rose and lunged past. The gun. In her purse. But her hands closed on air. It wasn't there. In the dark, she whirled, facing the heavy breathing between her and the door.

The monster, between her and the escape to the street . . .

She pushed the terror down and kept backing away. Scream. But who would hear? This deep in the steel belly of the ship. The J-phone . . . behind him, not her.

A click at the door. He was locking them in.

A sliding whisper, soft-soled shoes, slipping toward her. Backing away, she half stumbled over something soft on the floor. Her purse? She bent, felt for it, her very fingertips hoping for the hard outline of the 9mm.

But it was too soft. For a moment she gripped it, mind empty.

A blanket?

Yes. A soft, soft blanket.

Spread on the floor of her cabin.

The fear rose then, and clutched her throat like strangling fingers as he strode across the tiles toward her, brushing past one of the chairs by the round table, skirting it.

The head! With a lock on the door. But as she dashed for it he altered his course, as if guessing her intention. Hard fingers on her shoulders, and a shove in the dark thrust her back against the desk. The computer, keyboard, monitor—

A hand gripped her shoulder, and something cool and sharp pressed against her upper chest. "Don't fight me," a strange low voice growled. Deep. Reverberating. "Or I'll have to kill you."

Not a voice she recognized, but that deep bass . . . "Kaghazchi?" she muttered. But got no answer. Realizing, too late, that if it was him, she'd just asked for her own death.

She thought desperately, searching for some advantage, a way to call for help. She couldn't see, but at least she knew where things were. But oddly, he seemed to also. He hadn't stumbled over the chairs. He'd changed his stride when she'd edged toward the lavatory.

No more time to think. He was on her, both hands at her throat. He was much bigger than she was. Taller.

So it was going to be a fight. Either that, or give up and let him rape her.

Most encounters went to the ground, and if your opponent was stronger, you ended up being punched or wrestled to the floor. Then, basically, kicked and stomped to death. Or in her case, raped. And if this was the Iranian, most likely killed afterward.

She'd gotten some defensive/offensive tactics in the academy, half based on mixed martial arts, the other half boxing. She hadn't done well. Some agents kept on with MMA, aikido, karate . . . but once graduated, the only self-defense training they were actually required to do was expandable baton recertification.

The baton, in the desk! She felt behind her, clawed the drawer open with hooked nails. Groped for the smooth heavy cylinder.

A sharp thin edge at her throat. The knife. Both women had mentioned it. A smooth edge. A heavy, cloying breath, and the smell of . . . lemons? The softness sliding, giving way underfoot. Her left hand scrabbled at his back. Smooth cotton. A belt.

His hands were at her neckline, tearing at her clothes. She got an elbow between them and tried to lever him away. But he was too strong, and kept ripping downward. Cool air on her skin. The prick of the knife again. The bear growl. "Stop it. I'll cut your throat out."

She didn't want to go to the floor, but some remnant of advice surfaced from the certification. *Try to stay on your feet. But if you can't, turn the tables.*

She had just enough time to think, *Allah, help me. Help me fight. Amin.*

She levered his arm away, twisted, and buckled her knees, sliding instantly downward. Thrust her left leg out, and hooked his ankle. Reversed the baton, in her right hand, and slapped it down as hard as she could into the outside of his thigh. At the same time she bucked with all the power of her hips, with her haunches braced against the solid, bolted-down steel of the desk.

The leverage, and probably pain, too, reeled him back. She scrambled to her feet, left foot planted, panting, taking the ready position for the next strike. "You're under arrest!" she shouted, though the constriction in her throat made it choked and weak. "Stay back! Stop resisting. You're under arrest!"

The baton was an impact weapon. From the ready position, she could swing across her body both forward and back. They told you to aim for the extremities of the bad guy—elbow, knee, clavicle, upper arms, thighs, and shins. If she struck to the chest or head, that was deadly force. Still, against a knife, deadly force was justified. "Stop!" she yelled again, and stepped forward.

Flick the baton into extension . . . and *strike*. She couldn't see where, but she battered him again and again, flailing down in the dark, kicking with her boots at his legs. Stamp on an ankle, he'd be lamed. Get him in the crotch, and she could get cuffs on him. Take him right now.

Instead, he rolled up off the floor, and his harsh breath hovered a few feet off, level with her own. Like two battling wolves, each smelling blood, they crouched opposite each other. Stealing a moment to get their breaths.

"You're dead now," that strange voice grated. It *couldn't* be his normal voice. He was disguising it. But he didn't seem to have an accent. Maybe it *wasn't* Kaghazchi. "But first . . ." it trailed off into panting. Strange, the other seemed to be growing more tired than she was. She felt totally alive, totally focused. She could see in the dark. Her muscles possessed enormous power. He might kill her, yes. But she'd hurt him. Marked him out.

But who was it? Benyamin? Wenck? . . . *Lenson?* Certainly the captain would know his way around the unit commander's stateroom.

A little more trickled back from the annual

recert. The combatives trainer, a diminutive agent from the Philippines. Sergio? Regio? *Move and hit. Don't stand still. And when you hit, hit hard!* She took her stance, left foot out, right back, got her balance, backed to the left, getting the desk out from behind her. The baton made little circles. She cocked her arm, tracking ragged breathing in the dark, the squeak of soles on tile deck. If he got within arm's length, she'd go for face or neck. A side strike. Paralyze the shoulder, take out an eye. Then low, for the knee, drop him again.

Instead, there was a squeak and a clank, and a rush of air.

A heavy weight with steel protrusions crashed out of the dark into her face. She gasped and reeled back as the desk chair, swung a second time, caught her in the chest, knocked the baton out of her grasp. It rattled into the dark.

He came in after it. Something heavy and hard hammered down on her head. The butt of the knife . . . She gasped, trying to claw his face, but another chair-swing knocked her to her knees. And another, down onto cold tile. She gagged, his arm across her throat. His other hand tore at her pants. Buttons popped. A knee in her belly drove the last air from her lungs.

Helpless under his weight, she blinked as a jagged glare sectioned her vision, bright as lightning, the world come apart into light. A harsh hot breath in her ear.

His weight, on her.

Like before.

Just like before.

She screamed, only his arm pressed so hard she couldn't. Couldn't even *breathe*—

His outline above her, dark, crouched. The shape of his head.

More light, behind him.

The open door. A scream, but this one . . . not her own?

The weight shifted abruptly, then lifted. A swift movement above her; she rolled her head to the side, only just in time. The knife-point slammed into the tile beside her ear, dragging across it.

Then he was off her, and Ryan was screaming again. Something flew across the room and burst against the desk, shattered, throwing shards. Aisha got to one elbow, gagging, something broken in her throat. Dimly registering a scuffle near the door, a stumbling struggle, another scream.

Then the doorway was empty, and Ryan was groping toward the desk. The corpsman found the switch of the desk lamp, and light burst forth, dazzling. The freckled face, the blond-red eyebrows leaning close above her. "You all right? Aisha! You okay?"

"Who . . . who was it? Did you get a—"

"I couldn't see. Too dark. He ran past, almost knocked me down." Ryan helped her up. Helped her pull her pants up, put her clothing back together. "Um. Hm. Did he—"

"Not quite. You got here just in time." Aisha straightened, wheezing as pain lanced neck, head, throat. A jagged scar gleamed where the deck tile had been gouged open. He'd meant to bury the blade in her throat. She could almost see the blood, pooled, spattered on the white bulkheads. Her own.

Her knees buckled and she caught herself on the younger woman's shoulder. She squinted around, looking for something left behind. Something, anything, to identify her attacker.

But saw only a soft-looking blue blanket, lying rumpled on the deck.

22
Tysons Corner, Virginia

At seven in the morning, the China Emergency Group was back in session. But now not all the seats were occupied. Google had pulled out, along with the other commercial interests. There were more uniforms, fewer civilian suits.

Blair flexed her lower spine in the rather too-well-padded chair, wishing she'd brought her pain pills. But she had to be sharp for this.

Haverford Tomlin winked from across the table. She returned the general a half smile. Ms. Clayton was in a dark blue pantsuit, nursing a mug of tea. A sideboard held coffee, cinnamon buns, doughnuts, a bowl of oranges.

"Quickly then." The DIA staffer was finishing his daily update, reading from a briefing book. "The engagement last night. When allied naval forces advanced from their blocking position in the Miyako Strait to attempt an intercept of the invasion forces—"

Blair lifted a hand. "What ships were involved?"

"USS *Mitscher*, *Savo Island*, *Curtis Wilbur*, submarine *Pittsburgh*, plus Japanese and Korean naval units. I can give you their names—?"

"No, proceed," Ms. Clayton said, with a glance

at Blair that read *I know what you're wondering.*

"*Mitscher* was hit by three missiles, and heavily damaged. *Savo Island* was hit as well, but not as badly."

"Casualties?" Ms. Clayton said, with another glance at Blair.

"Fourteen wounded and seven dead aboard *Mitscher.* Two casualties reported from *Savo Island.* Minor burns fighting fires." The staffer glanced at his notes. "One of the Japanese destroyers, *Chokai*, was hit too. No report is available yet from her. A Korean frigate was sunk, though most of her crew was rescued. Republic of China naval surface forces attempted to coordinate with the attack, and also scored sinkings, but were largely destroyed. On the exhaustion of its ordnance, TG 779.1 withdrew.

"Meanwhile, our submarines carried out independent attacks farther west and south. We're not sure yet exactly who sank what, but altogether a heavy toll has been taken on the invasion force. Especially a group of transports carrying a Category One mechanized force ROC intelligence has tentatively identified as the 124th Amphibious Mechanized Infantry Division. Reports indicate two of the ships sunk carried most of the heavy armor intended for the invasion."

The retired Army general said, "That'll set back their timetable."

The DIA guy shook his head. "Not where they've landed, sir. That's rice cultivation. Very bad tank country."

"Then why bring them? They're not stupid, Jerry."

Blair interrupted. "We can argue that later. But they *are* ashore? I understood from the news, driving in this morning—"

The briefer nodded. "Correct, Ms. Titus. They've established two beachheads. One near the city of Hsinchu. The other, farther south. An airborne division is landing at the Hsinchu airfield. And Taipei estimates two more elite divisions are on their way across now. A second wave, again, with heavy air cover. The operational headquarters are in Putian, under a Lieutenant General Pei."

The general muttered, "I know him. A hard, ruthless Party man. Will the Taiwanese fight?"

"They seem to be doing so, sir," said the staffer. He was wearing a uniform today too, Marine greens. "Judging by the reports out of Taipei."

"Why, you're in uniform, Jeff," Ms. Clayton said, as if she'd only just noticed.

"I've been activated, ma'am. This will be my last day at SAIC. I'll be turning over to Miss Reich here." He nodded to an anxious-looking young woman in her twenties.

"Well, we'll miss your insights. But, actually, we may have to wrap up here, too. Pass our planning to the Chiefs and PaCom. Depending on—" She nodded to Blair. "Blair, you're in touch with Senator Talmadge. What's the status on the use-of-force resolution? You were involved in that, correct?"

"Actually, I wrote it. Rewrote, anyway." She put her hands to her lower spine, trying to adjust it herself.

"What does it cover?"

"Air and sea power, plus ground troops, with a one-year reauthorization on commitment." Something popped in her back, and she suppressed a wince. "He's bringing it to a vote this afternoon. I'd like to be there, if you can do without me."

"The taxis aren't running, and the Metro's still closed. We'll have you driven over. What's your opinion? How will it go?"

She remembered the conversation at the Monocle. "It'll be close. On one side, the hawks in our party, with the moderates in theirs. On the other side, our own peace wing, plus Tea Party types and libertarians. For different reasons, they're saying forget the Pacific. Concentrate on rearmament. Deal with whoever comes out on top."

The general stirred. "We abandon our allies, we're—"

"I told the senator that, General. But he's not sure the Taiwanese will fight. If they do, I think he'll support them."

Clayton murmured, "You're also getting close to your election."

Blair smiled unwillingly. "My main debate's tonight."

"Good heavens. Well, best of luck."

The staffer, still on his feet, cleared his throat. "If I may resume? As I was saying, they have two beachheads. Taipei reports fierce fighting. Heavy casualties on both sides. But ROC force numbers are eroding, while the mainlanders are still pouring in men."

Tomlin said, "China holds air and sea control in the strait now, correct?"

"That's correct, sir. Their sortie-generation rates are higher than prewar estimates. We still control the sea passages north and south of the island. But our numbers in theater are eroding too."

No one said anything. The general sketched silently on his notepad. Doodling, Blair noticed, something that looked like either a shark or a stylized rocket ship. Over and over.

"All right," she said at last. "Our mission here was to formulate a long-term strategy. In response to various possible Chinese moves. Now they've made one. How do we respond?"

"That, indeed, is the question." Clayton went to the sideboard, stirred sugar into a second mug of tea. "Bearing in mind that whatever we produce here goes to the Chiefs and the West Wing. Jeff?

You were going to work us up a detailed plan."

The DIA guy took a chair along the wall, parking his binder. The Marine staffer twisted in his seat, a motion that gave Blair's pelvis a sympathetic twinge. The slide he brought up on the far wall read SECRET NOFORN: OPERATION COMEBACK.

"As General Tomlin remarked several days ago, a breakthrough has to be contained at the flanks. Even if the invaders secure Taipei, it will take time, probably weeks, possibly even months, to establish control over the rest of the island. Especially if the ROC ground forces retreat into the uplands. The eastern half of Taiwan is quite mountainous.

"Our strategy will depend on what allies stand with us, and which bases remain when the dust settles. And also, what side Russia comes down on; if they back Zhang, the blockade will have less effect.

"However, if we can build a coalition, hold the second island chain, and cut off and isolate the invasion force on Taiwan, we might have the reserve capability, in terms of naval and air forces, to engineer another Stalingrad. As you directed, that's what this plan outlines. But it may be a longer, tougher struggle than anyone expected."

Blair said, "What about the force-reconstitution timeline? Logistics?"

"You're right, ma'am, major questions. Especially with the sabotage reported on the Canal locks, and since the Navy now suspects several nuclear submarincs made it out into the Pacific. We can expect the enemy to place every obstacle to our buildup that he can, up to and including diversionary attacks and raids on Hawaii or the continental U.S. This would impact not just our counteroffensive, but our ability to either reinforce or extract our troops in Korea and Okinawa."

The general said, "As an aside: the major here mentioned he was being activated. But I've arranged for him to be attached to the Joint Chiefs J-5, Strategic Plans. So the transition should be seamless from here to their planning cell."

Blair tapped her foot, trying to ignore the ache in her hips. Noting the arrows of attack. Noting, also, that all the forces listed were from Guam, Hawaii, or the continental United States.

As Clayton had directed, the staffer had planned for no one now in theater to survive or return. They were abandoning them. Bataan again. Corregidor, all over again.

She rested her chin on her fists as the slides flickered.

The car dropped her at C and First. She'd been to the Hart Senate Office Building many times, though Talmadge preferred the Russell. The hearing was closed, which meant she had to show her ID to the guards at the door.

The room itself was an immense, modern space with lofty ceilings, done in white and blue, with the senators elevated on a long dais. Most of their seats were filled, a signal that this would be an important session and end with a vote. They were leafing through briefing books. To her surprise, a lot of the blue-upholstered audience seats were vacant. She took one in the second row. Mindy shot her a smile. She was in Blair's old seat, behind Talmadge. Hu Kuwalay sat beside her, head down, scribbling something.

The chairman tapped the gavel. This would be a closed hearing under Rule 26, Paragraph 5(b), since they'd be discussing national security information. They had a quorum and were not in conflict with the floor schedule, but opening remarks would be limited to five minutes.

He continued, to outline the history of U.S.-China relations and their breakdown. Mindy winked past him at Blair, as if to say *I wrote that*. Blair wasn't impressed, except with a statement that U.S. policy toward that country had all too often been dictated by political and commercial considerations rather than any long-term strategy. All too fucking true . . . After some minutes, Talmadge got to the point. "Today's hearing will consider the proposed Authorization for the Use of Military Force against the People's Republic

430

of China. Are there any other opening statements by the members? . . . No? . . . Our first witness will be the national security adviser, Dr. Edward Szerenci."

Blair sat back, studying her old opponent. Szerenci wore a dark gray suit and a pale blue tie. A flag pin. The same heavy dark horn-rims. Since he was seated, you couldn't really see how short he was. Glancing back, he caught her eye and inclined his head, a half-smile playing around thin lips. Her nod in return was just as scant.

As usual, he spoke without notes. "Senator Talmadge, ranking member, Senators, I believe— and I saw it during both parties' chairmanships— that this committee makes the greatest contribution to our foreign policy when it addresses issues in a strong, bipartisan fashion. The chairman has made that point too, but I want to underline it. This is one of the moments in history when a united approach is absolutely critical.

"As you know, the president is committed to engaging with all of your colleagues in the House and Senate regarding an authorization for use of military force against recent aggressive moves of the People's Republic against India, against Japan, against Vietnam, the Philippines, and now, against Taiwan."

Blair made just an occasional note for the next few minutes, fully listening again only when she scnscd hc was winding up.

"I recognize all the work you've already done on this challenging issue. As I said, it's essential that this committee leads the Congress and the country into concerted action. This confrontation will not be over quickly. As the president said during his televised speech. We very much desire approval of this AUMF as a vehicle for further chamber action. I do note Chairman Talmadge has suggested that a one-year reauthorization be included. We're willing to support that, but with the reservation that we'll likely have to ask for an extension. I make that point now so there are no misunderstandings later.

"To sum up, Mr. Chairman, members, I ask for your approval with the strongest vote possible. Both our allies and our enemies will read messages into that vote—in connection with our campaign, and that of our coalition partners, to defeat a powerful and expansionist enemy of the sort we haven't encountered since the Cold War.

"Thank you. I'll be happy to answer any questions."

Talmadge shuffled papers as several of the members pitched softballs. When they were done, he asked Szerenci to stay, in case there was further discussion. Then he called a senior fellow from the Brookings Institution, who presented a backgrounder on Zhang Zurong.

A third witness, from State, outlined the administration's alliance building against the coalition of what he rather colorlessly called the Opposed Powers: China, Northern Myanmar, North Korea, Iran, and Pakistan.

She was closing her notebook, thinking about bailing, when Talmadge leaned into the mike. "Our next witness will be the honorable Dr. Blair Titus, former staff chair of this committee, more recently an undersecretary of defense from the De Bari administration, and currently a senior fellow at SAIC. Dr. Titus?"

The only open seat up front was next to Szerenci. He offered his hand. She hesitated, then took it. But didn't bother smiling.

Talmadge rumbled, "Dr. Titus, I understand you've been studying possible countermoves, and our strategic position vis-à-vis these Axis Powers." Mindy leaned forward and touched his shoulder. "Sorry . . . 'Opposed' Powers. Or whatever we're calling them. I'd like your estimate of our ability to hold our positions in the Pacific, and if we take losses, how we should regain the initiative."

She glanced back at the cameras, making sure they were off. "Mr. Chairman, thank you for inviting me to speak. However, I was not expecting to be called. I have no prepared remarks."

"That's all right. I called you because you've usually got good sense about these things."

She fiddled with her notes, playing for time.

Even in closed session, there were things she just didn't want to say. Outline plans for allied counterstrokes, when the issue on Taiwan was still in doubt? She finally murmured, "I can only say that we are being forced to make a definitive choice, for surrender or all-out conventional war. Zhang has breached the peace with the invasion of Taiwan. We're not formally pledged to intervene, but this is a bigger question than the wording of treaties.

"This aggression threatens the core interests of the United States. If Taiwan falls, South Korea's encircled and Japan's essentially neutralized. We stand to lose everything we fought World War II for: a stable Pacific, trading relationships, democratic allies. Right now, our position does not augur well. But I understand PaCom and the Joint Chiefs are formulating plans for downstream operations. Of course, these depend on Senate passage of this resolution."

A pat on her shoulder. "Well said," Szerenci whispered. She shot him a jaundiced look.

"Well, Dr. Titus, here is my question." The senior member from the other party, Senator McKane. "In my experience, it's easier to embark on a conflict than to end one. Certain members are drawing a parallel here with our war with Japan. But that was a different time, a different enemy. This may call for a different response."

"That's true, Senator. Quite true," Blair said. "Very wise remark."

"Well, what's your response? Can we win?"

She took a moment to choose the best words. "I have no crystal ball. And I hesitate to go on record as predicting the outcome of any conflict. But I believe the United States has the power to emerge victorious. At least if we define our objectives properly.

"The question will be whether we have the resolve to continue if faced, as we may well be, with painful reverses. I agree with both the chairman and Dr. Szerenci that this is not a partisan issue. It's a test of our ability to stand with our allies in a time of death and sacrifice. A test of our will to maintain an international order based on law, not force.

"But, given that, are we ready to make sacrifices on the scale of World War II? There are those who claim this isn't the same country it was then. That we're too used to peace. All I can say is, for once, I agree with Dr. Szerenci. We need to stand firm against aggression, no matter the cost."

No one asked her anything more. Several of the members seemed to be holding side discussions. At last Talmadge leaned to the mike again. "Our next witness will be General Ricardo Vincenzo, United States Air Force, chairman of the Joint Chiefs of Staff. General, have you prepared opening remarks?"

Vincenzo had. Halfway through them he hesitated, then drew a breath.

"This is highly classified. We can't reveal how we obtained this information. But General Zhang has ordered the rapid deployment of a new class of ICBM. The DF-41 is a surprise. In terms of throw weight, accuracy, and number of independently maneuverable warheads, it is superior to the heaviest missiles we have available. We'd heard rumors about its development, but had no indication it was this far along."

Talmadge said gravely, "This is indeed serious news, General. Do we have hard numbers?"

"We estimate at least fifty MIRVed ICBMs are being activated. All, presumably, targeted against major cities in the continental United States."

Szerenci held up a hand. Talmadge nodded. "If you will, Mr. Chairman. This accords perfectly with the premier's ultimatum of a few days ago. One: No American ally will be attacked unless it attacks China, or refuses to provide passage. Two: U.S. forces capable of delivering nuclear weapons will be dealt with 'by any means necessary.' Three: Any aggression against Chinese soil will be answered by a similar level of destruction visited on the American homeland.

"This underscores a point I've made in other venues: their breakout in nuclear delivery systems is quickly placing us in an inferior position. Until now, I thought this was some years out. Now it's happening sooner. Therefore, our goal must not be simply to restore the status quo. It must be to cap and, if possible, eliminate the Red Chinese nuclear deterrent. If we must take risks, better now than later. When we may be fighting from a position of disadvantage."

A stir on the dais; a murmuring. Talmadge tapped the gavel. They quieted. "Thank you, Doctor. General, any further remarks?"

Vincenzo said, "Our mobilization is proceeding. We'll bring a request to the Hill shortly for activation of the selective service system. We may be handicapped, though, by the recent data corruption discovered in their files. This may be a lengthy war. It's a long way out to the western Pacific, and we can no longer call on the shipping capacity we had in World War II."

The hearing wore on. The deputy director of the CIA. A Taiwan expert from Georgetown University. At last Talmadge called for a vote. One by one, the senators, in portentous tones, voiced their decisions.

It came out 11 to 2, with one member abstaining, to forward the force-authorization resolution to the Senate the next morning.

Looking exhausted, Talmadge declared the session closed. He lifted his head, seeming to search the audience for Blair. But she was already slipping out.

She had a debate to get ready for.

• • •

"This election is going to revolve around national security, Blair." Jessica looked anxious, frazzled, skinnier than when they'd first met. "He's going to scare them. Tell them their sons, and probably their daughters, are going to die in the Pacific. So we reassure them. Tell 'em nothing bad will happen. We'll win in a few weeks. It's under control."

Her campaign manager trotted alongside, talking on and on about what to say and what not to. Blair finally interrupted: "Did anyone from the party get in touch? About that funding Bankey promised?"

"I left four calls. No one's returned them. By the way, you look fantastic. Love that suit. Powerful. Remember, everything's going to be fine in the Pacific. Your dad said—"

"Not now," Blair muttered as the backstage door swung open and her makeup guy waved from a portable desk.

When she walked out onto the stage, smoothing her hair over the damaged ear, the auditorium looked much smaller than the hearing room in the Hart. But the audience was larger. In fact, standing room only. To the side waited a panel of students. They'd discuss the debate as soon as it was over. The local radio stations were carrying it live. Her opponent had wanted four meetings, but she'd cut it down to this one, citing her commitments in Washington. Which might or might not work against her. "Too busy to care about local issues"—that would be how he'd spin it. If he was smart.

She focused on her earnest-looking, dark-haired, awkwardly spindly opponent as they met in the middle of the stage, shook hands, and retreated to opposite sides. Gregory Beiderbaum owned a car dealership in Cheltenham. His family had sold Fords for generations. He'd been a state representative, then a state senator.

She won the toss and spoke first. In her opening statement, she made sure to mention Beiderbaum's coming out of the closet two years before, the first openly gay state senator in Maryland history. How courageous she found it. She smiled down at his husband, Fyodor, who was sitting in the front row. She kept it polite, outlining her experience at the Congressional Research Service, on the Senate staff, and in the Department of Defense, and pointing out that she'd just come from testifying about the war-powers resolution.

To her astonishment, Beiderbaum came out of the chute hungry for blood. His opening remarks painted her as a tool of the defense establishment. "Why docs 'the Honorable' Blair Titus—a title given her by the De Bari administration—care so much about what happens on a faraway island in Asia? One reason. It happens in every war: our freedoms erode, government prying and control increase. The national debt's skyrocketing. Those of you who depend on Medicare and Social Security, prepare to lose benefits. And those in our radio and TV audience, who've worked hard and accumulated investments: you see what's happening to their value."

He wheeled, and pointed at her. "This is nothing to the suffering Blair Titus will bring us. She talks about her family's history. Back to the slaveholders of the Civil War. But she's not even a Maryland resident anymore; she lives in Arlington." Beiderbaum licked his lips, glanced at his notes, beamed an earnest smile into the cameras. "Now let's talk about her husband. A 'Navy hero,' her office says. But, really, a left-wing agitator in his younger days, according to my good friend Congresswoman Sandy Treherne. More recently, he cravenly backed down from a confrontation with the Chinese in the Indian Ocean. And now he's dragging us into war, just like in the Tonkin Gulf. He recklessly risks his men's lives, the same cavalier way his wife— who distances herself by not taking his name— will endanger your children. She has, by the way, none of her own."

His voice rose; he pounded the podium with a clenched fist. "Blair just told you, with her own lips, who she is. The consummate Washington insider. The Senate. The Department of Defense.

Oh yes. Oh, *yes*. Her motto: Tax, spend, and herd other people's children to the slaughter, against the hordes of Asia.

"I call on the voters of this district, from both parties, to reject war. If you don't like me, write another name in on your ballot. But if you value the lives of your children, the value of your investments, and above all, your God-given freedoms, do not vote for Blair Titus."

A storm of applause, with many leaping up to cheer. Offstage, Kirschorn was pumping a fist at her, then clawing like an enraged raccoon: *rip his guts out*. Blair forced herself to breathe slowly. Concentrate. Attack, in her turn? Attack *what?* The guy had no national-level experience. Which was, of course, why he was shifting ground on her. Politics. In what other profession would being completely ignorant be presented as an advantage?

She could go personal. He wanted to compare families? He'd left three school-age kids behind when he'd abandoned his wife. After screwing her out of 160 acres of a trailer park that had been in her family for decades.

But if she took that route, she'd be portrayed as attacking his lifestyle choice. And lose one of her own bases of support. Check.

Instead, facing the by-now-hostile faces below her, she spoke calmly, to the issues. She defended the administration, which felt deeply wrong,

441

given her party. "I can't disagree that this war is being forced on us. We can't give the president a blank check. But neither can we walk away from our allies. That would be the beginning of our fall.

"We have to walk a middle path. It will be long. It may be harder than we like. The good news is that unemployment figures are down. Our manufacturing base is beginning to respond. Government spending, historically, is a stimulus to the economy."

But even as she explained logically and reasonably what they had to do, she saw it in their expressions. The rage. The naked fear. America was taking on a war no one wanted. Someone had to pay.

It looked as if that someone was going to be her.

23
Yongxing Island

Teddy came to only gradually. Someone was kicking him in the side, again and again. He submerged back into the darkness. He could still see the hurting up there, like a diver under ice. It was there, but it didn't really reach him. Not down here.

But the darkness rejected him. Buoyed him up, as if he wasn't yet heavy enough to stay, toward a jagged icy surface he didn't want to approach, but couldn't avoid.

He pried open swollen eyes to see a concrete floor. Close up, it was anything but flat. Wavy and bumpy, with hills and rugged valleys. Was he an ant? That hole would give him some cover. He tried to drag himself toward it, but his swollen body was too massive.

Black boots came into his field of view. Someone was yelling. The high voice was singsong. He didn't understand it. Ants didn't understand words. But he was starting to doubt his antness. Especially when the boot swung again, and his kidneys lanced. He barked and tried to roll away. But his hands were cuffed behind him. Knife-edged metal dug into his wrists.

443

More kicking, more screaming. Then one of them must have figured out, about his bad leg. Probably because he shrieked whenever the guy jumped on it. So, naturally, he was jumping on it again, yelling each time, grinding it into the concrete at that exact wrong angle. Teddy squeezed his eyes shut, feeling the tendons tearing out. Kiss all that surgery, physical therapy, good-bye. The gray concrete dissolved. He was blacking out again.

Until violent hands grabbed his arms and legs, yanked him off the deck, and rammed him into a chair. He blinked gritty eyelids, trying to focus. Glaring light. Brown concrete walls. Asians in grayish camo. Hard looking, and extremely pissed off, from the way they slapped him and backhanded elbows into his face.

Oberg let his head sag as it rushed back. The mission. The Package. Echo cut up and cut off. Crewing the machine gun. "Harch made it?" he muttered, realizing his lips were swollen too. What had happened to Knobby, Moogie, Mud Cat, the wounded? Had they made it out? And what about the MIA from Echo One, back at the causeway?

Then he shut up. These guys wouldn't tell him. *Nothing* they were going to tell him would be the truth. Something was wrong in his side. His leg was all fucked up. And his head reeled. The room spun like a chopper with an RPG in the tail rotor.

444

Loose teeth, too. Blood pooling in his throat. They must've been beating on him for a while already. Too bad he'd been out, couldn't enjoy it.

But he couldn't say that. Or anything like that. Not out loud.

He was going to have to watch that mouth of his, that was for sure.

You expected something like this from the moment you became a SEAL. That they'd capture you and, if you weren't fighting the Canadians or the Dutch, torture you. You might think that, since you'd been through BUD/S, it couldn't get worse. But then, at Survival, Evasion, Resistance, and Escape school in Coronado, you realized it could. *Much* worse.

He'd been through both levels at SERE. Level A. Escape and evasion. Eating lizards, biting the heads off snakes. Level C was for special operators, air crews, and others at high risk of capture. "Interrogation resistance," it was called.

The instructors had made it clear. It was about survival, not resistance. Those who spat in the interrogators' faces were going to die. Those who cracked—broke down, plcd for a break, or went along with the demands for signatures and confessions—weren't going to make it either. Those were the guys who were going to hang themselves in the latrine, or eat a bullet back in the States.

The only way to make it through alive, and with something resembling integrity, was to become the Gray Man. The Cipher. The Face in the Crowd. Maybe even, if you could pull it off, not the sharpest knife in the drawer. Cooperate just enough to stay alive. Tell as little as you could, stringing it out. While protecting any really important information with your life.

His problem at SERE had been taking it seriously. No matter how tough the guards acted, it was for show. They couldn't kill you, or even permanently hurt you, even as they messed with your mind, tried to play on your fears, and got you in stress positions. The endless tapes of crying babies and punk rock were annoying. But they *did* feed you, though not much. And it was only for five days. As long as you kept that in mind, how bad could it get?

This was going to be different. Glancing up from under bleeding eyebrows at the angry faces circling him, he figured: If I check out while these guys are at me, there won't be much of an investigation.

An hour later—chained to the chair for all that time, pissing in the rags that were all that was left of his black gear—the door banged open. The team who'd been beating him slammed their backs to the walls, at attention.

The guy who stepped through it was average

height, with black nerd glasses. His camos were the same as those of the others, but sharply creased. A holstered Makarov rode his hip. He wore a collar insignia that Teddy, blinking, found hard to make out. A star and two bars? A midgrade officer. Intel, security, or military counterintelligence. Most likely, attached to the unit that had garrisoned the island.

If they were still *on* the island. How long had he been out? More than long enough to get flown back to the mainland. The guy's hair was slicked back and he had a couple of days' wispy beard. Thirty-two, thirty-three, though it was hard to tell. Prominent cheekbones. He was carrying a can of something. It seemed to be Pepsi, though it looked smaller than U.S. cans. He spoke to the men along the wall, and they bowed and filed out. Only one remained. He brought a folding chair from somewhere, snapped it open, positioned it for the officer, and retreated behind Teddy, out of his field of vision.

Slick Man smiled as he took the seat. "My name is Kuo," he said, but with the K deep in the throat; it might have been Guo. "I am here to welcome you." His accent was southern, as if he'd spent time in Georgia or Alabama. He patted a pocket. "How about a smoke?"

Teddy cleared his throat and spat blood onto the concrete. There was plenty there already. "Thanks, don't use 'em," he mumbled through swollen lips.

"Didn't expect so. How about a drink?"

Teddy eyed the can. *Take it when it's offered,* they'd said at SERE. "Yeah, but my hands are sort of occupied at the moment."

Kuo, or Guo, laughed. He nodded to the guy behind Teddy. Chains rattled, and the cuffs came off his wrists, though his ankles were still shackled to the chair. Teddy shifted his weight as he massaged his wrists, trying to sense if it was bolted down. It didn't give. He got the Pepsi down in three long gulps, burped, and set it on the concrete, licking his lips. "Thanks."

"You're welcome." Kuo settled a tablet computer, an iPad if Teddy wasn't mistaken, on his lap. "Sorry about the shackles, but you're a dangerous guy, right?"

"Not so dangerous," Teddy said. "Obviously. If I'm here."

"You know, we can arrange to have things made much easier. I'd like you to see me as your friend. But first, let's see what we have here. I assume you're American. Correct?"

"Correct." Teddy made himself look at the floor. "Sir."

"Name and rank, please?"

"Theodore Harlett Oberg, master chief petty officer, United States Navy."

"Harlett, or *Hart*-lett? Spell the name, please."
He spelled it.

"And the serial number?"

Teddy gave it to him.

"Theodore, I'm sure you realize I'm a military intelligence officer. You are now a prisoner of war. But you're also a source. No doubt you have been trained to resist interrogation, as a SEAL. I respect that. You *are* a SEAL, correct?"

Teddy didn't answer. Kuo studied his iPad. "Born in Hollywood, California. Service in Saudi, Then Ashaara, then a break in service. Reactivated for service in Afghanistan and Iraq. Currently assigned to Echo Platoon, SEAL Team Eight, San Diego. Unmarried, no dependents?" He flicked a gaze at Teddy. "I'll take that as a yes. My job is to find out what Echo intended to accomplish on Yongxing. Or do you still call it Woody Island?"

Teddy didn't answer for a moment. He didn't see how—even the names of individuals on the Teams were confidential—but it sounded like the guy had his complete service record. Which meant that either they'd penetrated Team computers or they had someone on the inside. *Cooperate just enough to survive. Become the Gray Man.* He said, "We use both names."

Kuo nodded, looking pleased, and made a note. "Now, we have a slogan in the People's Republic: 'Kindness to those who confess, harsh discipline to those who resist.' Unfortunately, over twenty civilians, including women and children, were killed during your failed invasion. Certain of my

449

seniors are pressing for us to execute you and your teammate as war criminals."

Teddy didn't bother getting excited over the threat, and the obvious lie about civilian casualties. The Chinese were the enemy, but they probably weren't al-Qaeda. He could get kicked around, but at this stage of the war, a POW was more valuable alive than dead. But maybe Kuo had just let something slip he hadn't meant to. Teddy murmured humbly, "You captured someone else, sir?"

"One other SEAL, yes. He's wounded, but is receiving treatment. And cooperating fully. If your statements agree, we'll move you both to a special camp on the mainland. You will receive kind treatment. Your family will be notified via the Red Cross, in accordance with the Geneva Convention." Kuo shook the empty can. "Another?"

"Thank you, sir, one was good."

"Hungry? Something to eat?"

"I'm fine, sir, thanks just the same."

"A personal question, if you don't mind. Those scars on your face. Afghanistan?"

"Actually, it was at the pistol range," Teddy said. "A Beretta. The slide failed. But it improved my looks."

Kuo didn't chuckle. He said gravely, "I have to warn you, Teddy, your treatment depends on your attitude. If you don't cooperate, you won't be going to the camp I described. You will either be shot as a war criminal, or end up in a hard-labor camp. The treatment there . . . well, let's not talk about that." He smiled. "So. Will you help with our investigation?"

"I want to. But, see, I'm not actually part of the leadership. Low man on the totem pole, if you know what I mean. They tell me what to do, and I do it."

"What was your mission on Yongxing Island?"

"I didn't know that, sir. I'm just an admin puke. I get the guys ashore, and count noses when it's time to leave. The mustering petty officer, that's me. Guy who counts the bullets and types the requisition forms."

Kuo shook his head. "Let's not do this. You're a master chief. In the Teams, that ranks with officers. We need answers tonight. And believe me, we will get them. What was the mission?"

"I don't know," Teddy said again, gleaning, at least, that they hadn't captured Harch. They stared at each other.

Finally Kuo sighed. "Hands behind you, please."

He nodded to the trooper behind Teddy.

After about the fifth time they brought him up out of the water, Teddy had a come-to-Jesus moment. They weren't going to stop. This was just going to keep on. Time after time, until he drowned, or more likely his heart burst.

He'd been waterboarded at Coronado, during the training. But there was a difference, knowing the guys doing it would get busted if they actually hurt you. That there was a medic next door, ready to bring you back if you passed out or went into convulsions.

He didn't see any medics around here. Just furious, enraged sneers, as if some of the guys they'd taken down out on the dunes had been friends of theirs. Maybe they had. He was pretty sure now this was the 164th, and that he was still on Woody.

But he kept thinking about the brass bell. The one that hung at BUD/S, where, if you couldn't take it anymore, you walked over and rang it. You put your helmet down, with those of the others who *weren't good enough,* and walked away.

"Just shoot me," he mumbled, through the loose teeth, the clotted blood in his mouth. "Fuck you. Fuck all of you."

The big guy—his name seemed to be Lam—said something in Chinese. Kuo bent over, eclipsing the dangling bulb that glared into Teddy's eyes. "Theodore. My friend. Do you really want more of this?"

Oberg struggled to remember who this was. Oh yeah. Redneck Drawl. Probably had a Confederate flag sticker on his pickup. He tried to act like the good guy, like the others were hard-asses and he was only trying to save him. He grunted, "Rack that fucking Mak and shoot me, asshole. I fucking dare you."

"The mission," Kuo said, for about the hundredth time since they'd beaten him some more, with sticks this time, then dragged him down the hall into what looked like a cleaning-gear locker, to judge by the swabs and shelves of what smelled like cleaning chemicals. Strapped him to the board, and slid it over the deep sink.

You didn't need a lot of equipment. Just a sink, a faucet, and a towel. In a pinch, you could do without the sink. He'd done it with a towel and a canteen himself a couple of times. Persuading insurgents to share what they knew. Teddy didn't bother to answer. Fuck him. Fuck them all.

"The mission," Kuo whispered in his ear.

Teddy closed his eyes.

They always waited until he breathed out. This time too. The wet cloth, the struggle to get even a quarter of a breath around it. Then the water, going down his throat. Filling his sinuses. A lot of guys couldn't take that. They tapped out, thinking they were drowning. For a diver, though, it wasn't that terrifying. He gagged, and choked, but kept it wired.

It didn't matter what you did anyhow. You were going to die. You just had to buy into that. Think about something else. Like that platinum blonde he'd plowed in LA, at his grandmother's old house on Lookout Mountain. Loreena? Silvery hair. Shining breasts. Huge, dark nipples. Another wannabe songwriter, starlet. She'd fought him, tried to get away. He liked that. They never fought long.

But this time he couldn't stop his throat from opening. The water slid down his esophagus and into his lungs. Icy cold. He lost it and tried to scream. Mindless, panicking, he writhed and bucked on the board.

"You're shitting yourself," a voice said in his ear. "Theodore? You're disgusting. Listen. We won't let you die. And, no, we won't shoot you. Beg all you want. We know how this works. Your CIA showed us."

"Fuck you."

"Fuck *me? You're* the one who's fucked, Teddy. We can go all night if we have to. Just grunt, and this is over. Why wait? You know you're going to tell us. Even the SERE guys tell you that. Why not get it over with?"

Choking, writhing, blood tiding behind his eyes, Teddy Oberg slid back into the dark. Not knowing if he was coming back. And not caring.

He didn't know where he was. Or who. Or what was going on. Some strange noise was filling his head. A roaring, like under a ship. Was he diving, under a ship? What was the mission? What was the mission. Blackness. No air. Water, down his throat. He twisted and fought. Where was his regulator? Couldn't move his hands. Drop the weight belt. Drop the weight belt. Drop the . . .

"We're gonna take a little break now," someone was saying. Yanked the blindfold off, and slapped his face, hard.

Teddy coughed and choked, vomiting water and snot and stomach acid. His ribs flamed. The light glared. He blinked at a brown concrete wall, a rack of mops.

"Then we'll do it all over again. We have all night. There's no hurry."

He racked in a breath. Snorted what felt like thickened blood through his nose. He blinked at the crazy patterns chasing over the concrete. The room kept rotating. He was getting shadowed images again. Concussion? Or brain damage? It was hard to think, but he forced himself to, whipping his mind like a reluctant donkey. He couldn't feel his hands, which were still locked behind him. All the muscles in his painfully arched back had cramped hard as rocks. He sucked breath, head swimming. It would've been okay to die. He was *ready*. He'd dared them to shoot him. Practically begged.

But these guys weren't going to kill him. Just drown him, over and over.

"We can keep this up all night, Teddy," Kuo said, face leaning in. "All you need is to give us the mission. Come on. Throw me a bone here. I'm on your side, dude." Beads of sweat were running down his temples. Why was *he* sweating? I'm the one getting fucking tortured, Teddy thought. Higher-up must be turning the screws on the interrogator, too.

Someone was talking in the corner, arguing, it sounded like, although even at best the lingo sounded harsh and staccato. Smoke drifted toward the ceiling, but he couldn't smell it. Actually, he couldn't smell anything. Kuo seemed to be arguing for something, the others against. Teddy stared at the overhead, panting, building up the oxygen in his tissues.

The trouble was, the interrogator was right.

Sooner or later, he was going to give it up. Nobody could hold out forever. Not if your torturers knew what they were doing. Take you to the edge and hold you there, and sooner or later, everybody talks. Everybody.

Not Teddy Oberg, some dying, flaring remnant back in his brain screamed.

Yeah. Him too.

He could give them the EMP. That was only the cover, after all. After that, they'd let him alone.

'No," he mumbled, as they started to put the towel over his face again. "No. No. No."

"Going to cooperate, Teddy? Tell us everything?"

He nodded, but Kuo leaned in close. "I don't

456

believe you. Lam here says to do it anyway."

"No. No." He tried to roll away. He couldn't help it; he was weeping.

"You're going to cooperate?"

"Yeah. Yeah."

"You're fucked, right? You know that now?"

"Yeah."

Kuo exchanged glances with someone behind him. "Let's see. What is your commanding officer's name?"

"Harch. Bill Harch. Lieutenant. United States Navy."

"His commander?"

"Laughland. Richard T. Laughland."

"And his?" Kuo was busy making notes on his iPad.

"Uh, I guess that would be Group One: Captain . . . Culver. Yeah. Culver."

They kept going, right up to the president. Kuo made notes. "All right, good. Now we are making progress." He said something to the big guy, Lam, who chuckled. "But, you know, we can resume, if you prefer."

"Please don't," Teddy said. Weeping openly now. A part of his head was separate, watching, without judgment yet. He couldn't take this anymore, that was all. Yeah, he was ringing the fucking bell at last. After all these years.

"And your mission? What were you doing on Chinese soil?"

The bulb above them flickered.

Teddy lay with his mouth open. He stared at the bulb.

It flared, terrifically bright, then burned out with a *pop*.

In the hallway, from the dark, voices boiled, shouting. Something shook the walls, and dust sifted down.

"That," Teddy said.

From the dark, a gabble. One voice, Kuo's. "What was that? What just happened?"

He lay staring up as someone lit matches in the hallway. They'd forgotten him. If he could only get his hands free . . . but they were locked under him in the fucking sharp metal . . . his legs were strapped down too. He writhed, moaning. Crunched his eyelids. He wasn't the hard-ass anymore. Now he was the bitch. The pussy. He'd do anything they told him. Suck their dicks. Turn over and let them fuck him in the ass.

Then he remembered.

There was one thing he wasn't going to tell them.

But he had to tell them everything.

No. He couldn't tell them that.

But he would. Right now, he knew, he would.

Lying there, alone for just a few seconds in the dark, he doubled his tongue back and tried to swallow it. But it was too swollen. He couldn't get a grip on it. He bit down, hard, and blood filled his mouth.

458

• • •

A red glow behind his eyelids. A flashlight flicked around the room, then found him.

"Oh, Teddy, Teddy," Kuo said. Rapid Chinese, and hands grabbed him. Fingers in his mouth. He retched blood.

The bulb flickered. Everyone looked up. It flickered again, then lit, reduced in power, but lit.

"Sergeant Lam is going to be in charge now." Kuo hesitated, then reached out and patted Obie's shoulder. "I'm sorry." He said something else in Chinese, then left. Teddy blinked at the ceiling, too groggy and exhausted to respond.

But he couldn't miss the big hand grabbing his face. Turning it back and forth, the fingers digging into his eyes. "Hello, Oberg," Lam said, slowly, holding his gaze. So, he could speak English too. He was grinning, as if contemplating a steak dinner, something he was really going to enjoy.

Lam nodded to the guys behind Teddy. Metal clanked. A series of clanks, as if something was being wound up. He leaned close. "You left something in the dunes. It didn't hurt us, though. Just blew out a few circuits.

"But you never told us about it."

Teddy didn't answer. Real fear stirred in his gut now. The kind he hadn't felt for a long time.

Lam reached behind him, and metal clinked again. In a lazy voice he murmured, "You arc

459

helpless, my friend. There is no way out. Do you realize that now?"

"Hey," Teddy muttered. "Look, I'm cooperating. I'm your guy now."

Lam's eyebrows went up. "Yes? But now, you see, we do not care. It is too late. What Kuo did, those were the preliminaries. The major is a softhearted man."

Lam leaned close, and whispered into his ear, holding his gaze, smiling. "Now we will start the real interrogation."

24
USS *Savo Island*

The exec's stateroom was much smaller than Aisha's. Made sense; hers was a suite, to host a commodore or an admiral. Still, she felt trapped when the door closed and Staurulakis gestured her to the only other chair, between the sink and a filing cabinet. Diminutive Chief Toan lurked like an uncertain shadow in the open doorway. Until Aisha murmured, "I'm sorry, I know it's late, but . . . And maybe we'd better keep this private."

Staurulakis blew lank greasy-looking hair out of her eyes. "Sheriff? You mind?"

The door clicked closed. Aisha took the wrapped package out of her carpet-purse and set it on the exec's bed. Staurulakis eyed it. "What's that?"

"Something he left behind."

The commander folded small hands and glanced away. In the overhead light shadows were engraved under her eyes. "Tell me what happened. I got a partial report—"

"Probably not much more I can tell you. I was returning to my cabin from the wardroom. Where you and I were talking, over the chili."

"I remember." Glancing away again, at the file cabinet. What did the woman see in her face, that she kept evading her gaze? "Go ahead."

461

"I opened the door. It was unlocked. I didn't notice that at first, but when I hit the switch, the room stayed dark."

"Same as in the hangar. And the fan room. Then what?"

"I ran to my desk, for my gun, but he came out of the dark and grabbed me. Tall. A grating voice. Short hair. With a knife. There was a struggle. I got in a couple of licks with my baton. He may be marked."

"You told the chief corpsman? To watch for someone with wounds, bruises?"

"Seaman Ryan did. She came in. Just at the last minute. He was—" She took a breath, fighting not to show how she felt, what even then closed her throat as she remembered it. *The stairwell.* "He was on top of me, getting ready. She opened the door and he . . . tried for my neck, with the knife."

"Tried to kill you?"

"Yes. And it was a serious try. You can see the marks on the floor tile."

"Attempted murder as well as rape." When Aisha nodded, the exec said, "All right . . . and what's this?" She waved at the bunk.

Aisha undid the brown paper. She'd photographed it in place. Now it lay exposed, sealed in transparent plastic with evidence tape, marked for ID with her initials and the date. A worn-soft baby-blue blanket. Blue satin bindings banded the ends. So old patches were turning brown, although those might also be stains. She didn't want to think from what.

Staurulakis extended a hand, but Aisha grabbed her wrist. "The lab's going to want trace/touch DNA."

"It looks soft."

"There's a tag. Pure lamb's wool. Made in the U.S. Probably fifty years old, maybe older."

"This is what he put on the deck, to rape the victim on?"

"A compulsion. Part of the script he has to reenact."

Staurulakis trailed her fingers over the plastic covering, then turned brisk. "So who is it?"

Aisha grimaced. "On the basis of the voice, I'm going to eliminate one suspect. This guy was disguising his voice, but he's American. I caught a glimpse of his hair, from behind, in silhouette. When the door opened. Almost brush-cut. Which eliminates another . . . whose hair is . . . cowlicked, wild."

"Wenck," the exec said. "I know, you can't give me names. Which leaves who?"

Aisha tilted her head, not wanting to say it, then deciding she didn't have to. "There are still three names on my list. One more than I want to go to an Article 32 hearing with."

Staurulakis shook her head and sighed. A tap at the door. The exec flinched. "Who is it?"

From outside: "Me. For the trash."

"C'mon in, Longley."

The wardroom messman crept in, his ax-like costive face narrowly focused across the room. He grabbed the metal wastebasket, started back to the door, then glanced at the bunk. Turned back, picked up the blanket, and folded it over his arm.

"Longley," Staurulakis sputtered, jumping up, as did Aisha too, horrified. "What the . . . what the *fuck* are you doing?"

He halted, frowning at them. Looked at it, in his hands, then back at them. Murmured, angrily, "What are *you* guys doing with Dr. Noblos's blanket? Belongs at the foot of his bunk. What, did the laundry drop it here? Those assholes. Where's the laundry chit?"

The two women stared at him, mouths open.

An hour later, in the scientist's stateroom. Toan was with them. The exec had confirmed with a call that Noblos was in CIC. Aisha had her SIG, loaded and with a round in the chamber, stuffed into the back of her cargo pants. Just in case he returned, and caught them here.

The whole way down she'd been cursing herself. Though understanding why she'd missed him.

The civilian wasn't on the ship's roster. He was a supernumerary, a rider, like her. So he'd never

464

been given a questionnaire. Never popped in any of her investigations about who'd been on watch when. Because he didn't stand watches.

The Invisible Man. And one with the skills to account for the lacunae on the camera tapes.

His cabin was so clean as to seem uninhabited, full of shining, polished surfaces. The air-conditioned chill was enhanced by the absence of any photos, the lack of any stamp of personality. Longley, who was with them too, said he wasn't allowed to clean, only to pick up laundry and empty the wastebasket; Noblos did his own room. And the room was immaculate. The freshly waxed deck tiles reflected their faces. The clothing in the drawers was as neatly folded as if by a professional valet. Even the toilet articles were carefully arranged, with three toothbrushes, all with red handles, aligned in a rack to dry, as if employed in rotation.

Aisha told the master-at-arms and the steward to stand back, as chain-of-custody witnesses, while she tossed the place. Staurulakis was spinning the dial on the personal safe above the desk, peering at a slip of paper; the exec held the combinations to all the safes on the ship.

Hands sheathed in blue nitrile gloves, Aisha checked the usual hidey-holes: behind drawers, under the mattress, under the bunk frames. Inside the ventilator diffusers, which were easy to remove by unscrewing them. She'd seen some

465

imaginative uses made of common fixtures, for hiding drugs, but came up empty. She unscrewed the cover plates on the electrical outlets. Opened each book and binder, held them over the bed, and shook them.

"Nothing much in here." The exec closed the safe with a dull clank.

"He knows you have access. Does he have a computer? A notebook?"

"Carries it with him. Probably has it up in CIC right now."

She grimaced. If he had files about his activities, a log, they'd most likely be on his machine. But in the end, it was the exec who said, fingering through a small, perfectly aligned row of plastic software and video boxes, "We looking for media?"

"Digital media? With this guy, could be. Sure."

"Recordable DVDs. In boxes marked MDA— Missile Defense Agency?"

They were snapped into the jewel boxes. Sony recordable disks Magic Markered with four-digit numbers, not titles. "Good eye," she told Staurulakis. She didn't want to take them out of the cases until she could dust for prints. She photographed them in place. Then dropped them into evidence bags, sealed them, and ID marked them.

But there were no diaries. No letters. Most serial sexual offenders kept some sort of score sheet, or trophies, so they could reenact their fantasies. Unless the disks contained that. But then, wouldn't they have names, or dates?

Maybe she was assuming too much. "Longley, where did you see the blanket? You said it was his. Are you absolutely sure of that?"

"Right there at the foot of his bed. I started to take it once, to get it cleaned. He shouted at me to leave it there."

Aisha studied the foot of the bunk. She put her hands behind her back and bent closer, studying the seam where the frame abutted the bulkhead.

Then, with a yank, pulled it outward.

Metal clattered to the deck, and light spun from chromed steel. Staurulakis sucked air audibly. Toan murmured something under his breath in Vietnamese, and crossed himself.

The blade shone in the overhead glare. Aisha fitted the evidence bag around it, not touching it. "Chief, sign this form? Commander? This confirms you were present when I searched the room, and lists what we found. Four recordable DVDs. One Case-brand hunting knife, four-inch blade, chrome or nickel plated, with a bone handle."

Staurulakis signed the form and handed it to Toan. "Okay. What now?"

"Run prints on the jewel boxes. Check out what's on the DVDs."

"Confront him? Get a confession?"

467

She glanced at the door. "Chief, keep an eye on that passageway, will you? . . . It might be better to wait for him to notice they're missing. Then he has to find out if we have them, or if someone else does. I've done that before. Somebody this smart, he won't be easy to intimidate."

Staurulakis said, "I have to report this to the captain. He needs to know before we take any action."

Aisha looked around the space one last time. Spotless, almost sterile, filled with reflecting, polished surfaces. Like the blade that had almost killed her.

She nodded. "Then we'd better see him as soon as we can."

Dan lay exhausted in his sea cabin, listening to the mumble of voices from the next deck up. He longed to sleep, but worry kept hauling him back. He sat up, picked up the J-phone to ask the corpsman for something. Then hung up again without hitting the call buttons. He was groggy enough without meds. His chest felt tight. The cough was worse. Some of the crew had reported relapses. Legionellosis was notorious, Grissett had told him, for hanging on. Sometimes for months.

They were back off Miyako Jima, in nearly the same defensive positions as before the task group's incursion into the Taiwan Strait. But with a smaller and less capable force posture.

Mitscher had been hit hard during the action, with seven dead and many more injured. One missile had punched through the side by the boat deck, and torn a great hole just aft of CIC. Another had impacted aft. The third had struck the water close aboard and bounced into the hull. She had fire damage, antenna damage, and casualties from blast, burns, and smoke inhalation. Stony Stonecipher had reported he was no longer combat ready. Dan had detached her, and she was limping back to Guam.

He'd inspected *Savo*'s own damage as they departed the strait. Looked over the forecastle by the shielded light of a flashlight, at twisted, smoking steel, peeled back like the skin of an orange.

The skimmer had come in from astern, most likely from the sub they hadn't localized. Though Mills had pointed out it could also have been air-launched, programmed to loop the ship and approach from astern to maximize surprise.

At any rate, it had come in so fast—transonic, or even supersonic—and so low that they'd picked up on it only seconds before impact. *Savo*'s electronic countermeasures had managed to spoof it away from the centroid, the center of area most seekers calculated as their target. But not far enough to miss entirely.

Hitting at an angle, the warhead had penetrated to the paint locker before going off. The blast had blown off everything forward of the wildcat. Lifelines, bow bulwarks, bullnose, ground tackle, and both anchors. One entire anchor chain, which had run out with a grating rumble for several minutes after the hit. And the upper part of the stem, down to six feet above the waterline. When they'd gotten the fire under control, Dan had ordered them to cut away the damage. This left *Savo* with a gaping hole up forward, like a syphilitic's missing nose. "We'll have to call her Old Shovelnose from here on," Pardees had remarked. The damage-control teams were busy welding and shoring interior bulkheads, but he'd have to avoid taking any heavy seas head-on.

Lying in his bunk, Dan wondered how many more surprises the enemy had.

On the way out, the Japanese had reported receiving new orders. "Mount Shiomi" and "Mount Yari" had been withdrawn from his task force. Losing *Chokai* and *Kurama* left a big hole in his defenses. He couldn't help suspecting a lessening resolve on Tokyo's part.

The Koreans had lost a frigate. But, in a truly heroic action, Admiral Jung had ordered his flagship to stop dead in the water where it had gone down. He'd rescued every man before heading north again.

From what little Dan had heard, they'd scored hits. Whether with Harpoon or torpedo, he wasn't sure. Or so Fleet had said. Oh, not at first.

The first message had dressed him down for leaving station and exceeding orders. An hour later, PaCom had congratulated him on a daring action. The next message from Seventh Fleet had grudgingly withdrawn its condemnation, citing losses among the invasion transports and escorts, but left a sense that he was still on the carpet for leaving station.

The J-phone trilled. He flinched; unsocketed it. "Captain."

It was Singhe. *"Sorry to wake you, sir—"*

"Wasn't asleep. Talk to me, Amy."

"Uh, yessir. We're seeing more transports crossing."

"Reinforcements. More divisions."

"Uh, yessir, looks like it."

"What else?"

"They're beefing up on the Senkakus. We're also seeing increased air activity in the Wenzhou-Ningbo region. Across from Okinawa."

This was new. "How much? What kind? Significant?"

"I'm not sure. Just . . . increased activity."

"Set GQ early if you see a threat coming. Everybody's tired. We'll need more time to man up."

"Uh, I don't see any movement our way yet. But there seem to be a lot of aircraft transiting from south to north along the coast."

His fatigued brain gnawed at this. "Keep an

471

eye on it. Is Captain Fang there? Anything on the fighting ashore?"

"He's here. Stand by, I'll put him on."

Fang said the fighting on the beach was fierce. The ROC had sent in tanks against the perimeter. The mainlanders had heavy air cover, and were proving more adept at close air support of the beachhead than anyone had anticipated. They were also landing airborne troops at the airfield. He finished, *"What is your intent, Dan? Are you going to reattack?"*

A tickle in his throat; he cleared it. "Uh, not possible, Chip. We're down to the bottom of the shot locker on ordnance. The Japanese have pulled out. I'm standing by for orders, whether to hold on till the battle group gets here, or what."

"Roosevelt *is due soon, correct?"*

"That was the plan. They should arrive tomorrow."

"Their fighters will help us regain air superiority. Push the invaders back into the sea."

The tickle grew. He cleared his throat again, then started to cough. Uncontrollably, curling in his bunk like a deep-fried shrimp. White flares shot through his brain. "Crap," he whispered, unable to draw a full breath. His fucking trachea was closing up. Where had he put the fucking inhaler?

"You all right, Dan?"

"Yeah . . . yeah," he wheezed. "Uh, about air

472

support . . . above my pay grade, Chip. Like I said, we're about out of ordnance. And low on fuel again too. Any possibility we can get another drink from that tanker?"

"Bao Shan *was lost, Dan. Torpedoed and sunk on the way back to Hualien. Did I not tell you that?*"

"Oh—yeah, guess you did. Well, *Roosevelt* will have a combat-support ship. We'll refuel from her. Offload you, maybe to the battle group commander's staff? To be his liaison."

"*It is possible. I'll check with my command. They may want me back to fight.*"

"Then we'll probably be heading to Guam. Rearm, and get our bow repaired." He sighed, thinking, And maybe get some sleep, too.

"*Just a minute, Captain. The TAO wants the phone back.*" A rattle, then: "*Captain?*"

"Still here, Amy."

"Just came in. Chinese special forces have occupied Socotra Rock. The Ieodo Ocean Research Station."

"Socotra . . . where the hell's that?"

"There's another island by that name off Yemen, but this one's north of us. Halfway between the Chinese coast and Cheju-do, off Korea."

"All right . . . call me in an hour. Or if anything changes."

"Yes sir. Please get some sleep. You sound terrible."

He fumbled the handset into its socket, then lay

back in the dark. But far from relaxing, his mind tumbled and whirled anew.

Zhang wasn't limiting the war, but widening it. Grabbing another advanced position. This time from the Koreans.

To punish Seoul for Jung's attack? Or just to strike at another U.S. ally?

To intimidate Congress, meeting to vote on the force authorization?

Or just to stake another claim for the Greater China this new president and generalissimo had sworn to his troops was in their grasp?

He lay staring at the overhead, sweating, fighting down the cough. And gradually began the long dark oiled slide down into sleep. He turned over, rearranged his pillow.

Into blackness, at last. Here it came. Thank you. Thank you.

Then someone tapped on his door.

The CO's at-sea cabin was smaller than the scientist's, Aisha noted, and looked far more lived-in. Dirty laundry was stuffed into a corner. Books, binders, and papers were stacked under the folded-down desk, nearly to toppling.

Lenson stood in the doorway, a blue robe with yellow piping pulled over his underwear. His hair was rumpled and looked wet. He tapped the back of a fist against his mouth. "XO. Agent . . . Sheriff Toan. Fuck's going on?"

"Sorry to disturb you, sir."

"Whatever. I wasn't . . . well, I wasn't all the way asleep. Come on in."

After telling the chief to close the door, the exec briefed him in short sentences. Toan held up the evidence bags. Lenson's face grew stony. "In his stateroom? But . . . a lot of people carry knives aboard ship. And an old blanket . . . Not exactly open and shut. Is it?"

"The DVDs probably show the rapes," Aisha said. They'd tried to view them on a computer in Staurulakis's office. "But they're encrypted. We tried the numbers on them as passwords, but they didn't work. We know he's got a camera. If it has an infrared setting, that might be how he took video. We have cybertrained agents in the field offices; they can examine them. Or DCFL—the Defense Computer Forensics Laboratory."

"I told her she needs your permission to take him into custody," the exec added, slouching against the bulkhead as if her bones had softened.

Lenson fingered his chin. "But if they're encrypted . . . in MDA jewel boxes? Could be diagnostic software. Aegis patches."

"But those would be classified," Aisha said. "Should be in his safe, right? Plus, Longley's seen that same blanket every time he's picked up laundry. Terranova and Colón confirm it sounds exactly like what the rapist seated them on. Soft, with a satin border. Circumstantial, so far, but I'm convinced."

Lenson groped for a chair. "He's always had an attitude, but I never thought Noblos was capable of this."

"There's a shadow side to these guys," Aisha told him. "It's almost a cliché to say they seem like they couldn't do it. We need to make an arrest. Take him into custody before he attacks another girl."

"You think he would?"

"I guarantee it."

The CO rubbed his face with both hands—a habitual gesture, she'd noted, when he was buying a couple of seconds, especially when he was tired. If not sick, too. The cramped space smelled of sweat. "Is there still room for doubt? I mean, that he might not be our guy?"

"Not much," Aisha said. "The blanket, the knife, the disks. Once we break the encryption, that last two percent will disappear."

Lenson looked troubled. "The thing is, right now—I hate to say it, but we need him. We've got to keep those system numbers up. Under normal conditions, I'd notify Fleet Forces, get a replacement in the pipeline, and fire him off the ship. But that's not gonna happen. Not now."

"Operational necessity," Staurulakis said, not looking at Aisha. "I agree, sir. At least until we're out of the combat zone."

Lenson nodded. "Uh-huh. Also, now that I think about it . . . is he even under Navy jurisdiction?"

They all looked at Aisha. She said, "Um, to be honest, that's not a black-and-white situation."

Lenson closed his eyes. "What kind of 'situation' is it, then?"

"Well, Captain, first of all, you're right. He's not under UCMJ. Not as a civilian."

"He's a contractor, aboard a U.S. ship in international waters," Staurulakis said.

"That's true, yes ma'am. Which means we can possibly charge him under U.S. Code, under MEJA—"

Lenson interrupted, "Which is what?"

"The Military Extraterritorial Jurisdiction Act permits federal prosecution of crimes committed abroad by DoD civilian employees, or contractors thereof. There's also CEJA, the Civilian Extraterritorial Jurisdiction Act, which lets us prosecute employees of non-DoD federal agencies. I'm not clear yet who his employer is, or who he's subcontracted from."

Lenson said, shading his eyes, "Johns Hopkins, I think via the Missile Defense Agency. We can get the specifics off his clearance. Pull that from Radio, XO."

"Good, but it can be hard to get a case tried under either statute," Aisha added. "If we still had the DNA evidence, it would be easier."

"You just said you were ninety-eight percent certain." Staurulakis frowned.

Aisha smiled painfully. "My being sure, and persuading a prosecutor to take a case to trial, are two different things, Commander."

They gave her the same disbelieving stares she was used to from military people whenever she tried to explain civilian law. At last the captain sighed. "I don't doubt you're right. And I agree, we need to protect our female crew. But I just can't take him out of circulation right now. We're still on the firing line here."

"I understand you need him. But you've got to restrict his movements in some way," Aisha told him. "I can keep tabs on him if you want me to, but he's going to notice things are missing. Then what?"

Outside, in the passageway, the 1MC crackled. *"General quarters. General quarters. All hands man your battle stations."* Simultaneously the 21MC on the bulkhead said, *"CO, TAO: major movement here, multiple incomers. Need you in CIC, right away."*

"Gotta go," Lenson said, bolting for the door. He threw back over a shoulder, "Stay in your stateroom, Agent. We'll reconvene on this, all right? *If* we come out the other side."

25

The general quarters alarm rang on and on. Then cut off as abruptly as it had begun. *Savo* creaked like an aging carriage as she leaned into a slow turn.

Letting himself into CIC, Dan ran his gaze over the displays, the combat systems summary, the surface summary. On the far right, System Availability. Green across the board: SM-2s up, guns up, VLS, TLAM, Harpoon up, and Phalanx ready. But the weapons inventory was sobering. *Savo* had expended all her Harpoons. Her magazines held no more Sparrows, and only two Block 4 antimissile rounds. The seas were heavier tonight. The winds were increasing. The gun video showed the dead black of a night sea, the sparkle of stars. The forecastle camera was focused on the missing bow. The truncated, torn-up ground tackle was only just visible in the starlight.

On the rightmost display, the Aegis picture. As he sank into the command chair, tucking the worn blue plebe-issue bathrobe against the contact of bare skin with icy leather, a new constellation glittered at extreme range. Wenck and Terranova had their heads down at their console, palavering in low voices.

The callouts identified the USS *Franklin D. Roosevelt* battle group. The carrier. A cruiser. Three destroyers. And the replenishment ship that would refuel *Savo* before she and *Curtis Wilbur* headed back to Guam.

After that . . . it was out of his hands. For good, or ill.

"*FDR*'s three hundred miles away," Singhe murmured, beside him. "Call sign of battle group commander is 'Shangri-La.' Ten, twelve hours out, if the seas don't get any steeper, and they maintain speed." From the strike officer, the familiar scent of sandalwood. From him, he was afraid, the reek of sleep, perspiration, and unwashed underwear.

"Okay, but why'd you sound GQ?"

"We received a launch cuing, Captain."

"From where? All our satellites—"

"Not a satellite. From AWACS. Passed to us via the Slow Lead data link."

"Dave got that set up? I never heard—"

Singhe blinked. "I believe he told you, yessir—"

Dan twisted in his seat, cutting her off. "Donnie? Chief Wenck?"

"Yessir, we're lookin' for it." His and Terranova's intent frowns, lit a jaundiced amber, hovered above the console.

"Where do they cue it to . . . okay, yeah." He read the note, in Singhe's handwriting, on a message log beside the red phone. The launch coordinates were far inland, in the Wuyi Mountains. Farther than he'd thought AWACS could reach. They must be at extreme altitude, max radiated power. Trying to fill the gap left by the loss of the satellites. Or else the allies had some other reconnaissance asset out there. Perhaps a high-altitude drone.

"Shifting to ALIS mode," Wenck announced. "But it's probably out of range."

Dan took a last glance at the rightmost screen. "Put up the gun radar."

Terranova's soft voice: "All stations, Aegis control. Stand by . . . shift to BMD mode."

The god's-eye view vanished, succeeded, in the next blink of an eye, by the fanlike sector scan. The gun radar came up on the port display, providing at least a little local awareness. Dan felt naked without Stonecipher watching his back. But nothing threatened on either screen. Just the random freckle of terrain return from far inland. He flinched away as someone set coffee down next to him. When he looked up, it was Fang. The liaison's shoulders sagged.

"Thanks, Chip. You bearing up?"

"Doing okay. Look like you need a jolt, Captain."

Dan took a slug, monitoring the ALIS output on the rightmost display. The search beams clicked back and forth. The sea between *Savo* and the

Chinese coast gave nothing back. The coastline came up clearly, outlined in honey yellow. Behind it, a variegated clutter of mountain return. To southward, a ghostly-faint return from northern Taiwan.

The display blanked, changed. "These coordinates," Wenck announced at the same time the forward door creaked and someone else let himself in. Dan spared a quick glance. It was Dr. Noblos.

The man they'd just fingered as *Savo*'s resident rapist.

The scientist was in slacks and a homey-looking green cardigan sweater. His short white hair was brushed back. He leaned against the jamb with arms folded and chin up. "Those launch coordinates are out of your range," he said, with an air of being glad to say so.

Dan said, "Can we get on it when it's in range?"

"Doing that now, sir," the Terror muttered.

The forward door creaked open again. Really, he had to get somebody to check out the hinges and seals. A noisy watertight door was one ready to fail. *Savo* was getting weary too. She deserved a spell in port. An overhaul.

A slight figure in blue coveralls slipped in. Noiselessly, it drifted to a corner opposite the scientist. Chief Toan, the "sheriff." Keeping an eye on Noblos, as directed.

Dan shifted his attention back to the situation at

hand. "Good on ya, Terror. Amy, any way we can get updates on the track via—"

"On it, Captain. Those go to ALIS automatically as they're generated. This is just a slower data link than satcomm used to give us."

"Understood." He stared up at the screen, hands flat on the desk. Waiting for their cued target to come over the horizon, to where the radar could grab it.

"There it is," Terranova murmured at the same moment Wenck said, "Locking on. Jeez. Like a bat outta hell."

The brackets vibrated around a small, fast-moving white dot just off the coast. It clicked forward with each sweep, as if escapement-loaded. Headed toward Taiwan, but the altitude and speed from the swiftly climbing readouts told him, even in the absence yet of a predicted impact point, that it wasn't aimed at the island itself. "Missile lock-on, designate contact Meteor Juliet. Going way too fast, too high, for Taipei," Wenck called.

Singhe murmured, "Not coming our way, either. Azimuth's too far south."

Dan blew out and relaxed in his chair. Exchanged a relieved nod with Fang. "So . . . where *is* it aimed?"

Singhe typed, then studied her screen. "Someplace to the east. We'll know in a couple of minutes. Once ALIS generates aim point."

"Impact point. Not aim point. They're different,

Amy. Intent versus result. You hardly ever hit exactly where you aim."

"Thank you, Captain. Correction noted." She jotted something on her notepad.

Captain Fang lifted a headphone from one ear. "I have speed and altitude data from our Patriot battery. By voice."

"Good. Can they take it?"

"No. They can track, feed us data, but they are out of missiles, Dan. As I told you? They were all expended countering the attacks."

Why did everyone keep telling him they'd already told him things? Obviously, a conspiracy. To gaslight him. Or else *he* was missing stuff. He grunted, "Uh-huh, understand. Anybody got an ID?"

Terranova said, head down, "Seems to be a two-stager . . . we saw separation . . . but still, a pretty big return . . . could be a DF-21."

"Intermediate range. Solid-fuel, two-stage, road-transported," Chief Wenck added.

Dan leaned back and stretched, frowning. It was clearer with each second that the missile, still gaining altitude as it arched over the west coast of Taiwan, wasn't headed for that island. But if not, where? Or was it just a threat, a demonstration, on the order of "your antimissile capabilities are exhausted; Taipei is helpless now"?

Noblos, bending next to him. "You haven't figured it out yet, have you, Captain?"

Dan snapped, "If *you* have, Doctor, please enlighten us."

The scientist leaned forward, over his shoulder, and tapped Dan's keyboard. The screen jumped back.

Dan stared, his spine going rigid. The display jumped again, zooming away. Showing the missile's extended track.

Pointed almost due east.

Three hundred miles to the southeast of *Savo*, four hundred miles east of Taiwan.

At the battle group. And even as he watched, an IPP blinked into existence on the rightmost display. An oval, outlined in blinking yellow. Quivering at the edges, like some invertebrate alien life-form not yet decided on its shape as ALIS calculated and recalculated ten times a second.

Centered over the far-flung circular formation of the oncoming carrier and its screening units.

"Pass to *FDR*, pass to Fleet, pass to PaCom. Flash red. Incoming ballistic missile, type unknown, possible DF-21." But next to him, Singhe was already typing. He unsocketed his handset, waited for the red light, and went out on high-frequency Fleet Warning. "Shangri-La and all stations this net, Shangri-La and all stations this net: Flash, flash, flash. From Ringmaster. Ballistic-missile launch, targeted roughly 21 degrees, 46 minutes north, 123 degrees, 40 minutes east. Premliminary IPP, location Shangri-La. ETA one-one minutes. Flash. Flash."

He repeated it, then signed off without waiting for acknowledgment. Swung to yell across the compartment, "Donnie, can we take it?"

"It's a crossing engagement," Noblos observed. "You'd be wasting your ordnance."

"We only have two Block 4s left," Singhe murmured.

"That's *FDR* it's targeted on, Amy. Remember, intel said they were deploying on an anticarrier weapon." He pushed back and joined Wenck and Noblos as they huddled behind Terranova at the console. The chief looked worried. "Can we take it?" Dan asked again.

"Wait one . . . trying to get you an answer on that, Skipper. But the numbers aren't good."

Dan waited. Then, putting his revulsion aside, faced Noblos. "Doctor, we need your advice here."

The bristly eyebrows lifted. "Really? I don't see why. If you plan to throw your rounds away."

Dan tried for patience. He gritted his teeth. "How to maximize our probability of kill. If we take this guy on. Anything we can do?"

"Oh. Absolutely." The physicist nodded, all too smugly.

"Then *what?*"

"Be three hundred miles south of here." The physicist smiled. "Short of that, all I can say is, remember, the Block 4 is a terminal-phase interceptor. It's not designed for midcourse, in-space interception at the velocity and altitude this thing's traveling at. If you shoot too soon, the sustainer will burn out before it gets up there."

Noblos lifted his gaze to the overhead. "Your optimal intercept point will be the product of its closest slant-range point of approach to you. And long enough after it starts its descent so the terminal body still has enough fuel to maneuver to a collision. You can plot the vectors. A three-dimensional solution . . . On second thought, better let ALIS do that. Once your target crosses 125 degrees longitude, it'll be traveling away from you. Converting from a crossing engagement to a tail chase. In which case, it will actually be moving faster than your own warhead."

"I could have told you that, Dan," Donnie Wenck said. His cheeks were flushed; his hair was pawed into a roostertail. "We don't need this asshole to explain the obvious."

"This, from the *technician* who doesn't know how to tune for temperature differences across the array face." Noblos smiled sadly, and shook his head. "Fools," he whispered, just loud enough to be heard.

Dan slid between them, figuring Wenck was just hot enough to throw a punch. Not that he didn't feel like it too, but . . . "Leave it. Leave it! Yeah, we're just the button monkeys, Doctor. Help us out. Show us how it's done."

Noblos cleared his throat. With a superior smile, he leaned in to type rapidly on Terranova's keyboard. His left hand came to rest on her shoulder. She looked up, and her eyes widened. Dan tensed, began to grab for it, but the hand removed itself to enter another command.

Noblos straightened. "There. They'll still miss, but it's the best you're going to do."

"Donnie. Terror. Does that look good to you?" As they nodded he called across the slanting space, "Amy, did *FDR* roger on our flash?"

"Yes sir. They rogered up. Asked if we could intercept."

Terranova murmured, "ALIS is giving a probability of kill of less than ten percent."

"Thanks, Terror.—Tell 'em we're trying, but the odds are against it. Do what they can. It's"—he eyed the screen—"eight minutes out. Prepare to engage."

Singhe muttered, "Fire authorized?"

"Not just yet, Amy. Goddamn it, don't hurry me!"

He regretted the outburst at once, but set it aside as the CIC officer laid a red-bindered book atop the console. Pointed to a subhead. "It's probably just a warning shot," the officer muttered.

"I'd say so too," Singhe called across the compartment. "Just firing over our bow. They'd never dare . . . ?"

Dan was inclined to agree, but couldn't shake an ominous feeling. Zhang had threatened to take on anyone who intervened. *Savo* shuddered; she was slewing around, coming to a better launch bearing, a compromise between a course to clear the booster smoke and one that would smooth out her roll in these rougher seas. Theoretically, a Standard could exit its cell at up to a 15-degree angle. But the more nearly vertical, the less chance of a glitch or hang-up.

The salvo alarm began to ring, a steady drone far aft. *"Now set material condition Circle William throughout the ship,"* the 1MC announced. The vent dampers clunked closed, cutting off the air intakes from the exhaust plume, which seethed with toxic chemicals. The firing litany began.

Dan stood swaying as the deck slanted beneath his feet. He pressed his eyelids together and knuckled his eyeballs. Behind them fireworks bloomed. Coruscating scarlet and viridian shapes pulsated, migrating across the blackness of his visual field. Like the ionization trails that the warhead, traveling five or six miles a second, would shortly grow as it began its plunge, drilling down toward its target.

Time was running out. He tried to go over it again, to make sure he was right. Noblos said it was a waste. And they were his last two rounds. Despite his fatigue, his growing confusion, lack of sleep, he had to do this right.

Meteor Juliet, whatever payload it carried, whatever message it was meant to convey, was nearing midphase. The data callouts registered the unvarying speed consistent with ballistic flight. Coasting in a huge parabola, most of which lay outside Earth's atmosphere. His Standards would be trying to intercept it there, before reentry. But despite its terrific speed, there was no friction heating in the vacuum of space. The missile was infrared-dim, though seeing it from the side, its radar cross section should make it visible to the seeker head.

Another plus: ALIS indicated a solid lock-on. Since Standards began their flights depending on commands from the launching ship, both rounds should go out boresighted on the target. Or, rather, that patch of imagined space ahead of it, where it should be when their courses met, far above the last wisps of air.

And yet a third reason for optimism: the upper stage would still be in one piece. Once reentry began, temperature would build. The warhead's ablative sheathing would char off. The ionization plume would blur the radar return. At some point, also, the burnt-out engines would break apart into tumbling, burning debris. Sometimes releasing decoys, too.

If only the Patriot battery south of Taipei had had a couple of rounds left. They'd been in prime geometry for a boost-phase intercept.

On the very thin plus side, he didn't have to worry about interference from another anti-missile radar.

On this hand, on the other hand. But it didn't really matter, did it? This was what a U.S. Navy cruiser was built for. Protecting the carrier. This time, though, he wasn't being asked to throw his ship under the bus. Just expend his last rounds. However marginal their chances.

Singhe called, "One-minute warning. Fire gate selection. Launchers in 'operate.' Two-round salvo. Warning alarm sounded. Deselect all safeties and interlocks. Stand by to fire. On CO's command."

Dan crossed back to his desk. Bending past Fang, who was speaking urgently in Chinese on his net, he flicked up the cover over the Fire Auth switch. Even as it was tracking, ALIS was busily computing the probabilities of kill. He set his finger firmly on the switch, and snapped it to fire.

The bellow vibrated the stringers, the deck-plates. A brilliant sun ignited on the previously black camera display, lighting the fantail, illuminating *Savo*'s wake, whipped-cream white against a heaving midnight sea. "Bird one away," the combat systems coordinator announced. Another roar and rattle succeeded it. "Bird two away."

"That's it," Singhe breathed. "We're shit out of Block 4s."

Dan bent over the desk, watching the Aegis picture. Two symbols had departed *Savo*'s blue-circle-and-cross, heading south. He unsocketed the red phone again. "All stations this net, this is Ringmaster. Break. I have taken incoming missile with my last two Block 4 Standards. P-sub-K below ten percent. IPP remains centered over *FDR* strike group. Impact in six minutes. Over."

When a hollow voice acknowledged, he signed off. Snapped to Singhe, "Make a separate report. Magazines empty except for antiair rounds and land-attack Tomahawk. No fish left. Full loadout of gun rounds remains. Increasing air activity over the mainland, north of Taiwan. Fuel state nearing critical. Awaiting orders."

He lifted his gaze to meet Noblos's. The scientist was leaning against the door again, his habitual station, elbows cupped in palms. He gave back a lazy, insolent smirk. Glanced at Terranova. Then back at Dan, still smiling.

Dan straightened, suddenly ignited with rage. Shit! Was this asshole *laughing* at him? Had he discovered the missing DVDs? The missing blade? Did he *know* they knew?

No. He couldn't. Not yet. Noblos thought he was above suspicion. And, thanks to his equivocal status aboard, exempt from the Uniform Code. In international waters. Beyond prosecution.

But . . . fuck that! Dan gripped the back of his chair. He wouldn't give up until, somehow, the guy paid for what he'd done. To Terranova. To his other victim, Celestina Colón. For the fear and distrust he'd spread between men and women. And not least, for his violation of Dan's trust, and the duty and respect every sailor owed his shipmates.

"Stand by for intercept, salvo one," the Terror muttered. "Stand by . . . *now.*"

They stared up at the screen.

The brackets, blue for own-ship missile, red for target warhead, nearly merged.

Nearly. But the blue bracket seemed to lag.

Then fell behind, altitude callouts dropping. Slowly at first, then quickly.

"Maneuvering burnout," Wenck murmured, just loud enough to carry.

Noblos sniggered. Dan clenched his fists, but said nothing. Not yet.

ALIS's lock-on faltered. The brackets winked off, then back on. They jittered before locking on again. A nimbus of ionized gas was forming, a ghostly halo circling the now-plunging warhead. "Juliet, starting terminal phase," Terranova called.

The second set of brackets, where Aegis was tracking *Savo*'s other round, paced the speeding target for long seconds. The distance between them narrowed. Then held steady.

Then it, too, began to fall behind.

"Told you so," Noblos said cheerfully. "Another five million down the drain."

493

"I heard you, Bill," Dan said. "I had to try."

"Hey, it's only money. And now you all get to go home! I understand. Believe me." He chuckled. Waved a hand. Turned away, and undogged the forward door, before Dan could respond. The heavy steel protested as it came open, then thunked closed behind him. He didn't bother to operate the dogging bar. Chief Wenck stepped over and, in one swift, violent chopping shove, sealed it behind the civilian.

"Permission to self-destroy," Terranova said in a resigned voice.

Dan hesitated, wondering if it was necessary. If they shouldn't just let the terminal stage drop, vanish, into the wastes of the far Pacific. Then nodded. It was just conceivable it might endanger some lone fishing vessel. "Granted, Terror. Self-destruct."

"Mark, Meteor Juliet time on top," Amarpeet Singhe said in a subdued voice.

The Aegis display flickered, then blanked. They blinked up at a Blue Screen of Death. "What just happened?" Dan said.

Wenck muttered, "Not sure . . . suddenly lost power out. Maybe that hinky driver-predriver blew. Shifting to backup."

"Let's get out of BMD mode. Go to normal air," Dan ordered. He wanted a look around.

The screen came back on, but took several seconds to repopulate. The air activity over the mainland came up again, if possible, denser than before. It was concentrated opposite Okinawa now. Two U.S. F-15s were orbiting out in the strait, between Okinawa and Socotra Rock. Which, he recalled, the Chinese had just occupied.

"TAO, Radio." The 21MC on the command desk.

"Go."

"This is Radio. Dropped comms with Shangri-La."

"This is the captain. What did you lose? Data link? Slow Lead?"

"All comms, Cap'n. Tried to reestablish on voice coordination. They're not answering up."

Dan told them to keep trying. He was double-clicking off when another station came up. *"CIC, Bridge."*

"TAO, go," Singhe said into the remote in front of her. Glancing at Dan.

"Something funny up here . . . lookouts report a flash way out on the horizon. Bearing relative zero three zero. Still kind of a fading glow out there."

Dan glanced at the heading indicator, and converted the bearings in his head. To the southeast. The sun? He checked his Seiko. Too early. Their own self-destructing Standards? Not that small an explosion, that far away. "Bring up the aft camera."

It came up almost at once. The horizon was clearly visible, jagged with the growing seas. But it shouldn't be visible at all at this time of night. As they watched, the sky faded, very slowly, until all was dark again.

"What the hell," Wenck muttered, "was that?"

Fang breathed, "It can't be. Zhang's mad. Insane."

Dan gripped the edge of the command desk, breathing hard. Trying to keep it together. He clicked the Send lever again. "Radio, Captain. Any contact with the battle group yet?"

"Nothing heard, Skipper."

"Keep trying. All circuits. Keep me advised."

The Aegis screen jumped back, zoomed out. A patch of return shimmered. An elongated blob, where there'd been distinct contacts. Where six ships had steamed . . . "Ionization effects, bearing and range consistent with strike group," the Terror pronounced tonelessly.

No one else said anything. Until Dan said, "Make a voice report. Navy red flash. Nuclear detonation report. You know the drill."

26
Somewhere in China

Teddy Oberg stared at a steel chain inches from his eyes. It swayed and rattled. The metal floor beneath him, only thinly padded by shit- and piss-smeared straw, flexed and creaked as the bogies jolted slowly over a slanted roadbed.

"We're sending you for remolding," his final interrogator had said. "You are a war criminal, member of a criminal organization. Do you understand?"

"You mean . . . the U.S. Navy?"

"No, Oberg. I mean the SEALs. Do you understand why they are a criminal organization?"

"I understand now. Yes."

"What are they?"

"Terrorists. Assassins. Murderers of children and women."

"You deserve to die for your crimes. But perhaps you're not beyond help."

"Where?" he'd managed to whisper.

"You will see when you get there."

When they were done, they had turned him over to the political police. Flown him off the island, to the mainland, he assumed, though there were no windows in the cargo bay of the transport. His sessions with State Security, carried out with more leisure than the military had displayed, had left him with what he judged were torn rotator cuffs in his shoulders. This was from being hoisting into the air and dropped with his arms cuffed behind his back. When they weren't doing that, he was still pinioned, but in a way he'd never seen before. One arm was pulled up and over his shoulder, cuffed to the other, which was twisted up behind his back. Not only was it agonizing, it made it impossible to take a full breath. Along with no sleep, very little food, and the beatings.

Of course, the beatings. He'd blacked out several times during those weeks. Couldn't remember much now. A lot seemed to have been erased. Just blank. Where he'd had memories was now just animal terror.

They loved shackles, that was for sure. He hadn't spent half an hour without cuffs since Yongxing. The good news was that on the last pee-and-mush break, one of their car guards, a teenager with a round, pouch-cheeked face, had unlocked each prisoner, one at a time, as another guard stood aiming an AK. He'd locked the left or right cuff, depending on which side you lay on, to the chain. This left each prisoner with one hand free, so they didn't have to piss in their pants now; they could piss into the straw. The first time Teddy did, he wasn't surprised to find his urine was deep red with blood.

He was crammed into a boxcar with a hundred Vietnamese. The Viets, many wounded, had been captured during an action in the Paracels. A helicopter had strafed them after their ship went down, then been shot down in turn. Two crewmen had made it out of the crash. They hadn't lasted long, when they hit the water in the midst of the surviving Vietnamese.

This was the only news he'd had of the war since he'd been captured.

He lay on his back in the shit- and pus-fouled straw as the train jolted along, creeping uphill. The car was too cold at night to sleep, but too hot during the day to do much more than sweat. Two long chains ran fore and aft, padlocked into welded staples at each end. The prisoners were shackled to the chains. In four days since loading, they'd left the car three times. The guards unlocked the chains at the ends, then shouted the prisoners out to relieve themselves beside the right-of-way. Always in thick forest, or on a deserted, gravelly mountainside looking out over a bleak plain. At the head of the train, a black locomotive panted, venting steam and smoke as it took aboard water and fresh coal. The prisoners had been given bowls of cold cornmeal mush and murky water from pails. Several of the Vietnamese had died, but were still shackled to the snaffle. Obviously, to make the count come out right when they got wherever they were going. Teddy had eyed the mush. Started to scoop out a bowl; then handed it to the guy next to him. Who'd goggled at him, before wolfing it down.

From the position of the sun during these breaks, he figured they were headed north. He observed this from habit only. His apathy would have scared him if he'd cared. He could spring that padlock. An old German design they'd covered in lock-picking class. But what would be the point? Plus, every move hurt. His leg and shoulders were minefields of agony. His foot hung twisted, limp. He could barely generate the will to prop himself on an elbow to catch the occasional whiff of fresh air that came in from the barred grating high up on the side of the car.

He closed his eyes in the jolting darkness.

Wouldn't it be better just to die?

Some interminable time later, iron wheels clanked to a halt. The train stood motionless and silent for a long while. Someone wailed, far away, and the muffled coughing from the other prisoners never stopped. The Vietnamese seemed to have a lot of lung trouble. Maybe from inhaling fuel. Plus, each succeeding night seemed to get colder, the air less substantial. They were climbing, gradually, to some high plateau.

Suddenly the doors slid open, clanging and echoing. The guards' shouts caromed around, along with a racket they liked to make whacking the steel walls with batons. "*Du chulai*! *Du chulai*! *Pow, pow*!*" He wasn't sure what that meant literally, but it seemed to be pretty much like the "*raus, raus*" you heard the SS shouting in movies. The Viets scrambled up, those who could, and edged toward the bluish evening light at the door. Those who couldn't were hauled to their feet by their chainmates. Teddy's two nearest mates got up slowly. Both older, maybe officers, he couldn't be sure. One, Trinh, spoke some English. But Teddy didn't want to know them any better. No point to that, either.

Outside, it was evening. A barren waste stretched around them, made more haunting by a stiff wind that kicked up dust and tumbleweeds. The rails stretched into the distance. A water tower, a pile of coal, a ramshackle shed. The perfect setting for a rice Western. An ancient Chinese sat propped against a rusty loader, backdropped by immense heaps of brown dirt. He nodded, smiling and clapping as the guards beat the prisoners out of the cars and unshackled them. "*You mi bang*," the troops shouted, then louder, as if yelling harder would make them comprehend. "*You mi bang*! *Mi bang*!" They pushed, shoved, and clubbed them toward the piles.

Teddy figured it out. The stack of shovels. Seizing one, he was rewarded with a curt nod from a guard. Dragging the useless leg, he

501

hobbled to the heap and dug in. Under the brown dust, black coal. A husky Vietnamese with bandaged hands grabbed a wheelbarrow, and Teddy and the other prisoners started filling it, those without shovels using cupped hands.

When he glanced up, Teddy was startled to find himself looking into another European face. The other flinched back too. Stick-thin, almost ghostlike, with a narrow, projecting chin, a brown scraggy beard. Were his own eyes that haunted? "Where the 'ell'd you come from?" the wraith muttered.

"U.S. Navy. What're you . . . Australian?"

"Too right." They couldn't shake hands under the guards' gazes, but traded a word each time they passed. The guy's name was Pitchard, or Pritchard. "Mates call me Magpie."

"Obie."

"Guess their loader's cactus. Truly back o' Bourke here, eh?"

"Ass end of nowhere. You a pilot?"

"Radar-O. Shot down in the South Sea. You?"

"Diver."

Pritchard cast an eye around them. "Fella could walk off right here."

"If he could walk," Teddy said. Pritchard eyed his foot, then turned away to hammer with the point of his shovel at an immense solid block of coal, breaking it into pieces small enough to haul. A guard screamed and they separated, but kept track of each other as they moved about.

Teddy began to detect an unwelcome sensation, as if his guts were about to drop out. He hadn't had a bowel movement in a week. Why now? But it was undeniable. Immediate. He nodded to Pritchard and Trinh, and approached one of the guards.

The trooper eyed him as he neared, unslinging his AK. The old model with the wooden stock. Every SEAL trained with Kalashnikovs. If he could get his hands on it . . . He bowed. "Mister Honorable Guard, or whatever. Permission to take a crap."

"*Manwei bowgow.*" The guard made a threatening gesture with his rifle.

Teddy cringed. "Take a crap." He pointed to his ass.

The guard's eyes widened. "*Manwei bowgow,*" he shouted, face contorting. "*Manwei bowgow!*"

Teddy got it that time. He bowed again, lower this time. Murmured, humbly, "*Manwei bowgow,* you officious cat turd."

"*Zhe shi gang heshi de! Ni zhang yao shenme?*"

Teddy pointed to his ass again, then off to behind the coal piles. The guard shook his head, scowling. He nodded to the bare dirt by the rail line, where, Teddy saw, other prisoners had left their meager droppings.

As he trudged up the embankment, the first stars were coming out, low in the west. He blinked up at them, mind empty.

He was squatting, pants down, when shouting erupted. The guards were aiming at a distant figure. Arms pumping, it was shrinking into the desert. At a word of command, four shots popped in the stillness. The figure jerked, then toppled.

As Teddy had hoped, when it was time to reshackle, the guards didn't bother to match up names. They just counted a hundred heads into each car, and resecured them. He and Magpie drifted together and got locked into the same snaffle. They started a low conversation as the train jolted back into motion. Rolling north.

Away from the sea.

27
USS *Savo Island*

Aisha waited outside the unit commander's stateroom. As the appointed time approached, they showed up, one by one: Toan, the master-at-arms. His burlier assistant. Cheryl Staurulakis, pasty and shell-shocked. The command master chief, leathery-faced Tausengelt. They filed inside, grim-faced and unspeaking.

The news had raced through the ship. Three people had told her at breakfast. Apparently she was one of the last to know, since she hadn't been on watch, or in one of the berthing compartments, to be wakened and whispered to.

She'd tidied up the front room, and moved all her belongings into the smaller bunkoom. Leaving the coffee table cleared, and the chairs—including the one the intruder had clubbed her with two nights previous—ranged against the bulkhead. She shivered. It was so cold. Was something wrong with the heating? The engine noise seemed louder too, and the ship rolled from time to time, hard and long, as if something monstrous had it in its jaws and was tasting it before biting down in earnest.

Finally Lenson arrived. The CO murmured "Hello, Hal" to Toan, raising an eyebrow. The chief master-at-arms flashed shining metal cuffs from a jumpsuit pocket, then concealed them again. Aisha was wearing a loose flowered wrap over her jumpsuit, and under it, a shoulder holster. She reached in to check the loaded-and-locked 9mm. The baton was in the pocket of her cargo pants. She'd carried both ever since the attack.

A tap at the door. "Come in," Tausengelt called.

Dr. William Noblos half ducked to enter, then halted, glaring around. His escort, one of the junior masters-at-arms, closed the door and went to parade rest, blocking the exit. Aisha tracked the scientist's glance. It went around the room and dwelt on her. Then dropped—involuntarily, perhaps—to the knife-gouge in the tile.

"What the hell's this?" he said angrily. "They've left you staked out here, Dan. *Roosevelt*'s gone. The Philippines are under attack. The only way we're staying alive is if I can keep those radars going. Keep fighting until Washington gets the picture. We've lost, we're defeated, we have to pull back."

Lenson seemed to ruminate an answer, but looked to her instead. "Agent? You have the floor."

She stepped forward as Toan moved in from the other side. "William Noblos, you're under arrest."

He grinned. "Arrest? On what specious, idiotic charge?"

"Rape, malicious wounding, and attempted

murder." She glanced at Toan, and nodded.

Noblos stepped back as the chief approached. Under the wrap, Aisha's hand went for her pistol. But instead of resisting, the physicist raised his voice. "No need. I'm cooperating. But this is bullshit. Captain, think. Your ALIS team can barely read your AREPS data. Your radar's out of parameters. *Mitscher*'s gone. The Japanese have pulled out. You're putting your whole crew at risk. For what? Because some airhead says she got groped?"

Lenson, after a moment, put out a hand. "Chief. Stand down."

"Sir?" Toan halted, looking puzzled.

"He's not resisting. Let him have his say."

Aisha started to object, then glanced at the captain and didn't. Those gray eyes glittered like sea ice. "So, go on then. What are you saying, Bill? That you didn't rape Petty Officer Terranova, and try to murder the special agent here? Show me I've got the wrong guy. I'll be happy to call this off."

The J-phone on the bulkhead squealed, making everyone jump. Tausengelt answered in a low voice. Handed it off to the exec. Staurulakis nodded, glanced at Lenson.

"What is it, Cheryl?"

"They want one of us in CIC. I'll go?"

The captain nodded. "Call if you need me. . . . Okay now, where were we?"

507

As the door closed behind the exec, Noblos smiled frostily. "You were making threats, Dan. Accusing me of something I didn't do. If I can prove I'm innocent, you'll call it off? You'll have to call it off anyway! Why bother with this charade?" He grimaced. "Oh, I see. To rattle me. Make me come clean. Well, I don't think so."

He shifted that contemptuous grin to Aisha. "Or, wait. It was her idea, right? I'm going to break down, blurt out a confession. Does that work with the teenaged seamen you usually grill, Special Agent? Frightened ignoramuses who have no idea of their rights? Do you understand who I am, what I've done for the Ballistic Missile Defense Organization, the national missile defense program, the Defense Science Board?"

"It doesn't matter." Aisha tapped the toe of her boot on the scarred tile. "We have your knife. Your blanket. Your videos. Very interesting viewing. Plus gun-camera footage of you in the helo hangar, in the supply fan room, and in the Equipment Room on the 03 level with Terranova."

This wasn't actually true. The gaps in the taped record, which they were assuming showed him, had been deleted or overwritten. But the point right now wasn't to stick to facts, but to force an admission. "You were in here two days ago, with that knife. I identified you then. I'd say we're airtight, without any admissions from you at all."

She paused, reflecting once more that they still hadn't been able to break the encryption on the files. They were guessing what was on there. To that extent, he was right; she was bluffing, hoping for a breakdown, a confession.

Which she still might get, if she could play on that overweening pride. His conviction that he operated above everyone else's intellectual level, that they were ants creeping about his feet. "But you deserve to be on the record, Doctor. So what did you want to say? Now's your chance to tell us."

Noblos tossed his head, eyeing Toan, who still hovered between him and the captain. "Why should I say anything? As soon as those cuffs are on, I'm entitled to counsel. Correct, Special Agent?"

"Um . . . correct," she murmured. Not under the Uniform Code of Military Justice, but if they were going to charge him under MEJA, he was right. "You are so entitled." She added, "I see you've looked up the relevant statutes, in anticipation of your arrest. Still a step ahead of us, I guess."

He smiled. "It's not that hard." He tilted his head toward the chairs. "If you don't mind. Since you're obviously having second thoughts about staging your little drama. Dan?"

"Not a problem," Lenson said. After a moment, he pulled down a chair too, facing the physicist across the coffee table. She wasn't really sure how or when it had happened, but the confrontation was between the two men now, with the rest reduced to onlookers.

Noblos said, "All right, let's set up the problem. What exactly am I being accused of?"

"Like the agent said. Assault, rape, attempted murder."

"Ridiculous. You'd never bring me to trial."

Lenson regarded him steadily. Aisha remembered the scuttlebutt about this captain: that he'd actually once executed a murderer; hanged him, aboard an old destroyer. She didn't believe it, but something about his cold stare made her shiver. "Oh, I think we could," he said.

"You can't bullshit me, about those disks. None of you could break the encryption I put on them."

"The Justice Department can."

"No, Captain. Not even them. Maybe the NSA, but it would take years of supercomputer time. Which I doubt they'd be willing to commit, in the middle of a war. It's a block cipher with a 128-bit key. No one's ever going to see what's on there unless I give them the key."

"So what's on them?" Aisha put in. "Your home movies?"

The hard smile turned on her. "Test-results data. Tuning algorithms. Highly classified software."

"Not video footage? Your rape records?"

"What an imagination, Special Agent. You should write for television."

Lenson said, "What about the knife? The blanket? Longley identified it as yours."

Noblos rolled his eyes. "A knife? Someone planted it. I don't own one. The blanket? Yeah, that's mine. Someone stole it from my room. I'd like it back, by the way. There's nothing that proves it was at your crime scenes. Just the assertions of a couple of hysterical women." Noblos caught himself. "I mean, no doubt they were attacked. But not by me. The agent here needs to do her job. Not persecute someone who's out here at great personal risk to help his country."

"I believe her," Lenson said.

Noblos pulled a face. "So . . . what? You arrest me? Confine me to quarters? You can't."

"Try me," the captain said. "You're not getting away with these crimes. I promise you that."

Noblos addressed the compartment at large. "Let's sum up. None of you can prove a thing. But even if you could, you can't do without me. Not if you hope to survive out here.

"Actually, come to think of it, right now, arresting me would be the best thing for the ship all around."

Lenson blinked. "How do you reach that conclusion?"

Noblos spread his hands, as if explaining trigonometry to a first grader. "Simple. Confine me, and in a very short time, your Aegis

511

is useless. Your SPY-1 detunes. Especially Illuminator One. ALIS degrades.

"Therefore, your ship has no combat value. At which point you can retreat, and offload me. Everybody wins."

"Without charges?" Aisha put in, at the same time that Lenson said, "We're not retreating," in a flat voice. He interrupted himself and looked to her. "Sorry, Special Agent. This should be your show."

"Is that really what you expect?" she asked Noblos. Trying to take over again.

The physicist shrugged, still speaking to the CO. "Charge me, and I stop work. The next incoming missile, air strike, takes your precious ship out. Kills the crew you're worrying so much about. Your choice, Captain. But that's what they pay you for, right? To make the tough calls?"

Lenson glanced at her. She opened her hands to convey that, essentially, the scientist was right. She couldn't take him into custody against the wishes of the command.

Noblos looked from one to the other, then sighed. "Very well then. We're in agreement. And I'm free to go."

When he stood, Toan reached for the cuffs again. Tausengelt, too, went to stop him. But Lenson waved them off. "Belay that. He's got us over a barrel."

Toan gaped. "We can't let him remain free. Roaming the passageways. Sir?"

"I have no intention of that, Sheriff. We're shorthanded, but you'll just have to bird-dog him. Who do we—"

Aisha gripped the pistol under her wrap. "I'll do it."

Lenson frowned at her. "You, Special Agent?"

She swallowed. *The stairwell. His reeking breath.* "I, uh . . . don't have a general-quarters assignment. As far as fighting, I'm a sparc wheel. The least I can do is keep an eye on this . . . suspect."

"My own personal minder," Noblos said drily. "Aren't you afraid of me, Aisha? That I'll get you in a corner and work my will?"

She met his amused stare with as stony a glare as she could muster. "Not really. But if you did try it again, I'd have to shoot you."

Lenson nodded again. "Fair enough. All right, he's yours. CIC, Aegis spaces, his cabin, the wardroom. Nowhere else. He wants to sleep, lock him in. And once we get home, Doctor, I'm turning you in for prosecution."

"A deal I can't refuse." Noblos's sneer was open now. "And you imagine I'll go along with being railroaded? You have no evidence. Just this crazy woman's imagination. She can't come up with the real doer, so it's got to be somebody who's not in ship's company. Or is it actually you, Captain? Did you ever think of that, Special Agent? That it's really *him?*"

Aisha didn't answer. Just stood, looking to the skipper. Who put his hands down flat on the table and rose.

"You can't even answer." Noblos shook his head sadly. "Pathetic, the lot of you. Without me, you'd already be dead. You're fooling yourselves. I won't be prosecuted. They wouldn't dare."

Steel shuddered around them as the ship slammed into a heavy sea. "I'll be in Combat," Lenson said to no one in particular. Then, to her, "Let me know if you have any problems with him."

Noblos turned his back. She took advantage of that to reach under her wrap. Pretending to adjust her bra, she clicked the safety off the SIG, then followed her new charge out.

28
SAIC, Tysons Corner

B lair was in the conference room when the news arrived. She'd had to park some distance away. The lot, including where her space was, had been blocked off. Power diggers were gouging out earth. General Tomlin, the chair, Ms. Clayton, and the others were taking their seats when the new staffer barged in. Without a word, Reich turned on the television. They watched, appalled, as a stony-faced anchor spoke against a background still of a carrier departing port, sailors lining the rails, families waving from the pier.

"Details are sketchy. But the Department of Defense has confirmed that a possible nuclear explosion was reported early this morning. The presumed target was a U.S. task force on its way to support our allies in the Western Pacific. Five to six Navy ships are out of communication and may be lost. A Canadian ship reports heavy damage. It is searching for survivors, but encountering high seas and bad weather."

The anchor paused, then went on, tone of voice somber. *"Critics of the administration are already asking why the force was sent into a war zone without antimissile protection. Apparently an escort was planned, but was not yet ready for deployment. The group was directed to sail without it."*

"Let's see what Fox has to say." The general spoke soberly too, as if he'd suffered a personal loss.

The conservative network had little to add, except for a report that a Coast Guard cutter attempting to rescue survivors had been torpedoed. *"But if this dreadful news is confirmed, America must strike back."*

Clayton said acidly, "Yesterday everyone was saying we had no business in the Pacific. Nothing official yet?"

The aide shook her head, still watching the screen.

Which now showed a blue-suited officer against the seal of the U.S. Pacific Command. The banner read "Live from Pearl Harbor, Hawaii. Briefing by spokesperson for U.S. Pacific Fleet. Loss of USS *Roosevelt* strike group."

The officer began reading from a prepared text, gaze not meeting the camera. "A possible nuclear detonation was reported by units in the Western Pacific at approximately 0210 Pacific time this morning. A large explosion was confirmed from national sensing sources, localized to a position several hundred miles west of Guam.

"Five ships fail to respond to attempts at communication. The ships are: attack carrier USS

Franklin D. Roosevelt. Destroyer USS *Elisha Eaker*. Destroyer USS *Richmond P. Hobson*. USS *Crommelin*, a frigate. USS *Salisbury*, a littoral combat ship or frigate.

"A weak signal from HMCS *Protecteur*, a Canadian replenishment vessel that was part of the strike group, reports experiencing heavy damage from an explosion. She is searching for survivors, but encountering high seas, bad weather, and radiation contamination. Any further details must be considered as rumor until confirmed. We are attempting to reestablish communication, receive damage reports, and vector submarine and other units to the scene to assist in rescue of any survivors. Our communications are still degraded. However, even if their main comm links were damaged, U.S. Navy ships have enough backup systems that they should have reported in by now.

"Based on that fact, and on a report by a Saipanese fishing trawler east of the detonation area, we have to presume that at the very least, American forces have suffered heavy damage. Each Nimitz-class carrier carries upwards of six thousand personnel. Adding in the crews of the escort units, total casualties may be as high as seven to eight thousand.

"We . . . hope the numbers will not be that high. New Zealand and Australia have offered search and rescuc assistance, to add to those missions already being conducted by U.S. national forces."

The briefer lowered his head and coughed into a fist. Touched his eyes, then continued. "In comparison: About two thousand four hundred soldiers, sailors, and civilians were killed in the Pearl Harbor attack on December 7, 1941. And just under three thousand military and civilian dead on September 11, 2001.

"We will provide additional information as it becomes available."

The staffer switched from channel to channel but got only the same footage. Blair sat frozen. They hadn't mentioned *Savo*, and Dan's ship wasn't part of that strike group, as far as she knew. But a loss of this magnitude . . . it was devastating.

"We have how many carriers in the Pacific?" the general murmured.

"Two," Ms. Clayton told him. "Unless we find *Roosevelt* is still afloat."

"Which doesn't sound likely," Blair put in. "The reporters are giving us hope that they're just not answering the radio, but is there really any? With heavy seas, radioactivity—"

"Those ships are lost." Clayton's long fingernails scratched at the tabletop. "Seven *thousand* crew. Carriers. Destroyers. That . . . idiot . . . has nuked us. And there'll be no restraining Szerenci now."

Blair checked her phone. 9:01. She stood,

raking papers into her briefcase. "We're not going to continue to sit here any longer, are we? It's in JCS's hands now. I'm going over to the Senate."

Tomlin held up a hand. Looked at the aide, who seemed frozen, still staring up at the screen, where the anchors were repeating the same information. "Alex. *Alex!* What about our report?"

She flinched. "Um, sir, yes. The report . . . the fact is, I've been activated too. National Guard. I'll have to report in to my unit. This afternoon, I'm afraid."

Clayton said that was all right, she understood. "What's your MOS? Your specialization?"

"I'm an MP, ma'am. Virginia's activating us, I believe to protect the nuclear plant at Calvert Cliffs."

The general had the remote now. Fox was on again, a talking-head retired general saying this was another Pearl Harbor, another 9/11. Calling for resolve and vengeance. The streaming banner read "Stock market closed. Trading suspended by SEC. By presidential order."

They were still watching, silent and appalled, as she let herself out.

The streets were all but empty. Then she remembered: it was Election Day. But with this news, how many would turn out? Every flag was at half mast. She started to calculate whether a low turnout would help her or Beiderbaum, but made herself stop. Her worries seemed so petty, so selfish, in the face of what was happening.

PBS was streaming BBC World News. The soothing voice of Marion Marshall repeated what they'd just heard from the Pacific Command. Then reported that passengers on an Air Kiribati flight had witnessed a bright flash. The pilot turned away immediately, and the aircraft had suffered turbulence, but no damage.

Next Marshall read a release from Beijing. *"Xinhua News Agency, the official press agency of the People's Republic, reports that Premier Zhang has offered peace in the Pacific. Zhang is quoted: China has recently increased stability in Asia by the introduction of a new class of heavy intercontinental ballistic missiles. Fifty of these multiwarhead weapons, the equivalent of the Russian SS-19 or the U.S. Peacekeeper, are now fully operational, deployed in hardened bases proof against any attack."*

Marshall read on, *"China desires stability and peace in Asia and throughout the Pacific. As the premier, General Zhang Zurong, has repeatedly warned, those who attempt to upset the balance will be met with force. This was the fate of the recent aggressive American move to threaten China's coastal cities with a nuclear-armed carrier battle group.*

"China regrets the loss of life. However, we must insist on respect for our role in the rimlands of the Pacific, the territorial integrity of the province of Taiwan, and those islands and sea areas that remain historically and geographically Chinese. The United States must withdraw from the Western Pacific and refrain from additional provocations. This more equal relationship is our only precondition to a full and complete restoration of a stable, constructive bilateral relationship, maintaining the mutually advantageous commercial ties that are so necessary to a return to global prosperity."

That ended the communique. Blair braked hard, narrowly missing a barrier in front of the Capitol. Troops, not cops. A guardsman in BDUs, carbine slung, leaned into her window. "This road's blocked, ma'am. No entry."

"I'm a staffer."

"I'll need ID, ma'am." The trooper stepped back and waved someone over from a group of uniforms near a hulking armored vehicle.

They insisted on searching her trunk before letting her pass. Fortunately, there was nothing in there but her spare, and the jumper cables Dan always insisted she carry. At last, they waved her on.

The meeting area beneath the great dome was thronged. Apparently they were in a quorum call, which for most senators meant feeling free to leave their seats and even the floor. To mingle, discuss, try to reach compromises. Under the circumstances, she couldn't see this as a good sign.

Blair blinked around, thinking what a great target this would make for a suicide bomber. She recognized senators. Generals. Executives from major defense firms. All seemed torn between the requirement to display grief and the necessity of conducting pressing business. Four men surrounded Talmadge, who was holding court beside the statue of Dr. King. He favored that location for photographs, to appeal to his sizable African-American constituency. A tall black man stood beside him, with several other men. She almost didn't recognize Hu Kuwalay, the defense assistant.

"Missy." Talmadge extended a palm, but his gaze darted here and there, examining, calculating. "You know Hu. 'Bat' Jingell, majority leader, from the other side of the building. And Tony Venezelos, from Archipelago Defense."

She nodded greetings. "What's going on, Bankey? Aren't you voting?"

"Any minute now. That idiot woman from Seattle called for a quorum. Then we got word about the address."

"What address? This is the authorization bill?"

"No, it isn't," the old senator said. Now she noticed he was perspiring.

Kuwalay said, "The president's coming over."

She raised her eyebrows. "Coming *here?*"

"He wants war powers," Talmadge rumbled. "Wants that blank check. Should we give it to him? I don't honestly know."

"We've been attacked. There's really no other response." Jingell smiled down at her. She wondered why he was here. As far as she knew, the lower house didn't have a dog in this fight. The Senate approved treaties and declared war.

Then she remembered. This was Election Day. By midnight, she'd learn if she was Congresswoman Titus, or just plain Mrs. Lenson. She thought of asking again about funding. She'd borrowed heavily for a last-minute ad blitz. But no, she couldn't. Events were too big, moving too fast, to think about herself.

"Missy? You always gave good advice." Talmadge took her hand. "I don't want to send kids off to war. I went, to Korea. Fought the Chinese then. They're not gonna be a pushover like Saddam. And that security adviser . . . he scares me."

"I'll tell you exactly what he'll propose," Blair told him.

"What's that?"

"A nuclear strike on the mainland, in retaliation. I've heard him before. Do it while the balance still favors us."

Jingell said, "But does it? With the new missiles they announced?"

"Doesn't mean they're operational," Kuwalay put in. "It's a bluff, to scare us off. We still have the advantage."

Blair felt like gripping her head and howling. Did they have *any* concept of what all-out war could mean? She'd lived through 9/11. Barely. Nuclear exchange would be that, magnified ten thousandfold. "We don't want to play nuclear dare, Hu. Millions will die. In the most horrible ways. The time's past when we can isolate the homeland from the effects of a war."

"You're not saying let them have their way," the majority leader said.

"No. But we can't cave, either."

A stir swept the dome. Someone called from a nearby group, "Good news. One of the ships reported in. Damaged, but afloat."

A cheer rose, applause, then subsided. No one mentioned the other ships. She guessed they were still missing. And by now, presumed lost.

"The middle course is always tough." Talmadge waved to someone over her shoulder. "The party was soft on this even after they invaded. I offered the authorization resolution, but we only had forty-two members in support. So I put off the vote.

"But this attack, sinking the Pacific Fleet . . . we can't opt out. The country wants action. Demands it."

"I believe you're right," Jingell said, but not very eagerly.

Blair squeezed the old man's hand, not bothering to correct his military terminology. Knowing he wanted reassurance, not advice. But for once, the two were the same. "Zhang took this out of our hands, Bankey. He's rolled the dice. Now all we can do is see what numbers come up."

The old senator sighed. Before he could say anything else, an intern came trotting past. A live quorum had been called for. He gave her shoulder a squeeze, patted Kuwalay, nodded to the majority leader, and headed for the Senate antechamber.

The closed-circuit monitor in the visitors' center carried the floor proceedings. With two hundred others, packed shoulder to shoulder, she watched.

A hush. The president came in, flanked by Secret Service. Head down, he delivered a low-voiced, almost inaudible address that she caught only a few words of. "For the first time since World War II . . . unprovoked and dastardly attack . . . existential threat to national security . . . defend our allies to the utmost . . . topple the dictator, and bring democracy to all Asia."

She tightened her mouth, sensing overreach. Hubris. Or maybe, just hyperbole. This president had never been noted for skill with words, or insight into the way to deal with foreign countries. But at least his speech was short. So short that she, and apparently the others around her, hadn't quite grasped what was happening, by the time he stepped down.

"He's asked for a declaration of war," someone said.

"War . . . war . . ." The murmur eddied through the crowd. A lone spectator began to clap, but no one else joined in. He persisted for a few seconds, then stopped as those around shushed him.

She felt suddenly faint, and pushed her way through the throng to lean against a display case. Her head swam. Her knees trembled. What was it with human beings? They were like cattle thronging down a chute, with no idea what lay at its end. Distantly, through a hissing hum in her ears, she registered the question being moved. Seconded. Then, the roll call. Each senator going on record. Standing, to call out his or her vote, rather than simply pressing the usual button.

The final vote was for, but by only 54 in favor, 46 against. The narrowest vote for war in U.S. history, she was pretty sure. She stared to check the fact on her phone, then remembered: no service. And anyway, what did it matter? The room was emptying, gradually, then more swiftly. Almost a stampede. She limped along after them, hip aching now, feeling hollow. Alone.

And more frightened than she'd ever been in her life.

29
The Miyako Strait

Dan leaned on the splinter shield, gripping his cap against the buffeting of a cold wind. The temperature had fallen over the last few days as winds and seas built. The light was ebbing from the world. The shrouded sun was almost gone. He gripped the bulwark as a charcoal sea levered up. Smaller ripples, cat's-paws, complicated its heaved-up face. The damage-control teams had welded plating and shored bulkheads forward. But he still tensed as the damaged bow dipped once more. When that dark sea crashed into it, the ship shivered. White spray burst up through the gaps in the twisted metal as if from the blowhole of an immense whale. The wind blew the spray aft to spatter it against the pilothouse. He ducked, grabbing his cap at the last second as it flew off.

He took a last look around—racing clouds, carbon seas, failing light—and ducked into the pilothouse. "What's the prediction?" he asked Van Gogh.

The quartermaster chief turned from plotting his last radar fix, staggered as the deck reeled, but caught himself on the helm console. "Who knows. No satellite weather. Just hope it doesn't get any worse. Barometer's stopped falling anyway." The seaman on the wheel glanced at them, then back at his indicators.

"Keep an eye on it. Let me know if you see any change up forward, any more of that shell plating working loose."

"Uh, Cap'n, chief engineer called up here again."

"Fuel state again?"

"Yeah, I mean yessir. But not just that. Warning me to take it easy, and select a course that doesn't strain that shoring."

Dan watched the next sea bear down on them. Bigger than the last? Maybe about the same. "I can't do that and maintain station. Keep a thirty-degree angle to the prevailing seas. Use the screws if you have to."

The OOD nodded, and Dan monkey-groped hand over hand toward the ladder down. He paused at the radar repeater to check on *Curtis Wilbur*, twenty miles distant. SubPac had detached *Pittsburgh* for independent duty. His task group was down to two. The only allied forces left in the strait.

None of the news was good. Rit Carpenter had reported that the leak in their sonar dome, damaged during the grounding in the Med, was back. Worsened by the missile hit, no doubt. *Savo* had her sonar tail deployed. But she was increasingly deaf, handicapped in fighting the submarine threat. Dan was also getting low on fuel. Within a day, or at most a day and a half, they wouldn't have enough to reach Guam.

Worse yet, the enemy was on the move once more. Air activity over the mainland had increased. Combat air patrols had moved out over the northern strait. Clashes with the U.S. Air Force had taken down aircraft on both sides. Chinese numbers, though, were beginning to tell. According to Fang, Taiwanese intel reported the activation of a follow-on plan to Sheng Chi. By all accounts, it was a second cross-strait assault. But this time, not aimed at Taiwan or some remote island.

This time, they were heading for Okinawa.

A bridge too far? He clattered down the ladder toward Combat. Surely the Japanese would defend one of their home islands. Combined Japanese and U.S. air power would make a second landing impossible.

But the lack of response from Tokyo was worrying.

Back in his worn leather seat, he drowsed for an hour. Until Matt Mills reached across and shook him. "Captain. Cuing reports surface-to-surface missiles in the air. Multiple contacts."

They watched, helpless, as symbols popped into existence on the display. At least a dozen, with more behind them. A repeat of the bombardment that had opened the assault on Taiwan. But these weren't aimed at that battered island. He almost asked Wenck to shift to ABM mode, then didn't. Out of Block 4s; nothing they could do about it.

After some minutes Mills murmured, "Look at that patch of near-shore jamming again. They're trying to cover movement."

Dan massaged his eye sockets. Aegis's doppler function broke moving objects out of clutter, such as ground return. But the jammers on shore were boresighting his frequencies. Gaining familiarity with his system, and following his freq-hopping. Occasionally, now, even matching it, which broke the SPY-1 beam into inchoate, sparkling glitter.

His team was fighting it, though, and now and then managed to break through. When they did, the system could connect the dots to generate a track even through heavy interference.

What it showed now was a flotilla setting out from Hangzhou Bay. Surface vessels, with heavy air cover. Simultaneously, Mills reported an HF request from Kadena Air Force Base, asking *Savo* for ABM protection.

Dan sighed. "Tell them I'd like to help. But we're out of rounds." He blinked up at the display, realizing now why the Chinese had occupied Socotra. It would protect their flank as they invaded Okinawa. Beijing was playing six moves ahead. Everyone else was reacting late, with outdated plans and inadequate, uncoordinated forces.

And, of course, losing. "What did you just say, Matt?"

Mills got a funny look. "They say they're under bombardment. Incoming missiles are targeted on them."

"Right, I see that. How about their Patriots?"

"All rounds expended. They're scrambling aircraft off the strips. Sending them north, to the main islands, or back to Guam." He tensed, frowning, listening to his headphones. "They're passing a nuclear alert now."

"Keep an eye on those launch sites," Dan told him. "We could be next."

He sat back, rubbing his forehead. If *Savo* was targeted, about all he could render was the sailor's mythical final salute: bend over, and kiss his ass good-bye. Zhang was pushing hard. Following up on destroying the battle group. Okinawa . . . a second link shattered in the inner island chain. They'd thought a U.S. base there would protect it. Now, it seemed, the Chinese juggernaut might grind that trip wire into the mud.

Heavy fighting on Taiwan, to the south. In Korea. And an invasion of Okinawa, to the north.

Meanwhile, Task Group 779.1 was hanging out here, twisting in the wind. He couldn't hold the strait, nor help in the struggles in the air and on the ground. About all he could hope for was to get his ship and crew out alive. And each hour that passed made that less likely.

531

Plunking down next to him, in the seat Fang had warmed nearly continually for the last two days: a spectral-looking Cheryl Staurulakis. The exec muttered, "So what do we need to do? Want me to draft a message?"

He felt as tired as she looked. "How exactly would we phrase that, XO?"

"Empty magazines. Battle damage. Low-fuel state. Inability to continue mission."

"Then what?"

"Request permission to retire."

"Believe me, Cheryl, they're asking themselves, back at J-3, whether to send those orders. They don't need me squeaking in their ears."

He saw the question in her gaze. Almost, the contempt. "It's no shame to say we're out of ammunition. Out of fuel. Sir."

He shifted in the chair. "I know what you're thinking. But this isn't macho posturing, XO. Fleet has to realize the risk. The fact they haven't pulled us back means we're still here for a reason. To demonstrate commitment."

But he couldn't help thinking about another cruiser. USS *Houston*. Surrounded in the Sunda Strait, outnumbered, without air cover, she and HMAS *Perth* had fought together to the bitter end. Gone down with guns blazing in the dark.

He shook himself. They were still better situated than the doomed and heroic Captain Albert Rooks. They still had antiair rounds, and

Dan doubted the Chinese would waste a nuclear warhead on one ship. Which was why he'd stationed *Curtis Wilbur* forty thousand yards away.

The radio beeped. *"Ringmaster, this is War Drums. Over."* The signal was faint, all but overlaid by noise jamming. But it was Min Jun Jung, no doubt about it. Dan grabbed the handset, noting the time: nearly midnight. "War Drums, Ringmaster. Over."

"This is War Drums. Are you taking on these units coming out of Shanghai? Proceeding roughly one two zero."

"This is Ringmaster. That's a negative."

"War Drums. If we were to take them on, could you provide a diversion?"

"He's *attacking* them?" Staurulakis muttered, incredulous.

Dan said. "No surprise there. What surprises me is that the . . . This is Ringmaster. Interrogative. Do you have Japanese participation in your attack? Over."

"That's a negative. They decline to participate. Over."

"Jesus," Mills murmured. "They're writing off Okinawa?"

Dan shrugged. "If they can't defend it . . . But we're going to have to make a choice too."

"You can't seriously be thinking about supporting his attack," Staurulakis said.

"I'm considering it, XO. Yeah."

"With what? The five-inchers?"

Dan said, "We could cover him with our remaining regular Standards."

Staurulakis shook her head so hard her hair bounced. "Against that many aircraft? cruise missiles? A ticket to the bottom of the East China Sea, Captain."

He rubbed his face. "Fuck . . . I can't leave him in the lurch. Not when he backed us up, before."

"We had full magazines then." He started to lift the handset; she grabbed his hand. "Don't. You're tired. This is the wrong decision."

Dan breathed deep, trying to tamp down his rage. At what? At the universe, for being a place where men killed each other? *Only the dead have seen an end to war.*

Staurulakis, speaking so low no one else in the space could overhear: "I'll execute, if you order it. But it's the wrong decision. Zhang will fall. Someday. You want to be there to help topple him."

He drew another breath, deep, down to his belt buckle, and clicked back to the HF net. "This is Ringmaster. I can't advise you, my friend. But good luck, Min. Over."

"This is War Drums. We will meet again. War Drums, out."

He must have dozed off again. The next time he swam up out of the void, Captain Fang stood

534

before him. Dan coughed, long and hard, until something in his side spasmed and cramped. He inhaled cautiously. Glanced around. Long past midnight. The invasion fleet was still moving out from the coast. "Chip. What is it?"

"Premier Zhang has proposed peace."

"What? I'm not sure—"

"A cease-fire in place. Followed by a conference of foreign ministers. To decide the future of the Pacific."

"He's proposing that you surrender. And that we acknowledge it."

Fang looked distant. "They're rounding up officials in the cities they've captured. Special teams, with lists of street addresses. Taking the families, too."

That didn't sound good. "But the army's holding out, right? You're still fighting?"

"Our redoubts are strong. We have ammunition and determination. But they hold two perimeters, where they landed. Now they are trying to link the zones up, before pushing toward Taipei." Fang glanced away. "I need to fight alongside my comrades. And see to my family's safety."

Dan told him he understood, he'd start making arrangements.

"I've already contacted my headquarters," the liaison said. "They will have a fishing craft meet us. Off Miyako Jima. Early tomorrow, if possible."

Dan checked the display, calculated transit times and air-defense coverage in his head; nodded. "You can use one of our boats for transfer. I'll have the first lieutenant get a RHIB ready."

Fang extended a hand; Dan took it. And for the second time that night, feeling like Judas on the eve of the Crucifixion, he muttered, "Good luck."

At 0100 someone shook him awake again. Dave Branscombe this time, with the radio messenger behind him. Dan coughed himself back into consciousness and felt around for his mug. The coffee was cold, but he slugged it back anyway as he ran an eye down the clipboard. Then read it again. Feeling sick, and not from the rancid brew.

The message was from JCS, forwarded by PaCom to Seventh Fleet and from Seventh to Commander, Ryukyus Maritime Defense Coalition Task Group.

All U.S. forces were ordered to withdraw from forward positions, except for specifically tasked patrols, and submerged forces, which were to act in accordance with a separate reference. TG 779.1 was to pull back to Guam, conducting active ASW operations, transiting via a certain latitude and longitude. Dan said, "What's this 'Checkpoint Zulu'? . . . oh. Where the battle group last reported from."

"So we're pulling out." Branscombe looked stricken.

Dan glanced around, at other stunned expressions as the news filtered down the consoles. Lips shaped the words *retreating . . . running*. They turned to him, blinking, as if appealing for rebuttal. As if he, somehow, could obviate, deny, ameliorate the news.

He swallowed the impulse to throw up. Or to panic, struggling under an avalanche of reverses.

Then steeled himself.

It had happened before. Defeat. Humiliation. Retreat. But always followed by reconstitution, resolve, and return. His job now was to save the lives entrusted to his care. Bring them home, to fight another day.

He bent to pull up Fleet Weather on his terminal, then grimaced, remembering. Still, the seas seemed to be lessening, and the wind indicator had dropped to twelve knots.

Which reminded him, he had to get Red Hawk in the air. Scout and sanitize their route out. Staurulakis, tousled and flushed, came in. "Exec. Glad you're here. Orders on the clipboard. Review them and backstop me. Matt: I need a current fuel state. Distance to Point Zulu. Thence, to Guam. Figure six hours' linger at the checkpoint. Expanding square, starting at the checkpoint coordinates. Next: draft a message requesting refuel en route, if possible. Otherwise, most economical speed, estimated transit time. Call Wilker. Get Red Hawk in the air, loaded out for ASW."

"Right away, Captain." Mills hesitated. "Do we want *Curtis Wilbur* to accompany us to the checkpoint? Or head direct for Guam?"

"We'll travel in company. Mutual support. In case the worst happens, if . . ." He trailed off, not wanting to say *if the forward bulkhead gives way* or *if one of us gets torpedoed.* "Mutual support," he repeated, forcing a confidence he didn't feel. "A fighting withdrawal. Where's Chip? Captain Fang? As soon as we get him off, we'll pull in to close interval and haul ass."

"In his stateroom, I think. Throwing stuff in his duffel."

"Okay, good . . . Cheryl?"

She lowered the clipboard. Shook her head. "It might be good if you could get on the 1MC. Give the crew the word personally."

"Good suggestion. This is going to be an all-hands effort. When they say 'conduct active ASW operations,' they mean—"

" 'Don't get yourself sunk on the way.' "

"Exactly." He pried himself up out of the chair, which seemed to have fastened a grip on him that was harder to break the more tired he got. He looked past the frightened faces at the consoles, peering between the curtains to Sonar. "Listen up! This will be an opposed transit, without air cover. We know they have subs loose out here. Let's not fall victim." He turned back to his command team. "And if there are any survivors,

I want to find them. I know there's some kind of multinational SAR effort going, but we'll be the first surface units on scene." He stopped, searching a zombified brain for the next order. "Uh, like I said, we're gonna be on our own, once we leave Air Force cover. They're closing down anyway—Kadena's under attack.

"That means Condition One both antiair and ASW. Look at what systems both ships have operational. Set up a steaming formation that gives us three-sixty threat coverage."

He saw his orders take hold. The faces lowered, spoke into microphones, regained some semblance of business. He paced back and forth, swilled down the last of the tarry midnight brew, and replenished his cup. At least the fucking waiting was over. And with the seas lessening, maybe they could get back to safety before that bulkhead went.

Unfortunately, a retreat was the most difficult military maneuver of all. When your back turned to the enemy, it was easy for a unit to disintegrate into panic, demoralization, and then, surrender.

He had to get the crew on board. He left Cheryl organizing things and slowly clambered up red-lit ladders to the bridge. Thoughts milled. He tried to kick and shove them into some logical order. But he was so fucking tired. . . . The bridge was dark. He blundered into bodies. Seizing him, Nuckols steered him to the 1MC panel. The boatswain put the mike in his hand and flicked a switch. "You're on, Skipper."

Dan cleared his throat, then wished he hadn't. Coming over the bridge speaker, it sounded horrible. But at least it would wake up anybody who was still asleep.

"This is the captain speaking.

"We've received new orders. Leave the Miyako area. Proceed to Guam for rearm and repairs. En route, carry out ASW operations, and also, check out where the Roosevelt *battle group was last reported, looking for any survivors.*

"I won't kid you. We no longer have air cover or antimissile defenses. We do have some self-defense capability left, but we'll have to use it wisely to get out of what, just between you and me, is a hell of a jam. We'll all need to work together to get home safe.

"But we will *make it out. And we'll be back. The U.S. Navy has had to retreat before. But we've never given up. We've endured, rebuilt, come back, and, eventually, prevailed."*

He paused, fighting renewed nausea. He wasn't sure he could make it to the bridge wing in time if he had to. Maybe the trash can was a better bet. Yeah . . . okay . . . He was still holding the fucking mike. . . . What else? *"I know I can count on you. Let's do our best, get through this, and . . . may God help us all."*

When he clicked off there was absolute silence

540

for a moment. Then someone began clapping. It spread, and the southerners added rebel yells. All over the ship the clamor rose, mingled, and slowly died away.

He was throwing cold water on his face in his sea cabin when Nuckols came on the 1MC. *"Now flight quarters, flight quarters. All hands man your flight quarters stations. Remove all covers topside. The smoking lamp is out on all weather decks. Muster the crash and salvage team with the team leader in the helo hangar. Muster the ready boat crew on the starboard boat deck."*

Dan contemplated shaving, but was too exhausted. Red-rimmed eyes stared back from the mirror. The battered, frightened face of a defeated, skedaddling commander. "Fuck that," he muttered, but couldn't say whom he was talking to. "Pull it together, Lenson. Pretend you know the answers."

The trouble was, he wasn't at all confident he did.

When he got back to CIC it was filled. The off watches had turned out to help. Well, he'd said they'd need to work together. But this was overdoing it. He told the CIC officer to clear the space unless someone had a good reason for staying. Then headed for the chair again, looking forward to another nap. That soft leather would suck him down like padded quicksand. . . .

But as he passed the air controller's station the talker held up a hand. "Sir, ready boat crew reports—" The petty officer stopped, frowned, listening.

"What is it?" Dan said.

"There's no RHIB."

"What? What?"

"The boat deck's empty. Davits are down. Ready fuel's gone. Somebody already put it in the water."

Dan rubbed his face. "What the heck? But—"

Then he understood. He told the crew to shift to the other boat, get it ready instead. Then pulled his Hydra off his belt. "Master-at-Arms, Captain."

A sleepy voice. *"Sheriff Toan, sir."*

"Who's on duty, guarding Doctor Noblos?"

"Uh . . . that would still be the Special Agent, sir."

"Check on her. Right now."

Toan said he was on his way. Dan leaned back as Mills brought *Savo* around to launch course. Cautiously, since the seas were coming from that direction and he didn't want to stress the damaged bow.

"Captain, CMA."

"Go."

"Sir, one of my men is here, in the passageway, but looks like somebody knocked him out. Noblos's door is open. But he's not in his cabin."

542

Dan exchanged glances with Staurulakis. He told Toan, "Okay, get him medical attention. Then roust the agent. Get her up here ASAP."

The little Vietnamese and his assistants hustled Aisha along the red-lit corridors as if she were the criminal. She'd been in her cabin, asleep, after handing off the guard duty. But then been awakened by a pounding at her door, and orders to dress as quickly as possible. Which she'd done so haphazardly, pulling on the coveralls and over-wrap she'd left on the floor, that she realized only halfway down the passageway she'd forgotten a head covering. She halted. "Wait. I forgot—"

"Never mind. CO wants you."

"Don't be so rough. Who's got a bandanna?" She patted her shoulder, where the holster would be. She'd forgotten her gun, too. No, she'd given it to the petty officer who'd relieved her on guard duty. At last, in her pocket, her fingers closed on her baton.

CIC was almost bright after the passageways. She looked around for the physicist's angular form, his brush-cut hair, but didn't see him. A flash hood lay over the back of an empty chair. That would do. "Where is he?" she asked Toan as she draped it over her head, arranged it so her hair was covered again.

"You were supposed to guard the prisoner."

"Goree offered to relieve me so I could sleep.

Why?" A presentiment pricked her. "He didn't do away with himself? In his cabin."

"Noblos? No. Unfortunately."

"Then what's going on?"

The Vietnamese nodded behind her, and she spun to face Lenson. The captain looked ashen. Drawn. Those gray eyes barely seemed to note her. He muttered past her, to Toan, "Did you get hold of Medical?"

"Yessir. Hospitalman Ryan's on the way."

"What's Ryan got to do with this?" Aisha asked. "What happened? Is Goree okay?"

A man at a console called, "Sir, boat officer reports the port RHIB manned and ready, with one exception."

"Go," Lenson said.

"The mechanic, EN1 Benyamin. Which is weird, 'cause usually he's first on station. They sent a guy down to check, see if he's in his bunk."

Dan told Toan to get Chief McMottie up and looking for Benyamin. But a suspicion was growing. He crossed to the surface warfare supervisor's station. Put a hand on the operator's shoulder. "Any close-in contacts?" Past him he caught the special agent's quizzical stare. She was in one of her dark wraps, with a flash hood over her head, so all he could see was her eyes. As though she wore a burqa.

"What's going on, Captain?" she asked.

He held up a finger. "Just one minute."

The operator was pointing at a speckle on his screen. Only a faint one, among a lot of random returns. They discussed it. The captain straightened, and ran his hands through his hair. Sighed.

"What's going on?" she said again.

"Special Agent. The situation is . . . not totally clear at the moment. But we have a missing boat."

She frowned. "Missing?"

"The starboard inflatable. It was swung out and fueled. But when we went to man up, it was gone. Along with one of the crew, apparently."

"Who?"

"An engineman. Benyamin."

"One of our original suspects," she murmured.

"Excuse me?"

"He was on the short list. A serious misogynist. A rape-game player. With access to the electrical system."

"But you cleared him? As a suspect, I mean?"

Aisha said carefully, "No sir. Only found better evidence pointing elsewhere."

Toan put in, "Somebody knocked Goree out, Special Agent. Dr. Noblos is missing too."

Aisha said, "Did Goree have a pistol on him, Chief? I loaned him mine. To stand guard with. Did you find it on him?"

"We found an empty holster," Toan said, not meeting her eye.

Lenson tapped the screen. "Great. So he's armed, too. . . . We're checking bunks now. But it looks like both Noblos and Benyamin must be out there. Headed west. It'll be rough, but they're traveling with the prevailing seas; that'll give them a smoother ride."

She contemplated the screen, imagining it. In the dark. Amid the waves that were even now tilting the space they were in. "Where would they be going? What's west of here?"

"China," the captain said. He looked stern.

"Surely they can't make it. It's too far, isn't it?"

"It's a ways. Yeah. But small boats have made astonishing voyages. And there's a sizable piece of the Chinese navy between us and the coast right now. They might get picked up. Especially . . . if they signal. Or use the radio in the boat."

"Actually, it's only a hundred miles," Mills put in from behind them. "He doesn't have to make the mainland. Just the Senkaku group. He could be there tomorrow."

Aisha said, astonished, "You're saying, he's . . . deserting? Defecting?"

Lenson smiled grimly.

"And the petty officer?"

"I know him, but not well," Lenson said. "He could just be a hostage. If Noblos found him there checking the engine, decided a mechanic would be good to have along, and forced him aboard at gunpoint. Or, yeah—they could be accomplices.

546

I didn't think of that angle. Since I didn't know he was a suspect."

He kept rubbing his face, so hard she wondered why there weren't holes in his skin. Apparently that was how he kept himself awake. He still looked like Death. "Okay, and you want from me . . . what?"

Dan blinked. What was she asking? Oh, right. What he wanted her for . . . "I need some advice here. We've been ordered to retire."

"You can't go after him?"

"Coming alongside a small boat, in the dark, one that doesn't want to be caught, isn't easy. Not trying to maneuver ten thousand tons of cruiser. He'll just skip out of the way. Plus, he's armed. If I drop my visit and search team on him, he might not be the only one who gets hurt."

Aisha looked away, feeling both guilty—it *was* her pistol out there—and angry. But then, they'd always known Noblos was smarter than the average criminal. "I should have anticipated this. Why should somebody with his ego wait around for trial, imprisonment, even a death sentence?"

"You really think he was facing death?"

"Rape, attempted murder, they're capital crimes. And once we established jurisdiction, this would be a federal charge. Even a twenty-year sentence, for someone his age, would mean life in prison."

Dan said, "Whereas if he defects, he's a

noted scientist. With a hell of a lot of valuable knowledge about our most advanced systems."

"There you have it," Aisha said. They stared at each other.

Dan turned back to the console operator. "Range to the RHIB."

"Stand by . . . twelve thousand five hundred yards. Speed, ten knots. Course, two eight zero."

Setting course for the Senkakus, all right.

Only a hundred miles away.

"Take with guns," Dan said.

The petty officer hesitated. "Say again, Captain?"

"Designate to guns. Take with the after five-inch. Radar control. Is that sea return going to foul you up?"

"We've got a decent lock-on," the petty officer said. "And with proximity-fuzed high explosive . . . I wouldn't wait until the range opens much more, though. You're going to lose him in this clutter. And fifteen thousand yards is pretty much max range."

Dan grabbed the agent by the shoulder, felt her flinch away under his hand; but held on, and led her to the command desk. A weary Cheryl Staurulakis glanced down from the displays. "XO, Dr. Noblos is defecting in the boat. He stole the agent's pistol. There's one crewman with him. May be an accomplice. May be just a hostage. Backstop me?"

"We can't let him go," Staurulakis said. "He knows the whole fucking system! Aegis. ALIS. Block 4. ABM cuing. And how to disrupt them, too, I'll bet."

"Maneuver to recapture?"

The exec frowned. "He's armed? In the dark? He'll take people with him. May be blue-on-blue casualties, too."

"We're on the same page, then." He looked to Ar-Rahim. "Agent?"

She shook her head. She couldn't believe this. "You want my blessing? On a summary execution? I can't give you that."

"So we let him go over to the enemy? With everything he knows?"

She closed her eyes; said a short *du'a* asking for wisdom. "I'm not a judge. Or a jury. And neither are you, Captain. With all due respect." She looked at the overhead. Black as the night outside. "I am bound to advise you . . . if you do what you seem to have in mind, I'll have to prefer charges. Once we make port."

"What charges?" the exec said. "Bearing in mind that this is wartime."

"Murder, of course. Two counts. Wartime has nothing to do with it."

"To prevent defection? Protect sensitive information?"

"Those would be extenuating arguments at the trial," she admitted.

The exec said, "A warning shot, then."

Dan nodded, suddenly relieved. Of course. "Good call, XO. Matt, take control. One round, ahead of the RHIB. And call on the boat channel. See if they have the radio on. Come back along-side, right now, or we take him down."

"He's not coming back," Aisha said. "Not him. But I agree. Giving him the chance, that's a *sadaqah*. A good deed."

Dan blinked, taken aback by the interjection. But maybe she was right. "One round, high explosive, variable time, batteries released," he said.

The jolt carried faintly back through the metal around them. Dan strolled through the ranks of bent backs, glowing screens, to the gun-control console. He got there in time for the petty officer to point to a bright patch that appeared in the clutter, ahead of the fleeing boat. It grew, then faded. "Splash."

"Range?"

"To the boat, fourteen thousand two hundred yards. Splash, about two hundred yards ahead of it."

"Good shooting. Think they saw it?"

"Saw it, heard it . . . yessir. But . . . starting to lose it. Too much sea return. And it looks like they've jettisoned their radar reflector."

An encapsulated metal shape that let *Savo* track her boats more clearly at a distance. Yeah, Noblos would think of that. "Is he changing course? Coming back?"

"Wait one . . . no. Steady course. Speed may be picking up."

Dan turned his head to the agent, beside him. She was making notes. He sucked cold air. Sweat trickled under his clothes. "I can't let him go. Not with all he knows. I can't hand the enemy that advantage. His crime's really beside the point."

"I can't judge you," Aisha said. She looked at her watch, noted the time. "But I'll present the facts."

"We have to leave station. Even getting back to Guam is going to be questionable."

"You are the captain," she said. "No one can really know what is right, in the end. Only Allah knows the whole. But He gives it to you to decide. You must do the best you can, and trust in God."

Well, there it was. Nothing left he could say to that.

"Batteries released. Five rounds. Fire for effect," he told the petty officer. Trying not to feel whatever his gut was urging: vengeance; righteousness; anger; even regret.

In the end, none of those could claim a place in his decisions. Only the rules of engagement and operational necessity. Those alone had to guide his actions, as coldly and rationally as if he himself were an autonomous computer, working through millions of lines of passionless code. That was the basis on which he would be judged. On earth, as in heaven? And what about Benyamin? Was he guilty at all, or just collateral damage?

He couldn't know that now. Might never know. But the agent was right, wherever she was coming from.

He was the captain.

The responsibility was his.

The bangs sounded tinny and remote. He had time for a couple of breaths between each round; the Mark 45 fired slowly for a fully automatic gun. They sounded too distant and trivial to be seventy-pound chunks of steel and high explosive going out at three thousand feet per second. Reaching out in ballistic arcs over the dark sea, as second after second ticked out. Sensing their target, and calculating the distance. Until a circuit closed.

One after the other, green returns blossomed around the contact. Soundless. Almost lost, in the speckle of heaving sea.

When at last they faded, the pip was no longer there.

30
Western China

The train didn't stop again for two days. More Vietnamese died, and were stacked at the far end of the car. Teddy could hardly smell them over the stink of the rest of the locked-in POWs. All that time the train climbed. It got colder, until breath crackled and urine froze on the steel floor. He slept spoon-fashion with Pritchard, who talked less and less as time went on.

But the day finally came when the train jolted to a halt again, and they were rifle-butted out into a blinding daylight.

To Camp 576.

His first impression was of a teeming of gray lice festering a desolate landscape of gravel and sand. Vertical walls of pinkish crumbling rock surrounded an immense bowl amid gray hills. The eroding walls looked natural, but were still fearsome barriers. A dull explosion reverberated as the guards herded the prisoners down a barbed-wire lane from the rail spur down into the depression. A trooper with a Kalashnikov watched each fifty yards.

On a second look down, Teddy changed his mind. This gigantic hole in the earth had been scooped out by human effort. The thin wind was chilly, the sky russet with the same shade of fine dust he'd seen in eastern Afghanistan. Beyond the pinkish outcrops rocky hills undulated toward the horizon. Past them, in the far distance, rose jagged, uneven intaglios of mountain, deep-cut ravine-shadows intercutting black with indigo and rose-petal.

As the prisoners were mustered into lines and counted, he wondered dully where exactly they were. Somewhere in far northwestern China was as close as he could come.

"*Gankai*! *Gankai*!" He knew what that meant now. "Hurry up!" But he couldn't hurry. He had to drag the ruined foot behind him, with it bent to the side opposite where the tendons had been torn from the bone. Walking on the butt end of his tibia, each step was a stabbing agony. He didn't want to be beaten again. They got enthusiastic with those rifle butts. But he was going to be tail-end Charlie in any line.

Not a good place to end up. Not if he wanted to survive.

Did he?

"Give us an arm, mate," Magpie Pritchard said, beside him. Another explosion thumped the air. It didn't sound far off, but it was strangely subdued. Neither artillery nor mortar. The Australian pulled Teddy's arm over his shoulders, but it didn't work. He towered above the Vietnamese, above the Chinese guards. "You stand out like a fucking lighthouse, Maggie," Teddy told him.

"*Chenmo, chenmo*!" the guards shouted. He knew that, too—it meant "shut up." Whoa, getting fluent, Obie. Another in your long list of fucked-up accomplishments.

The day progressed. They were herded into a corral and made to squat in the blowing grit, hands behind their heads. The guards strolled among them, slugging anybody who relaxed the posture. One by one, the POWs passed down a disassembly line of what he assumed were convict trusties. Many had flatter faces and darker complexions than the guards. Tibetans? They shaved his head, then made him throw all his clothes onto a fire. He was hosed down with icy water, then issued a thin gray cotton uniform. The pants hems came only to his shins. A Chinese character was stenciled on the back. No sign of underwear or socks, which wasn't going to be good if it got colder. Teddy kept pointing to his foot, but no one seemed to care. He was issued faded, torn blue canvas shoes with white rubber soles, like a geezer would wear in Palm Beach. And a pair of brand-new, beautifully sewn goatskin gloves with decorative red beads sewn on the back. They looked like high-end gardening gloves. He stood in line for a ladle of the same thin white corn mush they'd gotten on the train.

The guards pushed him down to a squat on the ground in front of a desk. The official, on a wooden chair, tried Teddy in Chinese, then in what must have been Vietnamese, because the other POWs in line giggled. The official reddened. He called over another man, maybe his supervisor. This latter fished a booklet from a pocket and leafed through it. Frowned down at Teddy, and said, enunciating very carefully, "You . . . American?"

"Yes. American. Prisoner of war."

"American criminal of war."

Teddy spoke slowly and loudly. "*Prisoner* of war. I need medical treatment. Geneva Convention."

The guy consulted his booklet. Looked pissed off. Finally he said, "Here at Camp Five Seven Six, work. What can do?"

"Not much. Not with this." Teddy lifted his leg; the official glanced at the dangling appendage. "POWs are entitled to medical attention."

"You *bing hao*?"

"Excuse me?"

"You sick one. Half food." He spoke to the guy at the desk, who nodded and made a note.

"Oh, fuck me," Teddy mumbled.

"You say what?" The official spat orders at two guards, who came to attention. "Fuck me? You say, fuck me? *Guanjao ta*!"

The beating this time was prolonged, severe, and by men who didn't care about leaving marks. When it was over they dragged him to a gravel

556

pile and left him there spread-eagled, like a poster child for Bad Prisoners.

He got some sleep. Not exactly restful, but it was nice to stretch out without someone else's dick pressed to your asshole.

Only when dark approached did a hand touch him. Help him up.

He pried open swollen eyelids to see Maggie, plus three of the Vietnamese he'd been chained up with on the train. "Come on, mate. They assigned us a doss. Let's get you under some shelter."

Their "doss" was a corrugated iron lean-to built against one of the inner walls of the depression. Blackened rocks circled a fire pit. Behind the roof, which formed a six-by-four partially sheltered anteroom, a cave went back about fifteen feet into the rock. The ceiling was just high enough that he could sit upright but couldn't stand. Dried turds littered the ground between it and the next cave. The hut-caves stretched out of sight around the jut of the bluff. A guard tower loomed at the top. Dried grass and a couple of weary quilted-cotton blankets constituted their bedding. Once again, he slept nestled with Pritchard and the Vietnamese, and was glad of the warmth.

The next dawn they were shouted out by a ragged little squint-eyed Chinese carrying a stick. A stakebed truck idled at the bottom of the bluff.

Most of the Vietnamese climbed up onto the bed. Teddy was pushed up into a much-abused Toyota pickup. Where the inevitable shackles waited. Pritchard tried to go with him, but the Chinese whacked and shouted him into the big truck, with the Viets.

The pickup drove slowly, rocking and creaking on clapped-out shocks. Glancing sideways as they trundled along a bumpy gravel track, he gradually grasped the layout. The camp proper was built around an open pit mine. The whole operation was much larger than he'd guessed the night before. It had to cover many square miles. He couldn't tell what they were mining, and didn't have the vocabulary to ask. An explosion thumped, not far away, but again, oddly muffled. He realized he'd been hearing them all night long, though at longer intervals. They were working a graveyard shift, too. At the far end of the vast depression, the glitter of sheet glass. Buildings? Maybe where the guards lived, where the camp was administered. If there was a road to anything like a town, it would lie in that direction. He glanced up at the sun for his bearings, but got a sharp "*Yangjing-lay!*" More than one rifle butt had taught him what that meant: "Drop your head, eyes down."

Eventually they left him at a tower sheathed in the same unrusting corrugated iron as roofed their lean-to. A deafening roar and chatter came

558

from within. A breaker, one of dozens that rose here and there across the floor of the immense pit. The rock came up out of the pits, where most of the prisoners were working, in big diesel dump trucks. From them, it went up a power conveyor to the top of the breaker.

A very old, tottering, rail-thin Chinese with a mask over his mouth and nose shepherded Teddy up steel stairs slick with powdery grit to a platform near the top. There, gigantic steel rollers rotated ceaselessly, shaking the whole building. The din was deafening. Huge driven wheels chewed the ore into progressively smaller pieces as it descended. The air seethed with powdered rock, so thick he could see only eleven or twelve feet in any direction. The old man handed him a rag, and gestured to him to tie it around his face. Pointed to the air, and grasped both hands to his neck in the universal symbol for choking. His hands were withered, scarred, and covered with nodule-like, whitish growths. He patted his own chest. "Lew."

"Teddy."

"Ted-ti?"

"Close enough. Ted-ti it is."

Old Lew closed his fingers around the handle of a push broom leaning in a corner and began acting out what to do. The ore emerged from the mill crushed to a gritty, sparkling powder, the particles like coarse, dirty sea salt. Carried along on a wide rubberized belt, it passed under a bank of electromagnets. Switched on, the magnets sucked up grains of a reddish-brown mineral out of the passing ore. At intervals, a mechanism extended a tray, the current in the magnets was switched off, and the reddish matter dropped into the tray. Teddy's task was to walk from one side of the breaker to the other with the push broom, brushing away what was left sticking to the magnets after the current cut off. Finally, Lew gathered the filings, or shavings, up with the broom, and ran them along the catch tray into a hole at the end.

He handed Teddy the broom and looked expectant. "*Ni mingbai ma, Ted-ti*?"

"*Shid-eh*," Teddy said. He took the broom and brushed a few grains off the magnets, then pushed them into the hole.

The old man beamed as if he'd just graduated med school. "*Tway. Ting hao! Ting hao!*"

"*Ting hao*," Teddy said, bowing. "*Manwei bowgow.*"

The old guy grabbed his gut, bent over, guffawing so hard Teddy was afraid he was going to choke. "*Manwei bowgow! Bu, bu. Wo bushi yigi huwei.*"

He ran the broom all that morning as the rollers rumbled like Niagara and the metal siding around him reverberated with distant booms. Until, at

560

noon by the sun, a whistle blew, echoing from bluff to bluff down the length of the immense pit.

The breaker shut down, first the diesels that ran the conveyors chugging down the scale, then the rollers and the gearing that drove them rumbling to a halt.

A bell clanged. Dozens of workers streamed out from nooks and machinery onto the ladders. Teddy followed, but slowly, supporting his weight on a handrail. At the bottom of the breaker, in the open air, a wooden table held two tureens. One was the white mush, the other a doubtful-smelling vegetable soup. The powder-fog was dissipating, blown away by a thin wind. He shivered. Even at noon, the breeze was cold outside the tower. Four husky Chinese immediately plumped down, pulling up empty wooden cable-spools as seats. They planted their elbows as old Lew dealt metal bowls from a rolling chest that also held wrenches, screwdrivers, saws. There were only five bowls. Teddy tried to sit down too, but they elbowed him back, chortling. At last Lew said something and they grudgingly let him dip a bowl, but Lew stopped him and poured half of it back. *"Bu, bu. Bing hao,"* he said. *"Ni pàng, ni bìng bù xuyào tài duo de shíwù."* He pointed halfway down the bowl. The husky guys guffawed and slapped their thighs, grinning at him.

Fuck this. He wasn't going to survive on two

561

mouthfuls of corn mush and rotten veggies. His mouth was bleeding again. No way to clean his teeth since Yongxing. He was going to lose them soon. But he let the thugs push him away, folded himself into a corner, and slurped his mush with his fingers. Eat everything they give you, they'd said at SERE. Yeah, but even there he'd lost ten pounds. His legs were starting to look wasted. His hands were numb most of the time. Too many hours in steel cuffs.

Teddy looked over at old Lew, whose hands dangled too, all but useless. When he grinned, just one blackened tooth showed. The guy wasn't actually that old. He might even be Teddy's age.

"*Ted-ti*," said Lew, grasping his shoulder and turning him toward the rest of the breaker gang. They frowned over their bowls. "*May-guo sheebing*," he added. Two or three registered, but most just blinked, then went back to eating.

When the whistle droned again everyone got up and headed for the ladders. Still ravenously hungry, Teddy followed, though more slowly, dragging his foot.

Over the next weeks, it got colder. Now and then, back in the hills, at night, the howling of wolves echoed eerily as the searchlights swung this way and that. Also, two other Americans arrived at Chu Shan, which Teddy learned was another name for Camp 576. Or maybe that was the name of the town whose lights he could see in the distance. Both were airmen, shot down over the Taiwan Strait. Teddy managed to get across to his production brigade leader, the squint-eyed guy with the stick, that they wanted to hut together. That made seven in the cave: Oberg; Pritchard; the three Vietnamese, Trinh, Vu, and Phung; and the airmen, Fierros and Shepard. Now it was cramped, but it wasn't important where you crawled to sleep, or where you worked.

What mattered was more basic.

Little lizards darted down occasionally from what might be greener pastures for them, at the top of the cliff. They were wary, but a thrown rock could stun them long enough to be picked up and have their heads bitten off. He sucked the juices before cramming them into his mouth and chewing them whole, skin and all. The salty crunch reminded him of Fritos.

Old Lew apparently lived outside the camp, or in some privileged area of it. He would bring a little can of rice, and sometimes fish or radishes, for his lunch. Teddy spent anguished hours at the top of the breaker, raking magnetized ore and mulling over how and whether to steal the lunch can. The prisoners never saw rice. But if he antagonized Lew, lost this easy job, he'd go to the pits with the others. Or worse.

And those guys weren't doing so well. It was pick-and-shovel work, with a quota of ten cubic meters a day. Like Teddy at the breaker, the others got mush and soup at lunchtime, and another bowl at knockoff. The toll of heavy labor and lack of nutrients was clear in their wasting arms, their drawn, bony faces. The Viets seemed to be taking it better than Pritchard. The Australian rolled off the truck at the end of the day, crawled to the hut, and lay with his eyes closed. As weeks passed, he began coughing, a nagging hack that brought up gray oysters.

Teddy decided to do something about his foot. He stole two yards of the thin rag they all wore over their faces at the breaker, stuffing it down inside his pants when the last whistle blew. Back at the cave, he rubbed a scrap of wood on a rock until it resembled the sole of a shoe, but with a bent piece sticking up along the back. He strapped his foot up so that it didn't hang, and the wooden brace gave him ankle support.

With it strapped on tight, very tight, he could limp. Not fast, and it still hurt like a sonofabitch, but it was better.

Each day, he tried to pick up a word. Most of the other prisoners refused to speak to him, but a couple would. One, he suspected, was Christian. He'd drawn something on his palm, hiding it from the others, but Teddy couldn't make sense of the ideogram.

How was "good," or used like "okay," to agree or say you understood.

Tway meant "you did that right," which they didn't say to Teddy very often.

Apparently *boo yow* meant something like "fuck, no" or "get out of my face."

"No" was *bu shi*, with a sort of upward singing note on the *bu* and a dropping note on the *shi*.

He tried to figure out "thank you" so he could say it to old Lew, but no one seemed to say that around here. Finally he noticed that the husky guys scratched the table with two fingers when they got their mush. He used the gesture, and got rewarded with a squint, then a clap on the shoulder from Chow.

Chow ran Teddy's level of the breaker. One of the muscular guys who got to sit on the cable spools. A mechanic. He kept the grinding wheels lubed and adjusted. He was always climbing in among the mill gears, even while they were in operation, reaching in here and there as if he didn't care about losing a hand. He was already down two fingers. What were these guys in for? Either politicals or regular criminals, but he couldn't figure which. His hutmate Thinh thought they were politicals, that this had been a re-education camp, but admitted he wasn't sure.

Then one day Chow wasn't there anymore. Teddy asked Lew where he'd gone. "*Na-li shi Chow?*"

Lew just looked away.

• • •

And the days passed.

There was no clock, only the whistle. No news. No calendar, so he didn't know what day or even what month it was. Just that it kept getting colder, and now and then fine icy crystals drifted down.

It was too dry to really snow. But their piss froze in the plastic buckets, and they shivered all day long. They scavenged anything that would burn: paper, broken shovel handles, dead grass.

One evening Fierros whispered, staring into the dying fire, "We have to get out of here."

No one said anything for quite some time. Until the pilot added, "It doesn't matter where. Probably just out there to die. But we're gonna die in this shithole anyway."

Teddy slumped against the cave wall, massaging his leg. He'd kept falling down all afternoon. Each time, the unit leader had kicked him back to his feet.

This wasn't the first time they'd discussed escape. He and Pritchard had talked it over on and off since they'd arrived. Each time, they'd concluded it might be possible to get up the bluffs and over the wire. But what lay outside? Desert, mountain, hostile locals?

"You heard the wolves howling out there," Pritchard observed. "We leave the wire, mates, what do we do about them?"

Teddy slid closer, until the embers scorched

his knees. But his ass was still freezing. "It's not time yet," he muttered. "The war's got to be over someday. It's got to be."

"How long do we wait?"

"As long as they're feeding us, we stay."

Fierros muttered, "And when they stop?"

Teddy blinked into the dying glow. Took a deep breath, and let it out.

"Then it'll be time to go."

31
Guam

The morning was bright as silver, cool and still. The flat, hazy sea lay dimpled only here and there with the nearly exhausted echoes of distant swells, tinted rose, and scarlet, and gold.

The sun grew from the horizon first as a suspicion, a glow; then blinking suddenly into existence like a great golden eye, lentil-shaped, quivering. Droplets of gold ran up to join the upper limb until it birthed from the placental sea, snapping into a deep-red, quivering sphere, crossed with bands of white gold, gold, rose, and bloody crimson.

On the bridge wing, Dan lowered his binoculars, blinking away coruscating afterimages. Far on the southern horizon, the dark mote of *Curtis Wilbur.* He'd pulled her in closer the night before, once they had air cover.

Beneath the granite-seam of fatigue he still felt nauseated, but no longer so afraid. Guam lay ahead, after a tense and agonizingly slow twelve-hundred-mile passage. The formation was speed-constrained to conserve fuel, and he'd spent a full day searching where the battle group had gone down. But found only debris and empty sea. A pile of recovered flotsam lay under tarps on the fantail. *Wilbur* had been attacked by a submarine, but spoofing gear had pulled the torpedoes off track. The destroyer had gone in to prosecute, and the crackle of collapsing bulkheads was probably still reverberating in the deep sound layer.

Against the odds, they'd come through. The contrails had etched the darkling sky the evening before. Bombers, heading west for Taiwan and Korea. Transports, headed east, though most of the U.S. garrison on Okinawa had evacuated to the Japanese home islands. *Savo* would reach port that afternoon.

But Fleet had sent a messenger ahead. "Hopscotch incoming." The OOD pointed. Dan got his glasses on it. Heavy-bodied, high-winged, it grew rapidly into a small seaplane.

"Call away for boat transfer," Dan told him. "Tell the special agent to report to the boat deck. Have somebody help with her gear." He'd thanked her the night before, saying how much he and the crew appreciated her efforts. And Ar-Rahim had seemed, for a moment, to relax that obstinate vigilance. She'd apologized for suspecting him, and shaken his hand with what looked like genuine, if still wary, respect.

The plane made a pass, waggled its wings, and reported in. Dan checked with Sonar and Combat, then cleared it for landing. It came in skimming the purple sea, throwing up a roostertail. Smaller than he'd expected, and painted bright colors.

Some civilian island-hopper, commandeered at the start of hostilities. *Savo*'s remaining inflatable bounded toward it like a skipping stone.

"Captain? Morning traffic."

Branscombe, with the clipboard. Dan climbed into his chair and flipped through it. Trying to impress into a tired brain that, behind them, the Western Pacific had changed.

The Koreans were fighting fiercely. China was consolidating its hold on Taiwan, imprisoning thousands in makeshift camps. More troops were still streaming across from the mainland. But that fighting, though lessening in intensity, wasn't over. Some units had fallen back into the mountains, holding out in prepared redoubts.

The Philippines had neutralized itself. Manila had renounced all claims in the South China Sea, and offered to cede the still-occupied Itbayat Island as well in return for a nonaggression pact. Beijing had announced it welcomed this acknowledgment of the Empire's supremacy, but might have further demands.

"The *Empire?*" Dan muttered, incredulous.

"That's what Zhang's calling it now. According to some translators. The People's Empire of China."

He glanced to where the boat was heading back. The seaplane was gathering speed, lifting off for its return trip. He grunted, and read on. . . . India was debating Zhang's proposal. Japan had recalled its navy to home ports, and accepted the offer of a cease-fire in place in the Senkakus. Only Vietnam and South Korea seemed game to fight on. But the Koreans were isolated, with no access to the outside world. Jung's fleet had retreated east, announcing its intention to fight on at the side of the U.S. Navy.

The whole allied position in the Pacific had crumbled. With Taiwan and Okinawa in mainland hands, the U.S. had been forced back to the second island chain. Palau was being reoccupied by the Marines. That made the defensive line Palau–Guam–Saipan–Chichi Jima.

He read an analysis that speculated on Zhang's next move. Against Indonesia? Malaysia? Or the dictator could turn north, and seize the resources of Siberia.

The RHIB disappeared behind the ship, and Dan slid down from his chair. Hit the button on his Hydra. "XO? I'll be on the fantail. Tell Bart to convene the snipes, get the damage documentation together. We'll meet in the wardroom at 0700."

The seaplane's passengers were a mixed bag. Tiger Team engineers from Pearl Harbor Naval Shipyard. An investigator from DIA, who headed immediately to the pile of debris on the fantail. A rep from Raytheon, with a duffel of spares. And, to Dan's bemusement, a female journalist.

Presumably the "Chief of Information rep" the message had mentioned. Elfin. Dark-haired. "Maya Mao," she introduced herself, with a small hand clasping his. "And, yes, I'm of Chinese descent."

"I wasn't asking."

"I'm a pool reporter. Accredited by CHINFO. Here are my credentials."

He accepted the paper, but must have still looked bemused, because she added, "We're hoping for an interview. About the battle, and so forth."

"I have to get the engineers to work. We're going into drydock as soon as we get back in."

"I saw the damage. Amazing you made it home."

He said it wasn't he who had brought her back, but the crew. That she should really interview them, not him. Then excused himself, and headed for the wardroom.

When he left there Danenhower and McMottie, Carpenter, Uskavitch, Wenck, and the rest of his team were deep in the weeds with the shipyard people, translating the damage reports into statements of work, materials lists, parts orders. He'd planned to head for the bridge again, but halted in the passageway.

Sagging against a bulkhead, he closed his eyes. Giving up, just for a moment, now that he was alone. Tremors racked him. A spike of pain probed his cervical vertebra. He could hardly breathe. Fatigue, nausea, knees that just wanted to buckle . . .

Their orders read to refuel and make repairs, then await further orders. But in all honesty, he wasn't up to it. If he was realistic, he should request relief due to health reasons.

The more likely scenario: They'd relieve him for cause. The Navy had never saved room for losers. Those who oversaw the initial defeats of any war, responsible or not—and usually they weren't, just victims of the complacency, penuriousness, and misjudgments of those in higher office—were blamed, cast aside, and obliterated.

He leaned there, eyes closed, fighting the impulse to just open the safe in his cabin and load his pistol.

But at last he acknowledged that he was not in control. The regret, he would carry for the rest of his life. But maybe he could serve in some humbler way. Training recruits. Writing reports. And he'd see his wife again, and his daughter.

At least he'd brought *Savo* home. Saved her, and their lives, against all expectations. Including his own. A lot of families would be overjoyed tonight, hearing from husbands, wives, fathers, mothers, sons, and daughters, after far too long without word.

Footsteps rattled down the ladder. He straightened. Cleared his throat. And became, once more, the captain.

"I was sent at the request of the media pool," Ms. Mao said. Sitting primly, ankles crossed, fingers on her little notebook computer. Ready to write the first draft of history.

They were in his in-port cabin. He coughed into his fist, realizing he hadn't bothered to check out her legs. Maybe he was in even worse shape than he'd thought. "All right. Shoot."

"I believe we have some mutual friends. Hu Kuwalay? Of Senate Armed Services?"

"Not sure I know him. My wife used to work there."

"I see. Well, shall we begin? Let's start with your attack on the Chinese invasion fleet."

He coughed again, and she waited politely. Finally he said, "I'd rather start from the setup of the blocking forces." He kept to his own movements and the sequence of the campaign. It took nearly an hour, and when at last he fell silent she looked down, seeming to commune with her reflection in the screen.

"What do you think led to this war?" she murmured at last.

"In a nutshell? Hmm. I guess . . . deterrence is the art of making someone not do what he wants to do. Convincing him the price will be higher than he wants to pay.

"But we lost sight of that. We assumed everyone else wanted peace as much as we did. We tried to keep on with business as usual. Looked away, while our enemies stole our secrets. Did nothing, as they built islands and claimed the seas around them. Eventually, they concluded we were so feeble, so divided, and so fearful, we'd never fight, no matter how far they went." He shrugged. "Just my opinion, though."

"Who do you think should bear the blame?"

"Blame? There's enough to go around. Anyway, that's for the historians. The real question is, what are we going to do now, since we've lost the first round?"

She nodded. "I agree. So . . . you probably know Zhang has proposed peace again. On the basis of the 'union and demilitarization' of Korea. He also offers to return Okinawa to Japan, though he will keep the Senkakus. Once a conference of ministers ratifies the settlement, that is. He proposes they meet in Beijing."

"Very magnanimous," Dan said. "Until he decides he wants the rest of the pie."

"There *are* reports of unrest in China. But also rumors of wholesale executions in Taiwan, and savage repression in Hong Kong and Tibet. Up to four hundred thousand people have been deported into the interior. Many were shot in the streets."

Dan nodded, closing his eyes. Like any tyrant,

Zhang was tightening control. "What about Washington? What's the feeling there?"

"We're starting to tool up again. But I have to say, many are still unconvinced that retaking the Western Pacific is worth the cost."

"It'll be a hard, bloody road," Dan said. "But they started this. We can't forget the *Roosevelt* battle group. Our allies need us. And America still hates warmakers." She waited, looking as if she expected more. "So . . . yeah. We'll be back. And I'm confident that somehow, dark though it looks right now, we'll win."

Dark arched eyebrows rose. "Mind if I quote you?" She tapped the keyboard.

Abruptly nauseated again, he hoisted himself to his feet. "I've got to lie down for a few minutes, I'm afraid. Hope you got what you wanted."

"I think I got exactly what I wanted. 'We'll be back.' And the rest. You'll confirm, that's a direct quote?"

He hesitated. Who was he, after all, to speak for a whole country? He wasn't even sure he believed what he'd just said. Maybe America *was* beaten. Counted out. As Zhang, and so many others, thought. Weak. Soft. Corrupt. Could she pour out again the blood and heroism, the innovation and treasure and brutal tenacity, that had defeated the Germans, the Japanese, the Soviets? But at last he just muttered, "Yeah. It's what I said."

She snapped the notebook closed and stood.

When he'd ushered her out, he staggered into the head. Bent over the sink and gagged. Lights flashed behind his closed lids. He wasn't sure why he felt this way. He'd been defeated. Dishonored. But it was more than that. Much more than anything that had to do with Daniel V. Lenson.

He stared at himself in the mirror. At his pasty, haggard cheeks. His tired eyes.

The world was at war.

And the horror had only begun.

Acknowledgments

Ex nihilo nihil fit. For this novel, I began with the advantage of notes accumulated for the previous books about Navy and joint operations; see *The Crisis*, *The Towers*, *The Cruiser*, and *Tipping Point*.

The following new sources were also helpful. For Aisha's chapters: A Q&A–type backgrounder with agents from the NCIS Hampton Roads office. Discussion of profiling from the FBI study "The Criminal Behavior of the Serial Rapist," by Robert R. Hazelwood and Janet Warren. Also "Profiling Rapists" in the blog *Forensic Talk.* Abandon-ship instructions from OPNAVINST 5100.19E. For MEJA and CEJA, CRS "Civilian Extraterritorial Jurisdiction Act: Federal Contractor Criminal Liability Overseas," by Charles Doyle, 2012.

For Blair's chapters: Information on SAIC from their Web site. Classification and security info from DoD Manual 5200.01-V3. Mau VanDuren contributed advice on campaign strategy. For Senate procedures, Elizabeth Rybicki, *Voting and Quorum Procedures in the Senate*, Congressional Research Service, 2013, and Valerie Heitshusen, *Senate Committee Hearings: Preparation*, CRS,

2015. On Operation Causeway, Maj. Robert B. Sheeks, USMCR (Ret.), in the *China News*, August 10, 1997.

For Teddy and Echo Platoon: "Carlson's Raid on Makin Island," by Col. David W. Haughey, USMC (Ret.), in August 2001 *Marine Corps Gazette.* Also Gordon Rottman's *Carlson's Marine Raiders*, Osprey, 2014. Institute for Defense Studies, "Yongxing Island: China's Diego Garcia in the South China Sea?" by Sarabjeet Singh Parmar, August 7, 2012. "I Know Waterboarding Is Torture" by Malcolm Nance, *Daily News,* October 31, 2007. For prisoner experience: *The Great Wall of Confinement*, by Williams and Wu.

Weapons, sensor, and operational details are either from open sources or are made up. Especially helpful were Dr. Carlos Kopp, "Defeating Cruise Missiles," *Australian Aviation*, October 2004. Also "Soviet/Russian Cruise Missiles," same author, August 2009, and *Air Power Australia*'s "Soviet Maritime Reconnaissance, Targeting, Strike and Electronic Combat Aircraft," by Dr. Kopp, 2012. For sonobuoy placement, "On the Design of Multistatic Sonobuoy Fields for Area Search," by S. Ozols and M. P. Fewell, Australian government document. Discussion of ABM geometry: Gerald Brown et al., "A Two-Sided Optimization for Theater Missile Defense," *Operations Research,* September–

October 2005. Info on Japanese marines from "Japan's Amphibious Buildup," by Kyle Mizokami, *US Naval Institute News*, October 9, 2013. On Chinese TBMs: "PLA Ballistic Missiles," Technical Report APA-TR-2010-0802, Sean O'Connor, 2009, Air Power Australia Site for fuel specifications. Joseph Sermarini, "The Universal Fuel at Sea," Naval Post graduate School thesis, June 2000. EXTAC 1000, "Maritime Maneuvering and Tactical Procedures" (unclassified) was useful for command relationships and maneuvering. For background on operating areas: "Physical Oceanography of the Yellow and East China Sea" by Dr. Steven R. Ramp, Naval Postgraduate School. About River City: "Limited Online Access Stresses Sailors at Sea," *Navy Times*, April 15, 2012, by Joshua Stewart. For EW: U.S. Naval Academy, Weapons and Engineering Department, *Fundamentals of Naval Weapons Systems*, public information released by Raytheon, and NSWC Crane Electronic Warfare Center, "EW Maritime Fact Sheet," accessed March 2015.

Thoughtful discussions of how wars start, and how the United States typically responds, are found in *The Father of Us All* by Victor Davis Hanson, and *America's First Battles*, edited by Heller and Stofft.

Many sources have discussed a possible conflict with China. Among those I read were:

The Brookings Institution, "China's Growing Strength, Taiwan's Diminishing Options," by Yuan-kang Wang, November 2010.

RAND Corporation, *A Question of Balance: Political Context and Military Aspects of the China-Taiwan Dispute*, by David A. Shlapak et al., 2009.

The Diplomat: "Taiwan, Asia's Secret Air Power," by Ian Easton, September 25, 2014.

William S. Murry, "Revisiting Taiwan's Defense Strategy," *Naval War College Review*, Summer 2008, vol. 61, no. 3.

Office of the Secretary of Defense Annual Report to Congress, "Military and Security Developments Involving the People's Republic of China 2014," April 24, 2014.

F. Scott Hume, "Study of the Ability of the People's Republic of China to Conduct an Invasion of Taiwan," School of Advanced Military Studies, United States Army Command and General Staff College, Fort Leavenworth, Kansas, 2000.

Dennis Blasko, "PLA Amphibious Capabilities: Structured for Deterrence," *China Brief* 17, August 19, 2010.

For overall help, thanks to Charle Ricci and Stacia Childers of the Eastern Shore Public Library; Matthew Stroup of the Navy Office of Information, East; James DiAngio, N01P1, Commander, Naval Surface Forces Atlantic; and Paul O'Donnell, NCIS.

A deep bow to Mark "Dusty" Durstewitz, John Gibson, Anthony Ruta, and Bill Hunteman, who put in many hours commenting in detail. Others both retired and still on active duty supplied invaluable perspective. If I inadvertently left anyone out, my apologies!

Let me emphasize that these sources were consulted for the purposes of *fiction*. Likewise, the specifics of personalities, tactics, and procedures, and the units and locales described, are employed as the materials of story, not reportage. Some details have been altered to protect classified capabilities and procedures.

My deepest gratitude goes to George Witte, editor and friend of over three decades, without whom this series would not exist. And Sally Richardson, Ken Silver, Sara Thwaite, Naia Poyer, Adam Goldberger, and Anya Lichtenstein at St. Martin's Press. And finally to Lenore Hart, best friend, anchor on lee shores, and my North Star when skies are clear.

As always, all errors and deficiencies are my own.

Books are produced in the United States using U.S.-based materials

Books are printed using a revolutionary new process called THINKtech™ that lowers energy usage by 70% and increases overall quality

Books are durable and flexible because of Smyth-sewing

Paper is sourced using environmentally responsible foresting methods and the paper is acid-free

Center Point Large Print
600 Brooks Road / PO Box 1
Thorndike, ME 04986-0001 USA

(207) 568-3717

US & Canada:
1 800 929-9108
www.centerpointlargeprint.com

DATE DUE